T. Steward

The
Greatest
Escape Stories
Ever Told

Other Books in the Greatest Stories Series

The
Greatest
Escape Stories
Ever Told

EDITED BY
DARREN BROWN

THE LYONS PRESS
Guilford, Connecticut
An imprint of The Globe Pequot Press

The Globe Pequot Press, P. O. Box 480, Guilford, CT 06437.

The Lyons Press is an imprint of The Globe Pequot Press.

Printed in the United States of America.

1 3 5 7 9 10 8 6 4 2

The Library of Congress Cataloging-in-Publication Data is available on file.

Permissions Acknowledgments

Paul Brickhill, excerpt from *Escape or Die: Authentic Stories of the RAF Escaping Society.* Copyright 1952 and renewed © 1980 by Paul Brickhill. Reprinted with the permission of W. W. Norton & Company, Inc.

Robert E. Burns, "Georgia Chain Gang Fugitive" from *I Am a Fugitive from a Georgia Chain Gang!* (New York: Vanguard Press, 1932) Copyright 1932. Reprinted with the permission of the William Morris Agency.

Henri Charriere, excerpt from *Papillon,* translated by June P. Wilson and Walter B. Michaels. Copyright © 1970 by June P. Wilson and Walter B. Michaels. Reprinted with the permission of HarperCollins Publishers, Inc. and Editions Robert Laffont.

Dieter Dengler, excerpt from *Escape from Laos.* Copyright © 1979 by Dieter Dengler. Reprinted with the permission of Presidio Press.

Andre Devigny, excerpt from *A Man Escaped,* translated by Peter Green. Copyright © 1958 by Peter Green. Reprinted with the permission of W. W. Norton & Company, Inc.

Major Damon Gause, excerpt from *The War Journal of Major Damon "Rocky" Gause.* Copyright © 1999 by Damon L. Gause. Reprinted with the permission of Hyperion Press.

Billy Hayes with William Hoffer, "Out of a Turkish Prison" from *Midnight Express* (New York: Dutton, 1977). Copyright © 1977. Reprinted with the permission of IMG/Bach Literary Agency .

Ward Millar, "Down in Korea" from *Valley of the Shadow* (New York: D. McKay, 1955). Copyright © 1955 by Ward Millar. Reprinted with the permission of Sterling Lord Literistic, Inc.

Baroness Emmuska Orczy, "A Question of Passports" from *The League of the Scarlet Pimpernel* (New York: George H. Doran, 1919). Copyright 1919 by Baroness Emmuska Orczy. Reprinted with the permission of A. P. Watt, Ltd..

Pat Reid, "Escape Strategy" from *The Colditz Story.* Copyright 1952 and renewed © 1980 by P. R. Reid. Reprinted with the permission of Hodder Headline, plc.

Walter Babington Thomas, "Bid for Freedom" from *Dare to be Free.* Copyright 1952 by Walter Babington Thomas. Reprinted with the permission of Pan Books.

Since man invented prisons and slavery, the prisoners and the slaves have always attempted to escape, regardless of the price of failure. The battle has gone on for thousands of years. It will go on for thousands of years to come.

—ROBERT E. BURNS
I Am a Fugitive from a Georgia Chain Gang

How unhappy is that poor man who loses his liberty! . . . No degree of material comfort, no consciousness of correct behavior can balance that hateful degradation of imprisonment. Before I had been an hour in captivity I resolved to escape.

—WINSTON CHURCHILL
My Early Life, A Roving Commission

Acknowledgments

I would like to thank Tony Lyons and Jay Cassell of The Lyons Press for making this book possible. Thanks also to my wife, Pam, for listening to so many tales of escape as this project unfolded and my mother (and the librarian in the family), Jan Brown, for all her support.

Contents

The
Greatest
Escape Stories
Ever Told

Introduction

Hope and love of liberty never become extinct in the heart of man.

—HENRI MASERS DE LATUDE

As soon as the first man was imprisoned, he undoubtedly sought to escape. The Bible is full of narrow escapes; so are mythology and the history of the ancient world. Despite all the advances in technology through the centuries, modern prisoners continue to escape with amazing, sometimes unsettling, regularity.

The tools of escape have evolved over time, as have the settings, but the daring and romance inherent in the story of a man seeking his liberty against long odds remains constant. Even when hardened criminals escape, a part of us often admires the ingenuity and boldness of their deeds. John Dillinger was as much hero as criminal when he used a carved wooden gun to break jail and continue his bank robbing in the 1930s. Billy the Kid became a national folk hero of sorts—despite his carelessness for the lives of those around him and the violence of his escapes. And the mystery surrounding the escape of three criminals from the "escape-proof" island prison at Alcatraz captivated the nation in the 1960s.

The successful escaper is not necessarily one who is well trained or physically strong; much more important is an adaptable, independent mind and a readiness to rely on one's own talents. Many escapers failed repeatedly before finally making their way to freedom. Other talented escapers never made it, but they never quit trying.

Luck almost always plays a role in an escape. When Henry "Box" Brown—the southern slave who mailed himself to abolitionist friends in Philadelphia in a wooden box just three feet by two feet—was placed head down during shipment, he nearly died. Just as he was about to lose consciousness, the box was righted again. The famous French general Lafayette was recaptured after a break from prison in Austria when he misinterpreted the name of the town that would serve as the rendezvous point. He charged away on horseback in the wrong direction, completely missing the safe passage that had already been arranged for him.

One thing that sets many escapers apart is a pure love of adventure. Many soldiers seemed relieved at safely reaching a prison camp, content to wait until the end of hostilities to be free. Others chafed at the enforced boredom of prison life, preferring to risk death or torture to avoid idling away the days. Often this had creative and amusing results. Lieutenant Jones in *The Road to En-dor* tells of his adventures in the supernatural in a Turkish prison camp in World War I. He built a ouija board and convinced the camp commander that a spirit had used it to tell him the location of a buried treasure. After leading him on a hilarious treasure hunt around the compound, guided by the spirit, Jones and a companion parlayed the prank into an escape bid. With an enormous effort, which evolved into faking mental illness, they gained their release—just two weeks before the war ended.

Almost every war ever fought has included colorful escapes. World War I and II, in particular, saw an amazing array of escapes, many inspired by fictional stories and those from previous conflicts. Two of the best are told in *The Wooden Horse*, by Eric Williams and *The Great Escape*, by Paul Brickhill—both from Stalag Luft III in World War II. As the barracks were far from the barbed wire that surrounded the camp, Williams and a friend came up with the idea to build a vaulting horse that the men could carry out and use on the same spot each day near the fence. The men concealed themselves within the "horse" and were able to dig a short tunnel that allowed them to escape.

The Great Escape was just that. Several very long tunnels were built, complete with air ventilation, railroad tracks, and lighting. The Germans found most of the tunnels and shut them down, but 76 of the 200 men planning to escape were finally able to make it out during a single night in 1944. Mass escapes make reaching safety much more difficult, and only three of the men made it to the frontier. So much publicity was generated by the escape that the German high command decided to set an example that would deter future escapes—fifty of the recaptured men were taken to a field and gunned down, including Roger Bushnell, the principle organizer. (I still remember watching Steve McQueen jump his stolen motorcycle over a barbed wire fence as he was retaken in the film version.) The books by Williams and Brickhill make excellent reading, with far too much of interest to be able to include excerpts of the full stories in this collection.

Only three fictional escapes are included here, as they are rarely more intense or daring than those made by desperate people facing very real life-and-death consequences. The slave Eliza's escape in *Uncle Tom's Cabin* by leaping from iceberg to iceberg in the frozen river makes for interesting reading, but not nearly as much as the two real escapes Harriet Beecher Stowe likely borrowed from to create it. Even the most imaginative fictional escapes, such as *Peter Simple* from the Napoleonic Wars, are often based on real events. Moments of wild desperation, where lives hang in the balance, create outrageous situations that can't be easily duplicated from the comfort of a writing desk. They are usually dismissed as too improbable.

Many escapes, like the Emperor Napolean's from exile, had a huge impact on history but just aren't that exciting. (Napoleon simply boarded a ship and sailed back to France.) Other escapes, like Slavomir Rawicz's in *The Long Walk* or Benuzzi's in *No Picnic on Mount Kenya*, seem almost incidental to the unbelievable journeys that would follow.

The stories included here haven't necessarily changed the world, but they do share the bold, resolute spirit that marks all of history's most creative and ingenious escapes.

—Darren Brown
March 2002

Escape from the Tower of London

JOHN BUCHAN

Along with several other leaders, Lord Nithsdale was sentenced to death for his role in the Jacobite Revolt of 1715 in England. He was held in the Tower of London pending his execution, which was to include partial hanging and disembowelment while yet alive—among other things. The Tower was a formidable prison and the site of several famous escapes through English history.

Lady Nithsdale, just 26 years old, but bold and determined, came to London hoping to petition King George on her husband's behalf. Finding herself rudely treated and her petition cast aside, she decided to take matters into her own hands. The clever and successful escape she concocted surprised all of England.

The first of the great Jacobite rebellions, that of 1715, was grossly mismanaged from the start. The invasion of England by the Scottish Catholic lords and the Northumbrian Jacobites came to a dismal close at Preston, and the Tower of London was soon full of exalted personages—the English Earl of Derwentwater, who was a grandson of Charles II, and the Scottish Earls of Wintoun, Nithsdale, and Carnwath, and Lord Kenmure, who was head of the Galloway Gordons. The trial of the Jacobite lords was not a masterpiece of English justice. The method followed was impeachment, and it was clear from the start that with a Protestant House of Commons Catholic rebels had no kind of chance. Without proper proof they were condemned—a political, rather than a legal, verdict. They were advised to plead guilty, which as it turned out was an unwise course, for thereby they trusted their lives to the Crown and not to the English law, and King George's

5

Government were determined to make an example of them as a matter of policy. Wintoun alone refused to plead.

But the people of England were more merciful than their government, and the popular feeling in favour of leniency was so strong that Walpole was unable to send all the lords to the scaffold. For Derwentwater there could be no mercy; he was too near in blood to the royal house. Nithsdale and Kenmure were also marked for death, partly because they were devouter Catholics than the others, and partly because of their great power in the Lowlands. On Thursday, February 23, 1716, the Lord Chancellor signed the warrants for their execution on the Saturday.

Derwentwater and Kenmure duly lost their heads, and two famous houses were brought to ruin. But when the guards arrived to summon Nithsdale to the scaffold they found that he was gone. This is the story of his escape.

The Countess of Nithsdale had been Lady Winifred Herbert, the youngest daughter of the first Marquis of Powis. At the time she was twenty-six years of age, a slim young woman with reddish hair and pale blue eyes. Her family had always been Catholic and Royalist, and she had shown herself one of the most ardent of Jacobite ladies.

When the news came of the rout at Preston she was at Terregles, the home of the Maxwells in Nithsdale. She realized at once that her husband could expect no mercy, and that his death must follow his imprisonment as certainly as night follows day. It was a bitter January, with snowdrifts on every road. Without wasting an hour she set off for the south after burning incriminating papers. Her only attendant was a Welsh girl called Evans, from the Powis estate, who had been her maid since childhood.

The two women and a groom rode through the wintry country to Newcastle, where they took the coach for York. Presently the coach stuck in the snow and word came that all the roads were blocked. But by offering a large sum Lady Nithsdale managed to hire horses, and pushed on into the Midlands. The little company suffered every kind of disaster, but the lady's resolute spirit overcame them all, and after some days of weary travel they reached London.

Lady Nithsdale went straight to some of the Scottish great ladies, such as the Duchess of Buccleuch and the Duchess of Montrose, and heard from them that the worst might be expected. She realized that no appeal could save the prisoner, and that, unless he could break bar and bolt, in a week she would be a widow. The first step was to get admission to the Tower. Walpole refused to let her see her husband unless she was prepared to share his captivity to the end. She declined the condition, for she understood that if she was to do anything she must be free. At last she succeeded in bribing the keepers, and found herself in her husband's chamber. As she looked round she saw that there was no chance of an ordinary escape. One high barred window gave on the ramparts and Water Lane, and a sentry was on guard in front. If Lord Nithsdale were to leave the Tower he must leave it by the door. That in turn was strongly guarded. A halberdier stood outside and two sentries with fixed bayonets, and the stairs and the outer door were equally well held. Force was out of the question. The only hope lay in ingenuity.

The weak part of any prison is to be found in the human warders, more especially in a place so strong as the Tower, where the ordinary avenues of escape are few and difficult. The Lieutenant, trusting in his walls, was inclined to be negligent. The prison rules were often disregarded, and the wives and children of the officials wandered about the passages at will. This gave Lady Nithsdale her plan. She proposed to her husband to dress him up in cap and skirt and false curls and pass him as a woman through the soldiers. Very soon she had worked out the details. She had women friends who would assist: a Miss Hilton, and the landlady, Mrs. Mills, at her lodging in Drury Lane. The latter was tall and inclined to be stout, and a riding-hood that fitted her would fit Lord Nithsdale, while a red wig would counterfeit Mrs. Mills's hair. The prisoner's black eyebrows could be painted out, his chin shaved and his skin rouged.

Lord Nithsdale stubbornly refused. The scheme seemed to him crazy. How could a stalwart soldier with a rugged face and a martial stride imitate any woman? He might do something with a sword in his hand, but, raddled and painted, he would only be a laughing-stock. Far better let his wife get a petition from him placed in the royal hands. There might be some hope in that.

Lady Nithsdale pretended to agree, though she knew well that the King's clemency was a broken reed. For George had given strict orders that no petition from Lord Nithsdale should be received, and she found her friends very unwilling to disobey the King and act as intermediary. Her only hope was to see George himself; so she dressed herself in deep black, and, accompanied by Miss Hilton, who knew the King by sight, went to Court. They reached the room between the King's apartment and the main drawing-room, and when George appeared she flung herself before him. "I am the wretched Countess of Nithsdale," she cried. The King stepped back, refusing to take the petition; but she caught him by the skirt of his coat and poured out her story in French. George lost his temper, but she would not let go, and suffered herself to be dragged along the floor to the drawing-room door. There the officials unclasped her fingers and released his angry Majesty.

Lord Nithsdale now turned his hopes to the House of Lords. The Countess went from peer to peer; but once again she failed. Lord Pembroke, indeed, who was a kinsman, spoke in favour of the prisoner, but the thing was hopeless from the start. Nithsdale was utterly intractable and impenitent, and would never beg for his life.

Her husband's counsels having failed, it remained to follow her own. She drove to the Tower and told all the guards and keepers that Lord Nithsdale's last petition to the House of Lords had been favourably received, and that His Majesty was about to listen to their prayer. The officials congratulated her, for she had made herself very popular amongst them, and their friendliness was increased by her gifts. But to her husband she told the plain truth. The last moment had come. Next day was Friday, when the King would answer the petition. If he refused, as he was certain to do, on Saturday the prisoner would go to the scaffold.

On that Friday morning she completed her plans with Mrs. Mills, and as the January dusk drew in Miss Hilton joined them in Drury Lane and the details were finally settled. Miss Hilton was to be a friend, "Mrs. Catherine," and Mrs. Mills another friend, "Mrs. Betty." With the maid Evans all three would drive to the Tower, where Evans would wait inconspicuously near the Lieutenant's door, and the other three women would go to the earl's chamber. Miss Hilton, being slim, was to wear two riding-hoods, her own and that of Mrs. Mills. When she was in the room she was to drop her extra clothes and leave at once. Mrs. Mills was then to go in as "Mrs. Betty," wearing a riding-hood to fit the earl. She was to be weeping bitterly and holding a handkerchief to her face. Everything depended upon Miss Hilton being able to slip away quietly; then Mrs. Mills, having diminished in size, was to depart as "Mrs. Catherine," while the earl was to go out as "Mrs. Betty." The vital point was to get the sentries thoroughly confused as to who had gone in and out.

They drove in a coach to the Tower, and Lady Nithsdale, in order to keep the others from doleful anticipations, chattered the whole way. When they reached the Tower they found several women in the Council Chamber who had come to see Lady Nithsdale pass, for they had a suspicion, in spite of her cheerfulness, that this was the last occasion on which she would see her husband alive. The presence of these women, who were all talking together, helped to confuse the sentries. Lady Nithsdale took in Miss Hilton first, naming her "Mrs. Catherine." Miss Hilton at once shed her extra clothing and then left, Lady Nithsdale accompanying her to the staircase and crying, "Send my maid to me at once. I must be dressed without delay or I shall be too late for my petition." Then Mrs. Mills came up the stairs, a large fat woman sobbing bitterly and apparently all confused with grief. She was greeted by the Countess as "Mrs. Betty," and taken into Lord Nithsdale's room. There she changed her clothes, dried her tears, and went out with her head up and a light foot. "Good-bye, my dear Mrs. Catherine," Lady Nithsdale cried after her. "Don't omit to send my maid. She cannot know how late it is. She has forgotten that I am to present the petition to-night." The women in the Council Chamber watched Mrs. Mills's departure with sympathy, and the sentry opened the door for her to pass.

Now came the great moment. If any single keeper in the outer room had kept his wits about him the plot must be discovered. Everything depended upon their being confused among the women, and believing that "Mrs. Betty" was still with the Countess in Lord Nithsdale's chamber. It was nearly dark and in a few minutes lights would be brought in, and a single candle would betray them. The Countess took off all her petticoats save one and tied them round her husband. There was no time to shave him, so she wrapped a muffler round his chin. His cheeks were rouged; false ringlets were tied around his brow; and a great riding-hood was put on. Then the Countess opened the door and led him by the hand. Her voice was now sharp with anxiety. "For the love of God," she cried, "my dear Mrs. Betty, run and bring her with you. You know my lodgings, and if ever you hurried in your life, hurry now. I am driven mad with this delay."

The sentries in the dim light were unsuspicious and let them pass; indeed, one of them opened the chamber door. The Countess slipped behind her husband in the passage, so that no one looking after him should see his walk, which was unlike that of any woman ever born. "Make haste, make haste," she cried, and then, almost before she had realized it, they had passed the last door and the sentries.

Evans, the maid, was waiting, and, seizing Lord Nithsdale, *alias* "Mrs. Betty," by the arm, hurried him off to a house near Drury Lane. There he was dressed in the livery of a servant of the Venetian Minister, and started for the coast.

The Countess, dreading lest some keeper should enter her husband's room and find him gone, rushed back there with a great appearance of distress and slammed the door. Then for a few minutes she strolled about with the step of a heavy man, and carried on an imaginary conversation, imitating his gruff replies. Now came the last stage. She raised the latch, and, standing in the doorway so that all the crowd in the Council Chamber could hear, bade her husband good-night with every phrase of affection. She declared that something extraordinary must have happened to Evans, and that there was nothing for it but to go herself and see. She added that if the Tower were open she would come back that night. Anyhow, she hoped to be with him early in the morning, bringing him good news. As she spoke she drew the latchstring through the hole and banged the door. "I pray you, do not disturb my lord," she said in passing. "Do not send him candles till he calls for them. He is now at his prayers." The unsuspicious sentries saluted her with sympathy. Beyond the outer gate was a waiting coach in which she drove at once to tell the Duchess of Montrose what had been done. Meantime Lord Nithsdale, dressed as an Italian servant, was posting along the road to Dover, where, next morning, he found a boat for Calais. It was not long before his wife rejoined him in Rome.

Lady Nithsdale's bold escapade was received by the people of England with very general approval. Even the Government, who were beginning to have doubts about the wisdom of their policy, were not disposed to be too severe on the heroic wife. When the Duchess of Montrose went to Court next day she found the King very angry. But the royal anger was short-lived. Presently he began to laugh. "Upon my soul," he said, "for a man in my lord's situation it was the very best thing he could have done."

Jack Sheppard Earns Fame

PHILLIP ALBAN

Jack Sheppard was a none-too-discreet petty thief born in London in 1702. Although his robberies showed little forethought and netted few successes, his two clever and determined escapes from Newgate Prison made him one of the most famous men in 18th-century England. Newgate was a huge, ancient, and imposing prison that for centuries housed many of England's most notorious criminals. When Jack Sheppard made his first surprising escape the day before he was to be hanged in the summer of 1724, with the help of a file slipped in by a girlfriend, he became an instant celebrity.

Instead of leaving the city, however, he chose to stay and revel in his new status in the underworld. After the crude theft of a few watches, he was recaptured and again brought to Newgate. His second escape—from the strongest cell in the prison, known as "the Castle"—still stands as one of the most impressive in history.

He was carried back at once to Newgate. It is hardly necessary to say that such steps were now taken as were considered effectual to prevent him ever escaping again. Yet he had not been twenty-four hours in the prison before one of his friends managed to hand him the tools for effecting his release. On 12th September a small file was discovered between the leaves of his Bible; four days later a complete outfit of escaper's tools was revealed in the rush seat of his chair. Accordingly, he was put into the strongest cell, known as 'The Castle,' handcuffed, manacled with heavy leg irons, and chained by these irons to a staple fixed in the floor.

Jack had now reached the height of his fame—a fame that had spread through the town. On Sunday, 13th September, a 'vast concourse' flocked to the prison to see him, and the chapel was crowded. He was visited by all manner of people: literary men and Fleet Street dwellers came to talk with him, and hardly anyone left without making him a present of some kind or other. But in spite of the fact that these presents enabled him to obtain luxuries which were unheard of in Newgate, the one dominating idea in his mind was—escape. His fertile brain soon suggested a plan.

On the 14th October the Sessions began at the Old Bailey, and as the gaolers were kept busy in continually attending the Court, he judged that this was a propitious moment in which to attempt his escape, seeing that the gaolers would have little time to visit him. Accordingly, about two o'clock on the following afternoon, as soon as one of the gaolers had brought him his dinner and, having examined his irons, had gone out and locked the door, Jack set about his great exploit. It was undoubtedly a great exploit—one of the greatest in prison-breaking that has ever been recorded.

His first object was to free himself from his handcuffs. This he accomplished by holding the chain that connected them between his teeth, and, squeezing his fingers as closely together as possible, drawing his hands through the manacles. He next twisted the heavy links of the ankle-chain round and round, and partly by main strength, partly by a dexterous and well-applied jerk, snapped asunder the central link by which they were attached to the staple in the floor. Taking off his stockings he then drew the anklets up as far as he could and tied the chains to his legs to prevent them from clanking and impeding him.

A brief inspection of the chimney showed him that escape that way was prevented by an iron bar which was fixed across it a few feet up. To remove this obstacle it was necessary to make a hole in the wall big enough for him to crawl through. With the broken link of the ankle-chain as his only tool, he began operations just above the chimney-piece and soon managed to pick a hole in the plaster. As he suspected, he found that the wall was solidly constructed of brick and stone, and with such a tool as he possessed it was a work of infinite labour to get out a single brick. But he knew that when once that was done the rest would be comparatively easy, and he set to work with a will, and presently succeeded in removing the first brick.

Heartened by this success he set to work more vigorously, and the rapidity of his progress was soon evident by the heap of bricks, stones, and mortar which littered the floor. At the end of an hour he had made so large a hole in the chimney that he could stand upright in it. He was now within a foot of the bar, and squirming himself into the hole he soon worked his way to it. Regardless of the risk he ran by heavy stones dropping on his head, and paying no heed to the noise made by the falling rubbish which might well have attracted the attention of the gaolers, he continued to pull down large masses of the wall, which he flung upon the floor of the cell.

Having worked thus for another quarter of an hour, half stifled by the clouds of dust which his exertions raised, he found he had made a hole about three feet wide and six high, and had uncovered the iron bar. Grasping it with both hands he wrenched it from the stones into which it was mortised, and climbed down again to the floor. On examination it proved to be a square bar of iron, nearly a yard long, and more than an inch thick. Seeing that his only tool so far was quite inadequate for the purpose of breaking out of prison, he must have thought all his efforts to obtain this bar were well worth while.

Jack knew that it was impossible for him to escape by any other way than the roof. And to reach it would be a most difficult undertaking. Still, it was possible, and it was essential that he should escape. Blueskin. . . . He grasped his bar and started again.

He had a fair idea of the prison buildings, and he guessed that he would have to break open five or six heavily ironed doors. But he now had a tool that would serve as a useful 'jemmy,' and possibly the thought of what a stir his escape would make acted as a strong incentive. He was only twenty-three.

The heap of bricks and rubble which now littered the floor of his cell amounted almost to a cartload, and stepping over this he climbed once more into the chimney, and having reached the level of the room above recommenced operations as vigorously as before. The bar proved a serviceable tool, and with it he soon managed to make a hole in the wall. Before proceeding with this task he had considered whether it would be possible to barricade the door, but the bar was the only instrument with which he could have effected this, and as it was indispensable for his further efforts he gave up the idea, and determined to rely on the good fortune which had hitherto attended him.

The cell which he had now reached was called 'The Red Room' from the fact of its walls having been once painted that colour. Like 'The Castle,' which it resembled in respect of size, it was destitute of furniture; for it was reserved for state prisoners and had not been occupied since 1716, when the gaol was crowded with the Preston rebels.

Having made a hole in the wall sufficiently large for him to pass through, Jack tossed the bar into the room and crept after it. In stepping across the room he trod on something sharp which pierced the sole of his shoe, and stooping to see what it was found that it was a long rusty nail which projected from the boards. This he picked up, and reserved for future use: indeed he endeavoured presently to pick the lock of the door with it, but being unsuccessful he prised off the lock plate with the bar and, inserting his fingers, managed to draw back the bolt. Opening the door he stepped out into a dark narrow passage, leading, as he knew, to the chapel.

On the left there were doors communicating with the King's Bench Ward and the Stone Ward—two large rooms on the master debtors' side. The sound of voices coming from them cautioned him to go quietly, and he tip-toed to the end of the passage. Here his progress was checked by a strong door several inches thick, and nearly as wide as the passage. Running his hand over it he found to his dismay that the lock was on the other side. After several careful attempts to burst it open he decided to break through the wall on the side nearest the lock. This, however, was a much more serious task than he anticipated. The wall was a stone one and of considerable thickness; moreover, the noise that he made was so great that he feared it would be heard by the prisoners in the King's Bench Ward. However, it was neck or nothing, so he went to work again with more vigour than ever. At the end of half-an-hour's severe labour, during which he was obliged several times to stop for breath, he had managed to make a hole wide enough to admit his arm up to the elbow. Luckily, his fingers soon touched the bolt, and working it up and down he managed to push it back. To his delight the door instantly yielded, and passing on he hurried into the chapel.

The chapel of Old Newgate was situated at the upper part of the south-eastern angle of the gaol, and was divided on the north side into three grated compartments, or 'pens' as they were called, which were used by the felons and common debtors. At the end of these there was a small pen for female offenders, and on the south side of the chapel there was a larger enclosure which was used by the master debtors and strangers. Immediately beneath the pulpit was a large circular pen where criminals under sentence of death sat to hear the condemned sermon delivered at them, and where they provided a spectacle for the crowds drawn thither by curiosity on these occasions.

The door through which Jack had entered the chapel opened into one of the pens on the north side. The enclosure surrounding it was about twelve feet high, the under part being composed of oak planks, the upper part of a strong iron grating surmounted by iron spikes. In the middle was a gate, which of course was locked. Jack soon prised this open with the iron bar, and presently reached the condemned pew—where it had been his fortune to sit not so long before. A strange whim drew him to take his seat there again, and he sat down for a few moments and closed his eyes. But the vision of his previous occupancy of this pen, the three companions who had shared it with him, the clank of the heavy fetters as they shuffled uneasily beneath the gaze of the crowd of visitors, the droning voice of the chaplain imploring him to prepare for eternity,—all was so vivid that he started up and instinctively took refuge in the pen from which he had just emerged. Presently, recovering himself, he made his way to a gate on the south side of the chapel, managed to break off one of the spikes, and then climbed over it. A short flight of stairs brought him to a dark passage down which he went. Here he came up against another strong door, making the fifth he had encountered. Naturally the doors affording egress from the prison were considerably stronger than those within it, so he was hardly surprised to find that this door was fastened with a lock of unusual strength. After repeatedly attempting to remove the plate, which was so strongly bolted that it resisted all his efforts, and vainly attempting to pick the lock with the nail and the spike which he had broken off the passage door, he at length, after half-an-hour's hard work, prised off the box containing the lock; whereupon, as he laughingly told one of his visitors later, the door became 'his humble servant.'

Unhappily for him this door was not the last which he was to encounter, for just as he anticipated stepping out on to the roof, he came to door number six. He guessed that there might be another door here, but he was not prepared for its appearance. Running his hand over it he found that it was a complicated mass of bolts and bars. It seemed, indeed, as if all the precautions previously taken to prevent prisoners from escaping had been collected here. He was hardly as fresh as he had been at the start and his hands were sore with the labour he had already accomplished. For a moment or two he must have contemplated giving up the attempt. But a short rest revived his spirits and he went at the door with renewed vigour. First of all he passed his hands slowly and carefully all over it, making a mental picture of all the contrivances which held it in place. The lock appeared to be more than a foot wide, it was strongly plated, and was fastened to the door with thick iron hoops. Below it an enormously thick bolt was shot far into a socket, and in order to keep it there it was fastened to the hasp by an immense padlock. In addition to this the door was criss-crossed with iron bars bolted to the oak. A thick iron band secured the bolt socket and the tongue of the lock to the main post of the doorway. The hinges were un-get-at-able, being fixed to the door from the outside. It was an obstacle that would have daunted most escapers.

Jack set to work upon the lock and attacked it with all his implements in turn, the bar, the nail and the spike, but made not the slightest impression upon it. After an hour's toil he had broken the nail, and had slightly bent the bar. He was also considerably overcome by fatigue, had strained the muscles of his arms, and had made his hands so sore that he could hardly hold his tools. He was streaming with perspiration, and his lips and tongue were so dry that he asserted afterwards he would have parted with years of liberty for a drink of water. Apparently he had a moment's panic here, being quite certain that he could hear rapid footsteps making their way towards him, but presently he recovered his self-possession and sat down to think out the best way of getting through this door.

After a few minutes' thought it occurred to him that he might possibly be able to loosen the iron fillet which held the bolt socket and the tongue of the lock to the main post of the doorway. At length, with incredible labour and by the aid of both spike and nail, he succeeded in getting the point of the bar underneath this fillet. With one foot against the doorpost, and exerting every muscle in his body, he at last managed to lever up the iron band. It was seven feet long, seven inches wide, and two inches thick. After a short rest he went at it again, and inserting the bar now here now there between the fillet and the doorpost, he at length prised the whole of this band from its seating. In its fall it brought with it the bolt socket and the box containing the tongue of the lock. Next moment, Jack was on the other side of the door. A short flight of steps led to the roof, and at the top of these was a door bolted on the inside. He opened this, and the fresh air of London blew upon his face.

Sheppard had now reached what was called the tower leads, a flat roof which covered that part of the prison contiguous to the gateway, and surrounded on all sides by walls about fourteen feet high. On the north stood the battlements of one of the gate towers, and on this side a flight of wooden steps protected by a handrail led to a door opening upon the summit of the prison. This door was crested with spikes and guarded on the right by a semicircle of similar obstacles. Running up the steps Jack found the door, as he anticipated, locked. He could easily have forced it, but preferred a more expeditious way of reaching the roof. Mounting the door which he had last opened, he placed his hands on the wall above and drew himself up. In a moment he was on the roof of the prison. At this instant the clock of St. Sepulchre's struck eight: Jack had thus been six hours in breaking out of the gaol.

It was nearly dark now, but there was still enough light to enable him to discern surrounding objects. Proceeding along the wall he reached the southern door, climbed over its battlements, and dropped down upon the roof of the gate. He then climbed the north tower and made his way to the roof of that part of the prison which fronted Giltspur Street. Arriving here he found that he was overlooking the flat roof of a house, which roof, so far as he could judge in the darkness, was about twenty feet below him. Realising the risk of so great a drop, he turned about to see if he could find any more favourable place to descend, but could see nothing beyond lofty walls without a single projection. The roof of the house *looked* about twenty feet below him, but it might have been a good deal more, and prudence reminded him that to undergo six hours' excessive labour in breaking out of Newgate only to lie with a broken thigh on the roof of a house adjoining would have been foolish in the extreme. The only thing to do, therefore, was to go back for his blanket, and make a rope. This resolution must have taken a good deal of courage, for it was quite likely that his absence from his cell had been noticed by now, and although the contemporary accounts are silent on this point, it is safe to wager that Master Jack must have thought three, four, or more times before he could bring himself to go back to his cell. Yet go back he did. In fact, there was no alternative.

But he took the iron bar with him in case he met anybody on the way. . . .

As he passed the doors leading to the master debtors' side of the prison, he heard someone singing a roistering song which was followed by boisterous laughter, and this somewhat reassured him. The news of an escape passes quickly through a prison, and Jack was so notorious that even a rumour of his flight would have caused suppressed excitement. Entering the Red Room he crept down the chimney into the Castle—and found that his blanket was buried underneath the cartload of rubble encumbering the floor. However, he discovered the blanket at last, and presently he once more found himself looking down on the roof of the house in Giltspur Street.

Having torn his blanket into wide strips which he knotted together, he fastened one end of this improvised rope to the wall with the spike which he had broken off in the chapel, hammering it into the mortar with his bar. This done, he let himself carefully down and dropped lightly on to the leaden roof. After listening for a few minutes he stepped cautiously forward and found a small garret door in the roof which was open. Entering this, he passed through a bedroom, opened the room door and proceeded to go quietly downstairs. Half-way down his leg chains rattled slightly. 'Oh, Lor! what's that!' cried a woman's voice in an adjoining room. 'Only the dog,' replied the rough tones of a man, and all was silent again. Jack waited a little, and muffling the chains as best he could, he stole down the remaining stairs and had nearly reached the hall when a door suddenly opened and two people appeared, one of whom held a candle. Retreating as quickly as possible, Jack opened the first door he came to, and searching in the dark for somewhere to hide was lucky enough to discover a screen behind which he crept. Having lain here for some considerable time he at length ventured out on to the landing and downstairs once more—this time to see a man at the open front door taking leave of the family.

As soon as the maid had retired with the candle, Jack crept into the hall, stumbled, recovered himself, opened the door, and found himself in the street.

Sheppard again stayed in London to enjoy his fame. He was caught four weeks later and this time there was no escaping the hangman's noose. He died at the age of twenty-three.

Escape from Leads

CASANOVA

Remembered mostly for his legendary romantic escapades, Jacques Casanova also put his clever mind and glib tongue to use in escaping from the Leads, one of the most feared prisons in Europe. The charges against him were more or less crimes against religion during the time of the Inquisition, and in 1755 he was sentenced to five years in prison.

Being just thirty years old and chafing at the interruption of his flamboyant lifestyle, Casanova resolved to free himself, despite the fact that the Leads was widely considered escape-proof. Using a small bit of discarded iron, he cut a tunnel beneath his cell over the span of several months. Just before his planned exit, he was unexpectedly moved to another cell. His tunnel was discovered, but he was able to hide his cutting tool. When confronted by Lorenzo, his jailer, about what he had used to make the hole, Casanova used his famous cunning to turn the tables, calmly telling Lorenzo that it was he himself who had provided the tool and that it had been returned to him after the cutting was complete. Lorenzo was stumped, as he quickly saw the accusation could do him great harm with his superiors, even though he was completely innocent. The matter was dropped.

Casanova quickly conceived a new plan, one that would have to be acted upon from outside his now closely watched cell. Smuggling the tool to a monk named Balbi in a neighboring cell, he convinced this man that if he would cut his way into Casanova's room, he would have a plan worked out for both of them to escape. Just before Balbi was ready to break through, Casanova was surprised again; this time with a new cellmate, Soradaci. In a hilarious scene, Casanova convinces this simple-minded informer that an angel has assumed human form to reward him for his supposed piety by breaking into their cell to allow them to escape. Lo and behold, the angel (Balbi) appears right on cue at the newly opened hole, and all three men prepare to leave the prison. Casanova then cuts a hole into the attic and makes ready to crawl out onto the sharply angled roof. Angel or no angel, Soradaci balks at the danger inherent in leaving via the steep, slick lead roof and elects to stay behind. Happily rid of this foolish man but still needing at least one companion, Casanova cajoles Balbi, the monk/angel, into continuing on despite his strong dislike for the man's weak will and deceitful nature.

While the details of the escape, taken directly from Casanova's voluminous memoir, may certainly have been embellished to some degree, it is likely that the events themselves did occur. Either way, it is hard not to appreciate his considerable style and cunning. Once free, Casanova again took up his life of excess and debauchery, aided greatly by the fame of his escape.

It was now time to start. The moon was no longer visible. I tied half the cords on one of Balbi's shoulders, and his packet of clothes on the other, doing the same for myself; then the two of us, in our shirt-sleeves, our hats on our heads, went through the opening.

I went out first, Balbi followed me; Soradaci had orders to put the sheet of lead covering the hole back into its place, and then to go and pray with all his might to Saint Francis. I crawled along on all fours, pushing my tool into the cracks between the leaden roofing, and dragging the monk after me. With his right hand he firmly clutched the band of my breeches, so that I was in the painful position of a pack-horse and saddle-horse combined, and this on a steep lead roof made more slippery by the damp of a thick fog! Half-way up the monk called out to me to stop; one of his packages had slipped, but he was in hopes it had lodged in the gutter piping. My first impulse was to give him a kick and send him after it, but I checked myself, and asked him if it was the packet of cords; he said no, it was his clothes and a manuscript which he had found in the prison attic, and which he expected to sell for a high price. I told him he must bear his loss patiently; he sighed, and we crawled on. By and by we got to a gable, on which we could sit astride; two hundred feet in front of us were the cupolas of Saint Mark, which is, properly speaking, the private chapel of the Doge, and no monarch in the world can boast of a better or finer. Here my unfortunate companion lost his hat, which rolled over and over till it joined his clothes in the canal. He declared this was a bad omen, but I cheered him by pointing out that if the hat had fallen to the left, instead of to the right, it would have tumbled at the very feet of the guards in the courtyard. It was a proof, I told him, that God was protecting us, and at the same time, it was a lesson to him to be more prudent.

I left Balbi perched on the gable, while I explored the roof in search of some skylight or window, by means of which we could enter the palace.

After searching for more than an hour without finding any point to which I could fasten my cords, the canal and the courtyard were not to be thought of; to get beyond the church, towards the *Canonica,* I should have to climb such perilous slopes that I abandoned this idea also. Nevertheless, something must be done. I fixed my eyes on a garret window facing the canal, about two-thirds from the top of the roof. It was far enough away from our part of the palace for me to feel sure it was not connected with the prisons. If I could get in through it I should probably find myself in some attic, inhabited or otherwise, belonging to the apartment of some one of the palace functionaries, and at break of day the doors would be opened. I was morally certain that any of the palace servants, even those of the Doge himself, so far from giving us up to justice, would only help us in our flight, even had we been the worst of criminals, so hateful was the Inquisition in the eyes of all men. I let myself slide down the roof till I arrived astraddle the garret window; by leaning over I could feel it was filled with small panes of glass, behind which was a grating. The glass was easily disposed of, but in my nervous state of mind the grating, slight though it was, filled me with dismay. I was weary, hungry, overexcited, and this obstacle seemed insurmountable. I was beginning to lose my head, and my courage, when the simplest incident imaginable restored my mental equilibrium. The bell of Saint Mark's struck twelve! The day now beginning was All Saints, the prediction of the Jesuit father flashed through my mind, and at the same moment I remembered the line from Ariosto—

"Fra il fin d'ottobre e il capo di novembre."

The sound of the bell was as a speaking talisman to me, bidding me be of good heart, and promising me victory. I broke the glass, and after a quarter of an hour's hard work with my pike I lifted out the entire grating; blood was streaming from a wound in my left hand, but I was too excited to notice it.

I got back to my companion, who welcomed me with the grossest insults, for having left him so long, at the same time assuring me he was only waiting for seven o'clock to return to the prison. "And what did you think had become of me?"

"I thought you had fallen over."

"And this is how you show your joy at my safety! Follow me now, and you will see where I have been."

We scrambled to the garret window, and held a consultation as to the best means of entering it; it was easy enough for one, as the other could lower him by the cords, but how was he to follow after?

"Let me down first," said the amiable Balbi, "and when I am safe inside you will find some means of rejoining me." His brutal selfishness made me feel like digging my pike in his stomach, but I again restrained myself, and silently did as he asked. When I drew up the cord, I found the height from the window to the floor was thirty feet, the window was high in the roof of an immensely lofty gallery. Not knowing what to do, I wandered over the leads, where, on a sort of terrace I had not visited before, I found a tub full of plaster, a trowel, and a ladder. I dragged the ladder after me to the window, and managed to push it in as far as the fifth rung, but beyond that it was impossible, as there was an interior beam, which barred its entrance. The only thing was to push it from below instead of from above, as I was then doing. I fastened the cord to the ladder, and let it slip, till it hung balanced on a point of the gutter piping, and then slid gently along till I was beside it. The marble gutter offered a slight rest to my feet, and I lay on my stomach up the roof; in this position I had the strength to raise the ladder and push it before me. I got about a foot of it inside, which diminished the weight sensibly, when in my efforts to force it I slipped, and rolled over the roof, hanging only by my elbows to the gutter. In this frightful position I remained, as it seemed to me, some moments, but did not lose my presence of mind; the instinct of self-preservation made me, almost against my will, use all my strength in the supreme effort of hoisting myself back on the roof. I succeeded. I now lay along the gutter, panting and exhausted, but safe for the moment, though not out of danger, or at an end of my troubles, for the effort I had made caused a nervous contraction of my muscles, which resulted in a cramp so painful I completely lost the use of my limbs. I knew that immobility is the best remedy for cramp, and I had the sense to remain perfectly still until it passed away. What a terrible moment it was! By and by I was able to move my knees, and as soon as I had recovered my breath, I raised the ladder (which had fortunately been held in place by the frame of the window), and managed to introduce several more rungs of it through the opening, until it leaned parallel with the sill.

I then took up my pike, and once more climbed slowly and painfully up the slippery leads, till I got to the window, where I had no further difficulty with the ladder. I pushed it all in, and my companion held the other end of it firmly.

I flung into the attic the remaining parcels of clothes, the cords, and such *débris* and rubbish caused by my demolitions as I could gather up. I was particularly anxious not to leave any marks of my passage behind me on the roof. It was there that the archers, led by Laurence, would first search for us, and it was possible that we might still be lurking in the attic when they came that way.

This done, I descended the ladder into the garret, where the monk received me, more graciously this time.

Arm in arm we walked round the shadowy place in which we found ourselves. It was about thirty feet long by twenty wide; at one end was a door barred with iron; this, however, was not locked, and we went through it into another room, in the middle of which was a big table surrounded with chairs and stools. We opened one of the windows, but could see nothing but precipices, so to speak, between the windows. I closed the window, and went back to where we had left our baggage. Perfectly incapable of further effort, I fell on the floor; with a roll of cords to serve for a pillow, I gave myself up to sleep. Had I been certain that death, or torture, awaited me on waking, it would have made no difference. Even now I can remember the heavenly sensations of rest and forgetfulness which came over me as I sank to slumber.

I slept for three hours and a half; the monk aroused me by shouting and shaking me. He told me it had struck five, and he could not understand how, given our position, I could sleep! *I* could, though! For two days and nights I had not closed my eyes, and for the same length of time had eaten nothing; the efforts I had made were enough to wear out the strength of any man. My nap had restored my vigour, I was able now to think and to act.

"This place," said I, "is not a prison, so there must be some way out of it."

There was a door at one end, through which we passed into a gallery lined with shelves filled with papers: these were the archives, as I afterwards learned. A little stone staircase took us to a second gallery, and a second staircase into a large hall, which I recognized as the ducal chancery. On a desk lay a tool, a sort of long slim chisel which the secretaries use to pierce parchments with, so as to attach the lead seals of the chancery to them. I forced the desk with it, and found a letter to the *proveditor* of Corfu, announcing the despatch of three thousand sequins, which he was to spend on the restoration of the old fortress. Unfortunately the money was not there; God knows with what pleasure I should have taken it had it been otherwise.

I tried to force the door of the chancery with my chisel, but soon saw that it was impossible. I decided to make a hole in the panelling. With my pike I smashed and battered as well as I could, the monk helping me with the chisel, and both of us trembling at the noise we made.

In half an hour the hole was large enough, but it presented a terrific appearance, for the edges were splintered and broken, and bristling with sharp points, like the spikes on the top of a wall; it was about five feet from the ground. Putting two stools one on the other, we mounted on them, and taking Balbi first by the thighs and then by the ankles, I managed to lower him in safety. There was no one to help me, so I stuck my head and shoulders through as far as I could, and told the monk to drag me over the splinters, and not to stop, even if I reached the other side in pieces; he obeyed, and I arrived in frightful pain, with my hips and thighs torn and bleeding.

We ran down another staircase, at the bottom of which was the great door of the royal staircase. At one glance I saw that it was impossible to get through that without a mine to blow it up, or a catapult to beat it down. My poor pike seemed to say: *Hic finis posuit.*

Calm, resigned, and perfectly tranquil, I sat down, saying to the monk: "I have done, it is for God or fortune to do the rest. I don't know if the palace sweepers will come to-day, as it is a holiday—All Saints Day, or to-morrow, which is All Souls. If any one does come, I shall make a run for it as soon as I see the door open, but otherwise, I shall not move from here, if I die of hunger."

At this speech the poor man flew into a rage, calling me madman, seducer, liar. I let him rave without paying any attention to him. Even if some one opened the door, how to pass unnoticed in the state I was in!

Balbi looked like a peasant, but he was at least intact. His scarlet flannel waistcoat and his violet skin breeches were in good condition, and he was un-scratched, whereas my appearance was horrible. I was covered with blood, and my clothes were in ribbons. I had torn my stockings, and scraped all the skin off my knees while I was hanging from the gutter piping; the broken panel of the chancery door had caught and rent my waistcoat, shirt, and breeches into rags. My thighs were furrowed with deep wounds.

I bandaged myself up as well as I could with handkerchiefs, smoothed my hair, put on a clean pair of stockings and a laced shirt with two others on the top of it, stuffed as many handkerchiefs and stockings as I could into my pockets, and flung the remainder into a corner.

I must have looked like a reveller who had wound up the evening in some wild orgy! To crown all I put on my fine hat, trimmed with Spanish gold lace, and a long white feather; and thus attired I opened a window. It is not surprising that I immediately attracted the attention of the loungers in the courtyard, one of whom went to tell the concierge. The good man thought he must have locked some one in by mistake the night before, and ran off for his keys. I heard them jingling as he came upstairs; I could hear him puffing at every step. I told Balbi to keep close to me, and not to open his mouth. I stood, my pike in my hand, so that I could get out of the door the moment it was opened. I prayed to God that the concierge would make no resistance, as I was prepared to kill him if need were.

The poor fellow was thunderstruck at my aspect. I rushed past him and down the stairs, the monk at my heels. I went rapidly, yet avoiding the appearance of flight, down the magnificent steps called the Giant's Staircase, paying no heed to Balbi, who kept saying, "To the church, to the church." The door of Saint Mark's was not twenty paces away, but one could no longer take sanctuary there. The monk knew that, but fear had spoilt his memory. I went straight through the royal gate of the palace, across the little square, and on to the quay, where I got into the first gondola I saw, saying to the boatman, "I want to go to Fusina quickly; call up another gondolier." While the boat was being unfastened I flung myself on the cushion in the middle, while the monk took his place on the seat. We must have been an odd-looking couple: he with his extraordinary face and bare head, my beautiful cloak flung over his shoulders, and I with my most unseasonable elegance, plumed hat, and ragged breeches, laced shirt and bleeding wrists. We must have looked like a pair of charlatans who had been in some drunken fray.

When we were well started I told the boatman I had changed my mind, I would go to Mestre. He replied that he would take me to England if I would pay him enough, and we went gaily on.

The canal had never seemed to me so beautiful, more especially as there was not a single boat in sight. It was a lovely morning, the air was fresh and clear and the sun had just risen. My two boatmen rowed swiftly. I thought on the awful nights I had passed, the dangers I had traversed, the hell in which only a few hours before I was imprisoned; my emotion and my gratitude to God overcame me, and I burst into tears. My worshipful companion, who up till then had not spoken a word, thought it his duty to console me. He made me laugh.

At Mestre I arranged for a post-chaise to take us on to Treviso; in three minutes the horses were in. I looked round for Balbi, he had disappeared; I was on the point of abandoning him when I caught sight of the scamp in a coffee-house, drinking chocolate and flirting with the waiting-maid. When he saw me he called out to me to come and join him, and to pay for what he had consumed, as he was penniless. Speechless with rage, I grasped him by the arm and marched him up to the post-chaise. We had not gone many yards before I met a man I knew, Balbi Tomasi, a decent fellow, but reported to have dealings with the inquisitors; he recognized me and cried out: "Hallo! what are you doing here? I am delighted to see you, have you run away?"

"I have not run away, I was set at liberty."

"Impossible! I was at M. Grimani's only yesterday, and I heard nothing of it."

Reader, it is easier for you to imagine the state of mind I was in than for me to describe it. I thought this man was paid to arrest me; that in another moment he would call up the police, who were all over Mestre, and I should be ignominiously marched back to "The Leads." I jumped out of the carriage, and asked him to step to one side with me. As soon as we were at a safe distance from the others I seized him by the collar; he saw the pike I was brandishing and guessed my intention; with a violent effort he wrenched himself away, and ran with all his might down the road, jumping over a wide ditch, from the other side of which he kissed his hand to me several times, as a sign that I had his good wishes. I was glad I had been saved from committing murder, for I began to think he meant me no harm. I got back into the chaise, looking disdainfully at the cowardly monk, who saw now the danger he had exposed us to, and we went on in silence to Treviso.

There I ordered a chaise and pair for ten o'clock, though I had no intention of taking them, firstly, because I had not enough money, and, secondly because a post-chaise is easily tracked; it was merely a ruse. The landlord asked if we wished breakfast, but though I was fainting with hunger I had not the courage to eat anything; a quarter of an hour's delay might prove fatal. I wanted to get out into the open country where one man, if he is clever, can defy a hundred thousand.

We passed out of Treviso by Saint Thomas's gate, and struck across the fields. After walking for three hours I fell down exhausted. I told Balbi to get me something to eat or I should die; he said contemptuously that he had thought I was braver. He had filled his own stomach full before leaving "The Leads," and he had taken some chocolate and bread since. However, he found a farmhouse not far off, and brought me back a good dinner for thirty sols; after which we walked for another four hours, and then stopped by the roadside, twenty-four miles from Treviso. I was exhausted; my ankles were swollen and my shoes worn through.

I felt that it was impossible for me to continue to travel with Balbi; to think for him as well as myself, and to be constantly bickering and reproaching one another. His presence irritated me in my worn and nervous state, and I felt willing to pay any price to be rid of him.

"We must go to Borgo di Valsugano," I said; "it is the first town across the frontier of the Republic; we shall be as safe there as if we were in London; but we must use every precaution, and the first is to separate. You will go by the woods of Mantello, and I by the mountains; you will take the easiest and shortest way, and I the longest and most difficult; you will have money, and I shall have none. I make you a present of my cloak, which you can easily change for a coat and a hat; here is all that is left of the two sequins I took from Asquini. For to-night I shall trust to luck to find me a bed somewhere. I am absolutely in need of rest and peace, which I can't get with you. I am, moreover, certain that they are looking for us, and that if we show ourselves together at any inn we shall be arrested. You go your way, and let me go mine."

"I have been expecting some such speech," said Balbi, "and shall answer it by reminding you of all your promises. You said we should not separate, and I do not intend to; your fate shall be mine, and mine yours."

"You are determined not to take my advice?"

"Most determined."

"We shall see."

I took my instrument out of my pocket, and began quietly to dig a hole in the ground. After half an hour of this occupation I told him to recommend his soul to God, for the hole I had just made was to bury him in.

"I will get rid of you somehow—alive or dead."

He looked at me for some time in silence, wondering whether I was in earnest or not, then coming over to me—"I will do as you wish," he said.

I embraced him, and handed him the money.

I cannot say how pleased I was to see him disappear down the road.

The Bastille

HENRI MASERS DE LATUDE

Henri Masers de Latude, as he chose to be called, is one of the most famous escapers in history. As a clever but callow youth, he attempted a minor intrigue hoping to make a name for himself in France. Instead, he earned the lifelong enmity of Madame de Pompadour, and, hence, Louis XV. He would spend the next thirty-five years in prison, often under horrific conditions, before his eventual release from the Bastille in 1784. Latude made several spectacular escapes over the years, but he was always tracked down and returned to his fate—even beyond the borders of France—by the agents of Madame de Pompadour.

Through the long years of misery, Latude somehow managed to keep alive his determination to be free. In 1756, while housed in a cell within the imposing walls of the Bastille, he and a cellmate, D'Alègre, completed what has to be considered one of the most interesting escapes ever made. As this story from Latude's memoirs begins, D'Alègre is stricken with despair at the thought of spending the rest of his days in the Bastille.

My companion broke down under his grief; mine, however, produced a very different effect, giving me the courage and the energy of despair. In such circumstances, only two ways lay open to men yet youthful: to die, or to escape. To any man having the least idea of the Bastille and its position—of the enclosure, the towers, and the system, also the incredible precautions multiplied by despotism so to enchain its victims more surely—the project and the sole thought of escape must appear as the outcome of delirium and, seemingly, can inspire nothing but pity for poor wretches so destitute of sense as to risk such an attempt. Nevertheless I was thoroughly sane when I formed this resolve; and, as will be seen, a most uncommon mind and perhaps a very level head were necessary to devise, ponder, and to execute such a plan.

Here I pause, recalling to my readers the vow I have made to say no word incompatible with the most rigid truth. Whether they will believe themselves transported to some new sphere, in reading my subsequent narrative, or whether they may credit me with magical power, I leave to the free play of imagination; so far as I am concerned, I shall recount facts alone.

It was useless to think for an instant of escaping from the Bastille through the doors, since every physical impossibility combined to render that way impracticable: the last resort, therefore, led through the air. Certainly we had a chimney in our room, the shaft of which emerged at the top of the tower; but, like all Bastille chimneys, this was encumbered with gratings and bars, in several places barely allowing free passage even to the smoke. If we could reach the summit of the tower we should have an abyss of about two hundred feet beneath us; and, at the base, a moat dominated by an excessively high wall, which had to be scaled. We were alone, without tools, without materials, and spied on at each moment of the day and night; watched over meanwhile by a multitude of sentries who surrounded the Bastille, apparently investing it.

So many obstacles, so many dangers, did not discourage me. I sought to impart my idea to my comrade: who sank into a torpor, thinking I must be mad. Thus I was obliged to busy myself alone with this scheme, to think it out, foreseeing the host of frightful difficulties opposed to the execution, finding means to overcome all. To succeed, we must climb to the apex of the chimney, and in spite of the numerous and hampering iron gratings. A ladder of at least two hundred feet would be required for the descent from the top of the tower into the moat; and a second, necessarily of wood, to climb thence. In the event of my procuring materials, I must be able to hide them from espionage, and to work noiselessly, deceiving the crowd of attendants, cozening their senses, and for several months thus to trick their sight and hearing. How could I tell! It was essential to foreknow and to allow for a mass of obstacles continuously renewed, which, each day, and every instant of the day, would crop up, one created by the other, arresting and thwarting the application of my plan, maybe one of the boldest ever conceived by the imagination or carried through to an end by human industry. Reader, this I achieved! and, once again, I swear I am telling only the exact truth. Now let us follow all my operations in detail.

The first consideration was to discover a place where we could hide our tools and materials from sight, in the event of our being clever enough to get such things. By dint of hard thinking I grasped what seemed to me a most happy idea. I had inhabited several different rooms in the Bastille; and invariably when those above and below were occupied I could hear clearly any noise made in the one or the other. On this occasion I heard the movements of the prisoner above, and nothing whatsoever from below; I felt sure, however, that someone must be there. By calculation I hit on the notion of a possible double floor, divided by a little space. The following are the means I employed to convince myself.

In the Bastille there was a chapel where one mass was said each day, and three were said of a Sunday. This chapel had four small cabinets disposed so that the priest could never see any of the prisoners, who in turn, and by means of a curtain drawn aside only for the elevation, could never look directly at the priest. Permission to attend mass was a special favour granted only after much difficulty. This M. Berryer obtained for us, likewise for the prisoner who occupied room No. 3, the one beneath ours.

I determined to take a rapid survey of this room when, on coming from mass, I could steal a moment before the prisoner would be shut in again. I suggested to D'Alègre a means of helping me to this end: I instructed him to put his pocket-case in his handkerchief and, when we reached the second floor, to withdraw his handkerchief in such fashion that the case would fall to the bottom of the stairs; then he must ask the turnkey to go and pick it up. This man, Daragon, is yet alive. Our little manoeuvre was wholly successful. Whilst Daragon ran after the case I ascended quickly to room No. 3. I drew the bolt of the door, examined the ceiling, and noted that it was not more than ten and a half feet high; I closed the door again, and counted thirty-two steps from this room to our own; I measured the height of each step, and, as a result of calculation, found that there was a space of five and a half feet between the floor of our room and the ceiling of the one below. This could be filled neither with stones nor wood; for such weight would have been tremendous. Accordingly, I concluded that there must be a sort of drum, an empty space, of four feet between floor and ceiling.

We were shut in, the bolts were shot; and I fell on D'Alègre's neck and embraced him rapturously, drunk with hope and assurance. I said:

"My friend, patience, courage; we are saved!"

I told him of my observations and calculations, and continued:

"We can hide our ropes and materials—all I need. We are saved."

"What!" he said; "then you have not ceased to dream? Ropes, materials! Where are they? Where can we get them?"

I pointed to my trunk, saying:

"Ropes!—as many as we need. This trunk holds more than a thousand feet."

I spoke ardently; and, full of my idea, of the ecstasy provoked by my new hopes, I seemed inspired to him. He fixed his glance on me, and, in tones of the most touching and the most tender concern he said:

"My friend, return to your senses and try to calm this frenzy possessing you. Your trunk, you say, holds more than a thousand feet of rope. I know as well as you what it contains: there is not one single inch of rope."

"What! Have I not a large quantity of linen, thirteen dozen and a half shirts, a great many towels, stockings, caps, and other things? Will they not furnish us with ropes? We can unravel them—thus our ropes!"

D'Alègre, thunderstruck, understood at once the full extent of my plan and notions: hope and the love of liberty never die in the heart of man, and were merely numbed in his heart. Almost immediately I warmed him, I fired him, with my ardour. However, he could not keep pace with me: and I had to meet a huddle of objections, and to rid him of all his fears. He said:

"How are we going to wrench all the iron gratings from our chimney? Where shall we get the materials for the necessary wooden ladder, and find tools for all this work? We do not possess the happy art of creating."

I answered:

"My friend, genius creates, and we have the genius of despair to direct our hands. I repeat: we shall be saved."

We had a folding table, supported by two iron hinge-pins: these we sharpened by whetting them on a floor-tile; and in less than two hours, and with our tinder-box steel, we fabricated a good penknife, which served to make two handles to these hinge-pins, whose chief use would be to dig the iron gratings from our chimney.

In the evening, after all the daily inspections were over, we raised one of the floor-tiles with the aid of our picks, and set ourselves to delve in such sort that in less than six hours we had pierced the floor: then we saw that my conjectures were well founded, discovering a space of four feet between the floor and the ceiling beneath. We replaced the tile, which showed no signs of removal.

These preliminaries completed, we unstitched two shirts and their hems, and drew the threads out one by one; we knotted them together and so made a certain number of bundles, which, subsequently, we fashioned into two large balls, each having fifty threads sixty feet long: we plaited them together and so obtained a rope about fifty-five feet long, wherewith we made a twenty-foot ladder, destined to hold us suspended above while we removed the bars and the iron points arming our chimney. This task proved the most painful and the most troublesome, demanding six months' toil; and the mere thought of it makes one shudder. We could work only by doubling our bodies, racking them in exceeding awkward postures; nor could we endure this position for more than an hour, nor descend without bleeding hands. The iron bars were bedded in a very hard mortar, which could be softened only by blowing water from our mouths into the holes we made.

The laboriousness of our task may be imagined when I say that we were content if, in an entire night, we removed but a fraction of the mortar. As fast as we tore out a bar of iron, we had to replace it in its hole, so to avoid detection during the frequent inspections imposed on us; and in such fashion that we could remove the bars when the moment to escape arrived.

After six months of this cruel and stubborn work we occupied ourselves with the wooden ladder needed to mount from the moat to the parapet, thence to the governor's garden. This ladder must be twenty-five feet long. To such an end we used the wood supplied to warm us—logs from eighteen to twenty inches long. We could not do without pulley-blocks, and many other things for which, indispensably, we must furnish ourselves with a saw: and I made one with an iron candlestick, by means of the second half of the steel, the other having been transformed into a penknife, or small blade. With this piece of steel, the saw, and the pins, we reduced the size of our logs, morticed and tenoned them, and fitted one into the other, each mortice and tenon having two holes in which to fix a rung, and two bolts to prevent it from slipping. We made only one side for our ladder, and twenty rungs, each fifteen inches long; and, the upright being three inches in diameter, each rung jutted out six inches on either side. At every section of the ladder we bound the rung to its bolt with twine, consequently, we could easily mount at night. We hid each completed and perfected section under the floor as fast as we made it.

With the same tools we fitted our workshop, making compasses for ourselves, a square, ruler, winder, pulley-blocks, rungs, and so on, all things—as may be imagined—being always carefully hidden in our storehouse. One danger, already foreseen, could be avoided solely by rigorous precaution. I have previously mentioned that, apart from the frequent inspections made by the turnkeys and various officers of the Bastille, one of the customs of the place was to spy on the actions and to overhear the talk of prisoners, and at moments the least expected. We could shelter ourselves from view by doing our principal work only at night, and taking the utmost caution to hide the slightest trace; for a wood-shaving, any scrap of rubbish, might betray us; but, in addition, we had to cheat the ears of our spies. We talked without end of our project, and by necessity; and somehow we had to avoid, anyhow to avert, suspicion by confusing the notions of whoever might overhear us. Therefore we contrived a special dictionary for ourselves, assigning a name to each of the things we used. We called the saw *fawn,* the winder *Anubis*; the picks *Tubalcain,*

from the name of the first man who discovered the art of using iron; the hole
made in the floor to hide our materials in the drum became *Polyphemus,* an al-
lusion to the lair of the famous Cyclops; the wooden ladder, *Jacob,* recalled the
idea of the one named in Scripture; the rungs were *shoots*; our ropes, *doves,*
because of their whiteness; a ball of thread was *our little brother*; the penknife,
bow-wow, and so forth. If anyone came into the room and either of us saw
something lying in sight, he uttered the word *fawn, Anubis, Jacob,* etc., while the
other flung his handkerchief or a towel over the object, and so hid it.

We were ceaselessly on the watch, and were lucky enough to elude detection on the part of all our spies.

The first operations mentioned above being complete, we began on the
big ladder: this had to be at least 180 feet long. We set ourselves to unravel all
our linen; shirts, towels, caps, stockings, drawers, handkerchiefs—everything
that could furnish us with thread or silk. Immediately we had made a ball, we
hid it in *Polyphemus*; and, when we had a sufficient quantity, we spent an entire
night in twisting the rope. I defy the most clever rope-maker to fabricate one
with more art.

The Bastille was surrounded on the upper part by an edge that jutted out
three or four feet, which, naturally, would cause our ladder to swing and to
twist as we went down—more than enough to confuse and flurry the steadiest
head. To obviate this inconvenience, and to prevent ourselves from falling and
being mangled in the descent, we made a second rope, about 360 feet long.
This could be run through a pulley-block, a kind of wheelless pulley, so to
speak, thus to prevent the rope's getting caught between the wheel and sides of
the pulley, so that whoever descended might not find himself hung in the air
without means of continuing. Then we made sundry shorter ropes, with which
to attach our ladder to a cannon, or to supply unforeseen needs.

When all these ropes were finished, we measured them, having 1,400 feet:
subsequently we made 208 rungs, alike for the rope and the wooden ladder.
Another inconvenience to be avoided was the noise the rubbing of the rungs
against the wall might make as we were descending. We made a sheath for each
rung out of the linings of our dressing-gowns, vests, and waistcoats.

We spent eighteen entire months continuously at work on these preparations, nor was this all: we had made thorough provision for reaching the summit of the tower and for our descent to the moat, there being two methods for
issuing thence: one, to climb on to the parapet, and from it to the governor's
garden before descent into the moat near the Saint-Antoine gate; but this parapet, necessary to cross, was invariably lined with sentries. We could choose a
very dark and rainy night when the sentries would not parade to and fro,
hence we could manage to escape them; yet there might be rain while we

climbed our chimney, and calm, serene weather at the moment of our arrival on the parapet; we might meet the rounds-major, who inspected it continually, in which event we could not possibly hide ourselves, since lights were always carried, and so we should be lost forever.

The other expedient increased our difficulties, but was less dangerous and consisted in making our way through the wall that separated the Bastille moat from the moat of the Saint-Antoine gate. I realized that in the numerous floodings of the Seine—which, occurring, filled this moat—the water would probably dissolve the salt contained in the mortar, making it less difficult to break; therefore, and by this means, we might succeed in piercing through the wall. However, we needed a drill with which to make holes in the mortar for securing the points of the two iron bars, to be taken from our chimney, and with these two bars we could remove the stones and make a passage. We elected to try this expedient. Consequently, we made a drill with the pin from one of our beds, attaching a handle in the form of a cross.

The reader who has followed in detail these interesting occupations doubtless shares all our feelings of agitation; oppressed, like us, with hope and fear, he hastens the moment when finally we can attempt our flight. This was fixed for Wednesday, February 25th, 1756, the eve of Shrove Tuesday, when, the river being in flood, there were four feet of water in the Bastille moat, and in that of the Saint-Antoine gate, whither we sought deliverance. I filled my leathern portmanteau with a complete suit of clothes for each of us, so that we could make a change, if we were lucky enough to effect our escape.

Directly after dinner had been served, we put our major rope-ladder together, that is, we inserted the rungs; we hid this under our beds, and from sight of the turnkey, when he should come on his prescribed rounds during the day; then we arranged our wooden ladder in three pieces, slipped the iron bars necessary for piercing the walls into their sheath, to prevent them from making any sound; and we provisioned ourselves with a bottle of scubac with which to warm and to invigorate ourselves after labouring in water up to our necks for more than nine hours. These arrangements having been made, we awaited the moment when our supper would be brought to us; and at last the time came.

I climbed the chimney first, and, though I suffered from rheumatism in my left arm, I paid sparse attention to the pain, having soon to endure something much sharper; for I had taken none of the precautions customary among chimney-sweeps, and soot-dust almost choked me. These fellows protect their elbows and knees with leathern guards—and I had nothing of the sort; therefore I was skinned to the quick in all my limbs, and blood streamed down my hands and legs. In this state I reached the top of the chimney;

where, at once, I let down a ball of twine, having thus furnished myself. To this D'Alègre attached the end of the cord fastened to my portmanteau; which I drew up, untied, and flung on to the platform of the Bastille; and we raised the wooden ladder, the two iron bars, and the other packages, in a similar manner, ending with the rope-ladder, one end of which I let down, so to help D'Alègre in his ascent, meanwhile securing the rest by means of a thick bolt made for the express purpose: this I passed through the rope, laying it cross-wise on the chimney shaft—consequently my companion avoided covering himself with blood as I had done. Now I descended from the chimney-top, where I had been in a most uncomfortable position; and we found ourselves on the Bastille platform.

Here we arranged all our effects promptly; we began by coiling our rope-ladder, making a heap four feet in diameter and one foot thick. We rolled it on to the tower named the Treasure Tower, which, to us, seemed most suitable for our descent; and we fixed one end to a piece of cannon, let the ladder run gently down the length of the tower, attached our pulley-block with the 360-foot rope: I tied this pulley-rope around my body, and D'Alègre played it out by degrees as down I went; yet, in spite of this provision, I swung out into air at each motion. My position may be figured in accord with the shudders provoked by the mere thought of such a thing. Finally, and without mishap, I arrived at the moat. Immediately D'Alègre lowered my portmanteau and the rest of the stuff; and happily I found a slight eminence rising above the water—which now filled the moat—and on this I placed them. My companion then followed me in the same fashion, but with a greater ease; for, by holding the end of the ladder as firmly as I could, I prevented an excessive vacillation. When the pair of us had landed, we could not avoid a slight regret at the impossibility of taking our rope and the materials we had used* with us—these precious and rare memorials of human industry, and perhaps of virtues inspired by a love of freedom.

---

*On the 16th of July last, after the taking of the Bastille, I presented myself and found, with inexpressible delight, my rope-ladder, the wooden ladder of which I have spoken, and most of the other things; they were shut down under a kind of cage and had been kept as if they were precious, and made to provide a certain amazement and admiration: also, there was an official report, signed February 27th, 1756, by one Chevalier, major of the Bastille, and by the commissary Rochebrune, which verifies all the facts I have described. In addition, I found letters from the ministers, and other documents concerning myself, which I shall have to deal with in the course of these Memoirs.

All these things were carried to the Assembly of the Commune, who gave orders for the whole to be returned to me, and as a possession due to me by every right. They were exhibited subsequently at the last *salon,* where they attracted a general attention; and at the present time the rope-ladder is in the hands of a person who proposes to show it in the principal towns of France, and in England, as one of the most glorious trophies ever ascribed to liberty.

The rain had ceased. We heard the sentry as he walked at no more than a stone's throw from us; accordingly we were obliged to forgo our design of mounting on to the parapet, and of escaping by the governor's garden. We decided to use our iron bars and to attempt the second method, explained above. We went straight to the wall separating the Bastille moat from that of the Saint-Antoine gate; and, without respite, we began our toil. At this precise spot there was a small ditch six feet wide and a foot and a half deep, and this increased the height of the water. Elsewhere the water would not have reached above our middles, whereas here it came to our armpits. A thaw had set in only a few days ago, hence the water was yet strewn with pieces of ice; and here we remained for nine solid hours, our bodies exhausted by a task of exceeding great difficulty, our limbs numbed with the cold.

Scarcely had we begun when I saw a rounds-major approaching, twelve feet above our heads; and his lantern lighted our lair clearly. Our only resource, to prevent discovery, was to duck under water; and we were obliged to repeat this manoeuvre at each visit, thus several times during the night. May I be forgiven for narrating another vent of the same kind, which, in the first instant, gave me a mortal fright, but ended by seeming ludicrous to me? I recount it in a strict observance of the promise not to leave any detail untold, for my object is not to enliven this tale or to raise a smile.

A sentry, walking on the parapet, a very short distance from us, reached our particular spot and drew up immediately above my head. I thought we were discovered, and I had a frightful shock; but, instantly, I heard that he had paused only to make water, or, rather, I felt this, for not one drop escaped my head and face; and I was forced to throw away my cap and to rinse my hair as soon as he had passed on.

At last, after nine hours of work and of apprehension, and after having pulled out the stones one by one with an unimaginable toil, we succeeded in making a hole wide enough to pass through and in a wall four and half feet thick: and we dragged ourselves through. Already our spirits were beginning to rejoice; but we encountered a danger hitherto unforeseen, and before which we nearly succumbed. We were crossing the Saint-Antoine moat to reach the Bercy road, and had hardly gone twenty-five paces when we fell into an aqueduct in the middle, and with ten feet of water over our heads, and two feet of slime preventing us from movement or a step to reach the further edge of the aqueduct, one no more than six feet wide. D'Alègre threw himself on me, all but knocking me down: we were lost; for, without strength enough left to pick ourselves up again, we should perish in this bed of filth. I felt myself seized, and hit out violently and forced D'Alègre to release me; and, with a corresponding motion, I sprang, and managed to get out of the aqueduct. I plunged my arm into the water, seized D'Alègre by the hair, and drew him to my side. Quickly we were outside the moat; and we found ourselves on the high-road just as five o'clock sounded.

Trenck at Magdeburg

BARON TRENCK

Although he made just one successful bid for freedom, Baron Frederick von der Trenck remains one of history's most remarkable escapers. Born to privilege in 1726, Trenck quickly rose to a powerful position in Frederick the Great's Prussian Guard at just nineteen years of age. Misled by his own considerable ego and Frederick's hidden political agenda, Trenck was accused of treason and condemned to prison. After several bold escape attempts, including one that left him stuck to the waist in the muddy moat for a full day after a leap over the wall, he was finally able to break out with the help of one of the garrison soldiers. As these soldiers were often unhappy at being banished to the poverty and disgrace of garrison duty, it was not difficult for Trenck to enlist their help. He and the guard were able to escape and make their way to freedom through Bohemia.

Trenck was a man of vast skill with saber and pistol, and he eventually secured a position as a mercenary in a Russian regiment. Frederick's wrath, however, followed him across Europe and he was eventually retaken after a bit of treachery. He was placed in the prison at Magdeburg, where he would spend the next nine years. Although he never again successfully escaped, few others have matched his tenacity and determination in seeking liberty. The memoirs he later published describing his adventures and suffering made him one of the most famous men in Europe. This episode is taken from *The Strange Adventures of Frederick Baron Trenck*, edited by Philip Murray and based on a translation by Thomas Holcroft.

My dungeon was in a casemate, the fore part of which, six feet wide and ten feet long, was divided by a party wall. In the inner wall were two doors, and a third at the entrance of the casemate itself. The window in the seven feet thick wall was so situated that although I had light I could see neither heaven nor earth; I could only see the roof of the magazine. Within and without this window were iron bars, and in the space between was an iron grating, so close and so situated that owing to the rising of the walls it was impossible to see anyone outside the prison or for anybody to see me. On the outside was a wooden palisade six feet from the wall, by which the sentries were prevented from conveying anything to me. I had a mattress, and a bedstead which was immovably ironed to the floor, so that it was impossible to drag it under the window. Beside the door was a small iron stove and a night-stool, also fixed to the floor. I was not yet put in irons, and my allowance was a pound and a half of ammunition bread per day, and a jug of water.

From my youth I had always had a good appetite, but the bread was so mouldy that I could scarcely eat it. This was the result of Major Reiding's avarice; he endeavoured to make a profit even out of the scanty food of the prisoners. It is impossible to describe the tortures that, for eleven months, I endured through hunger. I could easily have devoured six pounds of bread a day; and after having swallowed my small portion I was as hungry as before I began, yet was obliged to wait another twenty-four hours for another portion. How willingly would I have signed a bill of exchange on my property at Vienna for a thousand ducats, only to have satisfied my hunger on dry bread! God preserve every honest man from sufferings like mine! Many have fasted three days; many have suffered want for a week or more; but certainly no one beside myself ever endured it in the same degree for eleven months. It may be thought that I should have become accustomed to eating little, but my experience is all to the contrary. My hunger increased every day, and of all the trials my whole life has afforded, this, of eleven months, was the most bitter.

Petitions were of no avail; the answer was: "We dare give no more; it is the King's command." When I entreated the Governor, General Borck, at least to allow me to have my fill of bread, he replied: "You have feasted often enough from the plate taken from the King by Trenck at the battle of Sarau; you must now eat ammunition bread in your dirty kennel. Your Empress makes no allowance for your maintenance, and you are not worth even the bread you eat or the trouble taken about you."

My three doors were kept perpetually locked, and I was left to such meditations as my feelings might inspire. Daily, about noon—once in twenty-four hours—my pittance of bread and water was brought. The keys of all the doors were kept by the Governor; the inner door was not opened, but my bread and water were pushed through an aperture. The prison doors were opened only once a week, on a Wednesday, when the Governor and Town Major paid their visit, my hole having been cleaned before they came.

Having remained thus for two months, I began to put in hand a project of escape which I had formed.

Where the night-stool and stove stood the floor was brick, and this paving extended to the wall that separated my casemate from the adjoining one, which was uninhabited. My window was guarded by only a single sentry, and I soon found among those who successively mounted guard two kind-hearted fellows who described to me the situation of my prison. Hence I perceived that I might effect my escape could I but penetrate into the adjoining casemate, the door of which was not locked. Provided I had a friend and a boat waiting for me at the Elbe—or if I could swim across that river—the frontier of Saxony was but a mile away. To describe my plan at length would be tedious, yet I must enumerate some of its details, for it was remarkably intricate and necessitated unusual labour.

I worked away the iron strips, eighteen inches long, by which the night-stool was fastened, and broke off the clinchings of the nails, but kept their heads so that I could put them back in their places and all would appear secure to my weekly visitors. This procured me tools with which to prise up the brick floor, under which I found earth.

I first attempted to work a hole through the wall, seven feet thick, behind and concealed by the night-stool. The first layer was of brick; then I came to large hewn stones. I numbered the bricks both of the flooring and wall carefully, so that I could replace them and make everything appear as it was before. This being done, I proceeded.

On the day before my weekly visitation I replaced everything carefully, including the intervening mortar. The wall had probably been whitewashed a number of times, and in order to fill up all the remaining chinks I flaked off and pounded up some of the whitewash, wetted it, made a brush of my hair, applied this plaster and washed it over to make the whole uniform. Then I stripped myself and sat with my naked body against the place, by which means it soon dried. While I was at work I placed the stones and bricks upon my bedstead, and had my visitors taken the precaution to come at any other time of the week I should inevitably have been discovered. But as no such ill accident befell me, in six months my Herculean labours assumed a prospect of success.

Means had to be found to remove the rubbish from my prison; for with a wall so thick it was impossible to replace all of it. Mortar and stone could not be removed, so I took the earth and scattered it about my room, then ground it underfoot the whole day long till I had reduced it to dust. This dust I strewed in the aperture of my window, making use of the loosened night-stool to stand on. I then tied splinters of my bedstead together with the unravelled yarn of an old stocking, and to this affixed my tuft of hair. I worked a large hole under the middle grating which could not be seen when standing on the ground, and through this I pushed the dust with the tool I had prepared. Then, waiting till the wind rose during the night, I brushed it away. By this simple expedient I got rid of at least three hundredweight of earth, and thus made room to continue my labours. I also made little balls of earth, and when the sentry was at the other end of his beat, blew them out of the window through a paper tube.

The difficulties I encountered when I had penetrated about two feet into the hewn stone were enormous. The only tools I had, in addition to the irons which had fastened my bedstead and night-stool, were an old iron ramrod and a sheath knife which a compassionate soldier had given me. The sheath knife did me excellent service, and with it I cut from my bedstead the splinters which enabled me to pick the mortar from between the stones. Yet the labour of penetrating through this seven-foot wall was incredible. The building was an ancient one, and the mortar was occasionally quite petrified, so that it was necessary to reduce the whole stone to dust. Yet after working unremittingly for six months the end was in sight, for I had reached the facing of brick which alone was between me and the adjoining casemate.

Meanwhile I found an opportunity of talking to some of the sentries, and among them was an old grenadier named Gelfhardt, who I afterwards discovered possessed qualities of the noblest kind. From him I learnt the precise situation of my prison and the circumstances which might best conduce to my escape. With money I learnt that I could buy a boat, cross the Elbe with him and take refuge in Saxony. By Gelfhardt's means I became acquainted with a kind-hearted girl, a Jewess and native of Dessau, Esther Heymannin by name, whose father had been in prison for ten years. This compassionate maiden, whom I had never seen, won over two other grenadiers, who gave her an opportunity of speaking to me every time they mounted guard. By tying my splinters together I made a stick long enough to reach beyond the palisade in front of my window, and by this means I obtained paper, another knife and a file.

I now wrote to my sister (wife of the beforementioned son of General Waldow), told her my awful situation and begged her to send three hundred rix-dollars to the Jewess, hoping by this means to escape from my prison. I then wrote another affecting letter to Count Puebla, the Austrian Ambassador at Berlin, in which I enclosed a draft for a thousand florins on my effects at Vienna, and desired him to remit these to the Jewess, having promised her that sum as a reward for her assistance. She was to bring the three hundred rix-dollars my sister should send me, and then concert measures with the grenadiers for my flight. Hope rose high in my breast, for I now had the power either to break into the adjoining casemate or, aided by the grenadiers and the Jewess, to cut the locks from the doors and thus escape from my dungeon. [Trenck was betrayed by the Secretary at the embassy, and all of Esther's help was of no avail.—*Ed*.]

I had heard nothing of what had happened for some days; at length, however, it was the honest Gelfhardt's turn to mount guard; but the sentries being doubled and two additional grenadiers placed before my door, told me that something untoward had occurred. In spite, however, of all precautions, Gelfhardt found means to inform me of what had happened to his two unfortunate comrades.

Shortly after this the King came to review troops at Magdeburg. He visited the Star Fort and ordered a new cell to be made for me immediately, himself prescribing the kind of irons by which I was to be secured. Gelfhardt heard the officers say that this cell was meant for me and told me about it, but assured me that it could not be ready in less than a month. I therefore determined to complete my breach in the wall as soon as possible and escape without the aid of anyone. The thing was possible, for I had twisted the hair of my mattress into a rope which I meant to tie to a cannon and thus descend the ramparts; then I could swim across the Elbe, gain the Saxon frontier, and thus escape.

On the 26th of May I determined to break into the next casemate. But when I came to work at the bricks I found them so hard and strongly cemented that I was obliged to defer the labour to the following day. I left off at daybreak, weary and spent, and had anyone entered my dungeon then they must infallibly have discovered the breach.

The 27th of May was a cruel day in the history of my life. My cell in the Star Fort had been finished sooner than Gelfhardt had expected, and at night when I was preparing to fly, I heard a carriage stop before my prison. O God! what was my terror, what were the horrors of this moment of despair! The locks and bolts resounded, the doors flew open, and I had only just time to conceal my knife. The Town Major, the major of the day, and a captain entered by the light of two lanterns. The only words they spoke were, "Dress yourself," which I immediately did. I still wore the uniform of the Cardova regiment. Irons were given me which I was obliged myself to fasten on my wrists and ankles; the Town Major tied a bandage over my eyes, and, taking me by the arms, they conducted me to the carriage. It was necessary to pass through the city in order to reach the Star Fort; all was silent but for the noise made by the escort; but when we entered Magdeburg I heard people running and crowding together to obtain a sight of me. Their curiosity was raised by the report that I was going to be beheaded. That I was executed on this occasion in the Star

Fort, after having been conducted blindfolded through the city, has since been both affirmed and written; in fact the officers had orders to spread this report in order that the world might remain in ignorance about me.

The carriage at length stopped and I was led into my new cell. The bandage was taken from my eyes. God in heaven! What were my feelings when I beheld by the light of a few torches the whole floor covered with chains, a brazier's furnace, and two grim men standing with hammers beside an anvil!

One end of an enormous chain was fixed to my ankle, the other to a ring built into the wall. This ring was three feet from the ground and only allowed me to move about two or three feet to the right and left. They next riveted another huge iron ring of a hand's breadth round my naked body, to which hung a chain fixed to an iron bar as thick as a man's arm. This bar was two feet long and at each end of it was a handcuff—the iron collar round my neck was not added till the year 1756.

Not a soul bade me good night; all retired in dreadful silence; and I heard the grating of four doors that were successively locked and bolted upon me!

I foresaw that my misery would not be of short duration. I had heard of the war that had lately broken out between Austria and Prussia. Patiently to await its termination appeared impossible amidst sufferings such as mine, and freedom even then was doubtful. Sad experience had I had of Vienna, and well I knew that those who had despoiled me of my property would anxiously endeavour to prevent my return. Such were my thoughts that night.

Day at length returned, but it brought small alleviation; for by its dim light I was able to behold the extent of my dungeon.

My cell was about eight feet by ten. Near me once more stood a night-stool, and in a corner was a seat, four bricks broad, on which I could sit and lean against the wall. Opposite the ring to which I was fastened the light was admitted by a semi-circular aperture, one foot high and two feet wide. This aperture reached to the centre of the wall, which was six feet thick, and in the middle of the wall was a close iron grating. From this grating the aperture descended outwards, its outer orifice being again secured by strong iron bars. My dungeon was built in the ditch of the fortification and the aperture by which the light entered was so covered by the wall of the rampart that instead of finding immediate entrance it gained admission only by reflection. This, in view of the smallness of the aperture and the impediments of the grating and iron bars, made the obscurity great, yet in time my eyes became so accustomed to this glimmering that I could see a mouse run. In winter, however, when the sun did not shine into the ditch, it was eternal night with me. Between the bars and the grating was a glass window, curiously formed, with a small central casement which could be opened to admit air. The name of Trenck was built into the wall in red brick, and under my feet was a tombstone with the name of Trenck also cut upon it and carved with a death's head.

The doors of my dungeon were double, of oak, two inches thick. Beyond these was an open space or front cell in which was a window, and this space was likewise shut in by double doors. The ditch in which this dreadful den was built was enclosed on both sides by palisades twelve feet high, the key of the door of which was entrusted to the officer of the guard, it being the King's intention to prevent all possibility of speech or communication with the sentries. The only movements I could make were those of jumping upwards or swinging my arms in order to warm myself. When I got more accustomed to these fetters I also found it possible to move from side to side about four feet, but this hurt my shin-bones.

It was only eleven days since the cell had been finished and plastered, and everybody thought it would be impossible for me to live there for more than a fortnight. I actually remained there for six months, continually wet to the skin with icy cold water that dripped upon me from the vaulted roof. In fact I can safely assert that for the first three months I was never dry; yet my health continued good. I was visited daily at noon after the guard was relieved, and the doors had then to be left open for some minutes, otherwise the dampness in the air put out the visitors' candles.

After some time my fortitude began to revive; I glowed with the desire of convincing the world that I was capable of suffering what man had never suffered before—perhaps of at last emerging from this load of wretchedness and triumphing over my enemies. So long and ardently did my fancy dwell on this picture that my mind at length acquired a heroism which Socrates himself certainly never possessed. Age had benumbed the sense of pleasure and he drank the poisonous draught with cool indifference; I was young and ambitious yet now beheld deliverance impossible or at an immense distance.

At noon my den was opened. Sorrow and compassion were depicted upon the faces of my keepers. No one spoke: no one bade me good day. Dreadful indeed was their arrival; for, unaccustomed to the monstrous bolts and bars, it was a full half-hour before these soul-chilling, hope-murdering impediments could be removed. It was the voice of tyranny that thundered.

My night-stool was taken out, a camp bed, mattress and blankets were brought to me; a jug of water and an ammunition loaf of six pounds weight were placed beside me. "You can have as much bread as you can eat," said the Town Major; "so you won't be able to complain of hunger any more." The door was shut and I was again left to my thoughts.

What a strange thing is the emotion which we call happiness! My joy was extreme when, after eleven months of intolerable hunger, I was again provided with a full feast of coarse ammunition bread. Fond lover never rushed more eagerly to the arms of his expectant bride, or famished tiger sprung more ravenously upon its prey, than I upon that loaf. I ate, rested; gloated over the precious morsel, ate again; and absolutely shed tears of pleasure. By evening I had devoured the whole loaf.

Alas, my enjoyment was of short duration! I soon found that excess is followed by pain and repentance. Fasting had weakened my digestion. My body swelled, my water jug was emptied; cramp, colic, and inordinate thirst racked me throughout the night. I poured curses on those who sought to refine their torture by inviting me to gluttony after starving me for so long. Could I not have reclined in some way upon my bed I should indeed have been driven this night to desperation; yet even this was but a partial relief, for I was unable to lie at full length. I dragged my fetters, however, together so as to enable me to sit down on the bare mattress. When they opened my dungeon next day they found me in a truly pitiable condition, yet they wondered at my appetite and brought me another loaf. I refused to take it, believing that I should never eat bread again; they, however, left it with me, filled my water jug, shrugged their shoulders and wished me farewell. Apparently they never expected to find me alive again, for they shut all the doors without asking whether I was in need of medical assistance.

Three days passed before I could eat again, and my mind, brave in health, became pusillanimous in a sick body, so that I determined on death. The irons round my body were insupportable and I could not imagine that it was possible that I should ever become accustomed to them or endure them long enough to expect deliverance. The King had commanded such a prison to be built as should preclude all necessity of a sentry, so that I might not be able to converse with one. I was, therefore, reduced entirely to my own resources, and those resources seemed now at an end. Every argument I could think of convinced me that it was time to put an end to my sufferings. I shall not enter here into theological disputes: let those who blame me imagine themselves first in my position. I had often braved death in prosperity, and at this moment it seemed the greatest blessing vouchsafed to mankind.

Filled with this conviction every minute's delay seemed foolish, yet I wished to be satisfied in my own mind that reason and not rashness had induced the act. I determined, therefore, in order to examine the question coolly, to wait another week and die on the 4th of July. In the meantime I revolved in my mind what possible means there were of escape.

I noticed next day when the four doors were opened that they were only of wood, and I therefore questioned whether I might not cut off the locks with the knife that I had so fortunately concealed. I also determined to make an attempt to free myself of my chains. Happily I was able to force my right hand through the handcuff, though the blood spurted out from beneath my nails as I did so. My attempts to free my left were for a long time ineffectual, but by rubbing with a brick on a rivet that had been negligently fastened I effected this also.

The chain was fastened to the ring round my body by a hook, one end of which was not inserted in the ring; therefore by setting myself against the wall I had strength enough to bend this hook back so far as to open it and force out the link of the chain. The remaining difficulty was the chain that attached my foot to the wall. The links of this I doubled, twisted and wrenched till at length, Nature having bestowed great strength upon me, I made a desperate effort and sprang up forcibly, when the two links at once flew off.

Fortunate, indeed, did I think myself. I hurried to the door and groped in the dark for the heads of the nails by which the lock was fastened, and soon discovered that the piece of wood which it was necessary to cut was not very large. I immediately set to work with my knife and cut through the oak door to ascertain its thickness. It proved to be only one inch thick and therefore it would be possible to open all the four doors in twenty-four hours.

Again hope revived in my heart! To prevent detection I hastened to put on my chains; but O God! what difficulties I had to surmount! After much groping about I at length found the link that had flown off, and this I hid. It had been my good fortune hitherto to escape examination, as the possibility of ridding myself of such chains was not suspected. The separated iron links I tied together with my hair-ribbon; but when I again endeavoured to force my hand into the ring it had swollen so that every effort was fruitless. The whole night was employed upon the rivet of this handcuff, but in vain. Noon was the time of the daily visit, and as my senses told me that this hour approached, necessity and danger again compelled me to attempt to force my hand in. At length, after excruciating pain, I effected it. My visitors came and everything appeared to be in order. I found, however, when they had gone that it would be impossible for me to withdraw my hand again until the swelling had subsided.

I therefore remained quiet till the day fixed, and on the 4th of July, immediately my visitors had closed the doors upon me, I disencumbered myself of my irons, took up my knife, and began my Herculean labour on the door. The first of the double doors that opened inwards was conquered in less than an hour, but the next was a very different matter. The lock was soon cut round, but it opened outwards, so there was nothing for it but to cut the whole door away above the bar. Incessant and incredible labour made this possible, though it was the more difficult seeing that everything had to be done by touch, as I was in pitch darkness. The sweat flowed from me in streams, my fingers were clotted with my own blood, and my hands were one continuous wound.

Daylight appeared. I clambered over the door that was half cut away and reached the window in the space or cell between the two doors. Here I saw that my dungeon was in the ditch of the first rampart. Before me I beheld the road from the ramparts, the guardroom but fifty paces distant, and the high palisade that would have to be scaled before I could reach the ramparts. Hope grew and I redoubled my efforts.

The first of the next double doors, which also opened inwards, was soon overcome; but the sun had set before I had finished with it and the fourth had to be cut away as the second had been. My strength began to fail; both my hands were raw; I rested awhile, began again, and had made a cut about a foot long when my knife snapped, and the broken blade dropped to the ground!

God of Omnipotence! What were my feelings at this moment! Was there ever, God of mercies, creature of Thine more justified in despair than I? The moon shone very clear; I cast a wild and distracted look to heaven, fell on my knees, and in the agony of my soul sought comfort in prayer. But no comfort was there for me; neither religion nor philosophy could give me that. I cursed not Providence, I feared not annihilation, I dared not the Almighty's vengeance. God was the disposer of my fate, and if He had heaped upon me afflictions which He had not given me strength to support, His justice would not therefore punish me. To Him, the judge of the quick and the dead, I committed my soul: I seized the broken knife, gashed through the veins of my left arm and foot, and sat quietly down and watched the blood flow. Nature overpowered my senses and I fainted.

How long I remained in this state I do not know, but suddenly heard my own name called and I sat up. It was my faithful grenadier, Gelfhardt, my friend of the citadel! The good fellow had got upon the ramparts that he might approach and, if possible, comfort me.

"How are you getting on?" asked Gelfhardt.

"Weltering in my own blood," I answered. "To-morrow you will find me dead."

"But why should you die?" said he. "It is much easier for you to escape from here than from the citadel. There is no sentry outside your door here and I shall soon find a way of providing you with tools. If you can only break out you can leave the rest to me. Whenever I'm on guard I'll make an opportunity to come and talk to you. There are only two sentries in the whole of the Star

Fort, one at the entrance, the other at the guardroom. Don't give in. God will help you. Trust me."

This discourse revived my hopes, and once more I cherished the possibility of escape. I tore up my shirt, bound up my wounds, and awaited the approach of day. When the sun rose it seemed to me that my prison was brighter than it had been before.

Till noon I had time to consider what might be done further; yet what could be done, or what expected but that I should now be much more cruelly treated and even more insupportably ironed than before, finding, as they must, the doors cut through and my fetters off. After mature consideration I evolved the following plan, which happily succeeded even beyond my hopes.

It is impossible to describe how exhausted I was. My cell swam with blood, and certainly very little was left in my body. Badly wounded, with swollen and torn hands, I stood there shirtless. The inclination to go to sleep was almost irresistible and I had scarcely strength to keep my legs, yet I had to rouse myself in order that I might execute my plan.

With the bar that kept my hands apart I loosened the bricks of my seat and heaped them up in the middle of my prison. The inner door was wide open and with my chains I so barricaded the upper half of the second one as to prevent anyone climbing over it. When noon came and the first of the doors was unlocked, my visitors were astonished to find the second door open. There I stood, smeared with blood, the picture of horror, with a brick in one hand and a broken knife in the other, shouting as they approached, "Keep off, major, keep off! Tell the Governor I won't have these chains on any longer and that he can shoot me if he likes, for I'll not submit to be chained again. I'll kill any man who comes in here: you see I've got weapons and I'll die rather than give in." The major was terrified: he hesitated a minute or two and then went off to report to the Governor. Meanwhile, I sat down on the bricks to await events. My intention, however, was not so desperate as I had made out: I only wanted to obtain favourable terms for capitulation.

Presently General Borck came in attended by the Town Major and some officers. He entered the outer cell, but sprang back as soon as he caught sight of me standing there with a brick in my uplifted arm. I repeated what I had told the major and he immediately ordered six grenadiers to force the door. The front cell was barely six feet wide, so that I could only be attacked by two at a time, and when they saw me waiting for them with my pile of bricks they leapt back terrified. A short pause ensued and then the old Town Major with the chaplain advanced to the door to soothe me. We parleyed for some time: whose arguments were the more satisfactory and whose cause the more just I

leave to the reader to determine. The Governor then grew angry and ordered a
fresh attack. I knocked the first grenadier down and the rest ran back to avoid
my missiles.

The Town Major again began a parley. "For God's sake, my dear Trenck,"
said he, "how have I injured you that you should thus seek to ruin me? I shall
have to answer for your having concealed a knife. Be friendly, I beg. You are
not without hope and not without friends." I answered him: "That's all very
well, but if I give in I know you'll load me with heavier irons than before." He
went out to speak to the Governor and returning presently gave me his word
of honour that no further notice should be taken of the affair, and that everything should be replaced exactly as it had been before.

Accordingly I capitulated. They took pity on my condition: my wounds
were examined, a surgeon sent to dress them, another shirt was given me, and
the bricks, clotted with blood, removed. Meantime, I lay half dead on my mattress. My thirst was appalling; the surgeon ordered me some wine; two sentries
were stationed in the front cell, and for four days I was left in peace, unironed.
Broth was also given me daily and how delicious was this change of diet! It is
impossible to describe how much it revived and strengthened me. For two days
I lay in a kind of slumbering trance, forced by unquenchable thirst to drink
whenever I awoke. My feet and hands were badly swollen and the pain in my
back and limbs was frightful.

On the fifth day the new doors were ready. The inner one was entirely
plated with iron, and I was fettered as before: perhaps they found further cruelty
unnecessary. The principal chain, however, which fastened me to the wall was
thicker than before. Except for this the terms of the capitulation were strictly
kept. They even went so far as to express their regret that they could not
lighten my afflictions without the King's express command, hoped that I
would have fortitude and patience, and barred up the doors.

My hands being fastened to and kept apart by an iron bar, and my feet
chained to the wall, it was impossible for me to put on my shirt and stockings
in the usual way. My shirt was, therefore, laced up in front and along the
sleeves, and changed once a fortnight. The coarse ammunition stockings were
buttoned up the sides; a pair of blue pantaloons, of sailor's cloth, and a pair of
slippers completed my outfit. The shirt was of army linen, and when I contemplated myself in this malefactor's garb, chained to the wall of such a dungeon,
and reflected on my former splendour in Berlin and Moscow, I was over-
whelmed with grief that might have hurried the greatest hero or philosopher
to madness or despair. Pride, the justness of my cause, the unbound confidence
I had in my own resolution and the labours of an inventive head and iron body

alone could have preserved my life. It was these labours, these continual projects of escape, which preserved my health.

Through serious bouts of illness, and always encumbered with the heavy chains that bound him, Trenck would go on to build several elaborate tunnels—each one discovered short of its goal. In a bizarre twist, just when he had secretly completed his final tunnel and made all the arrangements to escape, Trenck confessed his plans to members of the guard, asking them to tell a visiting prince that he was seeking the prince's intercession and protection, despite the fact that he could have escaped at will. One can only assume that after all his years of suffering, he had completely lost his senses. Those in charge of the prison, not wanting to show themselves negligent in their duty, never told the prince anything of Trenck's request. He was pulled from his cell and again placed in chains. But by some stroke of luck—his first bit of luck in nine long years—word finally came from Berlin that he was to be released.

Louis Napoleon

F. T. BRIFFAULT

Louis Napoleon, known as "the Pretender," was the nephew of the great Napoleon. After witnessing his uncle's defeat and banishment, he was determined to himself become emperor one day. He landed in France in 1840 with this goal in mind but was quickly arrested and sentenced to life in prison. He was taken to the fortress at Ham, which was surrounded by high walls and a moat and heavily guarded.

Louis spent five years at Ham in relative comfort, but depression and restlessness finally drove him to attempt a bold and clever escape. After making his way to safety in England, Louis Napoleon was finally elected leader of the French Republic in 1849, and he declared himself Emperor a few years later. In 1870, he was again made a prisoner, this time by the Prussians. He died just a few years later.

E scape having been decided, the plan was still to be settled; and the first thing to be done, was sedulously to instil into the mind of the Commandant the belief of an approaching amnesty, in order more effectually to conceal the prisoner's projects from his observation. It was easy to persuade him, after the information which the Prince had received from his friends in Paris, that the Ministers had determined to proclaim a general amnesty towards the month of June, just before the Elections, as sometimes happens. Several plans presented themselves to the Prince's mind, but he rejected them all, one after another, in order to adopt the simplest, which consisted in finding a pretext for introducing workmen into the prison, and to avail himself of the disguise of one of them to make his escape. Here accident marvellously contributed to promote his views, for at the very time in which he was thinking of finding a reason for persuading the Commandant of the necessity of some repairs, the latter came to inform him, that in compliance with his requests, the Ministry had at length resolved to have the staircase and corridors of the building occupied by the Prince, Count Montholon, Dr. Conneau and Charles Thélin, put into complete repair. Dr. Conneau's period of five years' imprisonment having expired, the two latter were free in their actions, and could go into the town.

Although the conduct of the Prince, during the five years of his captivity, which had now passed, was such as to disarm all suspicion of his attempting to escape, and in spite of the report of a general amnesty, generally spread and designedly circulated and cherished, the eager mind of the Commandant and his own interest sufficed to lead him to entertain suspicions, and adopt precautions, which his subalterns regarded as useless and ridiculous.

Night invariably brought with it double guards, and ten o'clock, no sooner struck, than the Commandant, who, as we have already said, usually came to spend the evening with the Prince, having seen that the keepers were on duty at the bottom of the stairs, retired, shutting up the whole within the building, and taking the key of the outer door in his pocket, as Lady Douglas did at Loch Leven.

Of the three keepers, to whom the immediate charge of the prisoner's person was entrusted, two were always stationed at the bottom of the stairs.

The Prince had observed, that on certain days of the week, one of the keepers whose duty it was to go and bring the public journals, absented himself for a quarter-of-an-hour, leaving the post at the bottom of the stairs in charge of his companion for this short space of time. This was to be the moment of escape, and a facility was thus given of turning away the attention of the single keeper. As to the sentinels, the Prince thought there was little to fear from them; but it must be said, that from the very commencement of his captivity, all the precautions and fears were directed against dangers from without. They were persuaded that the Prince did not wish to escape, but were, at the same time, afraid that partisans from without, might make an attempt to release him. The strictest orders were therefore given, to prevent all persons whatsoever from approaching the fortress, and from stationing themselves under its walls, and during the first years, especially, the sentinels' orders were not to obstruct persons going out, but carefully to prevent any from coming in.

With a view to carry out this arrangement, the sentinels were for the most part placed upon the top of the ramparts, and chiefly towards the outside, in order to guard against any possible surprise. The fortress, however, being small, it was easy to command it at all points. There was, therefore no other feasible means of escaping their observation than that of a disguise.

The plan was as follows: Charles Thélin, as he had several times done before, asked permission to go to St. Quentin; he was to go and hire a *cabriolet* for the purpose. As he was leaving the prison to go and find his *cabriolet,* the Prince was to go out at the same time, in the disguise of a workman. This combination had two advantages; it left Thélin at liberty to turn aside the attention of the keepers and soldiers from the pretended workman, by playing with *Ham,* the Prince's dog, which was well-known, and a great favourite with the garrison; and, moreover, it gave him an opportunity of always addressing himself to those, who, taking the Prince for a workman, might be disposed to speak to him.

The workmen had been already eight days engaged in making repairs within the prison, and these eight days had been carefully employed by the Prince and his friend, in observing the ways and measures of the extraordinary precautions adopted with respect to the workmen. They had observed that the precautions were very great on their coming in, and going out of the fortress in a body. On their passing through the first wicket, as they entered, they were obliged to defile one by one, and to pass under the inspection of a sergeant's guard, and a keeper especially appointed for that purpose. The same form was observed, and the same attention paid on their going out in the evening, besides then the Commandant himself was always present. They observed, moreover, that whenever any of the workmen went alone to any retired part of the citadel they were strictly watched, but when they went out for the purpose of fetching tools or materials of any description, by following the direct road, and thus exposing themselves to view for a considerable distance, they excited no distrust, and were allowed freely to pass through the wicket and over the drawbridge. The Prince, therefore, determined to adopt the last mentioned plan— the boldest, it is true, but offering the greatest chance of success.

The morning was selected, not only because at that time, the Commandant, all whose cares and anxieties were connected with the evening, was not up, not merely because this was the time in which they might expect to find only one keeper at the bottom of the stairs, but also because by adopting this course it would be easy to reach Valenciennes in good time for the four o'clock train to Belgium. As to General Montholon, the Prince, being anxious not to compromise him, would have found it somewhat difficult to conceal his project from his knowledge, had he not chanced to be unwell at the time.

All was then arranged for Saturday, the 23rd of May, one of the days on which, in the usual course, one keeper alone would be for a short time at the bottom of the stairs. By what at first appeared a very unfortunate accident, the Prince was visited on that day by some persons whom he had previously known in England, and whom he had expected to see sooner.

It became necessary to put off his departure till Monday, the 25th, although it was not then certain that there would be a sufficient number of workmen to cover the escape, and that two keepers would not be at the bottom of the stairs. The Prince, however, wishing to derive some advantage from the visit, asked his friends to be good enough to lend their courier's passport to his valet de chambre, who was about to take a journey. The request was complied with, with alacrity. The Prince himself, with the assistance of one of his friends in Paris, had already procured a passport, of which, however, he afterwards made no use. Sunday passed in the midst of great anxieties—for it was by no means certain that there was work enough for the Monday to require their attendance. Charles Thélin, however, asked them on this very day to be good enough to put up some shelves in a little recess, which was used for a cellar.

The difficulty did not merely consist in passing through the guards and doorkeepers,—it was also necessary to avoid being met by the workmen themselves, who were constantly on the stairs, and superintended by the contractor of the works and an officer of engineers. It is easy to understand what must have been the nature of the emotions by which the prisoner was agitated. Twice he had risked his life for a cause which he had thought it his duty to revive at the hazard of the greatest sacrifices; twice, the government had tried to throw ridicule on his failures—but if he failed on the morrow, they would no longer restrain their indignation and contempt. Neither six years of suffering, courageously endured, his studious works, nor even the sacred cause which called him through so many dangers would be accounted to him; the same gall, the same bitterness would cast blame and ridicule on the man failing in his attempt, and caught under a disguise.

On his part the excellent and noble Dr. Conneau had undertaken to play the diplomatic character necessary to screen the Prince's departure, and give him time to elude pursuit. We shall not here interrupt the course of the narration, in speaking of this faithful and devoted friend of the Prisoner of Ham.

At last, on Monday the 25th, early in the morning, the Prince, Dr. Conneau, and Charles Thélin, placed behind the window curtains, which they kept carefully drawn, and without shoes, in order to avoid noise, carefully watched the courtyard, and impatiently waited for the arrival of the workmen. All was still silent in the interior of the court—the sentries alone paced slowly up and down before their sentry-boxes. By a singular accident the only soldier in the garrison whom they were anxious to avoid, was this very morning on duty before the Prince's door. This man, who had long been a *planton* of the Commandant, was accustomed to exercise a very scrupulous *surveillance* over the workmen; and the Prince had already remarked him, when he was on duty, examining all their movements with the greatest attention, looking narrowly at their persons, and asking them where they were going.

It is easy to perceive how dangerous such a man might be. The Prince was so much the more annoyed at his presence, as it was probable that the soldier would not be relieved before seven o'clock, and it was of great importance to set out before that time, in order not to have a third keeper on their hands. Luckily, by another accident as singular, the hours of mounting guard had been changed in consequence of a review on Sunday, and the grenadier was relieved at six o'clock. It had been arranged, that after having brought the labourers and artizans into the dining-room to give them a morning dram, Thélin should go before the Prince, on to the stairs, in order to turn away the attention of the keepers. The Prince once in the courtyard, Thélin was to follow him closely, in order, as we have said, to call to him, any person who might be disposed to speak to the Prince, supposing him to be a workman.

A little after five, the workmen entered the fortress and passed between two files of soldiers under arms. At first they were not as numerous as usual—then, because it was Monday, they were better dressed than ordinary—as the weather was very fine, they had no *sabots,* moreover there were masons and painters, but no joiner among them, yet the Prince intended to put on a joiner's disguise; this gave some reason to fear lest the Prince's disguise should be remarked, as being dirty, and the Prince was anxious for a moment to give up the sabots (wooden shoes), which would have been very inconvenient—because those which had been prepared for him, and into which he was to put his high-heeled booth, increased his height at least four inches, which alone made a great change in his person. The plan, as we have described it, was a very simple one, but the principal difficulty of carrying it into execution lay in catching with resolution the favourable moment of going down stairs and getting out of doors, while the workmen should be kept drinking, and the attention of the keepers diverted by the Doctor and Thélin; it was, therefore, necessary that all should be in readiness before, in order not to lose the propitious opportunity. The Prince had to dress and have previously his moustaches cut; yet, on the other hand, should anything hinder his departure for that day, this very act of having cut his moustaches would betray his scheme in the eyes of the Commandant, and so render afterwards the departure impossible. The Doctor's earnest entreaties to the Prince were to delay this operation, so trifling in itself, yet bearing in the present circumstances such a fearful stamp of a settled resolution which was not to be withdrawn. Prince Napoleon Louis could not help smiling at the consternation of those who were around him when they saw the razor performing this unusual operation. And yet, in the hour which was yet to pass, how many accidents might happen, how many circumstances might occur, which would oblige them to put off their departure till the next day. From this moment dangers had commenced and all those palpitating emotions, which it is impossible to describe. Here then was no question about bayonets, through the midst of which the Prince was about to pass—for although the order in every prison is to fire at the escaping prisoner, such was not the fear by which the Prince was moved. Determined, however, to sell his life as dearly as possible, the Prince took a poniard. He was also about to place under his clothes a small portfolio, which contained two letters, one from his mother, and another from Napoleon—a sacred amulet which the Prince always carried about with him—the precious pledges of an abiding and constant affection, and of recollections the dearest to his heart. When he thought that those papers might betray him in case of search on the frontier, he experienced a moment's hesitation, and by look consulted the Doctor; but superstition for sacred objects prevailing in their hearts, prudence subsided, and Prince Napoleon Louis concealed carefully on his breast the only relic which he had, at that time, of the past grandeur of his family. The Emperor's letter is directed to the Prince's mother, Queen Hortense, and in speaking of his nephew the Emperor expresses thus, "I hope he will grow and make himself worthy of the destinies which await him."

How different those destinies proved from those anticipated by Napoleon! In how many trying occurrences had this wish to act as a talisman!

In the meantime, the preparation for concealing the Prince's person, by assuming a workman's dress, continued; of which Thélin gives the following account:—"The Prince put on his usual dress, gray pantaloons and boots; then he drew over his waistcoat, a coarse linen shirt, cut off at the waist, a blue cotton handkerchief, and a blouse, not merely clean, but somewhat elegant in its cut; and, finally, he drew on a pair of large trousers of coarse blue linen, which had been worn and were very dirty. Under these he concealed the lower part of the first blouse, and finally put on, over all, a second blouse, as much worn and dirty as the pantaloons. The rest of his costume consisted of an old blue linen apron, a long black-haired wig, and a bad cap. Being thus apparelled, and his hands and face painted with red and black, the moment of action being at hand, all emotion had ceased; and the Prince breakfasted as usually with a cup of coffee, put on his sabots, took a common clay pipe in his mouth, hoisted a board upon his shoulders, and was in readiness to set out!"

At a quarter before seven, Thélin called to him all the workmen who were engaged on the stairs, and invited them to go into the dining-room to take their morning dram, telling Laplace, his man-of-all-work, to pour out the liquor for them to drink. In this manner they got rid also of the latter. Immediately after he came to give notice to the Prince, that the decisive moment had come; and descended the staircase at the bottom of which the two keepers, Dupin and Issali, were posed by order of the commander, and where, besides, there was a workman occupied in repairing the baluster. Thélin exchanged a few words with the keepers, who bid him good morning, and seeing that Thélin had his overcoat on his arm, and was prepared to set out, they wished him a good journey. Thélin then pretended to have something to say to Issali, drew him aside from the wicket, and so placed himself that Issali, in order to hear, must have his back towards the Prince.

At the very moment at which the Prince quitted his chamber, some of the workmen were already coming from the dining-room, situated at the other end of the corridor; but Conneau was there to turn away their attention, and none of them observed the Prince, who was slowly passing down the stairs. When he came within a few steps of the bottom, he found himself face to face with Dupin, the keeper, who drew back in order to avoid the plank, which placed horizontally on the shoulder, prevented the profile of the face from being seen, and could not, therefore, observe the Prince's face. The Prince then passed through the two wicket-gates, going behind Issali, whom Thélin kept in close conversation. He then entered the courtyard, where a workman, who came down the stairs immediately after, followed him very close, and appeared as about to speak to him. This was a locksmith's boy, whom Thélin immediately called to him, and formed some pretext for sending him back again up stairs.

On passing before the first sentinel, the pipe dropped from the Prince's mouth, and fell at the soldier's feet; he stopped to pick it up; the soldier looked at him mechanically, and continued his monotonous pace. At the top of the canteen the Prince passed very near the Officer of the Guard, who was reading a letter. The Officer of Engineers and Contractor for the Works, were at a distance of some paces further, the officer busily occupied in examining some papers. The Prince continued his way, and passed through the middle of a score of soldiers, who were basking in the sun in front of the guard-house. The drummer looked at the man with the plank with an insulting glance, but the sentinel paid no attention to him whatever. The gate-keeper was at the door of his lodge, but he merely looked at Thélin, who kept a few yards behind, and, in order more surely to draw attention to himself, led the Prince's dog in a leash. The sergeant, who was standing by the side of the wicket, looked steadily at the Prince, but his examination was interrupted by a movement of the plank, which obliged the soldier who held the bolt to withdraw himself.

He immediately opened the gates, and turning round, the Prince went out—the door was closed behind him. Thélin afterwards wished the gate-keeper "good day," and passed out in his turn.

Between the draw-bridges the Prince met two workmen, coming straight towards him on the side on which his figure was not concealed by the plank. They looked at him with great eagerness from the distance at which they still were, and, in a loud voice, expressed their surprise at not knowing him. On his part, the Prince, pretending to be tired of carrying the plank on his right shoulder, moved it to the left; the men, however, appeared so curious that the Prince thought for a moment he should not be able to escape them, and when at last he was near them, and they appeared as if approaching to speak to him, he had the satisfaction of hearing one of them exclaim: "Oh! it's Bertou."

Success was now complete. The Prince was free beyond those walls, in which he had been immured five years and nine months.

Although the Prince had no other acquaintance with the neighbourhood than that which he derived from examining the map of the town, he did not hesitate, but immediately pursued the road along the ramparts, which joins the high-road to St. Quentin. In the meantime, Thélin went through the town to get the *cabriolet,* for which he had made arrangements the evening before, and which he was to drive himself.

Shall we now venture to speak of the tumultuous feeling which agitated the heart of the fugitive? Shall we attempt to depict the happiness of the deliverance, saddened by the melancholy thought of exile—regret for the loss of his country, softened down by the prospect of a dungeon, which the eye perceived in the distance? The mind may form some idea of these things, and of his situation, but no tongue can adequately describe them. The sudden joy of success followed the deep anxiety of expectation and the feverish excitement of action—a rapid transition, which, when it comes upon the mind unprepared, overwhelms all its faculties, and renders the trial more difficult to bear than all the strokes of misfortune. Are we not constrained to believe that the firmest mind would quail and sink in these great crises of life, was it not for the powerful instinct which hurries the mind away from all terrestrial concerns, and leads it towards God, the bountiful giver of every good and perfect gift? He had walked fast, and, in spite of the *sabots,* had reached a distance of about two miles from the town, near the cemetery of St. Sulpice, there he stopped for the carriage which was to save him; a rough crucifix stood in the middle of the burying-grounds; the fugitive prostrated himself before God, and offered up hearty thanksgiving to the master of all things, who had led him, as it were, by the hand, through the midst of so many dangers.

In the meantime the sound of an approaching carriage was heard, and Charles Thélin was seen approaching. The Prince was about immediately to get rid of his plank, when he perceived another carriage coming from St. Quentin. He, therefore, continued to walk, in order to give the other *cabriolet* time to pass, and Thélin, with the same intent, slackened his pace. At length the Prince threw his plank, which had been indeed that of his deliverance, into a corn-field, leaped into the *cabriolet,* shook off the dust with which he was covered, took off his *sabots* and threw them into the ditch, and, in order to commence his new character, which was that of a coachman, he seized the reins and began to drive. The travellers, at this moment, perceived two mounted *gensd'armes,* coming out of the village of St. Sulpice; but they, very luckily, took the road to Peronne, before coming up with the *cabriolet.*

The distance from Ham to St. Quentin, five leagues, was rapidly passed. At each change of horses Thélin concealed his face as much as possible in his handkerchief; it was, however, afterwards said, that he had been seen by several persons, and, among others, by the Commissary of Police from Ham, who was returning from St. Quentin; and we are assured that an old woman expressed great astonishment at seeing the Prince's valet de chambre, accompanied by a man so badly dressed.

Before entering St. Quentin, the Prince took off the old trousers, the dirty blouse, and the old cap, retaining the smaller blouse and the wig, and put on a braided cap. He then alighted from the *cabriolet,* in order to turn round the town of St. Quentin on foot, and to wait for Thélin again with fresh horses, on the Cambray road.

Charles Thélin drove to the post-house, from whence M. Abric, the post-master, had just come out; but Thélin was well-known to Madame Abric; he told her he was obliged to go, with all speed, to Cambray, to return early, and begged her to order a post-chaise and horses, with all possible haste, while he would leave at her house his horse and *cabriolet.* The kind Madame Abric showed the greatest alacrity to have Thélin served, and ordered horses to be put to her husband's small chaise. She pressed him very much to stay for breakfast; but, perceiving that he was anxious to proceed, she did not venture to urge her request. The traveller, however, with great politeness praised the remains of a cold pâté, which was on the table, of which she begged him to accept a slice, and which being carefully wrapped up, soon afterwards furnished an excellent breakfast for the Prince, for which his long walk had provided an excellent appetite.

In spite of his impatience Thélin dared not to hurry too much the post-people, for fear of awaking suspicions, yet the Prince had for some time arrived at the other end of the town of St. Quentin, and was waiting, not without some concern, for the carriage which was to overtake him. He laboured for a moment, and under fear of having been left behind while examining the town; but seeing a gentleman coming in a carriage from the Cambray road, he asked him whether he had not met with a post-chaise? This gentleman who answered him in the negative, was the Procureur du Roi of St. Quentin. Sitting on the road-side the Prince grew more concerned every minute, when, at last, he felt something by him; it was the little dog who, running before the horses, announced the arrival of the post-chaise.

M. Abric's small carriage, harnessed to two excellent horses, soon made its appearance; the Prince jumped up, and the postillion resumed his journey at a gallop. From this moment all risk of capture nearly disappeared. Notwithstanding the distance walked and the time lost in changing and procuring carriages, it was not yet nine o'clock; and even supposing that the Prince's escape had been discovered, immediately after his leaving the fortress, the authorities must have lost time in making a *reconnaissance,* in closely examining the fortress, in writing dispatches, sending off the *gensd'armes,* etc.

The travellers continued to make progress, inducing the postillion, by all possible means, to push his horses to their speed. He became, at length, impatient of their eagerness, and said to them, with warmth, *"vous m'embetez;"* but, nevertheless, he continued to make the pavement smoke under his horse's feet. Whilst they were changing horses at the first relay, a horseman with a forage-cap arrived at a gallop. They mistook him for a *gensd'arme,* and the Prince was preparing to avoid him; when they perceived that he was a non-commissioned officer of the National Guard.

No other incident worthy of notice occurred till the travellers reached Valenciennes where, thanks to his conductors, the Prince arrived at a quarter-past two. This was the only place where they were asked for their passports. Thélin presented that of the English courier, and the Prince was not called upon to show his.

As the train for Brussels did not leave till four o'clock, the Prince would willingly have taken post-horses to gain the frontier of Belgium; but this step might have led to remarks, as such a mode of travelling had become very rare since the opening of the railroad. The Prince, therefore, determined to wait at the station at Valenciennes, for the starting of the next train. The capture had now become an impossibility. Thélin, however, was wholly unable to turn away his eyes from that side from which *gensd'armes* might come. Suddenly, he heard himself named, he turned and recognised a *gensd'arme* from Ham, in the dress of a citizen. Thélin was as much surprised as he was *half-pleased*; he did not, however, lose his presence of mind and the *gensd'arme* soon after, asking him what news of the Prince's health, told him that he had quitted the service, and obtained an employment on the Northern Railroad, at the station of Valenciennes.

The Prisoner of Ham soon reached Brussels—then Ostend—and then England.

The Cemetery of the Chateau d'If

Few novels have had the timeless appeal of *The Count of Monte Cristo*, by Alexandre Dumas. The suffering and triumph of Edmond Dantès inspired an entire generation of future escapers, including Papillon. Dantès stands with Hugo's Jean Valjean as one of the most popular fictional escapers in literary history.

In this story, a young Dantès has been banished to an island prison on a trumped-up charge of conspiring to free Napoleon. After years of bitter suffering and despair, he finds a friend in the cleric Faria, who is imprisoned in a neighboring cell. Faria tutors Dantès in the ways of the world, and together they plan a variety of escapes with the clever tools Faria has fashioned in his cell. (The escapes of Trenck and Latude undoubtedly influenced Dumas's novel.)

Unfortunately, their intricate tunneling system still doesn't allow them egress without injuring or killing a guard, something the pious Faria won't submit to. Eventually, Faria dies, but not before telling Dantès the location of a secret treasure, hidden on the Isle of Monte Cristo. Still mourning his friend's sudden death, Dantès comes up with a daring plan to free himself and settle up with those who betrayed him.

On the bed, at full length, and fully lighted by the pale ray that penetrated the window, was visible a sack of coarse cloth, under the large folds of which were stretched a long and stiffened form; it was Faria's last winding-sheet—a winding-sheet which, as the turnkey said, cost so little. All then was completed. A material separation had taken place between Dantès and his old friend,—he could no longer see those eyes which had remained open as if to look even beyond death,—he could no longer clasp that hand of industry which had lifted for him the veil that had concealed hidden and obscure things. Faria, the usual and the good companion, with whom he was accustomed to live so intimately, no longer breathed. He seated himself on the edge of that terrible bed, and fell into a melancholy and gloomy reverie.

Alone! he was alone again! again relapsed into silence! he found himself once again in the presence of nothingness!

Alone! no longer to see,—no longer to hear the voice of the only human being who attached him to life! Was it not better, like Faria, to seek the presence of his Maker and learn the enigma of life at the risk of passing through the mournful gate of intense suffering?

The idea of suicide, driven away by his friend, and forgotten in his presence whilst living, arose like a phantom before him in presence of his dead body.

"If I could die," he said, "I should go where he goes, and should assuredly find him again. But how to die? It is very easy," he continued, with a smile of bitterness; "I will remain here, rush on the first person that opens the door, will strangle him, and then they will guillotine me."

But as it happens that in excessive griefs, as in great tempests, the abyss is found between the tops of the loftiest waves, Dantès recoiled from the idea of this infamous death, and passed suddenly from despair to an ardent desire for life and liberty.

"Die! oh, no," he exclaimed, "not die now, after having lived and suffered so long and so much! Die! yes, had I died years since; but now it would be indeed to give way to my bitter destiny. No, I desire to live, I desire to struggle to the very last, I wish to reconquer the happiness of which I have been deprived. Before I die, I must not forget that I have my executioners to punish, and, perhaps, too, who knows, some friends to reward. Yet they will forget me here, and I shall die in my dungeon like Faria."

As he said this, he remained motionless, his eyes fixed like a man struck with a sudden idea, but whom this idea fills with amazement. Suddenly he rose, lifted his hand to his brow as if his brain were giddy, paced twice or thrice round his chamber, and then paused abruptly at the bed.

"Ah! ah!" he muttered, "who inspires me with this thought? Is that thou, gracious God? Since none but the dead pass freely from this dungeon, let me assume the place of the dead!"

Without giving himself time to reconsider his decision, and, indeed, that he might not allow his thoughts to be distracted from his desperate resolution, he bent over the appalling sack, opened it with the knife which Faria had made, drew the corpse from the sack, and transported it along the gallery to his own chamber, laid it on his couch, passed round its head the rag he wore at night round his own, covered it with his counterpane, once again kissed the ice-cold brow, and tried vainly to close the resisting eyes which glared horrible, turned the head towards the wall, so that the gaoler might, when he brought his evening meal, believe that he was asleep, as was his frequent custom; returned along the gallery, threw the bed against the wall, returned to the other cell, took from the hiding-place the needle and thread, flung off his rags that they might feel naked flesh only beneath the coarse sackcloth, and getting inside the sack, placed himself in the posture in which the dead body had been laid, and sewed up the mouth of the sack from within.

The beating of his heart might have been heard if by any mischance the gaolers had entered at that moment.

Dantès might have waited until the evening visit was over, but he was afraid the governor might change his resolution, and order the dead body to be removed earlier.

In that case his last hope would have been destroyed.

Now his project was settled under any circumstances, and he hoped thus to carry it into effect.

If during the time he was being conveyed the grave-diggers should discover that they were conveying a live instead of a dead body, Dantès did not intend to give them time to recognise him, but with a sudden cut of the knife, he meant to open the sack from top to bottom, and, profiting by their alarm, escape; if they tried to catch him he would use his knife.

If they conducted him to the cemetery and laid him in the grave, he would allow himself to be covered with earth, and then, as it was night, the grave-diggers could scarcely have turned their backs, ere he would have worked his way through the soft soil and escape, hoping that the weight would not be too heavy for him to support.

If he was deceived in this and the earth proved too heavy, he would be stifled, and then, so much the better, all would be over.

Dantès had not eaten since the previous evening, but he had not thought of hunger or thirst, nor did he now think of it. His position was too precarious to allow him even time to reflect on any thought but one.

The first risk that Dantès ran was, that the gaoler when he brought him his supper at seven o'clock, might perceive the substitution he had effected; fortunately, twenty times at least, from misanthropy or fatigue, Dantès had received his gaoler in bed, and then the man placed his bread and soup on the table, and went away without saying a word.

This time the gaoler might not be as silent as usual, but speak to Dantès, and seeing that he received no reply, go to the bed, and thus discover all.

When seven o'clock came, Dantès' agony really commenced. His hand placed on his heart was unable to repress its throbbings, whilst with the other, he wiped the perspiration from his temples. From time to time shudderings ran through his whole frame, and collapsed his heart as if it were frozen. Then he thought he was gong to die. Yet the hours passed on without any stir in the Château, and Dantès felt he had escaped this first danger: it was a good augury. At length, about the hour the governor had appointed, footsteps were heard on the stairs. Edmond felt that the moment had arrived, and summoning up all his courage, held his breath, happy if at the same time he could have repressed in like manner the hasty pulsation of his arteries.

They stopped at the door—there were two steps, and Dantès guessed it was the two grave-diggers who had come to seek him—this idea was soon converged into certainty, when he head the noise they made in putting down the hand-bier.

The door opened, and a dim light reached Dantès' eyes through the coarse sack that covered him; he saw two shadows approach his bed, a third remaining at the door with a torch in his hand. Each of these two men, approaching the ends of the bed, took the sack by its extremities.

"He's heavy though for an old and thin man," said one, as he raised the head.

"They say every year adds half a pound to the weight of the bones," said another, lifting the feet.

"Have you tied the knot?" inquired the first speaker.

"What would be the use of carrying so much more weight?" was the reply: "I can do that when we get there."

"Yes, you're right," replied the companion.

"What's the knot for?" thought Dantès.

They deposited the supposed corpse on the bier. Edmond stiffened himself in order to play his part of a dead man, and then the party, lighted by the man with the torch who went first, ascended the stairs.

Suddenly he felt the fresh and sharp night air, and Dantès recognised the *mistral*. It was a sudden sensation, at the same time replete with delight and agony.

The bearers advanced twenty paces, then stopped, putting their bier down on the ground.

One of them went away, and Dantès heard his shoes on the pavement.

"Where am I then?" he asked himself.

"Really, he is by no means a light load!" said the other bearer, sitting on the edge of the hand-barrow.

Dantès' first impulse was to escape, but fortunately he did not attempt it.

"Light me, you sir," said the other bearer, "or I shall not find what I am looking for."

The man with the torch complied, although not asked in the most polite terms.

"What can he be looking for?" thought Edmond. "The spade, perhaps."

An exclamation of satisfaction indicated that the grave-digger had found the object of his search.

"Here it is at last," he said, "not without some trouble though."

"Yes," was the answer, "but it has lost nothing by waiting."

As he said this, the man came towards Edmond, who heard a heavy and sounding substance laid down beside him, and the same moment a cord was fastened round his feet with sudden and painful violence.

"Well, have you tied the knot?" inquired the grave-digger, who was looking on.

"Yes, and pretty tight too, I can tell you," was the answer.

"Move on, then."

And the bier was lifted once more, and they proceeded.

They advanced fifty paces farther, and then stopped to open a door, then went forward again. The noise of the waves dashing against the rocks, on which the Château is built, reached Dantès' ear distinctly as they progressed.

"Bad weather!" observed one of the bearers; "not a pleasant night for a dip in the sea."

"Why, yes, the abbé runs a chance of being wet," said the other; and then there was a burst of brutal laughter.

Dantès did not comprehend the jest, but his hair stood erect on his head.

"Well, here we are at last," said one of them. "A little farther—a little farther," said the other. "You know very well that the last was stopped on his way, dashed on the rocks, and the governor told us next day that we were careless fellows."

They ascended five or six more steps, and then Dantès felt that they took him, one by the head and the other by the heels, and swung him to and fro.

"One!" said the grave-diggers. "Two! Three, and away!"

And at the same instant Dantès felt himself flung into the air like a wounded bird, falling, falling with a rapidity that made his blood curdle. Although drawn downwards by the same heavy weight which hastened his rapid descent, it seemed to him as if the time were a century. At last, with a terrific dash, he entered the ice-cold water, and as he did so he uttered a shrill cry, stifled in a moment by his immersion beneath the waves.

Dantès had been flung into the sea, into whose depths he was dragged by a thirty-six pound shot tied to his feet.

The sea is the cemetery of Château d'If.

Dantès, although giddy and almost suffocated, had yet sufficient presence of mind to hold his breath; and as his right hand (prepared as he was for every chance) held his knife open, he rapidly ripped up the sack, extricated his arm, and then his body; but in spite of all his efforts to free himself from the bullet he felt it dragging him down still lower; he then bent his body, and by a desperate effort severed the cord that bound his legs at the moment he was suffocating. With a vigorous spring he rose to the surface of the sea, whilst the bullet bore to its depths the sack that had so nearly become his shroud.

Dantès merely paused to breathe, and then dived again in order to avoid being seen.

When he arose a second time he was fifty paces from where he had first sunk. He saw overhead a black and tempestuous sky, over which the wind was driving the fleeting vapours that occasionally suffered a twinkling star to appear: before him was the vast expanse of waters, sombre and terrible, whose waves foamed and roared as if before the approach of a storm. Behind him, blacker than the sea, blacker than the sky, rose like a phantom the giant of granite, whose projecting crags seemed like arms extended to seize their prey; and on the highest rock was a torch that lighted two figures. He fancied these two forms were looking at the sea; doubtless these strange grave-diggers had heard his cry. Dantès dived again, and remained a long time beneath the water. This manoeuvre was already familiar to him, and usually attracted a crowd of spectators in the bay before the lighthouse at Marseilles when he swam there, who, with one accord pronounced him the best swimmer in the port.

When he rose again the light had disappeared.

It was necessary to strike out to sea. Ratonneau and Pomègue are the nearest isles of all those that surround the Château d'If. But Ratonneau and Pomègue are inhabited, together with the isle of Daume; Tiboulen or Lemaire were the most secure. The isles of Tiboulen and Lemaire are a league from the Château d'If. Dantès, nevertheless, determined to make for them; but how could he find his way in the darkness of the night?

At this moment he saw before him, like a brilliant star, the lighthouse of Planier.

By leaving this light on the right, he kept the isle of Tiboulen a little on the left; by turning to the left, therefore, he would find it. But, as we have said, it was at least a league from the Château d'If to this island.

Often in prison Faria had said to him when he saw him idle and inactive: "Dantès, you must not give way to this listlessness; you will be drowned, if you seek to escape; and your strength has not been properly exercised and prepared for exertion."

These words rang in Dantès' ears even beneath the waves: he hastened to cleave his way through them to see if he had not lost his strength; he found with pleasure that his captivity had taken away nothing of his power, and that he was still master of that element on whose bosom he had so often sported as a boy.

Fear, that relentless pursuer, clogged Dantès' efforts; he listened if any noise was audible; each time that he rose over the waves his looks scanned the horizon, and strove to penetrate the darkness; every wave seemed a boat in his pursuit, and he redoubled exertions that increased his distance from the Château, but the repetition of which weakened his strength. He swam on still, and already the terrible Château had disappeared in the darkness. He could not see it, but he *felt* its presence. An hour passed, during which Dantès, excited by the feeling of freedom, continued to cleave the waves.

"Let us see," said he, "I have swam above an hour; but as the wind is against me, that has retarded my speed; however, if I am not mistaken, I must be close to the isle of Tiboulen. But what if I were mistaken?"

A shudder passed over him. He sought to tread water in order to rest himself, but the sea was too violent, and he felt that he could not make use of this means of repose.

"Well," said he, "I will swim on until I am worn out, or the cramp seizes me, and then I shall sink;" and he struck out with the energy of despair.

Suddenly the sky seemed to him to become still darker and more dense, and compact clouds lowered towards him; at the same time he felt a violent pain in his knee. His imagination told him a ball had struck him, and that in a moment he would hear the report; but he heard nothing. Dantès put out his hand and felt resistance; he then extended his leg and felt the land, and in an instant guessed the nature of the object he had taken for a cloud.

Before him rose a mass of strangely formed rocks that resembled nothing so much as a vast fire petrified at the moment of its most fervent combustion. It was the isle of Tiboulen.

Dantès rose, advanced a few steps, and, with a fervent prayer of gratitude, stretched himself on the granite, which seemed to him softer than down. Then, in spite of the wind and rain, he fell into the deep sweet sleep of those worn out by fatigue.

At the expiration of an hour Edmond was awakened by the roar of the thunder. The tempest was unchained and let loose in all its fury; from time to time a flash of lightning stretched across the heavens like a fiery serpent lighting up the clouds that rolled on like the waves of an immense chaos.

Dantès had not been deceived—he had reached the first of the two isles, which was in reality Tiboulen. He knew that it was barren and without shelter; but when the sea became more calm, he resolved to plunge into its waves again, and swim to Lemaire, equally arid, but larger, and consequently better adapted for concealment.

An overhanging rock offered him a temporary shelter, and scarcely had he availed himself of it when the tempest burst forth in all its fury. Edmond felt the rock beneath which he lay tremble; the waves dashing themselves against the granite rock wetted him with their spray. In safety, as he was, he felt himself become giddy in the midst of this war of the elements and the dazzling brightness of the lightning. It seemed to him that the island trembled to its base, and that it would, like a vessel at anchor, break her moorings, and bear him off into the centre of the storm.

He then recollected that he had not eaten or drunk for four-and-twenty hours. He extended his hands and drank greedily of the rainwater that had lodged in a hollow of the rock.

As he rose, a flash of lightning, that seemed as if the whole of the heavens were opened, illumined the darkness. By its light, between the isle of Lemaire and Cape Croiselle, a quarter of a league distant, Dantès saw, like a spectre, a fishing-boat driven rapidly on by the force of the winds and waves. A second after he saw it again approaching nearer. Dantès cried at the top of his voice to warn them of their danger, but they saw it themselves. Another flash showed him four men clinging to the shattered mast and the rigging, while a fifth clung to the broken rudder.

The men he beheld saw him doubtless, for their cries were carried to his ears by the wind. Above the splintered mast a sail rent to tatters was waving; suddenly the ropes that still held it gave way, and it disappeared in the darkness of the night like a vast sea-bird. At the same moment a violent crash was heard, and cries of distress. Perched on the summit of the rock, Dantès saw by the lightning the vessel in pieces; and amongst the fragments were visible the agonised features of the unhappy sailors. Then all became dark again.

Dantès ran down the rocks at the risk of being himself dashed to pieces; he listened, he strove to examine, but he heard and saw nothing,—all human cries had ceased; and the tempest alone continued to rage.

By degrees the wind abated; vast gray clouds rolled towards the west; and the blue firmament appeared studded with bright stars. Soon a red streak became visible in the horizon; the waves whitened, a light played over them, and gilded their foaming crests with gold. It was day.

Dantès stood silent and motionless before this vast spectacle; for since his captivity he had forgotten it. He turned towards the fortress, and looked both at the sea and the land.

The gloomy building rose from the bosom of the ocean with that imposing majesty of inanimate objects that seems at once to watch and to command.

It was about five o'clock; the sea continued to grow calmer.

"In two or three hours," thought Dantès, "the turnkey will enter my chamber, find the body of my poor friend, recognise it, seek for me in vain, and give the alarm. Then the passage will be discovered; the men who cast me into the sea, and who must have heard the cry I uttered, will be questioned. Then boats filled with armed soldiers will pursue the wretched fugitive. The cannon will warn every one to refuse shelter to a man wandering about naked and famished. The police of Marseilles will be on the alert by land, whilst the governor pursues me by sea. I am cold, I am hungry. I have lost even the knife that saved me. Oh, my God! I have suffered enough surely. Have pity on me, and do for me what I am unable to do for myself."

As Dantès (his eyes turned in the direction of the Château d'If) uttered this prayer, he saw appear at the extremity of the isle of Pomègue, like a bird skimming over the sea, a small bark, that the eye of a sailor alone could recognise as a Genoese tartane. She was coming out of Marseilles harbour, and was standing out to sea rapidly, her sharp prow cleaving through the waves.

"Oh!" cried Edmond, "to think that in half an hour I could join her, did I not fear being questioned, detected, and conveyed back to Marseilles. What can I do? What story can I invent? Under pretext of trading along the coast, these men, who are in reality smugglers, will prefer selling me to doing a good action. I must wait. But I cannot, I am starving. In a few hours my strength will be utterly exhausted; besides, perhaps, I have not been missed at the fortress. I can pass as one of the sailors wrecked last night. This story will pass current, for there is no one left to contradict me."

As he spoke, Dantès looked towards the spot where the fishing-vessel had been wrecked, and started. The red cap of one of the sailors hung to a point of the rock, and some beams that had formed a part of the vessel's keel, floated at the foot of the crags.

In an instant Dantès' plan was formed. He swam to the cap, placed it on his head, seized one of the beams, and struck out so as to cross the line the vessel was taking.

"I am saved," murmured he.

And this conviction restored his strength.

He soon perceived the vessel, which, having the wind right ahead, was tacking between the Château d'If and the tower of Planier. For an instant he feared lest the bark, instead of keeping in shore, should stand out to sea; but he soon saw by her manoeuvres that she wished to pass, like most vessels bound for Italy, between the islands of Jaros and Calaseraigne. However, the vessel and the swimmer insensibly neared one another, and in one of its tacks the bark approached within a quarter of a mile of him. He rose on the waves, making signs of distress; but no one on board perceived him, and the vessel stood on another tack. Dantès would have cried out, but he reflected that the wind would drown his voice.

It was then he rejoiced at his precaution in taking the beam, for without it he would have been unable, perhaps, to reach the vessel,—certainly to return to shore, should he be unsuccessful in attracting attention.

Dantès, although almost sure as to what course the bark would take, had yet watched it anxiously until it tacked and stood towards him. Then he advanced; but, before they had met, the vessel again changed her direction. By a violent effort, he rose half out of the water, waving his cap, and uttering a loud shout peculiar to sailors.

This time he was both seen and heard, and the tartane instantly steered towards him. At the same time, he saw they were about to lower the boat.

An instant after, the boat, rowed by two men, advanced rapidly towards him. Dantès abandoned the beam, which he thought now useless, and swam vigorously to meet them. But he had reckoned too much upon his strength, and then he felt how serviceable the beam had been to him. His arms grew stiff, his legs had lost their flexibility, and he was almost breathless.

He uttered a second cry. The two sailors redoubled their efforts, and one of them cried in Italian, "Courage."

The word reached his ear as a wave, which he no longer had the strength to surmount, passed over his head. He rose again to the surface, supporting himself by one of those desperate efforts a drowning man makes, uttered a third cry, and felt himself sink again, as if the fatal bullet were again tied to his feet.

The water passed over his head, and the sky seemed livid. A violent effort again brought him to the surface. He felt as if something seized him by the hair; but he saw and heard nothing. He had fainted.

When he opened his eyes Dantès found himself on the deck of the tartane. His first care was to see what direction they were pursuing. They were rapidly leaving the Château d'If behind. Dantès was so exhausted that the exclamation of joy he uttered was mistaken for a sigh.

As we have said, he was lying on the dock. A sailor was rubbing his limbs with a woollen cloth; another, whom he recognised as the one who had cried out "Courage!" held a gourd full of rum to his mouth; whilst the third, an old sailor, at once the pilot and captain, looked on with that egotistical pity men feel for a misfortune that they have escaped yesterday and which may overtake them tomorrow.

A few drops of the rum restored suspended animation, whilst the friction of his limbs restored their elasticity.

"Who are you?" said the pilot in bad French.

"I am," replied Dantès, in bad Italian, "a Maltese sailor. We were coming from Syracuse laden with grain. The storm of last night overtook us at Cape Morgion, and we were wrecked on these rocks."

"Where do you come from?"

"From these rocks, that I had the good luck to cling to whilst our captain and the rest of the crew were all lost. I saw your ship, and fearful of being left to perish on the desolate island, I swam off on a fragment of the vessel in order to try and gain your bark. You have saved my life, and I thank you," continued Dantès. "I was lost when one of your sailors caught hold of my hair."

"It was I," said a sailor, of a frank and manly appearance; "and it was time, for you were sinking."

"Yes," returned Dantès, holding out his hand, "I thank you again."

"I almost hesitated, though," replied the sailor; "you looked more like a brigand than an honest man, with your beard six inches and your hair a foot long."

Dantès recollected that his hair and beard had not been cut all the time he was at the Château d'If.

"Yes," said he, "in a moment of danger I made a vow to our Lady of the Grotto not to cut my hair or beard for ten years if I were saved; but to-day the vow expires."

"Now what are we to do with you?" said the captain.

"Alas! anything you please. My captain is dead; I have barely escaped; but I am a good sailor. Leave me at the first port you make; I shall be sure to find employment."

"Do you know the Mediterranean?"

"I have sailed over it since my childhood."

"You know the best harbours?"

"There are few ports that I could not enter or leave with my eyes blinded."

"I say, captain," said the sailor, who had cried "Courage!" to Dantès, "if what he says is true, what hinders his staying with us?"

"If he says true," said the captain doubtingly. "But in his present condition he will promise anything, and take his chance of keeping it afterwards."

"I will do more than I promise," said Dantès.

"We shall see," returned the other, smiling.

"Where are you going to?" asked Dantès.

"To Leghorn."

"Then why, instead of tacking so frequently, do you not sail nearer the wind?"

"Because we should run straight on to the island of Rion."

"You shall pass it by twenty fathoms."

"Take the helm, and let us see what you know."

The young man took the helm, ascertaining by a slight pressure if the vessel answered the rudder, and seeing that, without being a first-rate sailer, she yet was tolerably obedient,—

"To the braces," said he.

The four seamen, who composed the crew, obeyed, whilst the pilot looked on.

"Haul taut."

They obeyed.

"Belay."

This order was also executed, and the vessel passed, as Dantès had predicted, twenty fathoms to the right.

"Bravo!" said the captain.

"Bravo!" repeated the sailors.

And they all regarded with astonishment this man whose eye had recovered an intelligence, and his body a vigour they were far from suspecting.

"You see," said Dantès, quitting the helm, "I shall be of some use to you, at least, during the voyage. If you do not want me at Leghorn, you can leave me there, and I will pay out of the first wages I get for my food and the clothes you lend me."

"Ah," said the captain, "we can agree very well, if you are reasonable."

"Give me what you give the others, and all will be arranged," returned Dantès.

"That's not fair," said the seaman who had saved Dantès; "for you know more than we do."

"What is that to you, Jacopo?" returned the captain. "Every one is free to ask what he pleases."

"That's true," replied Jacopo. "I only made a remark."

"Well, you would do much better to lend him a jacket and a pair of trousers, if you have them."

"No," said Jacopo; "but I have a shirt and a pair of trousers."

"That is all I want," interrupted Dantès.

Jacopo dived into the hold, and soon returned with what Edmond wanted.

"Now, then, do you wish for anything else?" said the patron.

"A piece of bread and another glass of the capital rum I tasted, for I have not eaten or drunk for a long time."

He had not tasted food for forty hours.

A piece of bread was brought, and Jacopo offered him the gourd.

"Larboard your helm," cried the captain to the steersman.

Dantès glanced to the same side as he lifted the gourd to his mouth; but his hand stopped.

"Halloa! what's the matter at the Château d'If?" said the captain.

A small white cloud, which had attracted Dantès' attention, crowned the summit of the bastion of the Château d'If.

At the same moment the faint report of a gun was heard. The sailors looked at one another.

"What is this?" asked the captain.

"A prisoner has escaped from the Château d'If, and they are firing the alarm gun," replied Dantès.

The captain glanced at him, but he had lifted the rum to his lips, and was drinking it with so much composure, that his suspicions, if he had any, died away.

"At any rate," murmured he, "if it be, so much the better, for I have made a rare acquisition."

Under pretence of being fatigued, Dantès asked to take the helm; the steersman, enchanted to be relieved, looked at the captain, and the latter by a sign indicated that he might abandon it to his new comrade. Dantès could thus keep his eyes on Marseilles.

"What is the day of the month?" asked he of Jacopo, who sat down beside him.

"The 28th of February!"

"In what year?"

"In what year—you ask me in what year?"

"Yes," replied the young man "I ask you in what year!"

"You have forgotten then?"

"I got such a fright last night," replied Dantès, smiling, "that I have almost lost my memory, I ask you what year is it?"

"The year 1829," returned Jacopo.

It was fourteen years day for day since Dantès' arrest.

He was nineteen when he entered the Chateau d'If; he was thirty-three when he escaped.

A sorrowful smile passed over his face; he asked himself what had become of Mercédès, who must believe him dead.

Then his eyes lighted up with hatred as he thought of the three men who had caused him so long and wretched a captivity.

He renewed against Danglars, Fernand, and Villefort the oath of implacable vengeance he had made in his dungeon.

The oath was no longer a vain menace, for the fastest sailer in the Mediterranean would have been unable to overtake the little tartane, that with every stitch of canvas set was flying before the wind to Leghorn.

A Question of Passports

BARONESS ORCZY

Emmuska Orczy created the fictional Scarlet Pimpernel in 1903 and continued his adventures in a series of immensely popular books that saw the
British fop Percy Blakeney secretly dash off to rescue various French gentry
from the bloody guillotine during the French Revolution. His legendary
status and secret identity helped spawn a whole new generation of literary
super-heroes.

Virtually all of the Scarlet Pimpernel books contain dramatic escapes or
rescues and his adventures still make great reading today. Unlike many of the
real-life, life-and-death stories included here, this is a light-hearted escape
through the gates of Paris taken from *The League of the Scarlet Pimpernel*.

Bibot was very sure of himself. There never was, never had been, there
never would be again another such patriotic citizen of the Republic
as was citizen Bibot of the Town Guard.

And because his patriotism was so well known among the members of the Committee of Public Safety, and his uncompromising hatred of the
aristocrats so highly appreciated, citizen Bibot had been given the most important military post within the city of Paris.

He was in command of the Porte Montmartre, which goes to prove how
highly he was esteemed, for, believe me, more treachery had been going on
inside and out of the Porte Montmartre than in any other quarter of Paris. The
last commandant there, citizen Ferney, was guillotined for having allowed a
whole batch of aristocrats—traitors to the Republic, all of them—to slip
through the Porte Montmartre and to safety outside the walls of Paris. Ferney

pleaded in his defence that these traitors had been spirited away from under his very nose by the devil's agency, for surely that meddlesome Englishman who spent his time in rescuing aristocrats—traitors, all of them—from the clutches of Madame la Guillotine must be either the devil himself or at any rate one of his most powerful agents.

'Nom de Dieu! Just think of his name! The Scarlet Pimpernel they call him! No one knows him by any other name! and he is preternaturally tall and strong and superhumanly cunning! And the power which he has of being transmuted into various personalities—rendering himself quite unrecognizable to the eyes of the most sharp-seeing patriot of France must of a surety be a gift of Satan!'

But the Committee of Public Safety refused to listen to Ferney's explanations. The Scarlet Pimpernel was only an ordinary mortal—an exceedingly cunning and meddlesome personage it is true, and endowed with a superfluity of wealth which enabled him to break the thin crust of patriotism that overlay the natural cupidity of many Captains of the Town Guard—but still an ordinary man for all that, and no true lover of the Republic should allow either superstitious terror or greed to interfere with the discharge of his duties which at the Porte Montmartre consisted in detaining any and every person—aristocrat, foreigner, or otherwise traitor to the Republic—who could not give a satisfactory reason for desiring to leave Paris. Having detained such persons, the patriot's next duty was to hand them over to the Committee of Public Safety, who would then decide whether Madame la Guillotine would have the last word over them or not.

And the guillotine did nearly always have the last word to say, unless the Scarlet Pimpernel interfered.

The trouble was, that that same accursed Englishman interfered at times in a manner which was positively terrifying. His impudence, certes, passed all belief. Stories of his daring and of his impudence were abroad which literally made the lank and greasy hair of every patriot curl with wonder. 'Twas even whispered—not too loudly, forsooth—that certain members of the Committee of Public Safety had measured their skill and valour against that of the Englishman and emerged from the conflict beaten and humiliated, vowing vengeance which, of a truth, was still slow in coming.

Citizen Chauvelin, one of the most implacable and unyielding members of the Committee, was known to have suffered overwhelming shame at the hands of that daring gang, of whom the so-called Scarlet Pimpernel was the accredited chief. Some there were who said that citizen Chauvelin had for ever forfeited his prestige; and even endangered his head by measuring his well-known astuteness against that mysterious League of Spies.

But then Bibot was different!

He feared neither the devil nor any Englishman. Had the latter the strength of giants and the protection of every power of evil, Bibot was ready for him. Nay! he was aching for a tussle, and haunted the purlieus of the Committees to obtain some post which would enable him to come to grips with the Scarlet Pimpernel and his League.

Bibot's zeal and perseverance were duly rewarded, and anon he was appointed to the command of the guard at the Porte Montmartre.

A post of vast importance as aforesaid; so much so, in fact, that no less a person than citizen Jean Paul Marat himself came to speak with Bibot on that third day of Nivôse in the year I of the Republic, with a view to impressing upon him the necessity of keeping his eyes open, and of suspecting every man, woman and child indiscriminately until they had proved themselves to be true patriots.

'Let no one slip through your fingers, citizen Bibot,' Marat admonished with grim earnestness. 'That accursed Englishman is cunning and resourceful, and his impudence surpasses that of the devil himself.'

'He'd better try some of his impudence on me!' commended Bibot with a sneer, 'he'll soon find out that he no longer has a Ferney to deal with. Take it from me, citizen Marat, that if a batch of aristocrats escape out of Paris within the next few days, under the guidance of the d—d Englishman, they will have to find some other way than the Porte Montmartre.'

'Well said, citizen!' commented Marat. 'But be watchful tonight . . . tonight especially. The Scarlet Pimpernel is a rampant in Paris just now.'

'How so?'

'The *ci-devant* Duc and Duchesse de Montreux and the whole of their brood—sisters, brothers, two or three children, a priest and several servants—a round dozen in all, have been condemned to death. The guillotine for them tomorrow at daybreak! Would it could have been tonight,' added Marat, whilst a demoniacal leer contorted his face which already exuded lust for blood from every pore. 'Would it could have been tonight. But the guillotine has been busy; over four hundred executions today . . . and the tumbrils are full—the seats are bespoken in advance—and still they come. . . . But tomorrow morning at daybreak Madame la Guillotine will have a word to say to the whole of the Montreux crowd!'

'But they are in the Conciergerie prison surely, citizen! out of the reach of that accursed Englishman?'

'They are on their way, and I mistake not, to the prison at this moment. I came straight on here after the condemnation, to which I listened with true joy. Ah, citizen Bibot! the blood of these hated aristocrats is good to behold when it drips from the blade of the guillotine. Have a care, citizen Bibot, do not let the Montreux crowd escape!'

'Have no fear, citizen Marat! But surely there is no danger! They have been tried and condemned! They are, as you say, even now on their way—well guarded, I presume—to the Conciergerie prison!—tomorrow at daybreak, the guillotine! What is there to fear?'

'Well, well!' said Marat, with a slight tone of hesitation, 'it is best, citizen Bibot, to be over-careful these times.'

Even whilst Marat spoke his face, usually so cunning and vengeful, had suddenly lost its look of devilish cruelty which was almost superhuman in the excess of its infamy, and a greyish hue—suggestive of terror—had spread over the sunken cheeks. He clutched Bibot's arm, and leaning over the table he whispered in his ear:

'The Public Prosecutor had scarce finished his speech today, judgment was being pronounced, the spectators were expectant and still, only the Montreux woman and some of the females and children were blubbering and moaning, when suddenly, it seemed from nowhere, a small piece of paper fluttered from out the assembly and alighted on the desk in front of the Public Prosecutor. He took the paper up and glanced at its contents. I saw that his cheeks had paled, and that his hand trembled as he handed the paper over to me.'

'And what did that paper contain, citizen Marat?' asked Bibot, also speaking in a whisper, for an access of superstitious terror was gripping him by the throat.

'Just the well-known accursed device, citizen, the small scarlet flower, drawn in red ink, and the few words: "Tonight the innocent men and women now condemned by this infamous tribunal will be beyond your reach!"'

'And no sign of a messenger?'

'None.'

'And when, did—'

'Hush!' said Marat peremptorily, 'no more of that now. To your post, citizen, and remember—all are suspect! let none escape!'

The two men had been sitting outside a small tavern, opposite the Porte Montmartre, with a bottle of wine between them, their elbows resting on the grimy top of a rough wooden table. They had talked in whispers, for even the walls of the tumble-down cabaret might have had ears.

Opposite them the city wall—broken here by the great gate of Montmartre—loomed threateningly in the fast-gathering dusk of this winter's afternoon. Men in ragged red shirts, their unkempt heads crowned with Phrygian caps adorned with a tricolor cockade, lounged against the wall, or sat in groups on the top of piles of refuse that littered the street, with a rough deal plank between them and a greasy pack of cards in their grimy fingers. Guns and bayonets were propped against the wall. The gate itself had three means of egress; each of these was guarded by two men with fixed bayonets at their shoulders, but otherwise dressed like the others, in rags—with bare legs that looked blue and numb in the cold—the *sans-culottes* of revolutionary Paris.

Bibot rose from his seat, nodding to Marat, and joined his men.

From afar, but gradually drawing nearer, came the sound of a ribald song, with chorus accompaniment sung by throats obviously surfeited with liquor.

For a moment—as the sound approached—Bibot turned back one more to the Friend of the People.

'Am I to understand, citizen,' he said, 'that my orders are not to let anyone pass through these gates tonight?'

'No, no, citizen,' replied Marat, 'we dare not do that. There are a number of good patriots in the city still. We cannot interfere with their liberty or—'

And the look of fear of the demagogue—himself afraid of the human whirlpool which he had let loose—stole into Marat's cruel, piercing eyes.

'No, no,' he reiterated more emphatically, 'we cannot disregard the passports issued by the Committee of Public Safety. But examine each passport carefully, citizen Bibot! If you have any reasonable ground for suspicion, detain the holder, and if you have not—'

The sound of singing was quite near now. With another wink and a final leer, Marat drew back under the shadow of the *cabaret* and Bibot swaggered up to the main entrance of the gate.

'*Qui va là?*' he thundered in stentorian tones as a group of some half-dozen people lurched towards him out of the gloom, still shouting hoarsely their ribald drinking song.

The foremost man in the group passed opposite citizen Bibot, and with arms akimbo, and legs planted well apart, tried to assume a rigidity of attitude which apparently was somewhat foreign to him at this moment.

'Good patriots, citizen,' he said in a thick voice which he vainly tried to render steady.

'What do you want?' queried Bibot.

'To be allowed to go on our way unmolested.'

'What is your way?'

'Through the Porte Montmartre to the village of Barency.'

'What is your business there?'

This query, delivered in Bibot's most pompous manner, seemed vastly to amuse the rowdy crowd. He who was the spokesman turned to his friends and shouted hilariously:

'Hark at him, citizens! He asks me what is our business. Ohé, citizen Bibot, since when have you become blind? A dolt you've always been, else you had not asked the question.'

But Bibot, undeterred by the man's drunken insolence, retorted gruffly:

'Your business, I want to know.'

'Bibot! my little Bibot!' cooed the bibulous orator now in dulcet tones, 'dost not know us, my good Bibot? Yet we all know thee, citizen—Captain Bibot of the Town Guard, eh, citizens! Three cheers for the citizen captain!'

When the noisy shouts and cheers from half a dozen hoarse throats had died down, Bibot, without more ado, turned to his own men at the gate.

'Drive those drunken louts away!' he commanded; 'no one is allowed to loiter here.'

Loud protest on the part of the hilarious crowd followed, then a slight scuffle with the bayonets of the Town Guard. Finally the spokesman, somewhat sobered, once more appealed to Bibot.

'Citizen Bibot! you must be blind not to know me and my mates! And let me tell you that you are doing yourself a deal of harm by interfering with the citizens of the Republic in the proper discharge of their duties, and by disregarding their rights of egress through this gate, a right confirmed by passports signed by two members of the Committee of Public Safety.'

He had spoken now fairly clearly and very pompously. Bibot, somewhat impressed and remembering Marat's admonitions, said very civilly:

'Tell me your business, then, citizen, and show me your passports. If everything is in order you may go your way.'

'But you know me, citizen Bibot?' queried the other.

'Yes, I know you—unofficially—citizen Durand.'

'You know that I and the citizens here are the carriers for citizen Legrand, the market gardener of Barency?'

'Yes, I know that,' said Bibot guardedly, 'unofficially.'

'Then, unofficially, let me tell you, citizen, that unless we get to Barency this evening, Paris will have to do without cabbages and potatoes tomorrow. So now you know that you are acting at your own risk and peril, citizen, by detaining us.'

'Your passports, all of you,' commanded Bibot.

He had just caught sight of Marat still sitting outside the tavern opposite, and was glad enough, in this instance, to shelve his responsibility on the shoulders of the popular 'Friend of the People.' There was general searching in ragged pockets for grimy papers with official seals thereon, and whilst Bibot ordered one of his men to take the six passports across the road to citizen Marat for his inspection, he himself, by the last rays of the setting winter sun, made close examination of the six men who desired to pass through the Porte Montmartre.

As the spokesman had averred, he—Bibot—knew every one of these men. They were the carriers to citizen Legrand, the Barency market gardener. Bibot knew every face. They passed with a load of fruit and vegetables in and out of Paris every day. There was really and absolutely no cause for suspicion, and when citizen Marat returned the six passports, pronouncing them to be genuine, and recognizing his own signature at the bottom of each, Bibot was at last satisfied, and the six bibulous carriers were allowed to pass through the gate, which they did, arm in arm, singing a wild *carmagnole,* and vociferously cheering as they emerged out into the open.

But Bibot passed an unsteady hand over his brow. It was cold, yet he was in a perspiration. That sort of thing tells on a man's nerves. He rejoined Marat, at the table outside the drinking-booth, and ordered a fresh bottle of wine.

The sun had set now, and with the gathering dusk a damp mist descended on Montmartre. From the wall opposite, where the men sat playing cards, came occasional volleys of blasphemous oaths. Bibot was feeling much more like himself. He had half forgotten the incident of the six carriers, which had occurred nearly half an hour ago.

Two or three other people had, in the meanwhile, tried to pass through the gates, but Bibot had been suspicious and had detained them all.

Marat, having commended him for his zeal, took final leave of him. Just as the demagogue's slouchy, grimy figure was disappearing down a side street there was the loud clatter of hoofs from that same direction, and the next moment a detachment of the mounted Town Guard, headed by an officer in uniform galloped down the ill-paved street.

Even before the troopers had drawn rein the officer had hailed Bibot.

'Citizen,' he shouted, and his voice was breathless, for he had evidently ridden hard and fast, 'this message to you from the citizen Chief Commissary of the Section. Six men are wanted by the Committee of Public Safety. They are disguised as carriers in the employ of a market gardener, and have passports for Barency! . . . The passports are stolen: the men are traitors—escaped aristocrats—and their spokesman is that d—d Englishman, the Scarlet Pimpernel.'

Bibot tried to speak; he tugged at the collar of his ragged shirt; an awful curse escaped him.

'Ten thousand devils!' he roared.

'On no account allow these people to go through,' continued the officer. 'Keep their passports. Detain them! . . . Understand?'

Bibot was still gasping for breath even whilst the officer, ordering a quick 'Turn!' reeled his horse round, ready to gallop away as far as he had come.

'I am for the St Denis Gate—Grosjean is on guard there!' he shouted. 'Same orders all round the city. No one to leave the gates! . . . Understand?'

His troopers fell in. The next moment he would be gone, and these cursed aristocrats well in safety's way.

'Citizen Captain!'

The hoarse shout at last contrived to escape Bibot's parched throat. As if involuntarily, the officer drew rein once more.

'What is it? Quick!—I've no time. That confounded Englishman may be at the St Denis Gate even now!'

'Citizen Captain,' gasped Bibot, his breath coming and going like that of a man fighting for his life. 'Here! . . . at this gate! . . . not half an hour ago . . . six men . . . carriers . . . market gardeners . . . I seemed to know their faces. . . .'

'Yes! yes! market gardener's carriers,' exclaimed the officer gleefully, 'aristocrats all of them . . . and that d—d Scarlet Pimpernel. You've got them? You've detained them? . . . Where are they? . . . Speak, man, in the name of hell! . . .'

'Gone!' gasped Bibot. His legs would no longer bear him. He fell backwards onto a heap of street *débris* and refuse, from which lowly vantage ground he contrived to give away the whole miserable tale.

'Gone! half an hour ago! Their passports were in order! . . . I seemed to know their faces! Citizen Marat was here . . . He, too—'

In a moment the officer had once more swung his horse round, so that the animal reared, with wild forefeet pawing the air, with champing of bit, and white foam scattered around.

'A thousand million curses!' he exclaimed. 'Citizen Bibot, your head will pay for this treachery. Which way did they go?'

A dozen hands were ready to point in the direction where the merry party of carriers had disappeared half an hour ago; a dozen tongues gave rapid, confused explanations.

'Into it, my men!' shouted the officer; 'they were on foot! They can't have gone far. Remember the Republic has offered ten thousand francs for the capture of the Scarlet Pimpernel.'

Already the heavy gates had been swung open, and the officer's voice once more rang out clear through a perfect thunder-clap of fast galloping hoofs:

'*Ventre à terre!* Remember!—ten thousand francs to him who first sights the Scarlet Pimpernel!'

The thunder-clap died away in the distance, the dust of four score hoofs was merged in the fog and in the darkness; the voice of the captain was raised again through the mist-laden air. One shout . . . a shout of triumph . . . then silence once again.

Bibot had fainted on the heap of *débris*.

His comrades brought him wine to drink. He gradually revived. Hope came back to his heart; his nerves soon steadied themselves as the heavy beverage filtrated through into his blood.

'Bah!' he ejaculated as he pulled himself together, 'the troopers were well-mounted . . . the officer was enthusiastic; those carriers could not have walked very far. And, in any case, I am free from blame. Citoyen Marat himself was here and let them pass!'

A shudder of superstitious terror ran through him as he recollected the whole scene: for surely he knew all the faces of the six men who had gone through the gate. The devil indeed must have given the mysterious Englishman power to transmute himself and his gang wholly into the bodies of other people.

More than an hour went by. Bibot was quite himself again, bullying, commanding, detaining everybody now.

At that time there appeared to be a slight altercation going on on the farther side of the gate. Bibot thought it his duty to go and see what the noise was about. Someone wanting to get into Paris instead of out of it at this hour of the night was a strange occurrence.

Bibot heard his name spoken by a raucous voice. Accompanied by two of his men he crossed the wide gates in order to see what was happening. One of the men held a lanthorn, which he was swinging high above his head. Bibot saw standing there before him, arguing with the guard by the gate, the bibulous spokesman of the band of carriers.

He was explaining to the sentry that he had a message to deliver to the citizen commanding at the Porte Montmartre.

'It is a note,' he said, 'which an officer of the mounted guard gave me. He and twenty troopers were galloping down the great North Road not far from Barency. When they overtook the six of us they drew rein, and the officer gave me this note for citizen Bibot and fifty francs if I would deliver it tonight.'

'Give me the note!' said Bibot calmly.

But his hand shook as he took the paper; his face was livid with fear and rage.

The paper had no writing on it, only the outline of a small scarlet flower done in red—the device of the cursed Englishman, the Scarlet Pimpernel.

'Which way did the officer and the twenty troopers go?' he stammered, 'after they gave you this note?'

'On the way to Calais,' replied the other; 'but they had magnificent horses, and didn't spare them either. They are a league and more away by now!'

All the blood in Bibot's body seemed to rush up to his head, a wild buzzing was in his ears. . . .

And that was how the Duc and Duchesse de Montreux, with their servants and family, escaped from Paris on that third day of Nivôse in the year I of the Republic.

Three Years among the Comanches

NELSON LEE

In 1855, Nelson Lee, a former Texas Ranger and veteran of many battles, joined a group of men planning to take a horse herd from Texas to California. After some days on the trail, they were attacked by Comanches. Just four men, including Lee, survived from the original twenty or so. They were taken to a large Indian encampment where two of them were slowly hacked to death by a circling group of dancing braves. The other survivor was carried off and never seen again.

Lee's life was saved by pure luck. The Indians were fascinated by the fancy watch he carried, bought on a whim just before the trip, which rang like thunder on Lee's command. He was traded several times over the next couple of years to different bands of Comanches seeking to possess his magic. Still, he endured a great deal of torture. After one early escape attempt, he was tied down while the chief sawed through his hamstring to cripple him. He remained tied to the ground for several weeks while the wound was intentionally kept open to prevent healing. It was only partially effective.

In his third year of captivity, life improved somewhat for Lee. He was given a wife and made a sort of assistant to the chief, but he never gave up hope that he would one day have a chance to be free again.

At this time I had no apprehensions whatever in regard to my safety so long as I remained an obedient captive. A detected attempt at escape, however, I was aware, would be followed by the severest penalties. I had so long, and so intensely, contemplated the subject that there was no aspect of it that had not received my careful scrutiny. Of one thing I had become convinced: if I had been successful in escaping from the tribe of Spotted Leopard without the means of killing game or making a fire, I should most assuredly have perished from starvation among the mountains surrounding his town.

It became necessary, therefore, to devise some plan to provide myself with these indispensable conveniences. It is probable I could, on many occasions, have reached the mountains unperceived after my marriage. But it was utterly impossible to do so, providing myself at the same time with arms—the watchfulness over me in respect to them being strict and constant.

It was while indulging in these never-ending speculations that Rolling Thunder ordered me to saddle my mule and accompany him on a long journey.

His destination was a village three days' journey to the north. At this place a convention had been called of all the chiefs of tribes inhabiting the country between northern Mexico and the regions of perpetual snow. The object of the convention was to induce the Indian nations to bury the hatchet among themselves and unite in a universal bond of brotherhood to prevent the whites from passing through their territories to the Pacific Coast.

Rolling Thunder, before taking his departure, arrayed himself with extraordinary care. A dozen scalps were attached to his war shirt, silver trinkets representing the moon in all its phases were fastened on his breast; his feet were clad in new, cunningly embroidered moccasins, and on his head rested a crown of feathers dyed by his wives in all the colors of the rainbow. Of all the horses that grazed round his camp, he was mounted upon the most fleet and spirited. His weapons of war were a knife thrust through his belt, a hatchet suspended from the pommel of his saddle, and a Mexican rifle upon which he prided himself exceedingly.

I bestrode the same old mule that had so often borne me on her back, with nothing hanging from my saddle bow but a huge buffalo horn to furnish my master with cool draughts from the streams as we journeyed. Saluting Sleek Otter, who little thought it was the last nod she would ever receive from her long-haired spouse (I had not seen a razor for three years), we trotted away from the village, myself in advance.

Neither of us was destined ever to return.

From early morning, we traveled steadily. At sunset we entered a valley where a small tribe resided. The usual hospitalities were extended.

An Indian's dignity, whether chief or subject, never rises to that elevated degree which prevents his getting drunk every opportunity that offers. The sedate old chief became beastly intoxicated—forgot his customary decorum—vainly attempted to be funny—danced out of place—and whooped when there was no occasion for it—in fact, was as boisterous and silly as about half a gallon of bad Mexican whiskey could make him.

However, bright and early in the morning, the chief was again on his legs, ready to set forward on the journey. Very soon we passed out of the valley and entered the mountains. The last night's debauch had set the old chief on fire, and before the sun had halfway ascended to the zenith his throat was parched and he was mad with thirst.

But there was no water to be found. On and on we went, threading our way through thick bushes, around the sharp points of overhanging cliffs, across rough and rugged ravines, but nowhere did a spring or running stream greet his longing eyes.

We continued to press forward until about one o'clock in the afternoon, when, reaching the bottom of a deep hollow, we discovered water oozing from the base of a precipice and trickling down a little muddy channel through the grass.

Rolling Thunder called impetuously upon me to fill the horn at once. Though I attempted to obey his order with all possible speed, the rill was so extremely shallow that, with every dip I made, the contents of the horn would come up in the proportion of three parts mud to one of water.

Perceiving the difficulty, he leaped from his horse, directing me to hold him by the bridle. He threw his rifle on the ground and, lying down upon it in the grass, thrust his scorched lips into the little stream.

Standing by the horse's side, I observed the hatchet hanging from the pommel of the saddle.

The thought flashed through my mind quick as the fierce lightning that the hour of my deliverance had come at last.

Snatching the hatchet, in that instant, from its place, I leaped towards the chief and buried the dull edge a broad hand's breadth in his brain. A moment sufficed to draw the rifle from beneath him and jerk the long knife from his girdle.

Then, mounting his horse, I dashed wildly away over an unknown path towards the land of freedom.

I remembered that, some two miles back, I had seen a narrow ravine stretching to the west. I turned about and retraced the path we had followed. Coming to the ravine, I plunged into it and spurred on at a breakneck pace over piles of broken stones and through barricades of tangled thorns and brushwood. All the while the mule followed closely at the horse's heels. At the end of six miles I found my way blocked by a tall bluff extending entirely across the western end of the ravine.

Wheeling northward, I moved along the base of the bluff. Finally I reached an opening—a narrow crevice half filled with sharp-angled fragments of rock. With great difficulty, I, the horse, and mule managed to clamber up this until we gained a comparatively level spot. It was a kind of terrace, some twenty feet wide, about halfway to the summit. We followed this terrace as it wound around the precipice. The path became more and more narrow as we advanced, until, to my unutterable horror, it was less than two feet wide. Just in front of me it circled around a sharp point which hid the view beyond, but to all appearances the path ended there.

On one side were great, loose overhanging rocks impossible to ascend and threatening to fall. On the other, there was an almost sheer drop of at least a hundred feet. As if conscious of the danger, the horse hesitated to proceed. Between the wall of rock on the right and the precipice on the left there was not sufficient room for either horse or mule to turn around, and their bodies filled the path so completely that I could not turn back without pushing the poor brutes over the edge.

I turned my eyes away from the dizzy depth below. Then, closely hugging the upper side, I crawled carefully to the sharp point before me. I peered around it. To my enormous relief, it expanded into a broad, smooth road. With much urging and coaxing, I finally succeeded in inducing the horse to pass the point of danger. The mule followed cautiously.

I gazed around. Never had I observed a wilder or more dreary scene. On all sides, mountain was piled upon mountain as far as the eye could reach. Here and there, among the ravines, I discovered strips of timber, but the summits, in the distance, were bare and rocky, their bald peaks stretching to the clouds.

A narrow opening to the southwest attracted my attention, and I headed for it. It proved to be another ravine, over which cedar trees and clusters of thick bushes were scattered. By the time I reached the southwestern end of this little solitary valley, the sun had set. I pushed into the center of a dense thicket, the loneliest spot around, and halted for the night.

Securing the horse to a limb by the bridle, and removing the buffalo-skin saddle, I sat down upon it and tried to figure out what it was best to do. My safety depended much upon circumstances. If the body of the chief should be discovered immediately, my escape was doubtful. The moment it was found, a party would start upon my trail. At the same time messengers would be sent to all the tribes far and near, calling on them to keep a sharp lookout for me. I had as much to fear in front as in the rear.

I had the dead chief's rifle and ammunition, and consequently the means of kindling a fire and killing game. But doing either, at least for some days, would be a dangerous experiment, as the noise of the rifle or the light of the fire might expose me. Hunger, however, would force me to risk both. I was famished, not having eaten since early in the morning.

It was impossible at that hour to capture game. My thoughts turned to the mule. She had followed me unexpectedly and could be of no possible use. In all probability, she would prove an annoyance. Necessity suggested how I could turn her to account. Walking up to the unsuspicious beast, I pulled out the chief's long knife and drew it across her throat.

When the mule was dead, I cut long thin slips of flesh from her hams. Then I decided to run the risk of kindling a fire, trusting that the body of Rolling Thunder was still undiscovered. I gathered a pile of sticks and, withdrawing the charge from the rifle, ignited them with a priming of powder. I soon had a ruddy blaze going. After the mule meat was broiled and my appetite satisfied with a portion of it, I laid the rest carefully aside for future use. It occurred to me that I might suffer from lack of water on those thirsty mountains. I cut the bladder from the mule, blew it up, and dried it by the fire. Next I filled it from a sluggish pool and tied the mouth with a strong buffalo string. Now I had a serviceable canteen.

With the reloaded rifle in my hands, I sat down on the buffalo skin at the foot of a cedar tree and leaned against its trunk. Here a new terror awaited me.

The mule's blood had been scented by wolves and panthers. The panthers began to scream. The most terrifying sound that has ever fallen on my ears is the cry of these animals, it is so like the plaintive, agonized shriek of a human being. Nearer and nearer the beasts approached, until the horse snuffed and snorted. I could hear their teeth snap and the dry sticks crackle beneath their feet. A dozen times I was on the point of climbing the tree, expecting to be attacked at any moment. With such a crash would they break through the thicket that many times I bounded to my feet, thinking the Indians were upon me.

The fortunate resolution I had taken to build a fire undoubtedly kept the animals off. But it was a fearful night. It taught me an unforgettable lesson—never to encamp where I had killed my game.

In the morning, very early, I proceeded on my journey. In half an hour I again found my way blocked by a mountain. It was high noon when I reached the summit. During the afternoon I kept my course along the ridge of the highlands. The route was so rugged, that I probably had not traveled ten miles in a direct line from the place of departure in the morning when night again overtook me.

I passed the night under a ledge, in a little nook where a portion of the rock had fallen out. In such an exposed position as this it would have been madness to light a fire—nothing less than a signal to any in pursuit to come up and take me. The tough mule meat and the yet unemptied bladder furnished me with a repast. My poor horse, however, was not so well supplied, there being neither water nor grass here and few bushes on which to browse.

Wrapping the buffalo skin around me, I tried to sleep. But my slumbers were broken and troubled, full of fearful dreams in which I was clambering over rocks or pursued by Indians, yelling close on my trail, and yet I was unable to flee, having lost the power to move. I arose with the first faint glimpse of the rising sun, sore and unrefreshed.

For several days I wandered over these mountains, going from ridge to ridge until I attained and passed the summits. In the evening of the sixth day I descended into a dark, cavernous gorge, where I found a spring of water and many deer browsing around it. The mule meat was now nearly gone. Here, for the first time, I discharged the rifle, bringing down a plump doe. Leaving most of the animal for the wolves, I carried the skin and hindquarters four or five miles and halted for the night. Under an overhanging cliff I found a secluded spot hidden behind thick brushwood, and here I kindled a fire and prepared a meal of venison.

The seventh day found me toiling over a succession of mountains smoother and less steep than any I had yet crossed. My course here led southwest; I had conceived the idea (which proved very mistaken) that it would conduct me to the Mexican state of Chihuahua. At length I reached a point where I found a wide prairie unexpectedly spread out before me, over which numerous Indian horsemen were riding. At my feet stood an Indian town of at least three hundred tents.

I was anxious to escape at once from so dangerous a vicinity. In order to do so, however, I had to retrace my steps many rough and weary miles. Late in the evening of the next day I rounded the point of the prairie and encamped in a snug fastness of the mountains on its western side. Until I had passed far beyond this Indian settlement, I exercised the same caution as if I knew they had received news of Rolling Thunder's death and were on the watch for me.

For nearly two weeks now I was lost in a vast range of mountains. Sometimes I went forward, at others I was compelled to turn back. I often suffered from hunger and thirst. During the day I directed my course by the sun, always keeping in view, as far as I could, some prominent peak in the distance. At night I was guided by the North Star. However, there were many cloudy days and nights, during which I was unable to proceed with certainty and lost much time.

I encountered many hardships and dangers on this lonesome journey. For instance, I was frightfully annoyed by snakes. There was a flat-headed adder I frequently discovered on wet ground, and rattlesnakes were everywhere. But more terrifying than any of these was another species, a kind I had never seen before. It was brown, rather slim, and often over nine feet in length. It inhabited the clefts of the rocks, and stretched itself out on the ledges in the sun. One of its peculiar characteristics was to blow, when disturbed, emitting a loud disagreeable noise, half hiss, half bellow. Frequently, I would draw myself up a steep slope by grasping twigs that had sprung up in the crevices of the rocks; as my head emerged above the surface I was striving to reach, one of these monsters would raise itself to a height of three feet and blow directly in my face. It made my hair stand on end. Bears were numerous and occasionally I saw a panther stealing noiselessly through the underwood.

On the twentieth day, I discovered Indians again. I had reached another valley and was studying the terrain from a secure point when I saw a hundred horsemen, followed by a train of pack mules, moving towards the west. There was no village to be seen and the buffalo-hunting season was past, so I supposed they were a party on a visit to some neighboring tribe. I watched until the last one had disappeared. Then I hurried over the narrow valley and began to labor up the mountain on the other side.

By this time the horse had suffered so much from thirst and want of forage that he had become terribly emaciated. His hoofs, likewise, were broken, and he was lame and spiritless. My feet also were covered with bruises, and my whole body was sore and stiff. In this condition, one day we reached a deep basin among the hills. It was ten or fifteen acres in extent, covered with patches of grass and thickets of brush, and wholly shut in by tall mountains. A clear spring gushed from the base of the mountain on one side, and a number of deer were feeding at different points. I remained here twelve days.

Though I had no mirror with me to make a detailed examination, I expect my personal appearance was not especially attractive. Three years had elapsed since my beard or the hair on my head had known a comb, brush, or razor. My moccasins were worn out and my leggings and hunting shirt in shreds. I still retained the deerskin band which bound my head and fastened on the forehead with a clasp, preventing the hair from falling over my eyes. But the little painted feathers with which Sleek Otter had adorned it were long since blown to the winds of heaven.

Each day of my stay in this solitary place I toiled up the neighboring peaks to see if an enemy was approaching. In the center of the densest thicket I erected a fireplace of stone, my object being to kindle a fire where the thick shrubbery would conceal the light. Here I set to work to prepare provisions and replenish my wardrobe. I shot four or five deer, dried as much of the flesh as I planned to carry, and made the skins into clothing. The only tool I possessed was a knife. The moccasins were made of the hide while in its green state, applied to the foot with the hair inside. I inserted stout thongs of the same material through holes made with the point of the knife, tied them, and left the moccasins to dry. I was familiar with the Indian mode of dressing buckskin with the brains of the deer itself, and had no difficulty in preparing new leggings and a hunting coat. I delayed several days after this on account of the horse. But although he had plenty of pasture and water, he did not improve. He seemed completely broken down.

I set out again at the end of twelve days, dressed in my new clothes and with a bundle of dried venison hanging at the saddle bow. I wildly imagined myself in the neighborhood of Santa Fe. My course now led over a mountainous region, if possible more difficult and barren than any I had traveled before. Water was scarce, and in many parts there was not sufficient grass on a thousand acres to supply the horse with one night's forage. He became more and more tender-footed and lame. I was compelled to lead him, stopping frequently for him to lie down. At length the supply of water I had brought with me from the last spring was exhausted, and I was obliged to leave him.

Rolling up the buffalo skin enclosing my drinking horn and other articles and tying it into the form of a knapsack with the bridle reins, I threw it upon my back. Then I shouldered the rifle and, bidding the poor horse a sorrowful farewell, started on alone.

Now for the first time my heart died within me. For all I could discover, civilization was as far off as when I started the journey. I began to doubt myself, to fear that I had become crazed. Instead of pursuing a southwesterly course, I imagined I was only wandering around and around over the same everlasting solitudes. Moreover, since parting from the horse, who had been a companion to me—whose presence during the silent hours of the night, stamping and feeding around me, seemed like a protection—I was lonesome and desolate indeed. And I was sick in body as well as soul. My limbs had become swollen and the wounds and bruises that covered me were inflamed and painful.

Day by day I grew weaker as I advanced. Often I prayed God that when I fell asleep I might never wake again.

The fifty-sixth day brought me to a wide rolling prairie dotted with many small groves of timber. Into one of these I made my way to avoid the hot sun. I was lying in the shade, in a drowsy, half-sleeping state, when I was startled by the sharp crack of a rifle close at hand.

My first thought was: Is it possible they have chased me so far?

Bounding to my feet, I held the rifle in my hands, resolving, weak as I was, to defend myself.

In ten minutes, instead of being rushed by a band of Indians, I saw a mounted Mexican, wearing a wide-brimmed sombrero, come riding leisurely along. Thrown over his horse's back, behind the saddle, lay a deer which had received its death wound from the discharge that had so astounded me.

"How do you do?" he exclaimed in Spanish, looking greatly astonished.

I walked up to him and replied in his own language, with which I am familiar:

"Sick and dying. Will you help me, my friend?"

"How did you get here?" he inquired.

Not knowing the character of the company into which I had fallen, I decided to conceal my true story for the present.

"I have been lost among the mountains," I answered, "and have been trying to make my way to the settlements."

He informed me he was one of a party of three who had been on a trading expedition to the Apaches, and were now about to return to their home in San Fernandez, near the Rio Grande. He said his companions were not far off and invited me to accompany him to their camp. Seeing how difficult it was for me to go on foot, he dismounted and helped me into the saddle. He walked by the side of the horse, conversing kindly, and evidently much interested in my behalf.

His companions were cooking when we arrived, and were greatly astonished to behold me. They gave me a hospitable and generous welcome. Their kindness won my confidence at once, and I told them the whole story of my adventures. They were deeply moved and spared no pains to make me comfortable. The packs were rearranged to free one of the mules for me to ride and we started off.

The third day we crossed the Rio Grande on a raft, swimming the mules and horses. We passed through a number of frontier settlements, at all of which my misfortunes were related by the traders and I received the kindest treatment. On the seventh day we entered the town of San Fernandez.

I remained six weeks at San Fernandez under the care of a physician. At the end of this time one of the traders accompanied me to Matamoros. From here I proceeded to Brazos Santiago and shipped for Havana, where I obtained passage on the schooner *Elizabeth Jones,* and on November 10, 1858, reached the United States. I was home at last, and my adventures with the Indians were at an end forever, although I would never forget the awful scenes of agony and torture I had witnessed among them.

General Morgan's Flight from the North

THOMAS HINES

The American Civil War saw many spectacular escapes on both sides. The mixed sympathies of the people living in border states and the similarities between combatants allowed many prisoners to make their way home.

Confederate General John Morgan was one of the best cavalry raiders in the war, with an extensive spy network that allowed him to be in the right place at the right time with uncanny regularity. Thomas Hines, the author of this account, was a renowned spy and member of Morgan's staff. Morgan was captured following a series of battles with Union troops that resulted from an overextended raid across the Ohio River (the fast-flooding river prevented his escape). He was taken to the Ohio State Penitentiary—a slap in the face, as military officers were not usually placed in civilian prisons. (Morgan was often accused, and rightly so, of having motivations that went well beyond pure military goals.)

Several members of his staff quickly began to plot an escape.

On the 31st of July and the 1st of August, 1863, General John H. Morgan, General Basil W. Duke, and sixty-eight other officers of Morgan's command were, by order of General Burnside confined in the Ohio State Penitentiary at Columbus. Before entering the main prison we were searched and relieved of our pocketknives, money, and all other articles of value, subjected to a bath, the shaving of our faces, and the cutting of our hair. We were placed each in a separate cell in the first and second tiers on the south side in the east wing of the prison. General Morgan and

General Duke were on the second range, General Morgan being confined in the last cell at the east end, those who escaped with General Morgan having their cells in the first range.

From five o'clock in the evening until seven o'clock in the morning we were locked into our cells, with no possible means of communication with one another; but in the day, between these hours, we were permitted to mingle together in the narrow hall, twelve feet wide and one hundred and sixty long, which was cut off from the other portion of the building, occupied by the convicts, by a plank partition, in one end of which was a wooden door. At each end of the hall and within the partitions was an armed military sentinel, while the civil guards of the prison passed at irregular intervals among us, and very frequently the warden or his deputy came through in order to see that we were secure and not violating the prison rules. We were not permitted to talk with or in any way to communicate with the convicts, nor were we permitted to see any of our relatives or friends that might come from a distance to see us, except upon the written order of General Burnside, and then only in the presence of a guard. Our correspondence underwent the censorship of the warden, we receiving and he sending only such as met his approbation. We were not permitted to have newspapers, or to receive information of what was going on in the outside busy world.

Many plans for escape, ingenious and desperate, were suggested, discussed, and rejected because deemed impracticable. Among them was bribery of the guards. This was thought not feasible because of the double set of guards, military and civil, who were jealous and watchful of each other, so that it was never attempted although we could have commanded, through our friends in Kentucky and elsewhere, an almost unlimited amount of money.

On a morning in the last days of October I was rudely treated, without cause, by the deputy warden. There was no means of redress, and it was not wise to seek relief by retort, since I knew, from the experience of my comrades, that it would result in my confinement in a dark dungeon, with bread and water for diet. I retired to my cell and closed the door with the determination that I would neither eat nor sleep until I had devised some means of escape. I ate nothing and drank nothing during the day, and by nine o'clock at night I had matured the plan that we carried into execution. It may be that I owe something to the fact that I had just completed the reading of Victor Hugo's *Les Misérables,* containing such vivid delineations of the wonderful escapes of Jean Valjean, and of the subterranean passages of the city of Paris. This may have led me to the line of thought that terminated in the plan of escape adopted. It was this: I had observed that the ground upon the outside of the building, which was low and flat, and also that the floor of the cell was perfectly dry and free from mold. It occurred to me that, as the rear of the cell was to a great extent excluded from the light of air, this dryness and freedom from mold could not exist unless there was underneath something in the nature of an air-chamber to prevent the dampness from rising up the walls and through the floor. If this chamber should be found to exist, and could be reached, a tunnel might be run through the foundations into the yard, from which we might escape by scaling the outer wall, the air-chamber furnishing a receptacle for the earth and stone to be taken out in running the tunnel. The next morning when our cells were unlocked, and we were permitted to assemble in the hall, I went to General Morgan's cell, he having been for several days quite unwell, and laid before him the plan as I have sketched it. Its feasibility appeared to him unquestioned, and to it he gave a hearty and unqualified approval. If, then, our supposition was correct as to the existence of the air-chamber beneath the lower range of cells, a limited number of those occupying that range could escape, and only a limited number, because the greater the number the longer the time required to complete the work, and the greater the danger of discovery while prosecuting it, in making our way over the outer walls, and in escaping afterward.

With these considerations in view, General Morgan and myself agreed upon the following officers, whose cells were nearest the point at which the tunnel was to begin, to join us in the enterprise: Captain J. C. Bennett, Captain L. D. Hockersmith, Captain C. S. Magee, Captain Ralph Sheldon, and Captain Samuel B. Taylor. The plan was then laid before these gentlemen, and received their approval. It was agreed that work should begin in my cell, and continue from there until completed. In order, however, to do this without detection, it was necessary that some means should be found to prevent the daily inspection of that cell, it being the custom for the deputy warden, with the guards, to visit and have each cell swept every morning. This end was accomplished by my obtaining permission from the warden to furnish a broom and sweep my own cell. For a few mornings thereafter the deputy warden would pass, glance into my cell, compliment me on its neatness, and go on to the inspection of the other cells. After a few days my cell was allowed to go without any inspection whatever, and then we were ready to begin work, having obtained through some of our associates, who had been sent to the hospital, some table knives made of flat steel files. In my cell, as in the others, there was a narrow iron cot, which could be folded and propped up to the cell wall. I thought the work could be completed within a month.

On the 4th of November work was begun in the back part of my cell, under the rear end of my cot. We cut through six inches of cement, and took out six layers of brick put in and cemented with the ends up. Here we came to the air-chamber, as I had calculated, and found it six feet wide by four feet high, and running the entire length of the range of cells. The cement and brick taken out in effecting an entrance to the chamber were placed in my bed-tick, upon which I slept during the progress of this portion of the work, after which the material was removed to the chamber. We found the chamber heavily grated at the end, against which a large quantity of coal had been heaped, cutting off any chance of exit in that way. We then began a tunnel, running it at right angles from the side of the chamber, and almost directly beneath my cell. We cut through the foundation wall, five feet thick, of the cell block; through twelve feet of grouting, to the outer wall of the east wing of the prison; through this wall, six feet in thickness; and four feet up near the surface of the yard, in an unfrequented place between this wing and the female department of the prison.

During the progress of the work, in which we were greatly assisted by several of our comrades who were not to go out . . . I sat at the entrance to my cell studiously engaged on Gibbon's *Rome* and in trying to master French. By this device I was enabled to be constantly on guard without being suspected, as I had pursued the same course during the whole period of my imprisonment. Those who did the work were relieved every hour. This was accomplished and the danger of the guards overhearing the work as they passed obviated by adopting a system of signals, which consisted in giving taps on the floor over the chamber. One knock was to suspend work, two to proceed, and three to come out. On one occasion, by oversight, we came near being discovered. The prisoners were taken out to their meals by ranges, and on this day those confined in the first range were called for dinner while Captain Hockersmith was in the tunnel. The deputy warden, on calling the roll, missed Hockersmith, and came back to inquire for him. General Morgan engaged the attention of the warden by asking his opinion as to the propriety of a remonstrance that the general had prepared to be sent to General Burnside. Flattered by the deference shown to his opinion by General Morgan, the warden unwittingly gave Captain Hockersmith time to get out and fall into line for dinner. While the tunnel was being run, Colonel R. C. Morgan, a brother of General Morgan, made a rope, in links, of bed-ticking, thirty-five feet in length, and from the iron poker of the hall stove we made a hook, in the nature of a grappling-iron, to attach to the end of the rope.

The work was now complete with the exception of making an entrance from each of the cells of those who were to go out. This could be done with safety only by working from the chamber upward, as the cells were daily inspected. The difficulty presented in doing this was the fact that we did not know at what point to begin in order to open the holes in the cells at the proper place. To accomplish this a measurement was necessary, but we had nothing to measure with. Fortunately the deputy warden again ignorantly aided us. I got into a discussion with him as to the length of the hall, and to convince me of my error he sent for his measuring line, and after the hall had been measured and his statement verified General Morgan occupied his attention, while I took the line, measured the distance from center to center of the cells—all being of uniform size—and marked it upon the stick used in my cell for propping up my cot. With this stick, measuring from the middle of the hole in my cell, the proper distance was marked off in the chamber for the holes in the other cells. The chamber was quite dark, and light being necessary for the work we had obtained candles and matches through our sick comrades in the hospital. The hole in my cell during the progress of the work was kept covered with a large hand satchel containing my change of clothing. We cut from underneath upward until there was only a thin crust of the cement left in each of the cells. Money was necessary to pay expenses of transportation and for other contingencies as they might arise. General Morgan had some money that the search had not discovered, but it was not enough. Shortly after we began work I wrote to my sister in Kentucky a letter, which through a trusted convict I sent out and mailed, requesting her to go to my library and get certain books, and in the back of a designated one, which she was to open with a thin knife, place therein a certain amount of Federal money, repaste the back, write my name across the inside of the back where the money was concealed, and send the box by express.

In due course of time the books with the money came to hand. It only remained now to get information as to the time of the running of the trains and to await a cloudy night, as it was then full moon. Our trusty convict was again found useful. . . . His time having almost expired he was permitted to go on errands for the officials to the city. I gave him ten dollars to bring us a daily paper and six ounces of French brandy. Neither he nor any one within the prison or on the outside had any intimation of our contemplated escape.

It was our first thought to make our way to the Confederacy by the way of Canada; but, on inspecting the time-table in the paper, it was seen that a knowledge of the escape would necessarily come to the prison officials before we could reach the Canadian border. There was nothing left, then, but to take the train south, which we found, if on time, would reach Cincinnati, Ohio, before the cells were opened in the morning, at which time we expected our absence to be discovered. One thing more remained to be done, and that was to ascertain the easiest and safest place at which to scale the outside wall of the prison. The windows opening outward were so high that we could not see the wall. In the hall was a ladder resting against the wall, fifty feet long, that had been used for sweeping down the wall. A view from the top of the ladder would give us a correct idea of the outside, but the difficulty was to get that view without exciting suspicion.

Fortunately the warden came in while we were discussing the great strength and activity of Captain Samuel B. Taylor, who was very small of stature, when it was suggested that Taylor could go hand over hand on the under side of the ladder to the top, and, with a moment's rest, return in the same way. To the warden this seemed impossible, and, to convince him, Taylor was permitted to make the trial, which he did successfully. At the top of the ladder he rested for a minute and took a mental photograph of the wall. When the warden had left, Taylor communicated the fact that directly south of and at almost right angles from the east end of the block in which we were confined there was a double gate to the outer wall, the inside one being of wooden uprights four inches apart, and the outside one as solid as the wall; the wooden gate being supported by the wing wall of the female department, which joined to the main outer wall.

On the evening of the 27th of November the cloudy weather so anxiously waited for came; and prior to being locked in our cells it was agreed to make the attempt at escape that night. Cell No. 21, next to my cell, No. 20, on the first range, was occupied by Colonel R. C. Morgan. . . . That cell had been prepared for General Morgan by opening a hole to the chamber, and when the hour for locking up came General Morgan stepped into Cell 21, and Colonel Morgan into General Morgan's cell in the second range. The guard did not discover the exchange, as General Morgan and Colonel Morgan were of about the same physical proportions, and each stood with his back to the cell door when it was being locked.

At intervals of two hours every night, beginning at eight, the guards came around to each cell and passed a light through the grating to see that all was well with the prisoners. The approach of the guard was often so stealthily made that a knowledge of his presence was first had by seeing him at the door of the cell. To avoid a surprise of this kind we sprinkled fine coal along in front of the cells, walking upon which would give us warning. By a singular coincidence that might have been a fatality, on the day we had determined upon for the escape General Morgan received a letter from Lexington, Kentucky, begging and warning him not to attempt to escape, and by the same mail I received a letter from a member of my family saying that it was rumored and generally believed at home that I had escaped. Fortunately these letters did not put the officials on their guard. We ascertained from the paper we had procured that a train left for Cincinnati at 1:15 A.M., and as the regular time for the guard to make his round of the cells was twelve o'clock, we arranged to descend to the chamber immediately thereafter. Captain Taylor was to descend first, and, passing under each cell, notify the others. General Morgan had been permitted to keep his watch, and this he gave to Taylor that he might not mistake the time to go.

At the appointed hour Taylor gave the signal, each of us arranged his cot with the seat in his cell so as to represent a sleeping prisoner, and, easily breaking the thin layer of cement, descended to the chamber, passed through the tunnel, breaking through the thin stratum of earth at the end. We came out near the wall of the female prison—it was raining slightly—crawled by the side of the wall to the wooden gate, cast our grappling iron attached to the rope over the gate, made it fast, ascended the rope to the top of the gate, drew up the rope and made our way by the wing wall to the outside wall, where we entered a sentry-box and divested ourselves of our soiled outer garments. In the daytime sentinels were placed on this wall, but at night they were on the inside of the walls and at the main entrance to the prison. On the top of the wall we found a cord running along the outer edge and connecting with a bell in the office of the prison. This cord General Morgan cut with one of the knives we had used in tunneling. Before leaving my cell I wrote and left, addressed to N. Merion, the warden, the following:

"Castle Merion, Cell. No. 20, November 27, 1863: Commencement, November 4, 1863; conclusion November 24, 1863; number of hours for labor per day, five; tools, two small knives. *La patience est amère, mais son fruit est doux.* By order of my six honorable Confederates. /s/ THOMAS H. HINES, *Captain, C.S.A.*"

Having removed all trace of soil from our clothes and persons, we attached the iron hook to the railing on the outer edge of the wall, and descended to the ground within sixty yards of where the prison guards were sitting round a fire and conversing. Here we separated, General Morgan and myself going to the depot, about a quarter of a mile from the prison, where I purchased two tickets for Cincinnati, and entered the car that just then came in. General Morgan took a seat by the side of a Federal major in uniform, and I sat immediately in their rear. The general entered into conversation with the major, who was made the more talkative by a copious drink of my French brandy. As the train passed near the prison wall where we had descended the major remarked, "There is where the rebel General Morgan and his officers are put for safe keeping." The general replied. "I hope they will keep him as safe as he is now." Our train passed through Dayton, Ohio, and there, for some unknown reason, we were delayed an hour. This rendered it extra hazardous to go to the depot in the city of Cincinnati, since by that time the prison officials would, in all probability, know of our escape, and telegraph to intercept us. In fact, they did telegraph in every direction, and offered a reward for our recapture. Instead, then, of going to the depot in Cincinnati, we got off, while the train was moving slowly, in the outskirts of the city, near Ludlow Ferry, on the Ohio River. Going directly to the ferry we were crossed over in a skiff and landed immediately in front of the residence of Mrs. Ludlow. We rang the door-bell, a servant came, and General Morgan wrote upon a visiting-card, "General Morgan and Captain Hines, escaped." We were warmly received, took a cup of coffee with the family, were furnished a guide, and walked some three miles in the country, where we were furnished horses.

Despite the fact that Hines's version of designing the escape makes for great reading, it has often been disputed. Captain Hockersmith, who also participated in the escape, gave a very different account of its planning. According to Hockersmith, who had experience with masonry and engineering principles, he and Captain Taylor formulated the plan of escape based on their own knowledge of construction and not on Valjean's fictional sewer escape. Hines was taken into the plan, but he did not conceive it. Hockersmith later confronted Hines, who had used his self-proclaimed hero status in the escape to reach elected office, and Hines supposedly agreed to set the record straight. But he never did, of course, and his version has survived as the primary account of the escape.

Colonel Rose's Tunnel

FRANK MORAN

Before the more organized efforts made in both World War I and II, mass tunnel escapes were extremely primitive and chaotic. The American Civil War saw several attempts that devolved into free-for-alls. In Berry Benson's excellent memoir of his escape from a Union prison, the diggers were forced to guard their secret more carefully from their comrades than the prison guards. Previous attempts had resulted in a mad rush of prisoners, and it took Benson quite some time to discreetly join a small band of prisoners working on a new tunnel.

Colonel Rose's carefully executed tunnel allowed 109 men to break out of Confederate Libby Prison in Richmond, despite another mad rush that almost ruined everything. This account, penned by Frank Moran, who also escaped through the tunnel but was recaptured, gives an insider's perspective of how Rose persevered to make this incredible escape under very unpleasant conditions. Rose's tunnel became one of the most famous escapes of the Civil War, and it inspired several similar escapes carried out in the World Wars.

Thomas E. Rose, colonel of the 77th Pennsylvania Volunteers, was taken prisoner at the battle of Chickamauga, September 20, 1863. On his way to Richmond he escaped from his guards at Weldon, N.C., but, after a day's wandering about the pine forests with a broken foot, was retaken by a detachment of Confederate cavalry and sent to Libby Prison, Richmond.

Libby Prison fronts on Carey Street, Richmond, and stands upon a hill which descends abruptly to the canal, from which its southern wall is divided only by a street, and having a vacant lot on the east. The building was wholly detached, making it a comparatively easy matter to guard the prison securely with a small force and keep every door and window in full view from without. As an additional measure of safety, prisoners were not allowed on the ground-floor, except that in the daytime they were permitted to use the first floor of the middle section for a cook-room. The interior embraced nine large warehouse-rooms, 105 x 45, with eight feet from each floor to ceiling, except the upper floor, which gave more room, owing to the pitch of the gable roof. The abrupt slant of the hill gives the building an additional story on the south side. The whole building really embraces three sections, and these were originally sepa-rated by heavy blank walls. The Confederates cut doors through the walls of the two upper floors, which comprised the prisoners' quarters, and they were thus permitted to mingle freely with each other; but there was no communica-tion whatever between the three large rooms on the first floor. Beneath these floors were three cellars of the same dimensions as the rooms above them, and, like them, divided from each other by massive blank walls. For ready compre-hension, let these be designated the east, middle, and west cellars. Except in the lofts known as "Streight's room" and "Milroy's room," which were occupied by the earliest inmates of Libby in 1863, there was no furniture in the building, and only a few of the early comers possessed such a luxury as an old army blanket or a knife, cup, and tin plate. As a rule, the prisoner, by the time he reached Libby, found himself devoid of earthly goods save the meager and dust-begrimed summer garb in which he had made his unlucky campaign.

Such, in brief, was the condition of things when Colonel Rose arrived at the prison. From the hour of his coming, a means of escape became his constant and eager study; and, with this purpose in view, he made a careful and minute survey of the entire premises.

From the windows of the upper east or "Gettysburg room" he could look across the vacant lot on the east and get a glimpse of the yard between two ad-jacent buildings which faced the canal and Carey Street respectively, and he es-timated the intervening space at about seventy feet. From the south windows he looked out across a street upon the canal and James River, running parallel with each other, the two streams at this point being separated by a low and narrow strip of land. This strip periodically disappeared when protracted sea-sons of heavy rain came, or when spring floods so rapidly swelled the river that the latter invaded the cellars of Libby. At such times it was common to see enormous swarms of rats come out from the lower doors and windows of the prison and make head for dry land in swimming platoons amid the cheers of the prisoners in the upper windows. On one or two occasions Rose observed workmen descending from the middle of the south-side street into a sewer running through its center, and concluded that this sewer must have various openings to the canal both to the east and west of the prison.

The north portion of the cellar contained a large quantity of loose packing-straw, covering the floor to an average depth of two feet; and this straw afforded shelter, especially at night, for a large colony of rats, which gave the place the name of "Rat Hell."

In one afternoon's inspection of this dark end, Rose suddenly encountered a fellow prisoner, Major A. G. Hamilton, of the 12th Kentucky Cavalry. A confiding friendship followed, and the two men entered at once upon the plan of gaining their liberty. They agreed that the most feasible scheme was a tunnel, to begin in the rear of the little kitchen-apartment at the southeast corner of Rat Hell.

There was, in fact, but one plan by which Rat Hell could be reached without detection, and the conception of this device and its successful execution were due to the stout-hearted Hamilton. This was to cut a hole in the back of the kitchen fireplace; the incision must be just far enough to preserve the opposite or hospital side intact. It must then be cut downward to a point below the level of the hospital floor, then eastward into Rat Hell, the completed opening thus to describe the letter "S." It must be wide enough to let a man through, yet the wall must not be broken on the hospital side above the floor, nor marred on the carpenter's-shop side below it. Such a break would be fatal, for both of these points were conspicuously exposed to the view of the Confederates every hour in the day. Moreover, it was imperatively necessary that all trace of the beginning of the opening should be concealed, not only from the Confederate officials and guards, who were constantly passing the spot every day, but from the hundreds of uninitiated prisoners who crowded around the stove just in front of it from dawn till dark.

Work could be possible only between the hours of ten at night, when the room was generally abandoned by the prisoners because of its inundated condition, and four o'clock in the morning, when the earliest risers were again astir. It was necessary to do the work with an old jack-knife and one of the chisels previously secured by Rose. It must be done in darkness and without noise, for a vigilant sentinel paced on the Carey Street sidewalk just outside the door and within ten feet of the fireplace. A rubber blanket was procured, and the soot from the chimney carefully swept into it. Hamilton, with his old knife, cut the mortar between the bricks and pried a dozen of them out, being careful to preserve them whole.

The rest of the incision was made in accordance with the design described, but no conception could have been formed beforehand of the sickening tediousness of cutting an S-shaped hole through a heavy wall with a feeble old jack-knife, in stolen hours of darkness. Rose guarded his comrade against the constant danger of interruption by alert enemies on one side and by blundering friends on the other; and, as frequently happens in human affairs, their friends gave them more trouble than their foes. Night after night passed, and still the two men got up after taps from their hard beds, and descended to the dismal and reeking kitchen to bore for liberty. When the sentinel's call at Castle Thunder and at Libby announced four o'clock, the dislodged bricks were carefully replaced, and the soot previously gathered in the gum blanket was flung in handfuls against the restored wall, filling the seams between the bricks so thoroughly as to defy detection. At last, after many weary nights, Hamilton's heroic patience and skill were rewarded, and the way was open to the coveted base of operations, Rat Hell.

Now occurred a circumstance that almost revealed the plot and nearly ended in a tragedy. When the opening was finished, the long rope was made fast to one of the kitchen supporting posts, and Rose proceeded to descend and reconnoiter. He got partly through with ease, but lost his hold in such a manner that his body slipped through so as to pinion his arms and leave him wholly powerless either to drop lower or return—the bend of the hole being such as to cramp his back and neck terribly and prevent him from breathing. He strove desperately, but each effort only wedged him more firmly in the awful vise. Hamilton sprang to his aid and did his utmost to effect his release; but, powerful as he was, he could not budge him. Rose was gasping for breath and rapidly getting fainter, but even in this fearful strait he refrained from an outcry that would certainly alarm the guards just outside the door. Hamilton saw that without speedy relief his comrade must soon smother. He dashed through the long, dark room up the stairway, over the forms of several hundred men, and disregarding consequences and savage curses in the dark and crowded room, he trampled upon arms, legs, faces, and stomachs, leaving riot and blasphemy in his track among the rudely awakened and now furious lodgers of the Chickamauga room. He sought the sleeping-place of Major George H. Fitzsimmons, but he was missing. He, however, found Lieutenant F. F. Bennett, of the 18th Regulars, to whom he told the trouble in a few hasty words. Both men fairly flew across the room, dashed down the stairs, and by their united efforts Rose, half dead and quite speechless, was drawn up from the fearful trap.

Hamilton managed slightly to increase the size of the hole and provide against a repetition of the accident just narrated, and all being now ready, the two men entered eagerly upon the work before them. They appropriated one of the wooden spittoons of the prison, and to each side attached a piece of clothes-line which they had been permitted to have to dry clothes on. Several bits of candle and the larger of the two chisels were also taken to the operating-cellar. They kept this secret well, and worked alone for many nights. In fact, they would have so continued, but they found that after digging about four feet their candle would go out in the vitiated air. Rose did the digging, and Hamilton fanned air into him with his hat: even then he had to emerge into the cellar every few minutes to breathe. Rose could dig, but needed the light and air; and Hamilton could not fan, and drag out and deposit the excavated earth, and meantime keep a lookout. In fact, it was demonstrated that there was slim chance of succeeding without more assistance, and it was decided to organize a party large enough for effective work by reliefs. As a preliminary step, and to afford the means of more rapid communication with the cellar from the fireplace opening, the long rope obtained from Colonel White was formed by Hamilton into a rope-ladder with convenient wooden rungs. This alteration considerably increased its bulk, and added to Rose's difficulty in concealing it from curious eyes.

He now made a careful selection of thirteen men besides himself and Hamilton, and bound them by a solemn oath to secrecy and strict obedience. To form this party as he wanted it required some diplomacy, as it was known that the Confederates had on more than one occasion sent cunning spies into Libby disguised as Union prisoners, for the detection of any contemplated plan of escape.

The party, being now formed, were taken to Rat Hell and their several duties explained to them by Rose, who was invested with full authority over the work in hand. Work was begun in rear of the little kitchen-room previously abandoned at the southeast corner of the cellar. To systematize the labor, the party was divided into squads of five each, which gave the men one night on duty and two off, Rose assigning each man to the branch of work in which experiments proved him the most proficient. He was himself, by long odds, the best digger of the party; while Hamilton had no equal for ingenious mechanical skill in contriving helpful little devices to overcome or lessen the difficulties that beset almost every step of the party's progress.

The first plan was to dig down alongside the east wall and under it until it was passed, then turn southward and make for the large street sewer next to the canal and into which Rose had before noticed workmen descending. This sewer was a large one, believed to be fully six feet high, and, if it could be gained, there could be little doubt that an adjacent opening to the canal would be found to the eastward. It was very soon revealed, however, that the lower side of Libby was built upon ponderous timbers, below which they could not hope to penetrate with their meager stock of tools—such, at least, was the opinion of nearly all the party. Rose nevertheless determined that the effort should be made, and they were soon at work with old penknives and case-knives hacked into saws. After infinite labor they at length cut through the great logs, only to be met by an unforeseen and still more formidable barrier. Their tunnel, in fact, had penetrated below the level of the canal. Water began to filter in—feebly at first, but at last it broke in with a rush that came near drowning Rose, who barely had time to make his escape. This opening was therefore plugged up; and to do this rapidly and leave no dangerous traces put the party to their wit's end.

An attempt was next made to dig into a small sewer that ran from the southeast corner of the prison into the main sewer. After a number of nights of hard labor, this opening was extended to a point below a brick furnace in which were incased several caldrons. The weight of this furnace caused a cave-in near the sentinel's path outside the prison wall. Next day, a group of officers were seen eying the break curiously. Rose, listening at a window above, heard the words "rats" repeated by them several times, and took comfort. The next day he entered the cellar alone, feeling that if the suspicions of the Confederates were really awakened a trap would be set for him in Rat Hell, and determined, if such were really the case, that he would be the only victim caught. He therefore entered the little partitioned corner room with some anxiety, but there was no visible evidence of a visit by the guards, and his spirits again rose.

The party now reassembled, and an effort was made to get into the small sewer that ran from the cook-room to the big sewer which Rose was so eager to reach; but soon it was discovered, to the utter dismay of the weary party, that this wood-lined sewer was too small to let a man through it. Still it was hoped by Rose that by removing the plank with which it was lined the passage could be made. The spirits of the party were by this time considerably dashed by their repeated failures and sickening work; but the undaunted Rose, aided by Hamilton, persuaded the men to another effort, and soon the knives and toy saws were at work again with vigor. The work went on so swimmingly that it was confidently believed that an entrance to the main sewer would be gained on the night of January 26, 1864.

On the night of the 25th two men had been left down in Rat Hell to cover any remaining traces of a tunnel, and when night came again it was expected that all would be ready for the escape between eight and nine o'clock. In the mean time, the two men were to enter and make careful examination of the main sewer and its adjacent outlets. The party, which was now in readiness for its march to the Federal camps, waited tidings from these two men all next day in tormenting anxiety, and the weary hours went by on leaden wings. At last the sickening word came that the planks yet to be removed before they could enter the main sewer were of seasoned oak—hard as bone, and three inches thick. Their feeble tools were now worn out or broken; they could no longer get air to work, or keep a light in the horrible pit, which was reeking with cold mud; in short, any attempt at further progress with the utensils at hand was foolish.

Most of the party were now really ill from the foul stench in which they had lived so long. The visions of liberty that had first lured them to desperate efforts under the inspiration of Rose and Hamilton had at last faded, and one by one they lost heart and hope, and frankly told Colonel Rose that they could do no more. The party was therefore disbanded, and the yet sanguine leader, with Hamilton for his sole helper, continued to work alone. Up to this time thirty-nine nights had been spent in the work of excavation. The two men now made a careful examination of the northeast corner of the cellar, at which point the earth's surface outside the prison wall, being eight or nine feet higher than at the canal or south side, afforded a better place to dig than the latter, being free from water and with clay-top enough to support itself. The unfavorable feature of this point was that the only possible terminus of a tunnel was a yard between the buildings beyond the vacant lot on the east of Libby. Another objection was that, even when the tunnel should be made to that point, the exit of any escaping party must be made through an arched wagon-way under the building that faced the street on the canal side, and every man must emerge on the sidewalk in sight of the sentinel on the south side of the prison, the intervening space being in the full glare of the gas-lamp. It was carefully noted, however, by Rose, long before this, that the west end of the beat of the nearest sentinel was between fifty and sixty feet from the point of egress, and it was concluded that by walking away at the moment the sentinel commenced his pace westward, one would be far enough into the shadow to make it improbable that the color of his clothing could be made out by the sentinel when he faced about to return toward the eastern end of his beat, which terminated ten to fifteen feet east of the prison wall. It was further considered that as these sentinels had for their special duty the guarding of the prison, they would not be eager to burden themselves with the duty of molesting persons seen in the vicinity outside of their jurisdiction, provided, of course, that the retreating forms— many of which they must certainly see—were not recognized as Yankees. All others they might properly leave for the challenge and usual examination of the provost guard who patrolled the streets of Richmond.

The wall of that east cellar had to be broken in three places before a place was found where the earth was firm enough to support a tunnel. The two men worked on with stubborn patience, but their progress was painfully slow. Rose dug assiduously, and Hamilton alternately fanned air to his comrade and dragged out and hid the excavated dirt, but the old difficulty confronted him. The candle would not burn, the air could not be fanned fast enough with a hat, and the dirt hidden, without better contrivances or additional help.

Rose now reassembled the party, and selected from them a number who were willing to renew the attempt. Against the east wall stood a series of stone fenders abutting inward, and these, being at uniform intervals of about twenty feet, cast deep shadows that fell toward the prison front. In one of these dark recesses the wall was pierced, well up toward the Carey Street end. The earth here has very densely compressed sand, that offered a strong resistance to the broad-bladed chisel, which was their only effective implement, and it was clear that a long turn of hard work must be done to penetrate under the fifty-foot lot to the objective point. The lower part of the tunnel was about six inches above the level of the cellar floor, and its top about two and a half feet. Absolute accuracy was of course impossible, either in giving the hole a perfectly horizontal direction or in preserving uniform dimensions; but a fair level was preserved, and the average diameter of the tunnel was a little over two feet. Usually one man would dig, and fill the spittoon with earth; upon the signal of a gentle pull, an assistant would drag the load into the cellar by the clothes-lines fastened to each side of this box, and then hide it under the straw; a third constantly fanned air into the tunnel with a rubber blanket stretched across a frame, the invention of the ingenious Hamilton; a fourth would give occasional relief to the last two; while a fifth would keep a lookout.

The danger of discovery was continual, for the guards were under instructions from the prison commandant to make occasional visits to every accessible part of the building; so that it was not unusual for a sergeant and several men to enter the south door of Rat Hell in the daytime, while the diggers were at labor in the dark north end. During these visits the digger would watch the intruders with his head sticking out of the tunnel, while the others would crouch behind the low stone fenders, or crawl quickly under the straw. This was, however, so uninviting a place that the Confederates made this visit as brief as a nominal compliance with their orders permitted, and they did not often venture into the dark north end. The work was fearfully monotonous, and the more so because absolute silence was commanded, the men moving about mutely in the dark. The darkness caused them frequently to become bewildered and lost; and as Rose could not call out for them, he had often to hunt all over the big dungeon to gather them up and pilot them to their places.

The difficulty of forcing air to the digger, whose body nearly filled the tunnel, increased as the hole was extended, and compelled the operator to back often into the cellar for air, and for air that was itself foul enough to sicken a strong man.

But they were no longer harassed with the water and timbers that had impeded their progress at the south end. Moreover, experience was daily making each man more proficient in the work. Rose urged them on with cheery enthusiasm, and their hopes rose high, for already they had penetrated beyond the sentinel's beat and were nearing the goal.

The party off duty kept a cautious lookout from the upper east windows for any indications of suspicion on the part of the Confederates. In this extreme caution was necessary, both to avert the curiosity of prisoners in those east rooms, and to keep out of the range of bullets from the guards, who were under a standing order to fire at a head if seen at a window, or at a hand if placed on the bars that secured them. A sentinel's bullet one day cut a hole in the ear of Lieutenant Hammond; another officer was wounded in the face by a bullet, which fortunately first splintered against one of the window-bars; and a captain of an Ohio regiment was shot through the head and instantly killed while reading a newspaper. He was violating no rule whatever, and when shot was from eight to ten feet inside the window through which the bullet came. This was a wholly unprovoked and wanton murder; the cowardly miscreant had fired the shot while he was off duty, and from the north sidewalk of Carey Street. The guards (home guards they were) used, in fact, to gun for prisoners' heads from their posts below, pretty much after the fashion of boys after squirrels; and the whizz of a bullet through the windows became too common an occurrence to occasion remark unless some one was shot.

When the opening had been extended nearly across the lot, some of the party believed they had entered under the yard which was the intended terminus; and one night, when McDonald was the digger, so confident was he that the desired distance had been made, that he turned his direction upward, and soon broke through to the surface. A glance showed him his nearly fatal blunder, against which, indeed, he had been earnestly warned by Rose, who from the first had carefully estimated the intervening distance between the east wall of Libby and the terminus. In fact, McDonald saw that he had broken through in the open lot which was all in full view of a sentinel who was dangerously close. Appalled by what he had done, he retreated to the cellar and reported the disaster to his companions. Believing that discovery was now certain, the party sent one of their number up the rope to report to Rose, who was asleep. The hour was about midnight when the leader learned of the mischief. He quickly got up, went down cellar, entered the tunnel, and examined the break. It was not so near the sentinel's path as McDonald's excited report indicated, and fortunately the breach was at a point whence the surface sloped downward toward the east. He took off his blouse and stuffed it into the opening, pulling the dirt over it noiselessly, and in a few minutes there was little surface evidence of the hole. He then backed into the cellar in the usual crab fashion, and gave directions for the required depression of the tunnel and vigorous resumption of the work. The hole made in the roof of the tunnel was not much larger than a rathole, and could not be seen from the prison. But the next night Rose shoved an old shoe out of the hole, and the day afterward he looked down through the prison bars and saw the shoe lying where he had placed it, and judged from its position that he had better incline the direction of the tunnel slightly to the left.

Meantime Captain Johnson [who had missed roll call and was forced to stay at the tunnel site—*Ed.*] was dragging out a wretched existence in Rat Hell, and for safety was obliged to confine himself by day to the dark north end, for the Confederates often came into the place very suddenly through the south entrance. When they ventured too close, Johnson would get into a pit that he had dug under the straw as a hiding-hole both for himself and the tunnelers' tools, and quickly cover himself with a huge heap of short packing-straw. A score of times he came near being stepped upon by the Confederates, and more than once the dust of the straw compelled him to sneeze in their very presence.

On Saturday, February 6, a larger party than usual of the Confederates came into the cellar, walked by the very mouth of the tunnel, and seemed to be making a critical survey of the entire place. They remained an unusually long time and conversed in low tones; several of them even kicked the loose straw about; and in fact everything seemed to indicate to Johnson—who was the only one of the working party now in the cellar—that the long-averted discovery had been made. That night he reported matters fully to Rose at the fireplace opening.

The tunnel was now nearly completed, and when Rose conveyed Johnson's message to the party it caused dismay. Even the stout-hearted Hamilton was for once excited, and the leader whose unflinching fortitude had thus far inspired his little band had his brave spirits dashed. But his buoyant courage rose quickly to its high and natural level. He could no longer doubt that the suspicions of the Confederates were aroused, but he felt convinced that these suspicions had not as yet assumed such a definite shape as most of his companions thought; still, he had abundant reason to believe that the success of the tunnel absolutely demanded its speedy completion, and he now firmly resolved that a desperate effort should be made to that end. Remembering that the next day was Sunday, and that it was not customary for the Confederates to visit the operating-cellar on that day, he determined to make the most in his power of the now precious time. He therefore caused all the party to remain upstairs, directing them to keep a close watch upon the Confederates from all available points of observation, to avoid being seen in whispering groups,—in short, to avoid all things calculated to excite the curiosity of friends or the suspicion of enemies,—and to await his return.

Taking McDonald with him, he went down through the fireplace before daylight on Sunday morning, and, bidding Johnson to keep a vigilant watch for intruders and McDonald to fan air into him, he entered the tunnel and began the forlorn hope. From this time forward he never once turned over the chisel to a relief.

All day long he worked with the tireless patience of a beaver. When night came, even his single helper, who performed the double duty of fanning air and hiding the excavated earth, was ill from his hard, long task and the deadly air of the cellar. Yet this was as nothing compared with the fatigue of the duty that Rose had performed; and when at last, far into the night, he backed into the cellar, he had scarcely strength enough to stagger across to the rope-ladder.

He had made more than double the distance that had been accomplished under the system of reliefs on any previous day, and the non-appearance of the Confederates encouraged the hope that another day, without interruption, would see the work completed. He therefore determined to refresh himself by a night's sleep for the finish. The drooping spirits of his party were revived by the report of his progress and his unalterable confidence.

Monday morning dawned, and the great prison with its twelve hundred captives was again astir. The general crowd did not suspect the suppressed excitement and anxiety of the little party that waited through that interminable day, which they felt must determine the fate of their project.

Rose had repeated the instructions of the day before, and again descended to Rat Hell with McDonald for his only helper. Johnson reported all quiet, and McDonald taking up his former duties at the tunnel's mouth, Rose once more entered with his chisel. It was now the seventeenth day since the present tunnel was begun, and he resolved it should be the last. Hour after hour passed, and still the busy chisel was plied, and still the little wooden box with its freight of earth made its monotonous trips from the digger to his comrade and back again.

From the early morning of Monday, February 8, 1864, until an hour after midnight the next morning, his work went on. As midnight approached, Rose was nearly a physical wreck: the perspiration dripped from every pore of his exhausted body; food he could not have eaten if he had had it. His labors thus far had given him a somewhat exaggerated estimate of his physical powers. The sensation of fainting was strange to him, but his staggering senses warned him that to faint where he was meant at once his death and burial. He could scarcely inflate his lungs with the poisonous air of the pit; his muscles quivered with increasing weakness and the warning spasmodic tremor which their unnatural strain induced; his head swam like that of a drowning person.

By midnight he had struck and passed beyond a post which he felt must be in the yard. During the last few minutes he had directed his course upward, and to relieve his cramped limbs he turned upon his back. His strength was nearly gone; the feeble stream of air which his comrade was trying, with all his might, to send to him from a distance of fifty-three feet could no longer reach him through the deadly stench. His senses reeled; he had not breath or strength enough to move backward through his narrow grave. In the agony of suffocation he dropped the dull chisel and beat his two fists against the roof of his grave with the might of despair—when, blessed boon! the crust gave way and the loosened earth showered upon his dripping face purple with agony; his famished eye caught sight of a radiant star in the blue vault above him; a flood of light and a volume of cool, delicious air poured over him. At that very instant the sentinel's cry rang out like a prophecy—"Half-past one, and all's well!"

Recovering quickly under the inspiring air, he dragged his body out of the hole and made a careful survey of the yard in which he found himself. He was under a shed, with a board fence between him and the east-side sentinels, and the gable end of Libby loomed grimly against the blue sky. He found the wagon-way under the south-side building closed from the street by a gate fastened by a swinging bar, which, after a good many efforts, he succeeded in opening. This was the only exit to the street. As soon as the nearest sentinel's back was turned he stepped out and walked quickly to the east. At the first corner he turned north, carefully avoiding the sentinels in front of the "Pemberton Buildings" (another military prison northeast of Libby), and at the corner above this he went westward, then south to the edge of the canal, and thus, by cautious moving, made a minute examination of Libby from all sides.

Having satisfied his desires, he retraced his steps to the yard. He hunted up an old bit of heavy plank, crept back into the tunnel feet first, drew the plank over the opening to conceal it from the notice of any possible visitors to the place, and crawled back to Rat Hell. It was now nearly three o'clock in the morning. Rose and Hamilton were ready to go out at once, and indeed were anxious to do so, since every day of late had brought some new peril to their plans. None of the rest, however, were ready; and all urged the advantage having a whole night in which to escape through and beyond the Richmond fortifications, instead of the few hours of darkness which now preceded the day. To this proposition Rose and Hamilton somewhat reluctantly assented. It was agreed that each man of the party should have the privilege of taking one friend into his confidence, and that the second party of fifteen thus formed should be obliged not to follow the working party out of the tunnel until an hour had elapsed. Colonel H. C. Hobart, of the 21st Wisconsin, was deputed to see that the program was observed. He was to draw up the rope-ladder, hide it, and re-build the wall; and the next night was himself to lead out the second party, deputing some trustworthy leader to follow with still another party on the third night; and thus it was to continue until as many as possible should escape.

On Tuesday evening, February 9, at seven o'clock, Colonel Rose assembled his party in the kitchen, and, posting himself at the fireplace, which he opened, waited until the last man went down. He bade Colonel Hobart good-by, went down the hole, and awaited until he had heard his comrade pull up the ladder, and finally heard him replace the bricks in the fireplace and depart. He now crossed Rat Hell to the entrance into the tunnel, and placed the party in the order in which they were to go out. He gave each a parting caution, thanked his brave comrades for their faithful labors, and, feelingly shaking their hands, bade them Godspeed and farewell.

He entered the tunnel first, with Hamilton next, and was promptly followed by the whole party through the tunnel and into the yard. He opened the gate leading toward the canal, and signaled the party that all was clear. Stepping out on the sidewalk as soon as the nearest sentinel's back was turned, he walked briskly down the street to the east, and a square below was joined by Hamilton. The others followed at intervals of a few minutes, and disappeared in various directions in groups usually of three.

The plan agreed upon between Colonels Rose and Hobart was frustrated by information of the party's departure leaking out; and before nine o'clock the knowledge of the existence of the tunnel and of the departure of the first party was flashed over the crowded prison, which was soon a convention of excited and whispering men. Colonel Hobart made a brave effort to restore order, but the frenzied crowd that now fiercely struggled for precedence at the fireplace was beyond human control.

Some of them had opened the fireplace and were jumping down like sheep into the cellar one after another. The colonel implored the maddened men at least to be quiet, and put the rope-ladder in position and escaped himself.

My companion, Sprague, was already asleep when I lay down that night; but my other companion, Duenkel, who had been hunting for me, was very much awake, and, seizing me by the collar, he whispered excitedly the fact that Colonel Rose had gone out at the head of a party through a tunnel. For a brief moment the appalling suspicion that my friend's reason had been dethroned by illness and captivity swept over my mind; but a glance toward the window at the east end showed a quiet but apparently excited group of men from other rooms, and I now observed that several of them were bundled up for a march. The hope of regaining liberty thrilled me like a current of electricity. Looking through the window, I could see the escaping men appear one by one on the sidewalk below, opposite the exit yard, and silently disappear, without hindrance or challenge by the prison sentinels. While I was eagerly surveying this scene, I lost track of Duenkel, who had gone in search of further information, but ran against Lieutenant Harry Wilcox, of the 1st New York, whom I knew, and who appeared to have the "tip" regarding the tunnel. Wilcox and I agreed to unite our fortunes in the escape. My shoes were nearly worn out, and my clothes were thin and ragged. I was ill prepared for a journey in midwinter through the enemy's country: happily I had my old overcoat, and this I put on. I had not a crumb of food saved up, as did those who were posted; but as I was ill at the time, my appetite was feeble.

Wilcox and I hurried to the kitchen, where we found several hundred men struggling to be first at the opening in the fireplace. We took our places behind them, and soon two hundred more closed us tightly in the mass. The room was pitch-dark, and the sentinel could be seen through the door-cracks, within a dozen feet of us. The fight for precedence was savage, though no one spoke; but now and then fainting men begged to be released. They begged in vain: certainly some of them must have been permanently injured. For my own part, when I neared the stove I was nearly suffocated; but I took heart when I saw but three more men between me and the hole. At this moment a sound as of tramping feet was heard, and some idiot on the outer edge of the mob startled us with the cry, "The guards, the guards!" A fearful panic ensued, and the entire crowd bounded toward the stairway leading up to their sleeping-quarters. The stairway was unbanistered, and some of the men were forced off the edge and fell on those beneath. I was among the lightest in that crowd; and when it broke and expanded I was taken off my feet, dashed to the floor senseless, my head and one of my hands bruised and cut, and my shoulder painfully injured by the boots of the men who rushed over me. When I gathered my swimming wits I was lying in a pool of water. The room seemed darker than before; and, to my grateful surprise, I was alone. I was now convinced that it was a false alarm, and quickly resolved to avail myself of the advantage of having the whole place to myself. I entered the cavity feet first, but found it necessary to remove my overcoat and push it through the opening, and it fell in the darkness below.

I had now no comrade, having lost Wilcox in the stampede. Rose and his party, being the first out, were several hours on their journey; and I burned to be away, knowing well that my salvation depended on my passage beyond the city defenses before the pursuing guards were on our trail, when the inevitable discovery should come at roll-call. The fact that I was alone I regretted; but I had served with McClellan in the Peninsula campaign of 1862, I knew the country well from my frequent inspection of war maps, and the friendly north star gave me my bearings. The rope-ladder had either become broken or disarranged, but it afforded me a short hold at the top; so I balanced myself, trusted to fortune, and fell into Rat Hell, which was a rayless pit of darkness, swarming with squealing rats, several of which I must have killed in my fall. I felt a troop of them run over my face and hands before I could regain my feet. Several times I put my hand on them, and once I flung one from my shoulder. Groping around, I found a stout stick or stave, put my back to the wall, and beat about me blindly but with vigor.

In spite of the hurried instructions given me by Wilcox, I had a long and horrible hunt over the cold surface of the cellar walls in my efforts to find the entrance to the tunnel; and in two minutes after I began feeling my way with my hands I had no idea in what part of the place was the point where I had fallen: my bearings were completely lost, and I must have made the circuit of Rat Hell several times. At my entrance the rats seemed to receive me with cheers sufficiently hearty, I thought; but my vain efforts to find egress seemed to kindle anew their enthusiasm. They had received large reinforcements, and my march around was now received with deafening squeaks. Finally, my exploring hands fell upon a pair of heels which vanished at my touch. Here at last was the narrow road to freedom! The heels proved to be the property of Lieutenant Charles H. Morgan, 21st Wisconsin, a Chickamauga prisoner. Just ahead of him in the tunnel was Lieutenant William L. Watson, of the same company and regiment. With my cut hand and bruised shoulder, the passage through the cold, narrow grave was indescribably horrible, and when I reached the terminus in the yard I was sick and faint. The passage seemed to me to be a mile long; but the crisp, pure air and the first glimpse of freedom, the sweet sense of being out of doors, and the realization that I had taken the first step toward liberty and home, had a magical effect in my restoration.

I have related before, in a published reminiscence, my experience and that of my two companions above named in the journey toward the Union lines, and our recapture; but the more important matter relating to the plot itself has never been published.

Great was the panic in Libby when the next morning's roll revealed to the astounded Confederates that 109 of their captives were missing; and as the fireplace had been rebuilt by some one and the opening of the hole in the yard had been covered by the last man who went out, no human trace guided the keepers toward a solution of the mystery. The Richmond papers having announced the "miraculous" escape of 109 Yankee officers from Libby, curious crowds flocked thither for several days, until some one, happening to remove the plank in the yard, revealed the tunnel. A terrified Negro was driven into the hole at the point of the bayonet, and thus made a trip to Rat Hell.

Several circumstances at this time combined to make this escape peculiarly exasperating to the Confederates. In obedience to repeated appeals from the Richmond newspapers, iron bars had but recently been fixed in all the prison windows for better security, and the guard had been considerably reinforced. The columns of these same journals had just been aglow with accounts of the daring and successful escape of the Confederate General John Morgan and his companions from the Columbus (Ohio) jail. Morgan had arrived in Richmond on the 8th of January, exactly a month prior to the completion of the tunnel, and was still the lion of the Confederate capital.

At daylight a plank was seen suspended on the outside of the east wall; this was fastened by a blanket-rope to one of the window-bars, and was, of course, a trick to mislead the Confederates. General John H. Winder, then in charge of all the prisoners in the Confederacy, with his headquarters in Richmond, was furious when the news reached him. After a careful external examination of the building, and a talk, not of the politest kind, with Major Turner, he reached the conclusion that such an escape had but one explanation—the guards had been bribed. Accordingly the sentinels on duty were marched off under arrest to Castle Thunder, where they were locked up and searched for "greenbacks." The thousand and more prisoners still in Libby were compensated, in a measure, for their failure to escape by the panic they saw among the "Rebs." Messengers and despatches were soon flying in all directions, and all the horse, foot, and dragoons of Richmond were in pursuit of the fugitives before noon. Only one man of the whole escaping party was retaken inside of the city limits. Of the

109 who got out that night, 59 reached the Union lines, 48 were recaptured, and 2 were drowned.

After leaving Libby, Rose and Hamilton turned northward and cautiously walked on a few squares, when suddenly they encountered some Confederates who were guarding a military hospital. Hamilton retreated quickly and ran off to the east; but Rose, who was a little in advance, walked boldly by on the opposite walk, and was not challenged; and thus the two friends separated.

Hamilton, after several days of wandering and fearful exposure, came joyfully upon a Union picket squad, received the care he painfully needed, and was soon on his happy journey home.

Rose passed out of the city of Richmond to the York River Railroad, and followed its track to the Chickahominy bridge. Finding this guarded, he turned to the right, and as the day was breaking he came upon a camp of Confederate cavalry. His blue uniform made it exceedingly dangerous to travel in daylight in this region; and seeing a large sycamore log that was hollow, he crawled into it. The February air was keen and biting, but he kept his cramped position until late in the afternoon; and all day he could hear the loud talk in the camp and the neighing of the horses. Toward night he came cautiously forth, and finding the Chickahominy fordable within a few hundred yards, he succeeded in wading across. The uneven bed of the river, however, led him into several deep holes, and before he reached the shore his scanty raiment was thoroughly soaked. He trudged on through the woods as fast as his stiffened limbs would bear him, borne up by the hope of early deliverance, and made a brave effort to shake off the horrible ague. He had not gone far, however, when he found himself again close to some Confederate cavalry, and was compelled once more to seek a hiding-place. The day seemed of interminable length, and he tried vainly in sleep to escape from hunger and cold. His teeth chattered in his head, and when he rose at dark to continue his journey his tattered clothes were frozen stiff. In this plight he pushed on resolutely, and was obliged to wade to his waist for hundreds of yards through one of those deep and treacherous morasses that proved such deadly fever-pools for McClellan's army in the campaign of 1862. Finally he reached the high ground, and as the severe exertion had set his blood again in motion and loosened his limbs, he was making better progress, when suddenly he found himself near a Confederate picket. This picket he easily avoided, and, keeping well in the shadow of the forest and shunning the roads, he pressed forward with increasing hopes of success. He had secured a box of matches before leaving Libby; and as the cold night came on and he felt that he was really in danger of freezing to death, he penetrated into the center of the cedar grove and built a fire in a small and secluded hollow. He felt that this was hazardous, but the necessity was desperate, since with his stiffened limbs he could no longer move along fast enough to keep the warmth of life in his body. To add to his trouble, his foot, which had been broken in Tennessee previous to his capture, was now giving him great pain, and threatened to cripple him wholly; indeed, it would stiffen and disable the best of limbs to compass the journey he had made in darkness over strange, uneven, and hard-frozen ground, and through rivers, creeks, and bogs, and this without food or warmth.

The fire was so welcome that he slept soundly—so soundly that waking in the early morning he found his boot-legs and half his uniform burned up, the ice on the rest of it probably having prevented its total destruction.

Resuming his journey much refreshed, he reached Crump's Cross-roads, where he successfully avoided another picket. He traveled all day, taking occasional short rests, and before dark had reached New Kent Court-house. Here again he saw some pickets, but by cautious flanking managed to pass them; but in crossing an open space a little farther on he was seen by a cavalryman, who at once put spurs to his horse and rode up to Rose, and, saluting him, inquired if he belonged to the New Kent Cavalry. Rose had on a gray cap, and seeing that he had a stupid sort of fellow to deal with, instantly answered, "Yes," whereupon the trooper turned his horse and rode back. A very few moments were enough to show Rose that the cavalryman's report had failed to satisfy his comrades, whom he could see making movements for his capture. He plunged through a laurel thicket, and had no sooner emerged than he saw the Confederates deploying around it in confidence that their game was bagged. He dashed on as fast as his injured foot would let him, and entered a tract of heavily timbered land that rose to the east of this thicket. At the border of the grove he found another picket post, and barely escaped the notice of several of the men. The only chance of escape lay through a wide, clear field before him, and even this was in full view from the grove that bordered it, and this he knew would soon swarm with his pursuers.

Across the center of this open field, which was fully half a mile wide, a ditch ran, which, although but a shallow gully, afforded a partial concealment. Rose, who could now hear the voices of the Confederates nearer and nearer, dove into the ditch as the only chance, and dropping on his hands and knees crept swiftly forward to the eastward. In this cramped position his progress was extremely painful, and his hands were torn by the briers and stones; but forward he dashed, fully expecting a shower of bullets every minute. At last he reached the other end of the half-mile ditch, breathless and half dead, but without having once raised his head above the gully.

Emerging from this field, he found himself in the Williamsburg road, and bordering the opposite side was an extensive tract thickly covered with pines. As he crossed and entered this tract he looked back and could see his enemies, whose movements showed that they were greatly puzzled and off the scent. When at a safe distance he sought a hiding-place and took a needed rest of several hours.

He then resumed his journey, and followed the direction of the Williamsburg road, which he found picketed at various points, so that it was necessary to avoid open spaces. Several times during the day he saw squads of Confederate cavalry passing along the road so near that he could hear their talk. Near nightfall he reached Diasen Bridge, where he successfully passed another picket. He kept on until nearly midnight, when he lay down by a great tree and, cold as he was, slept soundly until daylight. He now made a careful reconnaissance, and found near the road the ruins of an old building which, he afterward learned, was called "Burnt Ordinary."

He now found himself almost unable to walk with his injured foot, but, nerved by the yet bright hope of liberty, he once more went his weary way in the direction of Williamsburg. Finally he came to a place where there were some smoking fagots and a number of tracks, indicating it to have been a picket post of the previous night. He was now nearing Williamsburg, which, he was inclined to believe from such meager information as had reached Libby before his departures, was in possession of the Union forces. Still, he knew that this was territory that was frequently changing hands, and was therefore likely to be under a close watch. From this on he avoided the roads wholly, and kept under cover as much as it was possible; and if compelled to cross an open field at all, he did so in a stooping position. He was now moving in a southeasterly direction, and coming again to the margin of a wide opening, he saw, to his unutterable joy, a body of Union troops advancing along the road toward him.

Thoroughly worn out, Rose, believing that his deliverers were at hand, sat down to await their approach. His pleasant reverie was disturbed by a sound behind and near him, and turning quickly he was startled to see three soldiers in the road along which the troops first seen were advancing. The fact that these men had not been noticed before gave Rose some uneasiness for a moment; but as they wore blue uniforms, and moreover seemed to take no note of the approaching Federal troops, all things seemed to indicate that they were simply an advanced detail of the same body. This seemed to be further confirmed by the fact that the trio were now moving down the road, apparently with the intent of joining the larger body; and as the ground to the east rose to a crest, both of the bodies were a minute later shut off from Rose's view.

In the full confidence that all was right he rose to his feet and walked toward the crest to get a better view of everything and greet his comrades of the loyal blue. A walk of a hundred yards brought him again in sight of the three men, who now noticed and challenged him.

In spite of appearances a vague suspicion forced itself upon Rose, who, however, obeyed the summons and continued to approach the party, who now watched him with fixed attention. As he came closer to the group, the brave but unfortunate soldier saw that he was lost.

For the first time the three seemed to be made aware of the approach of the Federals, and to show consequent alarm and haste. The unhappy Rose saw before the men spoke that their blue uniform was a disguise, and the discovery brought a savage expression to his lips. He hoped and tried to convince his captors that he was a Confederate, but all in vain; they retained him as their prisoner, and now told him that they were Confederates. Rose, in the first bitter moment of his misfortune, thought seriously of breaking away to his friends so temptingly near; but his poor broken foot and the slender chance of escaping three bullets at a few yards made this suicide, and he decided to wait for a better chance, and this came sooner than he expected.

One of the men appeared to be an officer, who detailed one of his companions to conduct Rose to the rear in the direction of Richmond. The prisoner went quietly with his guard, the other two men tarried a little to watch the advancing Federals, and now Rose began to limp like a man who was unable to go farther. Presently the ridge shut them off from the view of the others. Rose, who had slyly been staggering closer and closer to the guard, suddenly sprang upon the man, and before he had time to wink had twisted his gun from his grasp, discharged it into the air, flung it down, and ran off as fast as his poor foot would let him toward the east and so as to avoid the rest of the Confederates. The disarmed Confederate made no attempt at pursuit, nor indeed did the other two, who were now seen retreating at a run across the adjacent fields.

Rose's heart bounded with new hope, for he felt that he would be with his advancing comrades in a few minutes at most. All at once a squad of Confederates, hitherto unseen, rose up in his very path, and beat him down with the butts of their muskets. All hands now rushed around and secured him, and one of the men called out excitedly, "Hurry up, boys; the Yankees are right here!" They rushed their prisoner into the wooded ravine, and here they were joined by the man whom Rose had just disarmed. He was in a savage mood, and declared it to be his particular desire to fill Rose full of Confederate lead. The officer in charge rebuked the man, however, and compelled him to cool down, and he went along with an injured air that excited the merriment of his comrades.

The party continued its retreat to Barhamsville, thence to the White House on the Pamunkey River, and finally to Richmond, where Rose was again restored to Libby, and, like the writer, was confined for a number of days in a narrow and loathsome cell. On the 30th of April his exchange was effected for a Confederate colonel, and on the 6th of July, 1864, he rejoined his regiment, in which he served with conspicuous gallantry to the close of the war.

How We Escaped from Pretoria

CAPTAIN AYLMER HALDANE

Haldane was taken prisoner during the Boer War in South Africa in 1899 when the train he commanded was ambushed. Winston Churchill, acting as a war correspondent, was also captured. The prisoners were held in the state model school in Pretoria. After just a month in captivity, Churchill, Haldane, and another soldier had settled on a plan to scale the fence by timing the movement of the sentries. Churchill made it, but the others had to pull back. (Churchill's adventures trying to cover the 280 miles to freedom are told in his memoir *My Early Life: A Roving Commission*.)

Although he never became as well-known as his friend Churchill, Captain Haldane's account of his own escape from the same camp (told in *How We Escaped from Pretoria*) was probably the more interesting of the two. After Churchill's escape, security was tightened and several plans were considered and rejected before Haldane and two companions reluctantly began a tunnel. Their reluctance stemmed from the great length of time it would take to finish and because Haldane suffered acutely from claustrophobia. The tunnel quickly had to be abandoned when they hit water, but they got word that the camp was to be moved and hit upon an alternate plan. They decided to hide under the floor in the tunnel entrance to fool their captors into thinking they had somehow escaped, and when the camp was moved, they would simply come out and walk cleanly away. The plan worked, but, unfortunately, they mistimed their *faux* escape by three weeks and had to spend each day cramped together in a tight space under the floor. After a great deal of suffering, particularly for Haldane, the camp was indeed moved. . . .

The moment for our "moonlight flitting" had arrived. All above seemed still and deserted, but lest we might be mistaken we listened intently for some minutes. Sergeant-Major Brockie, who was deputed to reconnoitre the building, to make sure that no caretaker had been left in charge, now pushed up the trap-door; but so firmly had it been fastened down the previous night, that despite the greatest care he was unable to prevent it from making a loud noise, which echoed in the deathlike stillness. Creeping into the room above, he made his way out through the doorway into the passage, and shortly returned to say that all was clear.

Le Mesurier and I followed, carefully shutting the trap-door after us. We were astonished to find how weak the confinement and cramped position had made us. Le Mesurier's legs gave way and he fell down; and all of us, when we tried to walk, reeled like drunken men. Several minutes passed before we dared leave the room, and it was not till we were some distance from Pretoria that our limbs regained their wonted strength.

Leaving the room which we had lived in and under for four months, and threading our way with care along the passage, which was blocked with forms, we reached the back-door which opens on the yard. It was locked, but the absence of a large pane of glass, which had been broken and completely removed, provided an easy exit. Strange to say, after my long incarceration I felt almost reluctant to go forth into unknown dangers and difficulties; but such a feeling was of brief duration, and this no time to moralise. We now put on our boots, which we had been carrying, and passing through this opening gained the verandah. Pausing for a moment to see that no one was in the yard, we crossed over to the low buildings on the other side. The moon was full, and the electric lights not being turned off, as we had anticipated they would be, we felt unpleasantly conspicuous. The dog's kennel was in its usual place, but fortunately the occupant was gone.

We had intended to leave the yard by climbing over the iron paling into the next garden; but the moon was far too bright for this, and the windows of a house which looked on to the garden were open and some people were looking out. We therefore made our way to the railings, near which the police tents had been, and climbing over reached the street on the south side of the school. A couple happened to pass, just after we had got into the street, but they took no notice of us, and Le Mesurier told me afterwards that a special policeman slowly turned the corner of the Model School at that very moment.

Crossing the road, we went up the street which leads towards the fort guarding the southern entrance to Pretoria. Of the town itself we had a small scale plan, which many months before we had removed from a biography of

President Kruger, a book belonging to the Staats library. I stopped to light my pipe, and Brockie, keeping in the shadow of some trees, donned a white sling in which to place an arm, and this pious fraud, supported by his wearing the Dutch colours round his hat, gave him the appearance of a wounded Boer. We next bore to our left, then to the right, and finally struck a road which, from the plan, we conjectured would cross the Delagoa Bay Railway.

Brockie had warned us both that if we wanted to escape notice we must slouch along with knees bent and backs rounded, as is the manner of the Boer. This to me was somewhat difficult, for the exquisite sense of exhilaration which I was experiencing made me feel much more inclined to run, jump, or indeed do anything but walk soberly along.

So far, although we had passed a few special policemen, our appearance had seemed to attract no particular notice. In the Transvaal, as in many other parts of the world, the country bumpkin, when he honours his county town with a visit, puts off his workaday garments and comes in his Sunday best. Our garb could scarcely be said to come under the latter heading: we looked more like three moonlighters than anything else I can think of. Fortunately for us, the town had been depleted of many of its inhabitants, most of whom were at the front, and in consequence the streets presented a very deserted appearance; and although we knew that the Dutchman is abominably inquisitive, yet we hoped to evade his notice. Le Mesurier and Brockie kept to the middle of the road. I followed them on the pathway, a little behind. In this fashion we were tramping along towards the outskirts of the town, with the villas in gardens on our right and left, when we met a special constable. This one, instead of passing us as the rest had done, stopped, and turning round scanned us with suspicion. I expected every minute that he would ask us in Dutch who we were and whither we were bound. But Brockie, having noticed that we were running the risk of being challenged, turned half round, exposing to view his quasi-wounded arm. This seemed to partly satisfy the guardian of the peace, for he turned up a side street, stopped to have a good look at us, and ultimately moved off, unaware perhaps that

> "Them as is watched out of sight
> Bide away for many a night,"—

which proved to be the case. Perhaps he thought discretion the better part of valour, for we were three desperate men, and he was alone, with no help near. Whatever may have been his motives, his action was fortunate, for we were prepared to go to any length to avoid a hue and cry. Brockie had vowed that nothing would induce him to be captured a second time, and had armed himself with a sausage-shaped bag of cloth filled and jammed tightly with earth. He was burning to use it on some one, and must have lamented this lost chance.

The road along which we were travelling now began to leave the town, and the gates of a level-crossing, betokening the presence of the railway, were plainly to be seen. We halted for a moment to consider whether it would not be wiser to turn aside and avoid a spot where a patrol might possibly be met; but our anxiety to get clear of Pretoria without delay overcame the inclination to make a detour, and pressing on, we found that nothing barred our way. Crossing the railway-line, we sat down in some long damp grass to decide whether we should follow road or railway. I had a small medicine-bottle full of whisky, presented by a fellow-prisoner as a parting gift. The occasion was not one to be overlooked, and we proceeded to drink success to our venture; then, having decided to take the railway as our guide, we set off again, and found we were clear of Pretoria and its suburbs.

I inwardly congratulated myself that now no officer or man who wore the Gordon tartan was a prisoner in the hands of the Boers. But we were not yet out of the wood.

Straight before us, high up in the eastern sky, shone the moon, dimming the brilliancy of the evening star which followed closely in her wake; to the right the Southern Cross, and low down in the north-east Orion's Belt. With guides like these, to lose ourselves would not be easy. Reaching the railway, we walked along in single file, halting now and then to listen and make sure that all was clear in front. A coal-train from Balmoral, going westward, passed us, and soon after we had to throw ourselves down in a ditch beside the line to conceal ourselves from a Dutchman going home off bridge-guard,—for every bridge and every culvert from Pretoria to Komati Poort had its guard by day and night. These guards (we were afterwards told) had orders to fire on any one walking on the track at night.

When we had gone about three miles, and were covering the ground at a good rate, we almost walked into the arms of a sentry who was sitting on the parapet of a bridge which carried the railway over the road. We came upon him suddenly, as he was sitting partly hidden by a bush, and walked to within a few paces from him; and that he did not see us, unless he was asleep, is a miracle. We dropped like stones beside the rails, lay absolutely still for some moments, then softly crept back down the slope of the embankment in the direction whence we had come. Then along a muddy ditch until we had lost sight of him, climbed a barbed-wire fence beside the railway, which shook and rattled, after which, making a wide detour, and creeping through a mealie-field to avoid a Kaffir kraal, we passed along the face of a hill and found ourselves close to a telegraph-wire. This wire, we discovered later, ran like a Roman road over hill and dale to Komati Poort, and had we followed it we should have made our journey many miles shorter, and escaped the annoyance of losing our way in the dark. All around us dogs in the neighbouring farms were baying loudly at the moon, and this, and occasional shouts from afar, made us hasten on our way. We now followed the wire for a couple of miles, but thinking we were going out of our way, we left it and climbed a rocky ridge not far from Koodoespoort, where Churchill had caught the train when he escaped. Below us we heard the sound of running water. Hastily making our way to it, for we were growing thirsty, we came upon a muddy stream evidently used for irrigating the fields on the hillside, down which it flowed.

Unfortunately at this juncture Le Mesurier, who had got off the path among some rocks, twisted his ankle. Painful as it was, to walk on, however slowly, was better than to rest, and so allow it to grow stiff. Pluckily recognising this, he kept moving forward, and we made some progress, though slow. Our way led us over the open veldt, where the grass was long and wet. Brockie was growing tired, and insisted that he saw Boers under every tree and bush, and for some time we moved with great caution. We again struck the railway, crossed it, and a black patch in the distance told us we were approaching the first station, thirteen miles from Pretoria, and decided to halt there till next evening. I felt a good deal disappointed at covering so short a distance the first night; but it was no one's fault, and it was as well, perhaps, not to walk too far at first, for we were not in the best of training just then.

Reaching Eerste Fabriken, our farther progress was barred by a ditch some fifteen feet deep, with just beyond it a sluggish muddy river. Hunting up and down the ditch, we at length found a spot where, hidden by the thick bushes, it gradually sloped up to the ground-level. The bottom was damp, but that was soon remedied by covering it over with straw, which we found lying about. We had, however, got into a veritable hotbed of mosquitoes, for they attacked us with the greatest fury, and to sleep was impossible. The arrival of morning and dispersal of these greedy bloodsuckers was a great relief. At 6.30 A.M. the steam-horn of the Hatherly Distillery hard by sounded, bidding the workmen rise for another day of toil. At this establishment, I am told, strong waters of every variety, from Hennessey's three-star brandy to Long John of Ben Nevis fame, can be procured. It is merely a matter of labels, and they are not so hard to copy as bank-notes. Our hiding-place proved to be admirable, for though it was uncomfortable, it was improbable that anything but a dog would find it, and we were well sheltered from the sun. This was the first day for nearly three weeks that we had seen the sun, and we were not sorry to be protected from his burning rays by the thick foliage. During the day we ate a little chocolate and some meat lozenges; but as regards water we were as badly off as Tantalus, for the river, a few yards distant, could not safely be approached. Some one seemed to be fishing in it close to us—an Englishman we thought, for he whistled, one after another, many tunes that were familiar to us. His *répertoire* was somewhat antiquated, and included amongst others "Oh, what a surprise!" and "After the ball is over." Except for the occasional song of a Kaffir, the noise of cows busily cropping the grass, and the buzzing of many insects, all else was silent. The ubiquitous fly had of course marked us down, and did not spare us his objectionable attentions, and to drive him off by smoking was not considered safe. Even here, and indeed throughout all our travels, we never raised our voices above a whisper, lest some passer-by might hear and discover us. Our determination was if possible neither to see any one nor to be seen by any one till we reached the frontier. This would free us from incriminating explanations, if any were demanded.

Time passes slowly when one has nothing to do all day but brush off flies, and we regretted that a pack of cards had not been included among our baggage, for then we might have called the "demon" to our aid. A few trains passed up and down: these and the occasional sound of the distillery horn alone served to break the monotony. At half-past four Sergeant-Major Brockie, armed with Le Mesurier's field-glasses, which he had managed to secrete when taken prisoner, was despatched to do a little scouting, in order to find out whether there was a drift over the river near where we lay hidden. After a short time he returned, bringing the satisfactory news that the ford lay between us and the station, and across it several waggons were outspanned. There had been a heavy fall of rain during the afternoon, but we hoped insufficient to flood the river.

When darkness at length came, we sallied forth from our retreat, crossed the river, then the railway, and reached the road. By the small scale map we possessed, the railway appeared to make a considerable bend to the south-east, and as the road seemed to form the chord of the arc, it would be shorter to follow it. But Transvaal roads are not as other roads, and are as unlike their counterpart in England as a lane in Devonshire is unlike the turnpike to Bath. Looking at a map of the Transvaal, you are tempted to believe that once on the road, so clearly defined on paper, you have only to shut your eyes and go ahead. Try it, and you will find a close resemblance between yourself and the blind led by the blind. The highways in the South African Republic are innocent of metal—Macadam is a name unknown: they consist of nothing but deeply indented wheel-tracks left by the clumsy, ponderous transport of the country—the ox-waggon. As a Dutchman in wet weather leaves the main track where it has become swampy and marks out a line for himself, the natural consequence is that in time the vicinity of a road becomes a maze of tracks, and to find your way in the dark and in an unknown district is nigh impossible.

To-night we were to experience this. Sergeant-Major Brockie, who posed as a fairly good "pathfinder," took the lead, and we pushed boldly along; for our lame comrade was a little better, and had secured a bough as a walking-stick. We noticed that the track we were following went due south, but thought that doubtless it would soon change its course. A waggon coming towards us on the road, we had to turn off and wait until it had gone by. Not long after we had crossed the railway we came upon a large white wooden gate. Passing through it, we found we were on an avenue, both sides of which were lined with firs,— a most unusual luxury for a Dutchman; for the Boers have done almost nothing for their country in the way of wood-growing, and except for a few trees round a farmstead, you may travel miles without seeing a leaf or finding shade. A little farther on we noticed the lights of a cottage, which we took for the lodge of some larger building. Passing by as quietly as we could, we soon came to four crossroads, but we were beginning to lose faith in our conductor, and we turned north-east. Our route now led along what appeared to be a deer-park, for in the moonlight several of these animals could be seen to fly at our approach. We must have diverged considerably, for it seemed a long time ere we again met the railway, and both my companions were footsore and tired. Before us lay a range of hills in which was a *poort,* or gap, through which the railway passed, and on the name-board of the deserted station we read Pienaars Poort. As we drew nearer to the hills we heard the noise of rushing water, and once inside the *poort* we sat down by the river to refresh. The spot looked singularly picturesque. Road, railway, river—all were crowded together into the gap, which at its narrowest point was about two hundred yards wide; and on either side the hills, tenanted by chattering baboons, rose steep and bare. The ground ascended before us towards the farther entrance of this defile, and the gradient of the railway was steep. One felt instinctively that this would be a bad place in which to encounter a patrol, for the only way out of it seemed forwards or backwards.

Brand's essence and whisky worked wonders on my tired companions, and, reinvigorated, we started off full of the intention of reaching Elands River station, twenty-nine miles from Pretoria. I led the way along the railway-line. On our left, a stone's-throw distant, flowed the river, its surface shining like a mirror under the rising moon. Before me ran the double rails, looking like bars of silver; and beyond them, on the right, the road. As we trod softly and looked ahead as far as one could distinctly see, some tents appeared on the right of the railway, pitched close under the hill; one of them seemed larger than the rest. I turned to Brockie, who followed me, and asked his opinion. "Only a Kaffir kraal," he replied, so on we pressed. A few paces farther, and the stillness of the night was broken by the angry barking of a dog. Immediate action was imperative. Down we dropped into the long rushy grass which filled the space betwixt the river and the railway. The dog continued barking—he had evidently seen us. Presently voices became audible, one of them bidding the cur be silent. But he did not cease, and another followed suit. After lying in the grass about twenty minutes, for we did not care to move so long as the dogs remained on the alert, we heard voices coming in our direction, and the barking of the dogs became more distinct. A patrol was on its way to clear up the situation. A whispered conference was held, when it was decided to retreat, and then we dragged ourselves like snakes diagonally back towards the river. Fortunately the rushes had been beaten down by a recent flood, and our tracks were barely visible. Reaching a broad ditch full of water, Le Mesurier, who was following me, came alongside and asked me if I had seen Brockie, who had been following him. Being in front I had not, so we waited a few moments; but seeing nothing of him, and the enemy drawing near, we crossed the obstacle and found ourselves at the edge of the stream. Again we paused, this time for several minutes, and the searchers came in view, following our track. One of them, who was walking along almost bent double, we thought was Brockie, but looking through the rushes we quickly found our mistake.

At this moment many things rushed through my mind, and more especially one. Shortly before leaving Pretoria I had been reading again a very ancient friend, 'Tales of a Grandfather,' and now I instinctively remembered how the Bruce, when hunted by John of Lorne's bloodhound, had waded down a river and so destroyed the scent. My mind was quickly made up.

The crisis had come: to stay where we were meant probably recapture. I whispered to Le Mesurier to follow me silently and not to splash. Transferring my manuscript map from my pocket to the lining of my hat, the next minute I was in the river, which was out of my depth, and Le Mesurier dropped in beside me. Holding on to the roots of the reeds which lined the bank, we paused and watched the searchers, then carefully pulled ourselves some distance downstream, and paused again. The Boers and their dogs were evidently now at fault, and showed no signs of coming our way, so we continued our downward course, and ultimately swam across and into a ditch on the other side.

We had been a good half-hour in the stream, which seemed to us intensely cold, and our teeth were chattering so that we could scarcely speak. My wrist-watch had stopped; but Le Mesurier's—a Waterbury—was still going, for it had been provided by his care with a waterproof case. We now crept along the ditch up-stream again, and then turned off towards the hillside, which was dotted with large boulders. Coming round the corner of one of these, we found a tent in front of us, in which a light was burning, and not caring to pass it, we tried to climb up the steep face of the hill. Failing at one point, we found a kind of "chimney," up which we climbed, pulling and pushing each other till the top was gained. A few minutes' rest was necessary, for our clothes were heavy with water and the climb had made us breathless. Le Mesurier had done wonders with his ankle—the cold water had been most efficacious. Next we walked along the rocky face of the hill, parallel to the direction we had followed below, and gradually descended to the level and struck a path. While on the hillside we had looked down into the valley below, where all seemed quiet and nothing moved. Brockie was irretrievably lost, and it was useless to attempt to find him. He had with him a water-bottle and sufficient food, and knew both the Dutch and the Kaffir language. Following the path, we passed several clumps of bracken, one of which we selected as a suitable hiding-place. To have walked farther in our wet and clinging garments might have been wiser, but we decided that we had had sufficient excitement for one night without trying to add to it.

Carefully avoiding breaking down the fern, we took our way into the centre of the clump, and made ourselves as comfortable as was possible. I took as a prophylactic ten grains of quinine and four of opium, all that was not reduced to pulp by our recent immersion. The dose of opium, I have since been told, was a large if not indeed a lethal one, but it did not make me sleep. The night was bitterly cold—for where we lay was nearly five thousand feet above the sea-level—and, soaked as we were, we shook and shivered. Of course the mosquitoes did not spare us, and we spent the remainder of the night in fighting this useless scourge.

When day broke I found I was so stiff and rheumatic that I could not move, and Le Mesurier was not much better. However, when the sun rose and penetrated our wooden bodies we soon found movement possible, and by noon we were dry and ready for any more adventures that might come. We had suffered some loss by that unavoidable dip in the river. Le Mesurier had lost a pocket-book and I the contents of the whisky-bottle, the cork of which had come out when we were crawling along in the grass—by accident, not design.

I had also lost a triangular file, a memento of the Model School. Further, our food-supply was water-logged, our tobacco spoilt, and likewise our matches. We managed to eat some pulpy chocolate, which was becoming nauseous to us, besides creating a thirst we had no means of quenching. We had trusted to finding plenty of mealies growing; but the harvest was just gathered in, and this source of supply was lacking.

Our hiding-place, although overlooked by the hills, was a good one. Only a few Dutchmen and Kaffirs passed by along the paths, and they saw no sign of us. The want of proximity to water was its greatest fault, and we mutually agreed that howsoever uncomfortable a swamp might be as a sleeping-place, it was the only place in which to pass a day under the broiling sun, unless a shady nook were forthcoming. Few trains passed, as it was Sunday. One could not help carrying one's thoughts back to Pretoria, and wondering where our accomplices would think we had reached, and what they would think we were doing. Only too well we knew, at any hour of the day, how they were passing their time, and how unhappy many of them were. How light-hearted we felt at being free again! All that was necessary for us now was care and caution, and these we had been accustomed to when below the floor, and we were now determined not to leave anything to chance, or what people term luck, or to spare any trouble which might help to ensure our ultimate freedom.

In addition to the ordinary risks of being captured or shot—for being in plain clothes we ran the risk of treatment as spies—there were two others which now presented themselves. My fear was lest the trap-door, which we could not shut down very neatly, might have been noticed; and also that Sergeant-Major Brockie should get ahead of us, reach Lorenço Marques, and, forgetting that we were still behind him, talk. That the latter supposition was not devoid of foundation will appear later. On the whole, however, I felt exceedingly confident that our enterprise would prove successful: if we should have the misfortune to be recaptured, at least we would feel satisfied for ever after that we had made a determined bid for freedom.

The hour had now come round when it was time to continue our journey. It was decided to leave the railway and use the moon as a guide till near dawn, when by turning north we could regain the railway with certainty and reach Elands River station. The distant roll of thunder and the lightning-flashes gave every sign of a coming storm. The moon was not yet up; but the flashes which from time to time shot forth from the inky clouds made the bare veldt look as bright as day, and we felt that we were very conspicuous. Dropping down into the valley, we crossed at a narrow spot the same river whose waters we had encountered the night before. Soon we came to the railway, which we had decided not to follow, crossed it, and proceeded up a long steep hill. After we had covered between two or three miles, to my dismay I discovered that I had left my money-belt, containing some £18, and a compass, at our last hiding-place. The risk of returning to look for them was too great, for on quitting our hiding-place we had noticed many lights in the neighbourhood, and the probability of finding the clump of ferns in the pitchy darkness was remote. Besides which, both Le Mesurier and I were even now not entirely devoid of money, and it was doubtful if we should require what we still had. We therefore pushed on till by the light of the moon we saw in front of us a Kaffir kraal, and found that we were walking past a field of water-melons. The opportunity was too good to be lost. Since we left our hiding-place we had had no water save that which a shower had left in the hoof-marks of some cattle. We now sat down and simply gorged this thirst-quenching pulp. I have often eaten Afghan melons, which the caravans bring on their camels to Peshawur, and these more resembled them than any others that I have tasted. But we had been heard or scented, for the kraal dogs near by began to bark. I hastily tied up a melon in my handkerchief, and we walked silently away. Treading our way softly through some mealie-fields, we came to a deep donga at the bottom of which was a muddy rushing stream. We followed this for some time, till, thinking that our destination must be near, we crossed over and mounted a hill. Half-way up its side we heard a sound of galloping. The place was very open and the grass burnt short, but after a few moments of suspense nothing worse than a frightened horse appeared.

It seemed as if we were never going to strike the railway; but in this particular locality, where the ground is hilly and the gradients steep, I believe its windings are extraordinary. As with all the railways in South Africa, the contour of the ground was followed, cuttings and embankments being rare. Suddenly the glint of the moonlight reflected from the rails caught our eyes, then the black telegraph poles like spectres, and the wires, through which the chilly breeze was softly moaning. We had reached it at last.

But our last two nights' experiences with railway guards had had their effect, and we foolishly left the line and wandered far from our course. After some miles we saw in front of us a small wood, close to which some waggons were outspanned, and soon after passing them I had what cannot have been anything but a hallucination. Brockie was in my thoughts, and I was wondering where he was and if by any chance we should meet him to-night at Elands River, for we had talked with him of making for that place. On the ground a little to my left I saw what seemed to be a man lying at full length, his elbows resting on the ground, his head between his hands. Telling Le Mesurier what I saw, we went nearer, but the vision of my fancy had gone; yet it was so clear that I can recall it and the spot where it occurred with the utmost distinctness.

Not far from here we came to a ridge of grey rocks, where we sat down. I was tired out, principally from having slept badly when below ground, and from not having slept at all since we left Pretoria, and was prepared to lie down on the veldt and take my chance of discovery. But dawn was near, and before us we saw a signal-post and a little farther off a wayside station. Crossing the railway, we made for a clump of trees which rose prominently before us on the sky-line. No river was to be seen, although the name of the place betokened one: there was nothing in a liquid form visible save a tiny trickling stream. This, however, is a little way of their own that South African rivers have—at one time a roaring torrent, at another a microscopic stream.

Hard by a cock was shrilly crowing, betokening the presence of some inhabited dwelling, but, tired as I was, that was of no concern to me.

Nearing the trees, we walked into a barbed-wire fence, and crossing it, selected a small clump of blue-gum or eucalyptus trees for our lair. These were only saplings, six to eight feet high, interspersed with larger trees of a kind unknown to me. Behind us we had left two alarming tracks in the dew-sodden grass—but the sun would soon rectify that. Throwing ourselves down, we endeavoured to get some sleep before the mosquitoes found us and made repose impossible. We were far from comfortable, for the place was strewn with roots and stones; but my melon made such an excellent pillow that I was soon in the land of Nod, and awoke startled at 7 to hear Le Mesurier whispering, "I think we are discovered!" I could get no more from him just then, so lay thinking what was to be done, and hoping that he was mistaken.

He told me afterwards that some one had passed close by, and, he thought, had seen us. A heavy shower of rain now fell, perhaps hiding our footprints in the grass. Two hours later the sound of advancing footsteps became audible. It was a young Dutchman coming along a path not six feet from where our heads lay on the ground. He stopped when he came opposite to us, and a dog which accompanied him growled. How this animal did not immediately discover us will always remain a mystery to me, but perhaps the same shower which hid our tracks also spoilt the scent. Visions of bloodthirsty *vrouws* arose in one's mind; for now there were few men on their farms, and it was said on all hands that the women were more than Spartan in their severity. The lad now began shouting loudly what I supposed to be some Kaffir name, and after a brief interval was joined by some one with whom he talked for a space. It seemed to us as if he must have seen us, and, not daring himself to disturb the intruders, had called for help. But it is marvellous how, if one remains absolutely still, one may pass unnoticed, and our imaginations here had led us astray. Nothing happened, they moved away, and the incident only increased our confidence; for we felt that having had two such close shaves, we must eventually escape altogether.

All day long the Kaffirs worked near us, busy cutting wood and drawing water, and the Dutch lad passed more than once again. The Kaffir is more like an animal than a human being in the way he will detect a spoor and traces that would not catch a white man's notice; but we were completely unnoticed that day by black or white.

Of course, by now we knew that we had walked right into the middle of a Boer farm; but I had been too tired the night before to care where I went. The difficulty now was to leave it so quietly at night that even the dogs might not hear us. At 7 o'clock we quitted the gum-tree thicket and made our way through mealie-fields and hedges till we were quite clear of our dangerous surroundings. This took a long time, for each sun-dried mealie-stalk in our path had to be held aside, lest the rustling noise which they would have made if we had attempted to pass quickly through should rouse the watch-dogs. I eagerly scanned each plant as we made our way between them, but not one single corn-spike remained.

It might almost seem as if we had departed from our original plan of trying to catch a night train; but on the three preceding evenings we had wandered far from the railway, and had thought that during our absence from its vicinity the eastward-going train might well have passed. To-night, however, though some doubts had certainly arisen in our minds as to whether the train ran or not, it was our intention to lie in wait for it and board an empty truck as it moved slowly up a gradient. Should we be successful, it would bring us to near Balmoral by daybreak. But we were destined to pass that night and the two next on the veldt. We now made direct for the railway, which was near, and shortly after found a gradient of 1 in 57 for some hundred metres. Lying down close to it, and shielding our faces from the mosquitoes with our coats, we remained till 2 A.M., but no train passed. It now seemed certain that the night-service no longer ran, and there was nothing left but to go on walking. Our experiences of the previous evening decided us as to our route, and for a couple of hours we followed the line, and then began to look for water and a place to hide in. As there was a ganger's house close to the railway-line, it seemed probable that we should find water of some sort near. In this we proved to be right, for we nearly walked into a circular pit, at the bottom of which were some inches of the precious liquid. Quenching our thirst and filling the bottle, we looked everywhere for some place that would hide us. There was nothing for it but to lie down by an ant-bear hole upon which we fortunately stumbled. The dwelling of this animal is a hole like a badger's, with a trench about two feet deep, and as broad, leading to the entrance. Here we lay down and prepared, when the sun rose, to be grilled for nine or ten hours, for there was no shade, and we had no means of making it without attracting notice; and our ten-ounce water-bottle would not go very far. In two more marches we should reach Balmoral, and once there, we had a very good hope of hiding ourselves in a coal-truck bound for Portuguese territory.

Haldane and Le Mesurier eventually reached the same coal mines that Churchill had during his earlier escape. The helpful miners made the final arrangements for them to sneak to freedom.

A Gunman Breaks Jail

EDWARD H. SMITH

Harvey Logan, also known by the more colorful "Kid Curry," was one of the last famous outlaws associated with the Wild West. He started out as a cowboy with a wild streak before one thing led to another and he began to run with the notorious Wild Bunch. (He would eventually lead this famous group of bandits for a time.) He was first captured in 1897 following a holdup in South Dakota and held in jail in Deadwood awaiting trial for bank robbery and a lingering charge of murder in Montana. He made his escape by hacking through the cell bars with a saw provided by friends and rode quickly away to safety in the Hole in the Wall region, where lawmen were still afraid to follow.

Due to his jailbreak and the series of robberies and narrow escapes that followed, his legend, and that of the Wild Bunch, continued to grow. But the West was changing. Logan and his friends were hotly pursued by Pinkerton agents and various other law-enforcement groups. Eventually, he was traced to Nashville, Tennessee, through a large number of unsigned bank notes he had stolen and was attempting to forge. Authorities arrested the woman he was with, but Logan somehow slipped away. He stayed in the area, though, evidently hoping to break the woman out of jail.

Two months later, in December of 1901, a stranger was reportedly causing trouble in a Knoxville saloon and officers were called in. Two of them were shot in the ensuing holdup, and the stranger jumped a back fence to make his escape. Unfortunately, there was a 30-foot drop behind the fence, and the man was too injured to make his retreat. He was thrown in jail and held there pending a trial for shooting the policemen and holding up the saloon, but authorities had no idea they were holding Harvey Logan, one of the most wanted men in the country.

The Pinkertons finally arrived and identified Logan, and security was beefed up just in time. He was tried and sentenced to 130 years in prison. Knowing it would be much harder to escape after he was moved from

Knoxville, Logan made one last desperate attempt. His escape in 1903—with no outside help—was one of the most spectacular in America at that time and garnered national attention.

Knoxville did not at first appreciate its responsibilities. Harvey Logan was left in the county jail like any vagrant or pickpocket, and came very near escaping the first night after his identification. The Pinkertons, however, were soon on the scene and urged the local authorities to take the utmost precautions. Not only were all visitors to Logan quizzed, searched and not allowed to talk with him save in the presence of a keeper, but everything that was sent to him from the outside was rigidly examined. Finally, to make escape quite impossible, the detectives urged the Knoxville authorities to post a special armed guard before Logan's cell, and keep such a warder on duty day and night. Two men, working twelve-hour shifts, were employed for this purpose, and Harvey Logan found himself watched as only condemned men are guarded during the final weeks before the day of doom.

Logan was shortly brought to trial on charges of issuing falsified bank notes, robbing the government, and various other indictments which the Federal prosecutors had been able to get returned against him. It was decided that the local charges of assault on the two policemen and robbing the saloon should be held in abeyance until the government had tried its case. Logan was convicted on all counts, after a trial which was attended by great crowds, some of the populace waiting outside the courthouse in the streets and the square for news of the proceedings. He was sentenced to one hundred and thirty years in prison on ten counts, but, as most of the sentences were to run concurrently, it was calculated that Logan would spend about twenty years in the Federal keep. When this sentence had expired he was still liable to prosecution in Tennessee for assault and robbery, and there were various murder charges hanging over him in the Far West as a result of the Landusky affair and the killing of officers who had attempted to pursue Logan and his men. Obviously, unless this superbandit should escape again, he was doomed to live and die in prisons or on a gallows.

Logan took an appeal and was returned to the Knoxville jail to await the outcome of this legal manoeuvre. Now he began to plan escape in earnest, under circumstances that must have left the ordinary man no least glint of hope.

His confederates on the outside tried to corrupt the keepers who watched Logan, but these officers were themselves too closely watched by their superiors, even had they been inclined to malfeasance. Logan tried bribery from within the jail, but the warders turned deaf ears.

When Sheriff Fox and the Pinkertons heard of these overtures on the part of their famous prisoner they decided to take additional precautions, and they moved Logan to an upper and separate floor of the jail, where he was confined alone. This was done to prevent him from smuggling messages out of prison, through the aid of other prisoners whose terms were expiring, and from receiving tools or money from without, through fresh convicts arriving in jail.

So Logan was completely cut off from communication with the world outside. He wrote no letters save under the eyes of the guards, and he opened none that had not already been read and tested by the officials. No one could get near him, consult with him or communicate with him. He was, in effect, in solitary confinement. Sometimes, when he complained of ailing through long detention in his cell, he was allowed to leave it and walk about the corridor of his private floor, but there were always two and sometimes three armed keepers at hand when this liberty was granted. Most of the time he lay in his cell, with an armed man walking up and down before the door and another posted outside the entrance to the jail floor, to prevent Logan from reaching the main parts of the jail in case he should manage to overpower the inner guard.

But this intrepid man, with the prospect of perpetual immurement to goad him on, kept his courage high. His mind worked day and night upon any theory of escape that might open the way. Once he managed to keep a case knife with which he had been allowed to eat. A few days later it was found that he had been digging at the mortar between the stones in the rear wall of his cell. On another occasion, when he was allowed to walk about the corridor of his jail floor, he leaped upon one of the guards, while the others had momentarily turned to look out of the windows, but he was overpowered and put back into his cage, from which he was not again permitted to emerge. Sheriff Fox and Jailer Bell had been extremely watchful previously. These abortive attempts at escape made them ever more wary of this determined ward of theirs. They did not relax their vigilance for a moment, and they warned their keepers every morning and every night that there must be no lapse of precaution.

The friends of Logan outside prison contributed to keeping the bandit's guards awake, for they were active in many ways. One of the phenomena of the case was the interference of various persons who had no connection whatever with Logan, who were not criminals and had never seen the celebrated captive. They had merely come to be followers or partisans of the prisoner through his celebrity. Some of these emotional confederates even tried to smuggle into the prison articles which were intended to help Logan escape. The most notable of these attempts, which may not have been the work of one of these volunteers but was so set down, was the widely known episode of the pipes.

One morning half a dozen corncob pipes with extraordinarily long stems arrived for Logan. The pipes were still in what appeared to be waxed-paper cases or wrappers, and apparently had just come from a tobacconist's. Their sender wrote that they were merely intended for the comfort of the prisoner, and the officials came near being taken in. The pipes had already been passed and ordered delivered to Logan when a keeper, merely curious, tore off the wrapper of one. When he drew on the pipe there was an obstruction in the stem, and a little examination disclosed that each of the six pipes contained a long steel sawblade. It had been a close call, the officers thought, though it is a little difficult to understand how Logan might have used the blades with any good effect, since there was always a guard pacing outside his cell.

The appeal hung fire in the Federal courts. Logan, who had entered the jail on December 13, 1901, was still there when Christmas of 1902 rolled around. The public gradually lost interest in him, and apparently his free confederates gave up their attempts at aid. By doing so they played into the hands of the prisoner. Instead of keeping the jailers constantly stirred up and anxious in their vigilance, this new quiescence gave the jail a chance to settle down into a normal and easy routine. It also gave Logan the chance which every escaper needs, to sit alone and watch that routine for the little weak spot, the chink in the armour of the jail Achilles through which a bold man may strike to freedom.

The spring of 1903 passed without incident and without furnishing Logan with the chance he sought. In April he was informed that his appeal was up for argument, and a few days later the news came that his lawyers had been heard, and that the court had taken the decision under advisement. The time for action was at hand. Logan had little faith in a reversal. He must do his deed before the courts could decide against him, for he would immediately be transferred to a great penitentiary, whence escape would be a matter of the sheerest chance.

May came and went without any relaxation of discipline or vigilance, and the middle of June was at hand before Logan got even the first hint of a plan. Then one day when he was sweeping out his cell, one of the wires of the broom chanced to become loosened. In a twinkling he had unwound the wire and hidden it, neatly coiled, in a chink of his cell masonry, which he carefully covered with floor dirt, moistened with saliva. As soon as this was done he called gibingly to his guard:

"What kind of broom is this you gimme?"

The guard inspected the broom, which was coming to pieces at every swipe along the floor. Because it had been in use for some time, he took it, suspecting nothing, and got a fresh broom for the prisoner, who again took off as much of the wire as he dared and hid it with the rest.

Logan himself can have had no definite idea of what was to be done with these few yards of fine, strong wire, but he had the desperate man's confidence in trifles, and waited. After a time a plan formed itself vaguely in his mind. Perhaps he would have a chance to execute it.

Through the day, Logan observed, there were two men in his enclosure, outside his cell, of course. Only when one of them went away to his meals was there a lone guard on duty. At such a time, Logan decided, he must make his attempt.

Acting became part of the plan. Logan, who had been silent and threatening during his wait in jail, now seemed to become reconciled and communicative. Evidently, so he tried to make the keepers believe, he had given up hope and was trying to be cheerful about his lot. The officers could not guess the cheering power of those little strands of wire, or the histrionic abilities of the convict.

Logan soon found that his day guard was not an unsympathetic person, that he liked to talk and to listen, and that when Logan began to tell stories out of his adventurous life the guard would come to the grated door of the cell, lean against it, smoke his pipe indolently, and give close attention. This was obviously the man to be attacked, but the time and the circumstances must be precisely chosen if the attempt was to succeed.

On the afternoon of June 26, 1903, word was received at the Knoxville jail that the appeal of Logan had been rejected and the sentences of the lower court approved. With this notification came the order for the immediate transfer of Logan to the State penitentiary at Columbus, Ohio, where many Federal prisoners were held, while the big government prisons at Leavenworth and Atlanta were still in course of construction. Logan was somewhat tauntingly notified that he would be taken to Columbus the following afternoon, in charge of the sheriff and several deputies, one of whom was a keeper in the jail.

"Well," said Logan cheerfully, "I ain't exactly surprised."

He showed no emotion, settled down on the chair in his cell, lighted his pipe, and seemed cowed and resigned. The officers expected no further trouble from him.

Meantime, the city of Knoxville had awakened to a fresh interest in Harvey Logan. After all, this almost legendary rascal and hero was going to the penitentiary like an ordinary mortal. There was certain to be a crowd at the station the next afternoon to see him off, and probably to cheer him as he rode away to the gloom of his prison home.

Logan slept quietly on his last night in the Knoxville jail, and the guard who kept the dark vigil reported that the prisoner was evidently calm and stoic. He was licked and was going to take his medicine placidly. The truth was that this night guard had never once approached Logan's cell, so that the prisoner had found no opportunity to attack him. Consequently, Logan had got as much sleep as possible. He would need all his strength and endurance on the following day.

When morning came the guard was changed, and Logan's loquacious friend and one other guard took up the watch. The convict heard with some pleasure that one member of the force of keepers was at home ill, while another had gone to make ready for the trip to Columbus as part of the bad-man's escort. Warden Bell himself was on duty outside, while the regular guard of two men were on hand on Logan's floor.

Logan passed the morning packing up his few belongings and apparently making ready for his long term in prison. His food was brought in at noon, and the second guard left, as soon as the prisoner had eaten, to have his own luncheon. Only the friendly and communicative keeper remained.

Harvey Logan scratched the dirt away from the chink in the masonry, got out his two pieces of rusty wire, straightened them by pulling them over his knee, tested them for strength, joined the two pieces into one, and formed of the long strand a noose such as he had used a thousand times as a cowboy for lassoing cows and horses. This he concealed on his cot under the bundle he had prepared.

Logan began talking to his keeper in the usual familiar way, trying to draw the man to the bars. The fellow answered, but did not come near. Instead, he sat some distance away on a stool, cleaning and reloading one of his revolvers.

For a few minutes the prisoner's heart sank. The other guard would be back in less than an hour. In two hours the escort would be ready to take him to his prolonged incarceration. If he could not draw this guard to his cell door before the other man's lunch hour was past, all opportunity would be gone. Every chance must be taken. The issue was freedom or lifelong imprisonment.

Logan watched anxiously till the guard had cleaned his weapon and stuffed it back into his pocket. He began to talk with the keeper again. To his relief the guard rose and walked up and down. Logan sat on the end of his bunk and continued to talk in his usual confidential way. But the keeper did not come and lean against the cell door. Apparently either the Fates were against Logan or the guard was a bit wary on this last day.

Finally Logan asked for a pencil and a scrap of paper.

"I want to draw you a little map that will mean something to you," he said. "It's the best I can do before I go."

The beguiled keeper brought the paper and pencil and Logan spent a few minutes drawing a fanciful map, talking all the while.

"When 'Flat Nose' an' me got that bank in Sisley," he said, "they was purty hot after us, an' we had to drop the gold somewhere. There's about three thousand dollars of it that was never got back. We never had a chance to go after it. This here map'll show you where it is. All I want is one thousand so I kin get little things while I'm in stir."

With that he finished his map and poked it through the bars, whither the guard had been attracted.

"Look here," said Logan, drawing the man even nearer, "here's the railroad station at Sisley—see? Over this way goes the road toward Rat Gulch, where they chased us. See this cross here? That's a big red rock about the size of this room. Now follow this line here about twenty-five feet . . ."

The guard leaned his head close to the bars, and at the same time turned his back so that a light from above would shine on the crude, pencilled map. While he stood staring and listening to the prisoner's words, Logan slipped out his wire noose, twisted the free end about his right hand, tossed the noose quickly over the keeper's head, and threw himself back with great force, so that the wire caught the unhappy guard about the throat and pulled him back against the steel door of the cell, choking for breath and tortured as the fine, knife-like wire bit into his neck.

He tried to cry out, but the wire bound his throat, and he could make no sound. He struggled and writhed, trying to reach for his revolver. Logan pulled the wire a bit tighter with a low warning:

"Get out your keys and drop them inside the cell, or I'll cut your head off!"

The agonized keeper hesitated and obeyed. Logan got the keys, reached his hand through the bars, unlocked the cell, took two revolvers from his guard, and tied the hapless man to the cell door with the wire, loosening it only slightly so that the victim might not choke to death.

Logan put one revolver into his pocket and held the other ready for action. He took up a medicine bottle, put on the guard's hat, and walked to the outer door, where Warden Bell was on guard. This was a heavy, solid door, with a peephole in the upper panel, which the outside guard must open before he could unlock. Logan tapped, and Bell opened. He saw an arm extending the medicine bottle toward him and pulled the little trap of the peephole wide open. In that instant Harvey Logan's arm came through holding the revolver.

"Unlock the door quick and not a sound out of you!" Logan commanded. The jailer hesitated.

"I'll—give you three! One—two———"

The jailer could see the hammer of the revolver rising under the pressure of the bandit's thumb. He threw up his hands in token of surrender, picked up the key ring, unlocked the door, and let Logan out.

The sheriff's residence was attached to the jail, as it is in many communities. And there was also a stable in the rear, where Sheriff Fox kept a good riding mare, used for his excursions about the county. Logan knew the lay of the prison and the presence of the mare.

"Take me back to the stable," he ordered. "Go easy, and make no fuss. If anybody tries to stop us you're a dead man!"

The jailer led Logan back through the jail, out into the yard, which was empty at the lunch hour, and across to the stable. There he saddled the sheriff's mare and unlocked the door. Logan tied him up in one of the stalls, mounted the horse, and rode out through the open door with a taunt for his unhappy warder.

Within half an hour both the bound guards had been found and the alarm given. It was, however, fully an hour before the first posse could be organized, and it was not until late in the afternoon that a second and larger body of officers and citizens could be mounted, armed, and put on the road. Logan had a start, was a wonderful rider, and an eluder of posses without a peer.

Late at night the first posse came back from the chase without having picked up the trail of the fugitive, and in the first hours of the dawn the second outfit came straggling in, saddle-weary, thirsty, and hungry. The horses were ridden stale, but no one had seen Logan. Wild rumors of his flying passage at this point and that, all contradicting one another, came in to the police. But constant hard riding and the use of the telegraph were alike unrewarded. Toward noon of the following day the sheriff's mare, jaded, lame, and minus her saddle, came limping up to the door of the jail. Logan had abandoned her when she became winded, had thrown his saddle upon another horse found grazing in a field, and had fled for the mountains on this fresh mount.

Logan disappeared and did not resurface until 1904, when three bandits held up a train in Colorado. One man was wounded by the trailing posse, and his companions were forced to leave him behind. Before the posse could get to him, the man put a pistol to his head and pulled the trigger. He was later identified as Harvey Logan.

Eamon de Valera

FRANK KELLY

Eamon de Valera was born in New York City in 1882 and returned to his family's home in Ireland at age 2. He would eventually become one of the most revered men in Irish history. He was elected prime minister of the Republic of Ireland in the 1950s, after devoting most of his life to the cause of a free Ireland.

He spent his first stint in an English prison for participating in a small insurrection against British rule in 1916. He was released in a general amnesty after serving roughly a year. In 1918, British plans for the conscription of Irishmen for service in World War I caused the government to place Ireland under martial law to quell resistance. De Valera was arrested in the resulting turmoil. This time he was housed in Lincoln Prison, where he would stay until his escape in February of 1919.

His method of escape, with the help of Michael Collins and other Irish resistance leaders, was as clever as it gets.

The escape of Eamon de Valera from Lincoln Jail in February, 1919, was an affair of keys. Keys drawn on postcards; keys conveyed by cake. No disguises were used, no tunnel dug. Even the rope ladder, kept handy for emergency, never dangled from the prison walls. Nor did the initiative come from outside as so often happens in jail breaks. It was de Valera's own inspiration, planned by himself. Later on many others came into it.

Lincoln town is old and steep, full of odd and twisty by-ways. Outside the town stood the jail. Here, in this mediaeval city on the East coast of England, Eamon de Valera and other leaders of Sinn Fein had been imprisoned since May, 1918.

It was a stirring time. History was being made outside. World War No. 1 had ended in November, 1918. A General Election followed. In Ireland it resulted in an almost complete swingover to Sinn Fein. It was a Republican landslide. The first Dail Eireann met in Dublin in the following January, and adopted the Declaration of Independence.

But there were only 26 members present at that first meeting of the elected representatives of the people. Thirty-six more were held in various British jails. Others were deported, or "on the run."

The world was in a ferment. The countries of Europe, rising from the ruins of the war, were planning a Peace Conference. Every small nation in the world was getting its case ready—every small nation but Ireland whose leader was behind prison bars.

No wonder de Valera chafed in jail. Were he free he could bring Ireland's case for the first time into international politics. He could go to America, and there raise a national loan. At home, with the people now behind him, he could do so many things. There were so many things this newly-released nation could do.

Of all those things he was thinking day after day in Lincoln Jail. Thinking of the future, and of the immediate present with its constant urge to escape.

One morning his vague thoughts took form. One Sunday morning when he saw the prison chaplain's passkey lying in the sacristy beside the Chapel. Perhaps that key would fit the gate to freedom? But how to get an impression, and how to get a key made from it afterwards?

In a drawer in the sacristy were some wax candle ends thrown aside from the candlesticks. He collected them in an empty tin tobacco box. Then he waited his opportunity.

De Valera usually served Mass, but on the following Sunday he asked another prisoner to take his place. When the sacristy was empty he slipped quietly in. There was the Chaplain's key lying in its usual place. De Valera produced the wax which he had kept warm with the heat of his body. In a few moments he had taken an impression; not only an impression of the surface of the key but of its thickness and length as well.

The next problem was to get the impression out and a copy of the key in. The prisoners could not make a key there. It had to come from Dublin.

A snatch of an old music hall song came into de Valera's head. It went some way like this: "He couldn't get the latchkey in, he couldn't." The tag ran through his mind. It haunted him. Somewhere in that comic song lay the solution. But where? What did it suggest? He examined the matter in his mind. A drunken reveller coming home late at night, too unsteady in the hand to fit the latchkey of his home into the keyhole. That was it! He got the idea.

Sean Milroy, one of the prisoners, was a great hand at drawing comic sketches with pen and ink. So he got him to draw two postcards, sketches of a fellow prisoner, Sean McGarry. Sean was depicted in the first sketch with a key in his hand trying to open the door of his house. Underneath was written: *"Christmas, 1917—he can't get in."* In the second sketch McGarry was sitting disconsolate in a prison cell. He was staring at a large keyhole and the caption was: *"Christmas, 1918—he can't get out."*

The idea behind the sketches was clever. The key and the keyhole were full size. Everything else in the sketches was diminished. There was the plan.

The postcard was brought out by a warder who was quite unconscious of its importance. After many vicissitudes it was posted to Sean McGarry's wife in Dublin.

While this comic postcard, showing the good spirits of the Lincoln prisoners, was going the rounds of their friends in Dublin let us go back a little while in time.

Two of the men who escaped the May round-up were Michael Collins and Harry Boland. Since that month they had been on the run, but working like mad as the brunt of leadership and organisation had fallen upon them. It was a vital time at home. Suppression alternated with organisation, a tense and exciting time.

Collins and Boland had hourly expected the release of the prisoners following the end of the war. They thought, however, that the British would grudge them a glorious jail delivery, a mass return home with bands and banners and all the enthusiasm of a national welcome. More likely the British technique would be to release the men one by one from this or that jail, without notice.

This is where I came in. I was working at the old Sinn Fein Headquarters at 6 Harcourt Street, Dublin, at the time. Collins and Boland decided to have someone stationed in Lincoln to watch the jail closely and send word of de Valera's sudden release. My advance message would give them time to organise a mass welcome.

So I went to Lincoln City, took up my quarters at a hotel and haunted the jail gates from dawn till dark.

But the jail gates did not open. Two weeks passed and nothing happened. I got in touch with Collins for further instructions. The answer was the sudden appearance of Collins and Boland themselves.

There had been a change of plans. It now looked as if the British had no intention of releasing the prisoners until after the Peace Conference. This was alarming news. De Valera was urgently needed. The only thing was to get him out.

For back in Dublin Sean Milroy's comic postcard had found its mark at last. It had been going the rounds for weeks before somebody saw the point. I think it was Collins who spotted it first.

It was now clear to those outside that a jail escape was being planned by the prisoners themselves. But more must be known about it. We must try and get in touch with them. My orders were to stay in Lincoln and do this while Collins and Boland returned to Dublin to get their end ready.

Instead of watching the jail now I followed the prison warders around the town. I picked them up, talked to them in pubs, drank with them. I had to be careful, deadly careful, for a false move, a word, might ruin everything.

At last I decided on a more direct approach. I called on the prison chaplain and asked him to take a message in to John O'Mahony, who was a great friend of mine. The message was innocently worded, but I hoped that John would bite. John replied, but he did not bite.

Then a significant letter arrived in Dublin from Lincoln Jail. It had been smuggled out by a friendly official who used to carry small but harmless messages. This time he carried dynamite, though he did not know it. The letter was from John O'Mahony to a friend in Leeds. It was written in three languages, Irish, English and Latin. The Latin part asked that the enclosure be sent to Mrs. Sean McGarry. In English, it demanded a bottle of wine for John. The kernel was in the Irish. It explained the postcard and asked for a key. Details of the proposed escape were given.

But in the meantime the key had been made in Dublin. Mrs. McGarry had put it into a cake she had baked. And over to Lincoln travelled Fintan Murphy, a H.Q. staff man, with the key in the cake.

Fintan had a bad moment at the jail gate. For he had to sit in the waiting room while the warder prodded the cake with a long knife, the while remarking on the good food the so-and-so Sinn Feiners were getting while men doing their bit for 'King and Country' had to eat war bread. With all this talk, he missed the key. Had he spotted it then the whole game was up.

This first key was tried out by Sean McGarry on a cell door, but it broke in the lock. They dare not leave it there. So they prised it out hurriedly with wire before a warder came along.

Again a key was made, another cake was baked. I brought it to the jail gate.

At this point Collins and Boland arrived in Lincoln again. Another letter went in by the prison chaplain. It bore a code in Irish interspersed with English words. Back comes a letter from the prisoners asking for files and keys, blank keys this time.

So a third cake was baked. It was Mrs. O'Sullivan, housekeeper to Liam MacMahon of Manchester, who made it, and an Irish girl working in England who took it to the gate.

This cake held more hardware than raisins. Its weight was terrific. Instead of almond icing there was a thin coating of plaster of Paris to keep the cake from breaking. Why they didn't spot the fictitious nature of the cake was a miracle. Maybe they were tired of seeing cakes by that time. Anyway, many an Irish prayer went into those Lincoln cakes.

It was third time lucky. With the files and blank it contained Peadar de Loughrey, another prisoner, cut a perfect master key. He actually took the lock off a disused cell door with no other instrument than a little typewriter screw driver belonging to de Valera.

And so, many anxious weeks after the despatch of the postcard, a night was fixed for the escape. Now, we were to be up against the worst of it. Although the war was over, wartime conditions still prevailed in England. Lincoln was an armed camp. It was an R.A.F. base. Opposite the back wall of the prison, near the gate marked as the escaping gate, was a large emergency hospital for troops. Military traffic on it was unceasing. Every night the wounded Tommies would drift back to hospital. They'd linger outside for hours with their girls before they went in.

Now that the plan was ready the whole of Dublin Headquarters staff came on the job. Collins' genius for brilliant organisation came into full play. Every man was allotted his post and job. Every possible contingency was provided for. The whole lie of the land was mapped, roads drawn, distances and vital points marked.

The night of February 3rd, just before lock-up was the time chosen. All along the route of escape the Irishmen were at their posts. It was after dark when Collins and Boland arrived at the jail. Down in the town standing by with a taxi was Paddy O'Donoghue, then of Manchester.

Collins and Boland had guns. My weapon was a combined dagger and knuckle-duster, a nasty-looking thing. The final get-away might end in a fight. Among our equipment was a coiled rope ladder which made an enormous parcel, heavier than any of the Lincoln cakes. This was to be the last resort.

The back of the jail faced the Wraggly Road with fields in between. This was the road I mentioned which was crowded with military traffic.

Collins and Boland took the ladder and went towards the jail wall, while I scoured the Wraggly Road.

On the stroke of the appointed hour Collins and Boland flashed their torch upwards from the dark fields outside. From a high jail window a sudden light flashed in answer. This light, by the way, was made by a number of matches lit together which de Valera, who was watching from the window, himself ignited.

Down the long dim prison corridors de Valera hurried with the two men he had asked to escape with him, Sean Milroy and Sean McGarry. Like shadows across the grass sped Collins and Boland to meet them. Now Collins reaches their first objective, the lock in the postern gate of the back wall. He thrusts his duplicate key into it and turns it. But the key will not turn. It sticks. He tries again and to his horror the slight pressure snaps it. Both men stood in unspeakable dismay, Collins with the handle of the broken key in his hand.

Inside, the escaping prisoners were having better luck. De Valera's master key had already brought them safely through three inner doors each of which was opened and locked again with great precision. They had escaped from their own wing, and passed through its door; they had crossed a courtyard and then had to enter a second building. Out of this building they made their way and across the last yard which led to the jail wall. Here there was an inner door. Once more the master key did its work and it, too, swung open. But not to freedom, for there, between the prisoners and their rescuers, stood the last door of all, an iron-covered gate. And it was in this gate that Collins' key had broken and stuck.

In whispers they conferred through the iron gate. "I've broken the key in the lock, Dev," said Collins, with a sob in his voice. It was a terrible moment. Breathing a prayer, de Valera inserted his master key into the last lock. Very carefully he put it in, it met the stub of Collins' broken key, it pushed it before it and the lock turned. The outer gate swung open. They were free.

Five shadows now crossed the fields and bore towards the five-barred gate which separated them from the Wraggly Road. The Tommies were drifting back to hospital, lingering with their girls at the gate. There was no way out but through the groups of courting couples. As the five conspirators passed the cheery Harry Boland called out, "Good-night, Chums," as he went by.

Then, still on foot they walked down the steep streets of Lincoln to Paddy O'Donoghue and the first waiting taxi. Here they scattered, the escapers going off in the taxi, while Collins and Boland went for a train.

The rest of the de Valera escape was timing and organisation. The rest of the story belongs to Mr. O'Donoghue who took them on the first stage to

Worksop; and to Mr. Fintan Murphy, who put them on the road to Sheffield and to Mr. Liam MacMahon, who did the rest. It was much more difficult than it seems. There were heavy wartime restrictions on petrol and on the use of taxis. The late Neil Kerr, that trusty veteran, had charge of the Liverpool end.

In Liverpool, Collins' underground transport organisation was running to perfection. From Liverpool smuggling was easy. So three weeks after the Lincoln Jail break de Valera came home by that port. But not to public acclamation. His new position of escaped prisoner prevented that. But public welcomes were no longer necessary. His amazing prison coup had already set all Ireland aflame.

Georgia Chain Gang Fugitive

ROBERT E. BURNS

The chain gang is one of the classic images of Southern prison life in the early 1900s. Robert Burns was one of the first to escape and write about the brutal treatment inherent in this system. Born to a respected family, Burns served in World War I and came home traumatized by what he had seen. He wandered aimlessly in search of a job and a new start. In Georgia, he was tricked by two men into helping with a holdup that netted all of $5.80. They were caught 20 minutes later, and Burns was sentenced to six to ten years of hard labor on the chain gang.

Upon his arrival at a work camp, a heavy steel shackle was riveted on each ankle, and a heavy chain was permanently fixed to connect the shackles. With just thirteen links in the chain, it was impossible to take more than half a step. In the middle of this chain, another chain was fixed. This chain was 3 feet long and ended in a large iron ring. In order to walk, this chain had to be held off the ground. These chains weighed roughly 20 pounds and were never removed.

Beatings, poor food, and long, hard hours of work in heavy chains sucked the life out of most prisoners, and Burns quickly saw that if he didn't get out soon, he never would. Here is the story of how he made his first escape.

I was exhausted mentally, physically, and spiritually, and soon fell asleep. I thought I had been asleep about five minutes when I was awakened at 3:30 by the building chain being pulled through my ring.

Each day was an exact duplicate of the one preceding it. Only some nights more of us or fewer "got the leather," as it was called.

The dirty filthy "stripes" would stick to the wounds on the buttocks and cause inflammation and torture.

And that is what a chain gang is for, torture! Torture every day. Any idea of reformation, any idea of trying to innoculate ideas of decency, manners, or good and right thinking in the convict, is prohibited. All the convicts get is abuse, curses, punishment, and filth. In a few weeks all are reduced to the same level, just animals, and treated worse than animals.

I did not wash my hands and face, or comb my hair or change my clothes until Saturday, when we got a bath. A piece of borax soap about as large as a package of chewing gum was given to each convict to bathe with, and a clean suit of "stripes."

I traded a square plug of chewing tobacco for a shave. Tobacco is rationed twice a week—a plug of chewing on Wednesdays and smoking tobacco on Saturdays.

Personal hygiene or cleanliness was impossible. Cleaning your teeth was out of the question entirely, except on Saturdays or Sundays.

Sunday we were all locked in the building; but we were allowed to rest until about eight o'clock. This rest on Sunday morning was the only comfort one could find on the chain gang. Less than twenty per cent of the prisoners could read, so reading matter was scarce, and time to read scarcer, it being limited to Saturday evenings and Sundays.

So much for the Fulton County chain gang as it was then in 1922. What it's like now, I don't know. I take my oath that I have described it exactly—but mere words can never convey the true conditions as they were, the utter hopelessness and torture the convict suffers.

I have been in three different chain gangs (140 counties of the 161 counties in Georgia have them). State convicts are leased to these counties for their board and keep, with the County Warden in absolute command. Conditions are almost identical on all, as I found out later.

So many prisoners died from the beatings they received that Governor Walker of Georgia was obliged to abolish the leather in 1923 to still the national agitation against this medieval brutality.

The chain gang is simply a vicious, medieval custom, inherited from the blackbirders and slave traders of the seventeenth and eighteenth centuries, and is so archaic and barbarous as to be a national disgrace.

There was a saying on the chain gang, and it ran as follows:

"Work out"—meaning make your time.

"Pay out"—meaning purchase a pardon or parole.

"Die out"—meaning to die—or

"Run out"—meaning to escape.

I pondered on these four means of release. I had been a soldier and suffered torture and taken chances with my life for my country. Such studied torture as this, however, was too much for me. Death would have been a welcome relief. And so I pondered more and more each day. "Work out" was out of the question. Six years of this and I would return to society a worthless, defeated creature, unhuman and inhumane. "Pay out." By listening to the conversation of the native Georgians and old-timers, I found that $2,000 was the average price with which to "pay out" or buy freedom. And even then the convict must first serve a year. My parents had no $2,000 and I'd be free or dead in less than a year. That I knew only too well.

Not that I wanted to cheat justice. I leave that to the reader. If I had been sentenced to one year—which under the conditions of the chain gang and the extenuating circumstances of my crime, would have been plenty—I would have tried to make it. But six years—that was plain vengeance and also complete destruction.

"Well," thought I—"Die out."

I'll "Die out" trying to "run out." That was the definite conclusion I finally came to after two weeks at Fulton County.

I had heard from other convicts that in the smaller counties they had fewer prisoners and perhaps more opportunities of escape.

Promptly the following Sunday I wrote a letter to the Prison Commissioners. This Commission is similar to the parole board of other states. In Georgia the Prison Commissioners function as a parole board and also as a supervisory force over the one hundred forty-odd County Wardens of the chain gangs. The Commission consists of three members. In my letter to them I asked for a transfer to some other county gang.

Two weeks later I was transferred with eleven other convicts to Campbell County chain gang. Prior to our arrival at this camp, the County Warden, Sam Parkins, would only accept "niggers" and there had been no white convicts there for several years.

Conditions here were almost the same as at Fulton County, with these exceptions: Our sleeping quarters were worse. Twelve men slept in a "pie wagon" (a steel-barred wagon on wheels, four tiers of three bunks each) and we barely had room to turn around. The mess hall was simply a shed built inside a barbed wire stockade, and there was no wash-room at all. We washed in the open from a bucket.

The nightly whippings took place in the yard—the convict being laid on a semi-circular piece of corrugated iron.

The "pie-wagon" and bedding were lousy, full of vermin, and were old and decayed and had a foul odor.

We did not work on a squad chain as at Fulton County, as here we worked on the roads and were spread out a little more. We also worked with the Negroes.

Here, then, was a chance to run, if you could run with twenty pounds of chain or if you could remove the chain.

Blood-hounds were taken to the road each day and the guards were increased, two guards to each twelve convicts. For six weeks I racked my brain for a method of removing those chains. Two others of the twelve convicts in my group were also willing to take desperate measures to escape. One tried cutting the steel rivets in his shackles with an improvised saw made from a safety razor blade.

But as our chains and shackles were thoroughly examined once a day, he was discovered and received several terrific beatings. Besides, at night, we were so fatigued and exhausted that it was impossible to use any skill or strength for such delicate tasks.

At night, as we filed in through the entrance to the mess hall, blacks on one side, whites on the other, came a voice:

"Come by me—I want to smell you. Come by me—I want to smell you."

Meaning that the speaker wanted to smell the perspiration on each convict so as to be sure the convicts had "put out" a day of strenuous and fatiguing toil. If he didn't smell you, you got the leather.

From a thorough study of conditions I had also arrived at this conclusion: Any escape would have to be made on a Monday morning, for that would be the only time in the week that one would have the strength to hope for success. The rest on Sunday would refresh and quicken the brain—but by Tuesday morning this would vanish, and for the balance of the week the convict would go through his daily labors in almost a semi-conscious state—so great was the exhaustion and fatigue from the heat and long hours of toil.

That was the first fact I planted in my brain—*Monday morning when I was fresh*—some Monday morning—when? But Monday morning it must be! No other time would I try.

The next problem was the chains. How to get these off—when and where I wanted them off. Finally this idea struck me. The shackles around my ankles were circular in shape. I knew if they could be bent into an elliptical shape, that perhaps I could slip them over my heel, after removing my shoes. But how to bend them? That was a difficulty, for they were made of steel as thick as a man's finger.

Day in and day out—every conscious moment I studied, planned and discarded, planned anew, discarded again—plans—plans—but all seemed idle dreams. And thousands of convicts the whole world over are all dreaming the same dream: a successful escape from the tortures and obsolete treatment modern society deals out to its weaker element.

One day I noticed a certain Negro in my group swing a twelve-pound sledge hammer. He had been in the gang so long and had used a sledge so much that he had become an expert. Claimed he could hit a pin on the head with his eyes closed.

Suddenly, like a flash, an idea came to me. I might try to get that Negro to hit my shackles and bend them into an elliptical shape. If I could put my leg against something to take up the shock and hold the shackle against it. I determined to think this over.

Of course, if I were discovered, many brutal beatings were in store for me.

A week later we were tearing up an old railroad, ties, rails and all. And there was my answer—I could place my foot against the end of a railroad tie that was still embedded in the road ballast. This would give the support needed. The Negro could hit the shackle and perhaps it would bend. If he missed the shackle, it would mean perhaps the loss of a foot. Not pleasant thoughts, but life-or-death problems call for both daring and courage.

I maneuvered things so that I worked near this Negro at all times, waiting for a chance to speak to him.

One day in June, when the heat was terrific and the guards were half asleep from the humidity, I spoke to this nigger.

"Sam," I said. "Would you do me a favor?"

"Boss, if I can, I sho' will," he replies.

"Sam, I got six years; that's a long time, and I'm going to try to 'hang it on the limb,' and I need a little help. Will you help me?" I asked.

"Boss, it sho' is pretty rough, and I ain't much for hunting trouble, but if I's can help you, I sho' will," he answered.

"Well, Sam, here's the idea—if I put my leg against this tie—do you think you could hit my shackle hard enough to bend it and still not break my ankle?" I asked.

"Boss, if you can keep the shackle from turning, I can hit it right plump," he answered.

I looked up at the two guards; all was quiet and serene. I put my right foot against the tie—by spreading my legs the connecting chain became taut—one side of the shackle against the tie. I looked at Sam. He grinned. I looked at the guards. All was as it should be. I took a deep breath, closed my eyes, and said to

Sam, "Shoot, Sam." Sam shot. Bang went the sledge; I felt a sharp quick pain in my shins. One side of the shackle was embedded in the end of the tie. I looked at the shackle, but couldn't see much difference in the shape. Another look at the guards. All was well. "Again, Sam," I whispered. Another bull's-eye by Sam. "Again, Sam," I said. And again the sledge fell right on the shackle. Then the left foot. Three solid whacks of the sledge on the left shackle.

"Thanks, Sam," I said. "If they won't come off now we'll try again."

Night could not come quick enough. Would the shackles come off? Would the guard discover the change from circular to elliptical, when examining the chains when we returned for the night?

The day was over at last, supper finished and we were lined up single file in front of the "pie wagon," to be searched and our chains inspected. My heart was beating hard and fast. My turn came, I was searched, the chains were examined, I counted off and passed on. What a relief!

Ten minutes later, lying on my bunk, I tried to pass the shackle over my heel. What a thrill! *It would come off!* A little tight, but it would come off. Wet it with a little saliva and it would come off. This was Wednesday night. Monday was the day! Four days to lay my plans—four days till Monday. Monday was my day!

I had four dollars and twenty cents. The rules of the chain gang permitted the prisoners to receive money. All mail was opened by the Warden, he was the censor and the banker. If the family or friends of the convicts sent them any money the Warden would allow them as much as $2.00 per week of the funds sent. My family was sending me $2.00 each week. This $4.20 was saved by me from that allowance. Perhaps by Saturday or Sunday I would have a letter with $2.00 more. That would be $6.20. Sunday morning the Warden handed me a letter and the $2.00 was there. So much the better.

Now for the new difficulties. There were the blood-hounds; three of them, with us all of the time. In discussing means of escape, the native hill-billies fear the dogs. They would say, "You got to get off the ground, or the dogs will get you. You got to get off the ground or you can't make it because the dogs will be upon you in ten minutes. They are trained to howl and bite and betray you. You got to get off the ground." I listened to this but kept my own counsel.

Then there were the clothes to secure. Also, I was a Northerner and my speech would betray me. I didn't know the country. Georgia is a large state, sparsely populated, and a stranger with a Northern accent stands out and can be easily recognized. The guards also carry repeating shotguns and shoot at you too, that much was certain.

The whole thing presented many obstacles that seemed impossible to overcome. Frankly I estimated my chances at one to one hundred. But here again my army training and war experiences came to my rescue. A hundred times I had missed death by a hair over in France—I had seen my buddies die—death ended their troubles. Now they were sleeping peacefully. I'd shake dice with Fate and try to take advantage of every opportunity. Monday I was going—it was to be death, freedom, or capture. No matter how the die was cast, I couldn't have been much worse off than I was then.

Monday morning, June 21, 1922—the longest and hottest day of the year—we left the camp at 4 a.m. Twelve convicts, two guards and three blood-hounds.

Our job that day was tearing up a small wooden bridge over a creek about twelve feet wide. By 10:30 it was all up; only one stringer was still in place. Three convicts, one guard, and myself were on one side of the stream. The other guard, nine convicts and the dogs were on the other. The bridge served as a link in the county road which crossed the creek here. On either side of the road were bushes and shrubbery about four feet high. Back of the road were the hinterlands of Georgia. Pine-covered hills, corn and cotton fields on the flats, bayous and swamps in the lowlands.

When it was necessary for a convict to obey the call of nature while work-ing on the road he sang out to the guard, "Getting out here," and then waited for the guard to answer. The guard would look over both sides of the road, se-lect a particular spot and answer, "All right, get out here," and point to the spot. Not over two to three minutes were allowed, and the guards were then on the alert and watched the convict closely.

My heart was in my mouth, I was nervous and taut, my face was drawn—my voice rang out, "Getting out here." I was startled at the sound of it. My hour had struck. A chilly fear crept up my spine.

"All right, 'Shorty,' get out here, and don't be long," came back the guard's reply.

Laying down my pick, I glanced at the other guard, fifty feet away. Every-thing seemed regular and usual.

I went into the bushes, sat down, took off my shoes, slipped off the chains, put on my shoes, then on my hands and knees, Indian fashion, I started to crawl away. I kept crawling, hidden by the underbrush.

The two minutes were up. The guards called out, "Come on, Shorty, get back to work."

I was supposed to answer, "Yes, sir." If I didn't answer the guard would call for the dogs. If I did answer the guard could tell from the direction of my voice that I had moved from the place he designated. So when he called, "Come on, Shorty," I jumped to my feet and like a flash I broke into a run. The guard was startled, surprised, and I gained a few precious seconds. I ran at top speed, never looking back. Suddenly I heard the crack of the shotgun, *bang!*

Buckshot flew all around. I put on more speed. The cry went up, "Shorty's gone, bring on the dogs." Bang, bang! went the gun; but I was going like the wind and with the last shot I was under cover of the woods.

Never in my life did I run as I did that day. Ten minutes later the dogs were at my heels, howling, barking, and snapping. But instead of being afraid of them I talked to them, I called them and tried to make them think I was playing with them. I kept to the woods and fields using the sun as my guide to point north.

After twenty minutes I broke into a steady gait, the dogs still at my heels. Through bushes, briars, hills, dales, fields, swamps, and small streams I ran. The heat was terrific; I was burning up, and when I came to a stream, I lay in it full length for a second, taking a long drink. Refreshed, I started again, only to be scorched by the heat once more.

How light my feet and legs felt! For the first time in twelve weeks I was not carrying a twenty-pound chain.

All morning I kept going, never stopping but to drink for a second or two when I struck water. I was tired, exhausted, ready to quit, but this was not a race, this was life or death! Somehow I called on tired muscles, heaving lungs, a pumping heart, and they answered my agonized plea, and responded when I thought tey were through. What a race I ran that day.

It was about 5 P.M. and I was still going strong, through fields, woods, and swamps, and the dogs still with me, barking, howling, but apparently enjoying it immensely, for by this time they were my friends.

I came through a wood to a small clearing occupied by a Negro shanty. There were clothes hanging on a line. A Negro woman was bending over a wash-tub beside the shanty. I needed clothes. I ran up to the line, grabbed a pair of overalls and a man's shirt, and kept right on going, still heading North. Entering another small patch of woods I changed clothes. The overalls were much too large, and so was the shirt.

At about six o'clock, I struck a railroad trestle over a small river. I was so hot and so exhausted, having been on the run since morning, that this river looked like Paradise.

I couldn't resist the temptation of a cool plunge. Crossing the trestle to the center I jumped in, feet first, and started swimming slowly downstream. The dogs were dismayed by this turn of affairs, but followed along the bank. I stayed in the water about half an hour, still swimming downstream. By this time the dogs were quiet. They were somewhere back along the bank.

Crawling out of the river on the opposite side from which I had left the dogs, I started walking North again. Walking was quite a relief from running, and it gave me time to think. I was refreshed physically now from my great exertion, but it was still unbearably hot. So hot, in fact, that in ten minutes my clothes were practically dry.

Unexpectedly at about seven o'clock I came to a paved highway. Paved highways are rare in Georgia, so I knew this must be leading me to some large city. Considerable automobile traffic was flowing both ways. Seeing this I made an instant decision. I'd go out on this highway, flag some auto, and get a ride going in any direction. The direction wouldn't make any difference, I had to keep moving and get as far away from the camp as possible. To think was to act. I was on the road. A young man in a Ford coupé stopped to pick me up. On the door of the car, in small letters were the words "Standard Oil Company."

I got in. In order to sit down I had to pick up a large basket of peaches which was on the seat beside him, and hold the basket in my lap. The peaches looked so inviting, and I must have looked at them so longingly, that he said to me, "Eat a couple of them if you want."

"Thanks," I answered.

As I started to eat a peach, I wondered where he was going, and, afraid he'd ask me where I was going, I quickly framed the following question: "How far are you going?"

"Atlanta," he answered.

"Fine," I came back. "If you have no objections I'll thank you if I can go all the way with you."

"Sure," he answered. "But it isn't far, only about nine miles."

Nine miles! I must have covered about twenty-seven miles in my cross-country run.

As I ate the peach, speculating on what I'd do in Atlanta, two autos full of police, shotguns sticking out of the sides, whizzed by, going in the opposite direction. I recognized Chief Beavers himself in the first car with all his gold braid.

"I wonder who they're after," my friend said.

"Moonshiners," I answered, with my heart in my mouth.

Before I knew it we were in Atlanta. It was almost eight o'clock. We passed a General Clothing store. The sign read, "I. Cohen & Son." The store was still open. I got out at the next corner, and went into the store.

I bought a suit of overalls, pants, and a jumper that fit, and a fifty-cent cotton shirt, and changed clothes in the store. This set me back $2.50. I still had $3.70 left. Not much to get away on.

I went into a barber shop to get a shave. While I was being shaved a police-man came in. He was a regular customer and knew the barbers. After hanging up his coat and hat he said, "A New York gunman escaped from the Campbell County gang this morning. There are several posses out after him and I guess they'll get him!"

I couldn't see the speaker as I lay flat on my back, my face full of soap lather. A nervous tremor ran through my body, beads of perspiration started to roll down me, but I just sat tight.

The barber asked, "What does he look like?"

And the cop answered, "About thirty years old and a short stocky man, as near as I can find out. We have orders out to watch all railroads, bus stations, and exits from the city. They think he is heading toward Atlanta."

And there I sat in the chair, staring at the ceiling. Fear clutched every nerve and muscle. If I attracted suspicion I was done for. The barber finished and I got out of the chair. My legs were trembling and I was a nervous wreck. Without speaking I handed the barber a half dollar. He gave me thirty-five cents change. I took it and tried to walk as casually as possible to my jumper and black "gin house Stetson" cotton hat, hanging on the clothes rack. That hat was a prison hat, almost new, but it looked the same as any black felt hat. Would the copper notice this? If he had asked me any question I think I would have collapsed. How I got out of that barber shop without creating any suspicion I don't know. I was in a daze when I reached the street. I kept turning corners zig-zag fashion, and did not even breathe freely until I got about five blocks away.

Burns fled to Chicago by train. After years of hard work, he married and started his own magazine and became one of the city's leading citizens. But his marriage was one of coercion and convenience and when he fell in love with another woman and sought a divorce, his wife contacted the police and revealed his secret. He probably could have fought extradition back to Geor-gia and won, as he had been an upstanding citizen in Chicago for seven years, but he elected to go back and face the court in Georgia on the promise that he would be quickly pardoned and released to resume his life.

The state of Georgia, however, had other ideas. Burns was again sen-tenced to the chain gain while waiting for a pardon that never came. After a year and a half, he made another bold escape and continued to live on the run. The book about his experiences, *I Am a Fugitive from a Georgia Chain Gang*, was written while he was still in hiding.

Papillon

HENRI CHARRIERE

Henri Charriere, nicknamed Papillon, was part of the French underworld in Paris in the late 1920s. At the age of 25, he was convicted of murdering another criminal—a charge he denied his entire life—and sentenced to life imprisonment at the famous French penal colony in Guiana in South America. It was nearly impossible to escape from this brutal, isolated existence, and even if a prisoner broke away there was virtually nowhere to go. Neighboring countries either returned prisoners or used them as prison labor in their own countries before eventually turning them over. The surrounding jungle was impenetrable so almost all escape attempts focused on the sea.

Papillon made two spectacular sea escapes and tried to escape countless other times during his fourteen years of imprisonment. His amazing adventures were chronicled in *Papillon*, first published in 1969, which quickly sold more than a million copies in France and became a movie starring Steve McQueen and Dustin Hoffman. Critics questioned the veracity of some of the claims he made in his memoir, but there is no doubt that his life included incredible suffering and drama.

In his first escape, Papillon manages to get himself sent to the prison hospital upon his arrival in Guiana. With two companions, he plots a quick escape. After making arrangements with a local man, Jésus, to have a boat waiting, Papillon and Clousiot ambush an Arab guard who has been lured into a late-night tryst with their friend Maturette.

At eight in the evening Maturette said to the Arab, "Come after midnight. That way we can be together longer."

The Arab said he would. On the stroke of midnight we were ready. The Arab came in at quarter past twelve, went straight to

Maturette's bed, pulled his feet and continued toward the toilets. Maturette followed him. I yanked the leg off my bed; it made a noise as it fell. Clousiot's made no sound. I was to stand behind the door and Clousiot was to walk up to the Arab to attract his attention. After a twenty-minute wait everything went very fast. The Arab came out of the toilets and, surprised at seeing Clousiot, said:

"What are you doing in the middle of the room at this hour of the night? Get back into bed."

Then I whacked him on the head and he fell without a sound. Quickly I put on his clothes and shoes. We dragged him under the bed and, just before we pushed him completely under, I gave him another crack on the back of the neck. Now he was really out.

Not one of the men in the room budged. I went straight to the door, followed by Clousiot and Maturette, who were both in their smocks. I knocked, the guard opened up, and I swung my iron leg, whack! right on his head. The other guard facing us dropped his carbine; he must have been asleep. Before he could react, I smacked him. None of mine made a sound; Clousiot's said "Ah!" before collapsing on the floor. My two guards were still on their chairs, the third was stretched out stiff. We held our breaths. To us, that "Ah!" had been heard by the entire world. It was certainly loud enough, yet no one moved. We left them where they lay and took off with their three carbines, Clousiot first, the kid in the middle and me last. We ran down the dimly lit stairs. Clousiot had left his bed leg behind; I kept mine in my left hand, the rifle in my right. Downstairs, nothing. Around us the night was as dark as ink. We had to look hard to find the wall next to the river. We went as fast as we could. Once at the wall, I made a footrest with my hands. Clousiot climbed up, straddled the wall, pulled Maturette up, then me. We slid down the other side. Clousiot fell into a hole and hurt his foot. Maturette and I made it without trouble. We both got up; we had abandoned the rifles before jumping. But when Clousiot tried to get up, he couldn't. He said he had broken his leg. I left Maturette with Clousiot and ran toward the corner of the wall, feeling along with my hand. It was so dark that I didn't see when I came to the end of the wall, and when my hand kept on going, I fell flat on my face. Down by the river, I heard a voice:

"Is that you?"

"Yes. Jésus?"

"Yes."

He lit a match. I stepped into the water and waded over to him. There were two men.

"You get in first. Who are you?"

"Papillon."

"O.K."

"Jésus, we have to go back up. My friend broke his leg jumping off the wall."

"Then take this paddle and row."

The three paddles dipped into the water and the boat quickly made the hundred yards between us and the place where I thought they were—for we could see nothing. I called, "Clousiot!"

"For Christ's sake, don't talk. L'Enflé, use your lighter." A few sparks flew off; they saw them. Clousiot gave a whistle between his teeth—a Lyon whistle; it makes no noise, but you can hear it clearly, like the hiss of a snake. He kept whistling until we came abreast. L'Enflé got out, picked Clousiot up in his arms and placed him in the boat. Then Maturette climbed in and finally L'Enflé. We were five, and the water came to within two fingers of the gunwales.

"Nobody move without a warning," Jésus said. "Papillon, stop paddling; put your paddle across your knees. Let's go, L'Enflé!"

Helped by the current, the boat plunged into the night. A third of a mile downstream, we passed the penitentiary. We were in the middle of the river and the current was carrying us at an incredible speed. L'Enflé was feathering his paddle. Jésus kept the boat steady, the handle of his paddle tight against his thigh—not paddling, just steering.

Then Jésus said, "Now we can smoke. It went all right, I think. You're sure you didn't kill anybody?"

"I don't think so."

"Goddammit! You double-crossed me, Jésus!" L'Enflé said. "You said it was a simple *cavale*. Now it seems it's a *cavale* of internees."

"That's right, they're internees. I didn't tell you, L'Enflé, because you wouldn't have helped me and I had to have another man. Relax. If we're caught, I'll take all the blame."

"You'd better, Jésus. For the hundred francs you paid me, I don't want to risk my neck if somebody got killed or wounded."

I said, "L'Enflé, I'll make you a present of a thousand francs for the two of you."

"All right then, *mec*. That's fair enough. Thanks. We're dying of hunger in the village. It's worse being liberated than in prison. In prison you at least get food every day, and clothes."

"*Mec*," Jésus asked Clousiot, "does it hurt a lot?"

"Not too bad," Clousiot said. "But how are we going to make it with my leg broken, Papillon?"

"We'll see. Where are we going, Jésus?"

"I'm going to hide you up a creek about twelve miles from the mouth of the river. You stay there eight days until the guards and the man hunters give up looking. You want them to think you went down the Maroni and into the sea on the same night. The man hunters use boats without engines. A fire, talking, coughing could be fatal if they're anywhere near. The guards use motorboats; they're too big to go up the creek—they'd run aground."

The night grew lighter. It was nearly four in the morning when, after a long search, we finally came to the hiding place known only to Jésus. We were literally in the bush. The boat flattened the short brush, but once we had passed over it, it straightened up again, providing a thick protective screen. It would take a sorcerer to know that there was enough water here to float a boat. We entered the creek, then spent over an hour penetrating the brush and separating the branches that barred our passage. Suddenly we found ourselves in a kind of canal and we stopped. The bank was neat and green and the trees huge, their foliage so thick that daylight—it was now six o'clock—couldn't get through. Thousands of beasts we had never heard of lived under this impressive canopy. Jésus said, "This is where you stay for eight days. On the seventh I'll come and bring you supplies." He untangled the thick vegetation and pulled out a tiny dugout six feet long. Inside were two paddles. This was the boat to take him back to Saint-Laurent on the rising tide.

It was now time to do something about Clousiot, who was stretched out on the bank. He was still wearing only his smock, so his legs were bare. With our hatchet we split some dried branches to serve as splints. L'Enflé pulled on his foot and Clousiot broke into a heavy sweat. Suddenly he said, "Stop! It hurts less like that. The bone must be in place." We arranged the splints and tied them with a new hemp rope we found in the boat. The pain eased. Jésus had brought four pairs of pants, four shirts and four wool sweaters originally intended for *relégués*. Maturette and Clousiot put them on; I stayed in the Arab's clothes. We drank some rum. It was the second bottle since our departure. It warmed us. Mosquitoes attacked without mercy, forcing us to sacrifice a packet of tobacco. We put it to soak in a water bottle and spread the nicotine juice on our faces, hands and feet. The wool sweaters kept us warm in the penetrating damp.

L'Enflé said, "We're off. What about the thousand francs you promised?" I went off for a moment and returned with a brand new thousand-franc bill.

"So long. Don't move from here for eight days," Jésus said. "We'll be back on the seventh. On the eighth you go out to sea. While you're waiting, make your sail, your jib, and get the boat ready. Put everything in its place, fix the pins in the rudder and mount it on the rear. If we haven't come after ten days, we've been arrested. There'll be bloody hell to pay because you attacked those guards."

Then Clousiot told us that he hadn't left his carbine at the base of the wall. He had thrown it over the wall and the river was so near—which he didn't know then—that it must have fallen into the water. Jésus said that was a good thing, for if it weren't found, the man hunters would think we were armed. Now we could relax a little: they were armed only with revolvers and machetes, and if they thought we had a carbine, they wouldn't go out of their way to find us. Well, so long. If we were discovered and had to abandon the boat, we were to follow the creek upstream until we hit dry land. Then, with the compass, we should keep going north. There was a good chance that after two or three days we'd come to the death camp called Charvein. Once there, we'd have to bribe someone to tell Jésus where we were.

The two old cons left. A few minutes later their dugout had disappeared. We could hear nothing, see nothing.

Daylight penetrated the brush in a very peculiar way. It was as if we were in an arcade where the sun reached the top but allowed no rays to filter down. It began to get hot. And there we were, alone: Maturette, Clousiot and me. Our first reflex was to laugh—it had gone like clockwork. The only inconvenience was Clousiot's leg. But he said that with the strips of wood around it he was okay. He would like it if we made some coffee. It was quickly done. We made a fire and each drank a mug of black coffee sweetened with brown sugar. It was delicious. We had spent so much energy since the night before that I didn't have the strength to examine our equipment or inspect the boat. That could come later. We were free, free, free. We had arrived at the *bagne* exactly thirty-seven days before. If the *cavale* succeeded, my life sentence would not have been very long. I said, "Mr. President, how long does hard labor for life last in France?" and I burst out laughing. Maturette, who also had a life sentence, did too. Clousiot said, "Don't crow yet. Colombia is still far away, and this boat doesn't look all that seaworthy to me."

I didn't answer because up to the last minute I had thought this boat was only to bring us to where the real one was. When I discovered that I was wrong, I didn't dare say anything for fear of upsetting my friends. And also, since Jésus seemed to think it was perfectly normal, I didn't want to give the impression that I didn't know the kind of boats normally used for escapes.

We spent the first day talking and getting acquainted with this new unknown, the bush. Monkeys and a small species of squirrel made terrifying somersaults over our heads. A troop of small wild pigs came to drink and bathe in the creek. There must have been at least two thousand of them. They came down to the creek and swam, tearing at the hanging roots. An alligator emerged from God knows where and caught one of them by the foot. The pig started to squeal like a lost soul, and the other pigs attacked the alligator, climbing on top of him and trying to bite him at the corners of his enormous mouth. With each whack of his tail the alligator sent a pig flying. One of them was killed and floated on the surface with its belly in the air. His companions immediately set to eating him. The creek was full of blood. The spectacle lasted twenty minutes, until the alligator took off through the water. We never saw him again.

We slept soundly and in the morning made some coffee. I took off my sweater and washed with a big cake of Marseilles soap I found in the boat. Maturette gave me a rough shave with my lancet, then shaved Clousiot. Maturette himself had no beard. When I picked up my sweater to put it back on, an enormous violet-black spider fell from it. It was covered with very long hair which had tiny platinum-like balls at the ends. It must have weighed at least a pound; I crushed it in disgust.

We emptied everything out of the boat, including the barrel of water. The water was purple; Jésus must have put too much permanganate in it to keep it from going bad. We found matches and a striking pad in tightly closed bottles. The compass was no better than a child's; it showed only north, south, east and west, with nothing in between. Since the mast was only two and a half yards high, we sewed the flour sacks into a trapeze shape with a rope around the edges for reinforcement. I made a small jib shaped like an isosceles triangle. It would help to keep us pointed into the wind.

When we were ready to mount the mast, I saw that the bottom of the boat wasn't solid: the hole for the mast was completely eaten away. When I inserted the screws for the pin that was to support the rudder, they went right through—the wood was like butter. The boat was rotten. That son of a bitch, Jésus, was sending us to our death. Reluctantly I asked the others to take a look; I had no right to hide it from them. What should we do? When Jésus returned, we'd make him find us a better boat. We would disarm him; then I, armed with the knife and the hatchet, would go with him to the village to find another boat. It was taking a big risk, but it wasn't as bad as putting to sea in this coffin. At least we had enough food: a large bottle of oil and boxes of flour and tapioca. With that we could go a long way.

This morning we watched a strange spectacle: a band of gray-faced monkeys staged a battle with some hairy black-faced monkeys. While the fight was raging, Maturette was hit on the head with a piece of branch and got a bump as big as a nut.

We had now been here five days and four nights. Tonight it rained in torrents. We made a shelter of wild banana leaves. The water rolled right off their varnished surface and we stayed dry except for our feet. This morning, as I drank my coffee, I thought about Jésus and what a crook he was. To take advantage of our innocence by giving us this punky boat! For five hundred or a thousand francs, he would send three men to certain death. I wondered if, after I'd made him give us another boat, I shouldn't kill him.

The cry of jays startled our small world—such sharp, bloodcurdling cries that I told Maturette to take the machete and find out what was going on. He returned after five minutes and beckoned me to follow. We came to a place about a hundred and fifty yards away, and there, suspended in the air, was an extraordinary pheasant or waterfowl twice as big as a large rooster. It was caught in a lasso and hung by its claws from a branch. With one whack of the machete I cut its neck to stop the ghastly noise. I felt its weight and guessed it to be at least fourteen pounds. We decided to eat it, but then it occurred to us that the snare had been put there by somebody and there might be more than one of him. We went to see and found a curious thing: a barrier twelve inches high made of leaves and creepers woven together, about thirty feet from the creek and running parallel to it. Here and there was a door, and at the door, camouflaged by twigs, a lasso made of brass thread, attached at the other end to the branch of a bush bent double. I figured that the animal would run into the barrier, then walk along it, looking for an opening. When he found the door, he'd start through, but his claw would catch in the thread which would spring the branch back. The animal would then hang in the air until the owner of the traps came to get it.

This discovery was very disturbing. The barrier looked well maintained and quite new; we were in danger of being discovered. We should make no fires during the day, only at night when the hunter would surely not be attending his traps. We decided to mount a guard to watch them. We had the boat under some branches and secreted our provisions in the brush.

I was on duty the next day at ten. We had eaten the pheasant, or whatever it was, the night before. The bouillon had tasted marvelous and the meat, even though boiled, was delicious. We each ate two bowlfuls. So there I was, supposed to be on watch, but I became fascinated by some very large black tapioca ants, each one carrying a large piece of leaf to an enormous anthill. The ants were over a quarter of an inch long and stood very high on their legs. I followed them to the plant they were defoliating and I saw a vast organization at work. First there were the cutters, who did nothing but cut up the pieces. With great speed they sheared through the enormous leaves, which were similar to those of a banana tree, cut them with amazing dexterity into pieces of the exact same size, then let them fall to earth. Below them was a line of ants of the same general species but a little different. They had a gray line running down the sides of their jaws. Those ants formed a semicircle and observed the carriers. The carriers approached in a line from the right, then headed left toward the anthill. First they loaded up, then they got in line, but from time to time, in their hurry to claim their burden and get back into line, there was a traffic jam. This brought on the police ants, who shoved the worker ants into their proper places. It wasn't clear to me what grave error one of the worker ants had committed, but it was pulled from the ranks and two police ants took over, one cutting off its head, the other slicing its body in two at the waist. The police then stopped two worker ants, who dropped their bits of leaf and made a hole with their feet. Then the ant's three sections—head, chest and the rest—were buried and covered with earth.

I was so absorbed in watching this small world and waiting to see whether the police carried their surveillance as far as the anthill that I was completely taken by surprise when I heard a voice say:

"Don't move or you're dead. Turn around."

There stood a man naked from the waist up, wearing khaki shorts and red leather boots, and carrying a double-barreled shotgun. He was bald, sunburned, of medium height, thickset, and his eyes and nose were masked by a bright blue tattoo. A cockroach was tattooed in the middle of his forehead.

"Are you armed?"

"No."

"Are you alone?"

"No."

"How many are you?"

"Three."

"Take me to your friends."

"I can't, because one of them has a carbine and I don't want you killed before I know your intentions."

"Ah! Then don't move and talk quietly. Are you the three who escaped from the hospital?"

"Yes."

"Which one is Papillon?"

"I am."

"Well, your escape sure caused a revolution in the village! Half the *libérés* are under arrest at the police station." He came nearer and, pointing the barrel of the gun to the ground, held out his hand. "I'm the Masked Breton," he said. "You've heard of me?"

"No. But I can see you don't belong to the manhunt."

"Right. I set traps here to catch *hoccos*. A cat must have finished one off, unless it was you people."

"It was us."

"Want some coffee?" He took a thermos from a pack on his back, gave me a swallow and drank some himself.

I said, "Come meet my friends."

He followed me and sat down with us. He laughed over the scare I'd given him with the carbine. He said, "I believed you because the manhunt wouldn't go after you when they learned you'd left with a carbine."

He explained that he had been in Guiana for twenty years and liberated for five. He was forty-five. Stupidly he had had the mask tattooed on his face, so he had been forced to give up any idea of returning to France. He loved the bush and his whole life centered around it: snake and jaguar skins, collecting butterflies and, most of all, catching *hoccos* alive—the bird we had eaten. He sold them for two hundred to two hundred and fifty francs. I offered to pay him, but he refused indignantly. Then he told us about the *hoccos*: "This wild bird is a cock of the bush. Naturally he's never seen a hen, rooster, or man. So I catch one, take him to the village and sell him to someone who has a chicken coop. They're in great demand. O.K. You don't clip his wings, you don't do anything to him, you just put him in a coop at the end of the day and in the morning, when you open the door, there he is right in front, looking as if he were counting the hens and roosters as they file out. He follows them, and as he pecks along with them, he watches them high, low and in the surrounding brush. He's the best watchdog there is. In the evening he stations himself by the coop door, and how he knows that one or two of the chickens are missing is a mystery, but he knows it and he goes looking for them. And, hen or rooster, he drives them back with sharp pecks of his beak to teach them that it's time to go home. He kills rats, snakes, shrews, spiders, centipedes, and the moment a bird of prey is sighted in the sky, he sends everyone scurrying into the grass while he stares it down. And furthermore, he never runs away."

And we had eaten this remarkable bird as if it were a common rooster.

The Breton told us that Jésus, L'Enflé and about thirty *libérés* were in prison at the police station in Saint-Laurent, where they were being questioned about our escape. The Arab was in a cell, too, under suspicion of being an accomplice. The two blows that put him out had done no damage, but the guards had slight swellings on their heads. "Nobody bothered me because everybody knows I never get involved in *cavales*." He told us that Jésus was a bastard. When I told him about the boat, he asked if he could have a look at it.

When he saw it, he cried out, "He was sending you to your deaths, that son of a bitch! At sea, this tub wouldn't last an hour. The first big wave would break it in two. Whatever you do, don't leave in that thing; it would be suicide."

"So what do we do?"

"You have money?"

"Yes."

"I'll tell you what you do; better still, I'll help you. You certainly deserve it. And I'll do it for nothing because I want to see you and your friends succeed. First, don't go near the village, no matter what. To get a good boat, you'll have to go to the Ile aux Pigeons. About two hundred lepers live on the island. There are no guards there and no healthy person ever goes ashore, not even a doctor. Every morning at eight a boat brings them a twenty-four-hour supply of food. The orderly at the hospital gives a case of medication to their two orderlies—they're lepers too. They alone take care of the islanders. Nobody— no guards, no manhunts, no priests—ever goes to the island. The lepers live in little straw huts they make themselves and they have a common room where they get together. They raise chickens and ducks to supplement their ordinary diet. Officially they can't sell anything off the island, but they have a black-market trade with Saint-Laurent and Saint-Jean and with the Chinese at Al-bina in Dutch Guiana. They're all murderers. They don't often kill each other, but they commit lots of crimes when they're off the island, then they return to take cover. For these expeditions they have a few boats stolen from a neighboring village. The worst offense they can commit is to have a boat. The guards fire on anything they see going or coming from the Ile aux Pigeons. What the lepers do is they sink their boats by filling them with rocks; when they need them again, they dive down, take out the rocks, and the boats float up to the surface. There are all kinds of people on the island, all races, and from every part of France. This boat of yours is good only for the Maroni, and lightly loaded at that! To go out to sea, you'll have to find another, and the best place is the Ile aux Pigeons."

"How do we get there?"

"Like this: I'll go with you up the river until we come in sight of the island. Alone you'd never find it, or you might make a mistake. It's about sixty miles from the mouth of the river, so you'll have to backtrack. It's about twenty miles beyond Saint-Laurent. We'll attach my boat to yours. I'll bring you as close as possible and, after that, I'll get back into my own boat. Then you head for the island."

"Why can't you come to the island with us?"

"Oh, God," the Breton said, "all I needed was to put one foot on the wharf where the Administration boat docks. It was in full daylight, but what I saw was enough. Forgive me, Papi, but I will never set foot on that island again. I wouldn't be able to hide how I felt. I'd do you more harm than good."

"When do we leave?"

"At nightfall."

"What time is it now, Breton?"

"Three o'clock."

"O.K. I'll sleep for a little while."

"No, you don't. You've got to load the boat."

"No, I'm going with the boat empty. Then I'll come back for Clousiot, who'll stay and watch over our things."

"Impossible. You'll never find this place again, not even in broad daylight. And don't ever be on the river during the day. They're still looking for you. The river is still plenty dangerous."

Evening came. He went to find his boat and we attached it to ours. Clousiot sat next to the Breton, who took the tiller. Maturette sat in the middle. I went up front. We had trouble getting out of the creek and by the time we reached the river, night was falling. An enormous reddish-brown sun was ablaze on the horizon across the sea. We could see clearly, twelve miles ahead, the estuary of the majestic river as it threw off pink and silver sequins in its rush to meet the sea.

The Breton said, "The tide is out. In an hour it will begin to rise. We'll use it to go back up the Maroni. That way we'll reach the island with the least effort." Night fell suddenly.

"Push off," said the Breton. "Paddle hard to get into the middle of the river. And no smoking."

The paddles sliced the water and we sped across the current. The Breton and I pulled in rhythm and Maturette did his best. The farther we got into the middle of the river, the more we felt the rising tide push us. We were skimming along fast now. The tide grew stronger and pushed us even faster. Six hours later we were very close to the island and heading straight for it: a black spot, almost in the middle of the river, slightly to the right. "That's it," the Breton said in a low voice. Although it wasn't a very dark night, it would be hard to see us from that distance because of the mist on the water's surface. We came nearer. When the outline of the rocks was clear, the Breton got into his boat, untied it quickly and whispered, "Good luck, boys!"

"Thanks."

"Don't mention it."

With the Breton no longer at the tiller, the boat made for the island broadside. I tried to bring it around but couldn't, and with the current pushing us, we went sideways into the vegetation that hung down into the water. For all my frantic back-paddling, we struck with such force that, had we landed against rock instead of leaves and branches, we would surely have cracked up and lost everything. Maturette jumped into the water, pulled the boat under a thicket and tied her up. We shared a cup of rum and I climbed the bank alone, leaving my two friends in the boat.

I walked compass in hand, cutting back the brush and attaching strips of flour sacking to branches along the way. I saw a faint light ahead, suddenly heard voices and made out three straw huts. I moved forward, and since I didn't know how I should present myself, decided to let them discover me. I lit a cigarette. As the light flared, a small dog came barking at me and nipped at my legs. Just so long as he isn't a leper, I thought. Then: Idiot, dogs don't get leprosy.

"Who's there? Who is it? Is that you, Marcel?"

"It's an escaped prisoner."

"What are you doing here? You want to rob us? You think we're too well off?"

"No, I need help."

"For free or for pay?"

"Oh, shut up, La Chouette!"

Four shadows emerged from the hut.

"Approach gently, friend. I bet you're the man with the carbine. If you've got it with you, put it on the ground; you have nothing to fear from us."

"Yes, that's me. But I don't have the carbine now."

I inched forward. I was close now, but it was dark and I couldn't make out their features. Stupidly I put out my hand. No one took it. I understood too late that such a gesture was not made here: they didn't want to contaminate me.

"Let's go back to the hut," La Chouette said.

The little cabin was lit by an oil lamp on a table. "Have a seat."

I sat down on a stool. La Chouette lit three more lamps and placed one of them on a table directly in front of me. The smoke of the coconut oil had a sickening smell. The five of them stood, so that I couldn't make out their faces. Mine was well lighted because I was at the same height as the lamp, which is what they had intended.

The voice which had told La Chouette to shut up now said, "L'Anguille, go ask at the main house if they want us to bring him over. Come back with the answer right away. And make sure it's all right with Toussaint. We can't offer you anything to drink here, friend, unless you don't mind swallowing eggs." He placed a basket full of eggs in front of me.

"No, thank you."

Then one of them sat down near me and that's when I saw my first leper. It was horrible. I had to make an effort not to look away or otherwise show my feelings. His nose was completely eaten away, flesh and bone; there was only a hole in the middle of his face. I mean what I say: not two holes, but a single hole, as big as a silver dollar. The right side of the lower lip was also eaten away and exposed three long yellow teeth that jutted out of the bone of the upper jaw. He had only one ear. He was resting a bandaged hand on the table. It was his right hand. With the two fingers remaining on his left hand he held a long, fat cigar. He had probably made it from a half-ripe tobacco leaf, for it was greenish in color. Only his left eye had an eyelid; the lid of his right eye was gone and a deep scar stretched from the eye to the top of his forehead, where it disappeared into his shaggy gray hair.

In a hoarse voice he said, "We'll help you, *mec*. I don't want you to stay around here and become like me."

"Thank you."

"My name is Jean sans Peur. I was handsomer, healthier and stronger than you when I first came to the *bagne*. Look at what ten years have done to me."

"Doesn't anybody take care of you?"

"Sure. I'm much better since I started giving myself injections of chaulmoogra oil. Look." He turned his head and showed me his left side. "It's drying up there."

Feeling an immense pity for this man, I made a motion to touch his cheek as a sign of friendship. He threw himself back and said, "Thank you for wanting to touch me, but you must never touch a leper, nor eat or drink from his bowl." Of all the lepers, his is the face I remember, this man who had the courage to make me look.

"Where's the *mec*?" In the doorway I saw the shadow of a very small man not much bigger than a dwarf. "Toussaint and the others want to see him. Bring him to the center."

Jean sans Peur got up and said, "Follow me." We all set off into the night, four or five in front, me next to Jean sans Peur, more behind. After three minutes we arrived at a clearing faintly lit by the moon. It was the flat summit of the island. In the middle was a house. Light came from two windows. In front about twenty men waited for us. As we arrived at the door, they stood back to let us through. I found myself in a room thirty feet long and twelve feet wide with a kind of fireplace in which wood was burning, surrounded by four huge stones of the same height. The room was lighted by two large hurricane lanterns. On one of the stone stools sat an ageless man with black eyes set in a white face. Behind him on a bench were five or six others.

"I'm Toussaint, the Corsican; you must be Papillon."

"I am."

"News travels fast in the *bagne*. Almost as fast as you do. Where is your carbine?"

"We threw it in the river."

"Where?"

"Opposite the hospital wall, exactly where we jumped."

"So it would be possible to recover it?"

"I suppose so. The water isn't very deep there."

"How do you know?"

"We had to wade through it to carry my injured friend to the boat."

"What's the matter with him?"

"He broke his leg."

"What have you done for him?"

"I split some branches and made him splints."

"Is he in pain?"

"Yes."

"Where is he?"

"In the boat."

"You said you came for help. What kind of help?"

"A better boat."

"You want us to give you a boat?"

"Yes. I have money to buy it with."

"Good. I'll sell you mine; it's a great boat and brand-new. I stole it last week in Albina. It's not a boat; it's a transatlantic steamer. There's only one thing missing: a keel. But in two hours we can fix it up with a good one. It has everything else you could want: a rudder, a thirteen-foot mast of ironwood and a brand-new linen sail. What will you give me for it?"

"Tell me what you want. I don't know what things are worth here."

"Three thousand francs if you have it. If you don't, go find the carbine tomorrow night and I'll give you the boat in exchange."

"No, I'd rather pay."

"O.K. It's a sale. La Puce, let's have some coffee!"

La Puce, the near-dwarf who had first come for me, went over to a board fixed to the wall above the fire, took down a bowl, shining new and clean, poured in some coffee from a bottle and put it on the fire. After a moment he took the bowl and poured the coffee in some mugs. Toussaint leaned down and passed the mugs to the men behind him. La Puce handed me the bowl, saying, "Don't worry. This bowl is only for visitors. No lepers drink from it."

I took the bowl and drank, then rested it on my knee. It was then that I noticed a finger stuck to the bowl. I was just taking this in when La Puce said: "Damn, I've lost another finger. Where the devil is it?"

"It's there," I said, showing him the bowl.

He pulled it off, threw it in the fire and said, "You can go on drinking. I have dry leprosy. I'm disintegrating piece by piece, but I'm not rotting. I'm not contagious." The smell of grilled meat reached me. It must be his finger.

Toussaint said, "You'll have to stay through the day until low tide. Go tell your friends. Bring the man with the broken leg into one of the huts. Take everything you have from the boat and sink it. Nobody here can help you. You understand why."

I returned to my companions and we carried Clousiot to the hut. One hour later everything was out of the boat and carefully stowed away. La Puce asked if we'd make him a present of it and also a paddle. I gave it to him and he took it away to sink it in a special place he knew. The night went fast. All three of us were in the hut, lying on new blankets sent over by Toussaint. They were delivered in the heavy paper they'd been shipped in. As we lay there, I brought Clousiot and Maturette up to date on what had happened since our arrival on the island, and the bargain I had struck with Toussaint. Clousiot said without thinking, "Then this *cavale* is really costing six thousand francs. I'll pay half, Papillon, or the three thousand I have."

"We're not here to haggle like a bunch of Armenians. As long as I have money, I'll pay. After that we'll see."

During the night we were left to ourselves. When day broke, Toussaint was there. "Good morning. Don't be afraid to come out. Nobody can bother you here. There's a man watching for police boats on the river from a cocoa tree on top of the island. We haven't seen any so far. As long as the white rag is up, there's nothing in sight. If he sees anything, he'll come down and tell us. Pick yourselves some papayas if you like."

I said, "Toussaint, what about the keel?"

"We're going to make it from the infirmary door. It's made of heavy snakewood. The keel will need two planks. We brought the boat up while it was dark. Come see it."

We went. It was a magnificent boat sixteen feet long, brand-new, with two benches, one with a hole for the mast. It was heavy, and Maturette and I had trouble turning it over. The sail and the ropes were also new. There were rings on the sides for hanging a barrel of water. We went to work. By noon a keel, tapered from front to back, was solidly in place with long screws and four angle irons.

The lepers formed a circle around us, watching in silence. Toussaint told us what to do and we obeyed. There wasn't a sign of a sore on Toussaint's face; he looked perfectly normal, but when he talked you noticed that only one side of his face moved, the left side. He told me that he, too, had dry leprosy. His torso and right arm were paralyzed and he expected his right leg to go before long. His right eye was fixed, like a glass eye; he could see with it, but he couldn't move it.

I only hoped that no one who ever loved these lepers knew their terrible fate.

As I worked, I talked to Toussaint. No one else spoke. Just once, when I was about to pick up one of the angle irons, one of them said: "Don't touch them yet. I cut myself when I was removing one of them from a piece of furniture, and there's still blood on it even though I tried to wipe it off." One of the lepers poured rum on it and set it on fire, then repeated the operation. "Now you can use it," the man said. While we were working, Toussaint said to one of the men, "You've left the island several times. Papillon and his friends haven't, so tell them how to do it."

"Low tide is early tonight. The tide will start to ebb at three o'clock. When night falls, around six, you'll have a very strong current which in three hours will take you about sixty miles toward the mouth of the river. At nine o'clock you must stop. Get a good grip on an overhanging tree and wait out the six hours of the rising tide—that is, until three in the morning. But don't leave then; the current isn't moving fast enough yet. At four-thirty beat it into the middle of the river. You have an hour and a half before daybreak to do your thirty miles. This is your last chance. When the sun rises at six, you make for the sea. Even if the guards spot you, they won't be able to catch you because they'll be arriving at the bar just as the tide turns. They won't be able to get over it and you'll have made it. Your life depends on this half-mile headstart. This boat has only one sail. What did you have on your boat?"

"A mainsail and a jib."

"This is a heavy boat; it can take two more sails—a spinnaker from the bow to the mast, and a jib that will help keep the nose pointing into the wind. Use all your sails and go straight into the waves; the sea is always heavy at the mouth of the estuary. Get your friends to lie flat in the bottom of the boat to stabilize it, and you hold the tiller tight in your hand. Don't tie the sheet to your leg, but put it through the ring and hold it with a single turn around your wrist. If you see that the force of the wind plus the size of the waves is about to capsize you, let everything go—the boat will immediately find its own equilibrium. Don't stop; let the mainsail luff and keep going with your spinnaker and the jib. When the sea calms down, you'll have time to take down your sail, bring it in and move on after hoisting it again. Do you know the route?"

"No. All I know is that Venezuela and Colombia are northwest."

"Right. But be careful you're not driven back to the coast. Dutch Guiana, opposite us, turns in all escaped cons; so does British Guiana. Trinidad doesn't turn them in, but you can only stay two weeks. Venezuela will turn you in after making you work on a road gang for a year or two."

I listened closely. He told me that he left the island from time to time, but since he was a leper, he was always sent back in short order. He admitted that he had never been farther than Georgetown in British Guiana. He wasn't an obvious leper, having lost only his toes as I could see since he was barefoot. Toussaint made me repeat my instructions and I did so without making a mistake.

At that point Jean sans Peur said, "How much time should he spend on the open sea?"

I answered straight off. "I'll do three days north northeast. With the drift, that makes due north. On the fourth day I'll head northwest, which comes out to due west."

"Bravo," said the leper. "The last time I did it, I spent only two days going northeast and I hit British Guiana. If you take three days going north, you'll pass north of Trinidad or Barbados, you'll bypass Venezuela, and before you know it you'll find yourself in Columbia or Curaçao."

Jean sans Peur asked, "Toussaint, how much did you sell your boat for?"

"Three thousand. Is that too much?"

"No, that isn't why I asked. I just wanted to know. Have you got the money, Papillon?"

"Yes."

"Will you have any left?"

"No, it's all we have, exactly three thousand francs belonging to my friend, Clousiot."

"Toussaint, will you buy my revolver?" said Jean sans Peur. "I'd like to help these *mecs*. How much will you give me for it?"

"A thousand francs," Toussaint said. "I'd like to help them too."

"Thanks for everything," Maturette said, looking at Jean sans Peur.

"Thanks," said Clousiot.

I began to feel ashamed of my lie, so I said, "No, I can't accept it. There's no reason for it."

Jean looked at me and said, "Sure there's a reason. Three thousand francs is a lot of money, but even at that price Toussaint is losing at least two thousand, for that's a great boat he's giving you. So there's no reason why I can't give you something too."

Then a very moving thing happened. La Chouette placed a hat on the ground and all the lepers came and threw in bills and silver. They came from everywhere and every last one put in something. Now I was really ashamed. How could I tell them that I still had some money? God, what a fix! It was despicable to let this go on in the face of such generosity. Then a mutilated black from Timbuktu—his hands were stumps, he hadn't a single finger—said to us, "Money doesn't help us live. Don't be ashamed to accept it. All we use it for is gambling or screwing the girl lepers who come here sometimes from Albina." This relieved my guilt and I never did admit I still had money.

The lepers supplied us with two hundred hard-boiled eggs in a crate marked with a red cross. It was the same crate that had arrived that morning with the day's medicine. They also brought two live turtles weighing at least sixty pounds each, some leaf tobacco, two bottles of matches and a striking pad, a sack of rice weighing at least a hundred pounds, two bags of charcoal, a primus stove taken from the infirmary and a demijohn of fuel. Everybody in this miserable community was touched by our predicament and wanted to help. It was almost as if our *cavale* were theirs. The boat was pulled to where we had made our original landing. They counted the money in the hat: eight hundred and ten francs. I owed Toussaint only twelve hundred. Clousiot handed me his *plan* [a small tube used by prisoners to hide money—*Ed.*] and opened it before everybody. It contained a thousand-franc bill and four bills of five hundred each. I gave Toussaint fifteen hundred francs and he gave me back three hundred, saying:

"Here, take the revolver. It's a present. This is your only chance; you don't want to fail at the last moment for lack of a weapon. But I hope you won't have to use it."

I didn't know how to thank them, him first, then all the others. The orderly prepared a small box with cotton, alcohol, aspirin, bandages, iodine, a pair of scissors and some adhesive tape. A leper produced two small, carefully planed planks and two Ace bandages still in their original wrappings so that we could replace Clousiot's splints.

Toward five o'clock it began to rain. Jean sans Peur said, "You're in luck. This will keep them from seeing you. You can leave now and it will give you a good half hour's headstart. You'll be that much nearer the mouth of the river by four-thirty tomorrow morning."

"How will I know the time?"

"You'll know by the tide, by whether it's rising or falling."

The boat was put in the water. It was a far cry from our old one. This boat floated more than sixteen inches above the water line, fully loaded, us included. The mast was rolled up in the sail in the bottom of the boat since we weren't to use it until we were out of the river. We put the rudder and tiller in place and found a grass cushion for me to sit on. With the blankets, we fixed up a corner for Clousiot in the bottom of the boat, between me and the water barrel. Maturette sat on the bottom in the bow. Right away I had a feeling of security I had never had in the other one.

It was still raining, and I was to go down the middle of the river but a little to the left, toward the Dutch side. Jean sans Peur said, "Good-by. And get moving!"

"Good luck!" said Toussaint, and gave the boat a strong shove with his foot.

"Thanks, Toussaint, thanks, Jean, everybody, thanks a million!" We were off and away fast, for the ebb tide had started two and a half hours before and was now moving with incredible speed.

It continued to rain and we couldn't see thirty feet in front of us. There were two small islands lower down, and Maturette was leaning over the bow, his eyes straining for any sign of rocks. Night came. A large tree was going down the river with us—happily at a lower pace. For a moment we were entangled in its branches, but we freed ourselves quickly and resumed our lightning speed. We smoked, we drank some rum. The lepers had given us six straw-covered Chianti bottles filled with it. It was odd, but not one of us mentioned the lepers' terrible deformities. We talked only of their kindness, their generosity and honesty, and our luck in meeting the Masked Breton. It was raining harder and harder. I was soaked to the bone, but our woolen sweaters were so good that, even soaking wet, they kept us warm. Only my hand on the tiller was stiff with cold.

"We're going more than twenty-five miles an hour now," Maturette said. "How long do you think we've been gone?"

"I'll tell you in a minute," Clousiot said. "Wait—three hours and fifteen minutes."

"You're joking. How do you know?"

"I've been counting in groups of three hundred seconds since we left. At the end of each one I cut a piece of cardboard. I have thirty-nine pieces. Since each one represents five minutes, that means three hours and a quarter since we started. And unless I'm wrong, in the next fifteen or twenty minutes we won't be going down any more; we'll be going back up where we came from."

I pushed the tiller to the right in order to cut across the river and get closer to the Dutch coast. The current stopped just as we were about to crash into the brush. We didn't move, either up or down. It was still raining. We stopped smoking, we stopped talking. I whispered, "Take a paddle and pull." I paddled, holding the tiller under my right thigh. We grazed the brush, pulled on the branches and hid underneath. It was completely dark inside the vegetation. The river was gray and covered with a heavy mist. Without the evidence of the tide's ebb and flow, it would be impossible to tell where the river ended and the sea began.

The rising tide was to last six hours. Then we were to wait an hour and a half after the turn of the tide. That meant I had seven hours to sleep, if only I could calm down. I had to sleep now, for when would I have time at sea? I stretched out between the barrel and the mast, Maturette used a blanket to make a tent between the barrel and the bench, and thus well protected, I slept and I slept. Nothing disturbed me, not dreams, rain, or my uncomfortable position. I slept. I slept—until Maturette woke me and said:

"Papi, we think it's almost time. It's a long time since the ebb tide started."

The boat was heading downstream. I felt the current with my fingers; it was moving very fast. The rain had stopped and the light of a quarter moon clearly revealed the river three hundred feet ahead with its floating burden of grass, trees and unidentifiable black shapes. I tried to make out the demarcation between river and sea. Where we were, there was no wind. Was there any in the middle of the river? Was it strong? We emerged from under the brush, the boat still attached to a big branch by a slipknot. It was only by looking at the sky that I could make out the coast, the end of the river and the beginning of the sea. We had come down much farther than we thought and it seemed to me we couldn't be more than six miles from the mouth. We drank a good snort of rum. I felt around in the boat for where the mast should go. We lifted it and it fitted nicely through the hole in the bench into its socket. I hoisted the sail but kept it wrapped around the mast. The spinnaker and jib were ready for Maturette when we needed them. For the sail to open, I had only to let go the rope that held it to the mast. I could do that from where I was sitting. Maturette was in front with one paddle, I in the rear with another. We must work fast to get away from the bank which the current was pushing us against.

"Careful. Now let her go and God help us!"

"God help us," Clousiot repeated.

"We are in Your hands," Maturette said.

We cast off. Together we pulled on our paddles. I dipped and pulled. Maturette did the same. It was easy. By the time we were sixty feet from the bank, the current had taken us down three hundred. The wind hit us all at once and pushed us to the middle of the river.

"Raise the jibs and make sure they're both tied fast!"

The wind filled them and, like a horse, the boat reared and was off. It was later than we had figured for the river was suddenly bathed in broad daylight. We could easily make out the French coast about a mile and a quarter to our right and the Dutch coast about half a mile to our left. Before us and very clear were the white caps of the breaking waves.

"Christ! We were wrong about the time," Clousiot said. "Do you think we can make it?"

"I don't know."

"Look how high those waves are! Has the tide turned?"

"Impossible. I see things floating down."

Maturette said, "We're not going to make it. We don't have time."

"Shut up and hold the jibs tight. You shut up too, Clousiot."

Pan-ingh . . . pan-ingh. . . . We were being shot at. On the second round I could fix where the shots were coming from. It wasn't the guards. The shots were coming from the Dutch side. I put up the mainsail and it filled so fast that a little more and it would have taken my wrist with it. The boat was heeling over at a forty-five degree angle. I took all the wind I could, which was much too easy. Pan-ingh, pan-ingh; then nothing. We were being carried nearer the French coast—that must be why the shooting had stopped.

We moved ahead with dizzying speed, going so fast that I saw ourselves driven into the middle of the estuary and smack into the French bank. We could see men running toward it. I came about gently, as gently as possible, pulling on the sheet with all my strength. The mainsail was now straight out in front of me; the jib came by itself and so did the spinnaker. The boat made a three-quarter turn. I let out the sail and we left the estuary running before the wind. Jesus! We had made it! Ten minutes later the first wave barred our passage, but we climbed over it with ease, and the schuit-schuit of the boat on the river changed to a tac-y-tac-y-tac. We went over the high waves with the agility of a boy playing leapfrog. Tac-y-tac, the boat rose and fell with no vibration, no shaking—only the *tac* when it hit the sea after coming off a wave.

"Hurrah! Hurrah! We made it!" Clousiot shouted at the top of his lungs.

And to help celebrate our victory over the elements, the good Lord sent us a breathtaking sunrise. The waves kept up a continuous rhythm. The farther we got out, the smoother they became. The water was very muddy. Ahead of us to the north the sea was black; later it would change to blue. I didn't need to look at the compass: the sun was over my right shoulder. I was running before the wind in a straight line and the boat was heeling less, for I had let out the sail and it was now half full. Our great adventure was under way.

Papillon sailed more than 1,000 miles across open water and had many adventures, including seven months of living with a primitive Indian tribe, before being recaptured and placed on Devil's Island—one of the most hopeless places imaginable. After years of failed escapes and brutal treatment, Papillon made another incredible escape, throwing himself into the crashing waves off the island while perched on a sack of coconuts. He drifted almost 25 miles to reach the coast again and eventually made another sea voyage to Venezuela, where he gained citizenship after a shorter incarceration. Few fiction writers would be able to match the real-life adventure of Henri Charriere's life.

A Man Escaped

A N D R E   D E V I G N Y

Andre Devigny was a soldier and member of the French Resistance during World War II. He was captured by the Germans and imprisoned in Fort Montluc, in Lyons, France. He endured severe beatings and privation there and was eventually sentenced to death by the infamous Gestapo agent Klaus Barbie. Unbeknownst to the Germans, however, Devigny had found a way to take apart the heavy wooden door of his cell. Using just a small razor blade, he was able to make a clever dovetailed key to hold the pieces together during the day, which he could then disassemble at night to roam the prison searching for a way out.

On the eve of his planned escape, and just before his scheduled execution, Devigny was given a cellmate, Gimenez. He had no alternative but to convince this rather lazy and dull-witted young man that they had to escape together. Their escape, the only successful one made from Montluc during the war, was one of the most riveting in history. The full account of this escape is given in Devigny's excellent memoir, *A Man Escaped*.

Gimenez had finished the parcel. I checked it, and then we set about packing up the big rope. It had to be made into as small a parcel as possible so that it could go through the main skylight without difficulty; it also had to be done up in such a way that it could be unpacked in a matter of seconds. To solve this problem I tied the string in double bows; we could not afford to waste time over knots in the dark. I left one end out and fastened the spare hook to it, making sure that this, too, could be quickly removed when necessary.

Once I had reached the roof I intended to hang the roll containing the shorter rope on this hook, and let it down into the courtyard, thus leaving myself completely free and unhampered in my movements.

We ranged these parcels in a line along the wall, in the order in which Gimenez would pass them out to me: first the light rope; then the heavy one, and lastly our coats and shoes.

I gave Gimenez detailed instructions.

"When I pass you the boards and pieces of wood from the door, put them in that corner near the earth-closet, so that they don't get in our way."

"I understand," he said.

Slowly the hours chimed out in the stillness. All was quiet; the prison slept. The dismal, regular footfall of the sentries echoed on the cobbles.

Lights were lit in the town, and a dim glow penetrated into our cell.

Ten o'clock began to strike. I sprang to my feet, and nodded to Gimenez.

Seven; eight; nine; *ten*. Crouched in front of the door I counted the strokes. The infantryman ready to spring out of his trench, the parachutist slipping into space—both of them act instinctively, without thought; they lose their identity in a corporate movement, and are plunged at once into violent action. But I had no such support. My operation had to be carried out in cold blood. I was alone in this vast, menacing silence. My equipment was home-made, and I bore sole responsibility for my plan. The young man beside me symbolised the element of doubt and uncertainty. I had to remain absolutely cool-headed, controlling my enthusiasm, matching determination with patience. Every move had to be calculated logically, and executed at precisely the right moment. Only so could we ever cross the wall to freedom.

My heart was thudding violently against my rib-cage, and I felt myself trembling.

Gimenez was behind me, a little to my right. I tapped several times on the wall to tell Jeantet we were off, and heard a faint knocking in response.

As the last stroke faded I knocked out the wedges which held the boards in place. Now I was trembling no longer; the curtain had gone up, and the play was on.

Gimenez took the boards from me one after the other and stacked them away. In the half-light we could just see the faint, barred outline of the gallery rails; it was too dark to make out the cell doors on the other side. I put out my head and listened. Only the creaking of beds as sleepers turned over, and occasionally a bucket scraping along the floor, broke the silence—that hostile silence against which we had to struggle for what seemed like a century.

For two long minutes I remained motionless. Then I pushed one arm out into the corridor, turned on one side, and crawled forward like a snake. I stood up cautiously. The light was on down below; but, as usual, its feeble rays were swallowed up in the vast gloom of the hall.

Gimenez passed me the light rope, which I at once took over to the latrines. It was followed by the rest of our equipment. I went back to the cell door to help Gimenez. We both stood there for a moment, listening. All was still. Slowly we moved towards our starting-point.

I tied one end of the light rope round my waist—the end, that is, which had no grappling-iron attached to it. Three steps, and we were standing by the metal rod. The rope would pay out as I climbed; I left it coiled loosely on the ground. Gimenez braced himself against the wall and gave me a leg up. I stood on his shoulders, both hands gripping the rod, and tried to reach the edge of the skylight. I pulled myself up slowly, with all the strength I had. But it proved too much of an effort; I had to come down again.

The weeks of confinement I had undergone since my previous successful attempt must have sapped my strength more than I thought. We went back to the latrines to give me a few moments' rest. I inhaled deeply, waiting till I got my breath back before making a second attempt.

I had to get up there, whatever happened.

Jaws clenched, I began to climb. I got my feet from Gimenez's hands to his shoulders, and then to his head. My fingers gripped the metal rod convulsively. Somehow I went on, inch by inch; at last my fingers found the frame of the skylight, and I got my legs over the horizontal rod, which shook in its rings as my weight hung from it. I got round the ratchet supporting the skylight without touching it. I was sweating and panting like a man struggling out of a quicksand, or a shipwrecked sailor clinging desperately to a reef. Eyes dilated, every muscle cracking, I gradually worked my way through the opening. Then I stopped for a minute to get my strength back. I had managed to preserve absolute silence from start to finish.

A few lights twinkled in the distance. The fresh night air cooled my damp face. It was very still. Slowly my breathing became normal again. Carefully I put out one hand on to the gritty surface of the flat roof, taking care to avoid touching the fragile glass in the skylight itself; this done, I hauled myself up a little further and got my other hand into a similar position. With a final effort I completed the operation, and found myself standing upright on the roof, dazed by the clear splendour of the night sky. The silence drummed in my ears.

For a moment I remained motionless. Then I knelt down and slowly pulled up the rope. The shoes were dangling in their bundle at the end of it. I let it down again and brought up our coats. The third time I salvaged the big rope; it was a difficult job to squeeze it through the narrow opening.

Go slowly, I thought. Don't hurry. You've got plenty of time.

I unhooked the parcel and put it aside. Then I paid out the rope once more. We had agreed that Gimenez should tie it round his waist so that I could take up the slack and make his ascent easier. I waited a little, and then felt a gentle tug. I pulled steadily, hand over hand, taking care not to let the rope bear heavily on the metal edge of the skylight. We could not risk any noise. I heard the rods creaking under his weight; then, a moment later, two hands came up and got a grip on the sill. Slowly Gimenez's face and shoulders appeared.

I bent down and whispered: "Don't hurry. Take a rest."

He breathed in the fresh air, gulping and panting.

My mouth still close to his ear, I said: "Be careful how you pull yourself up. Don't put your hands on the glass."

He seemed as exhausted as I was.

I untied the rope from my waist, and he followed suit. I coiled it up carefully, took a piece of string out of my pocket, and ran a bowline round the middle of the coil.

There we both stood, side by side, in absolute silence. Gradually my breathing slowed down to its normal rate, and I began to recover my strength. It was hard to get used to this immense, seemingly limitless space all round me. The glass penthouse (of which the skylight formed a part) stood out from the roof and vanished in darkness only a few feet away. I made out one or two small chimney-cowls here and there. The courtyard and the perimeter were hidden from us by the parapet. We could walk upright without being seen.

I felt the shingle grit under my feet at the least move I made.

I took a coil of rope in each hand and picked them up with great care. Gimenez did the same with the shoes and coats. We stood there waiting for a train: it was five, perhaps even ten minutes coming.

Gimenez became impatient. I was just about to move when the sound of a locomotive reached us from the distance. It grew louder and louder; presently the train steamed past on the nearby track. We managed to get ten feet forward before it vanished into the distance again. The stretch of line which runs past Montluc joins the two main stations of Lyons. As a result it carries very heavy traffic, which had hardly slackened off even at this stage of the war.

We had nearly reached the middle of the roof now. We found ourselves standing by the far end of the penthouse. A little further on a second penthouse appeared, which stretched away towards the other side of the roof. My eyes were beginning to get accustomed to the dark. I could see the large glass dome above the penthouse; that meant we were standing above the central well. I thought then for a moment of our friends below in their cells: some asleep, lost in wonderful dreams; others, who knew of our plan, awake, waiting in frightful suspense, ears straining for any suspicious noises.

We had advanced with extreme care, putting each foot down as lightly as possible, bent double as if the weight of our apprehension and of the dangers we had to face was too heavy to be supported. Gimenez kept close behind me. I could hear his slow, regular breathing, and glimpse his dark silhouette against the night sky. We had to wait some time before another train came to our assistance. But this time it was a slow goods train. It enabled us to reach our objective—the side of the roof opposite the infirmary—in one quick move.

We put down our various packages. I turned back and whispered to Gimenez: "Lie down and wait for me here. Don't move."

"Where are you going?"

"To see what's happening."

Gimenez obediently dropped to his knees, and remained as motionless as the equipment stacked round him. I crept slowly round the corner of the roof, raised myself cautiously, and peered over the parapet. Below me I could see the stretch of the perimeter which flanked the Rue du Dauphiné. I lifted my head a little further, and quickly drew it back again at the sight of a sentry. He was standing on one corner near the wash-house. I had known he would be there; yet in my present situation he scared me nearly out of my wits.

Of course, he could not see me. I told myself not to be a fool.

I pressed my cheek against the rough concrete surface and slowly raised my head once more. Unfortunately, the wide shelf outside the parapet cut off my view of the part of the courtyard immediately below. As this was where we would have to climb down, it was essential to find a better observation-post.

But before moving I took another quick look at the soldier in the far corner. He seemed very wide awake. Soon a second sentry walked over to join him—probably the one who guarded the wooden barrack-block on the other side. I saw the glowing tips of their cigarettes. The lamps in the courtyard gave off so weak a light that the men themselves were mere shadows against the surrounding gloom.

Occasionally a twinkling reflection from buckle or bayonet hinted at their movements. I knew that the best way of remaining unseen was to keep absolutely still. If I had to move, it must be done as slowly as possible, with long and frequent pauses. It took me some time to get back to Gimenez, tell him to stay put, climb over the parapet, and crawl along the outer cat-walk till I was once more opposite the infirmary. A train passed by at exactly the right moment; I scrambled along as fast as I could to the corner of the wall. A loose piece of shingle, even a little sand going over the edge would have given me away. I would feel ahead with my hands, then slowly pull myself forward like a slug, breathing through my mouth.

In front of me the perimeter was clearly visible. Beyond it the tobacco factory and the buildings of the military court formed a broken outline against the horizon. Above them the stars shone out in a moonless sky. After a little I could just make out the roof of the covered gallery over which we had to pass. Gradually our whole route became visible. I spotted a familiar landmark—the fanlight of my old cell—and then, on the left, the workshop and women's quarters. Close by was the low wall between the infirmary and the courtyard. Soon, I thought, we should be climbing that wall. One room in the infirmary was still lit up; the light shone behind the wall in the direction of the covered gallery. I was, I realised, directly above cell 45, where my first few weeks of detention had been spent.

I wriggled forward inch by inch, so as to reach the outer edge of the cat-walk and get into a position from which I could observe the whole area of the courtyard. The two sentries were now out of sight round the corner of the block, smoking and chatting. I could see no one below me. The way was clear. My heart beat excitedly. A little further and I would be certain. My face against the rough surface, I peered cautiously over the edge.

I was horrified at the gulf stretching down below me; I could not help feeling that my rope must be too short.

Nothing was stirring. I examined every danger-point in turn—the shadowy corners by the wash-house and workshop, the women's quarters, the alley between the infirmary wall and the main block, the half-open doors leading from court to court, every conceivable hole or corner where a sentry might be lurking. Nothing. The cell windows were patterned on the façade like black squares in a crossword puzzle. Occasionally the sound of a cough drifted out from one or other of them. This, and the recurrent trains, alone broke the silence. Further down, on the left, some of the windows seemed to be open. The stillness was almost tangible.

Still I scrutinized the courtyard with minute care. Suddenly a dark shape caught my eye, in a corner near the door of the main block. I stared closely at it. After a moment I realised it was a sentry, asleep on the steps. The weight of this alarming discovery filled me with a sudden vast depression. How on earth were we to get past him? How could we even be certain he was asleep? How—in the last resort—could we surprise him without being seen?

At this point the sentry sat up and lit a cigarette. The flame from his lighter gave me a quick glimpse of his steel helmet and the sub-machine gun he carried. He got up, walked a little way in the direction of the infirmary, and then came back again.

Midnight struck.

It must have been the time when the guard was changed. The soldier passed directly beneath me, between the infirmary and the main block, and vanished in the direction of the guard-house. Four or five minutes later his relief appeared. His footsteps crunched grimly over the cobbles.

A frightful inner conflict racked me as I studied his every movement, like a wild beast stalking its prey. We could not retreat. The way had to be cleared.

The sentry's beat took him away into the shadows at the far end of the court, then back to the main door, where the lamp shone for a moment on his helmet and the barrel of his sub-machine gun.

I watched him for a whole hour, memorising the pattern of his movements. Then I raised myself on knees and elbows, climbed quietly over the parapet, and returned to Gimenez.

He was asleep. I woke him gently. "Time to move on," I said.

He got up without making any noise. I was busy untying the knot of the string lashed round the big rope.

"All set now," I whispered. "As soon as a train comes, we'll lower the rope."

I stood with one foot on the roof and the other on the cat-walk, the low parapet between my legs. This way I could control the rope with both hands and pay it out without it touching the edge. I left Gimenez to control the coil and see the rope was free from entanglements.

An eternity of time seemed to pass before the train came. At the first distant panting of the engine I began to lower away, slowly at first, then with increasing speed. When I felt the reinforced stretch near the end passing through my fingers I stopped, and lowered the rope on to the concrete. Then I hooked the grappling-iron on to the inner side of the parapet. It seemed to hold firm enough. The rope stretched away into the darkness below us.

Gimenez would sling the parcels containing our shoes and coats round his neck, and follow me down when I gave him the signal. I knew that the moment I swung out from the roof into open space the last irrevocable decision would have been taken. By so doing I would either clinch my victory or sign my own death-warrant. While I remained on the roof it was still possible to return to my cell. Once I had begun the descent there was no way back. Despite the cool night air, my face and shirt were soaked with sweat.

"Hold on to the grappling-iron while I'm going down," I told Gimenez. I took hold of his hands and set them in position.

Then I crouched down on the outer ledge, facing him, ready to go down the rope at the first possible moment, and waited for a train to pass. Gimenez leant over and hissed nervously in my ear: "There's someone down below!"

"Don't worry."

Then I looked at the sky and the stars and prayed that the rope might be strong enough, that the German sentry would not come round the corner at the wrong moment, that I would not make any accidental noise.

The waiting strained my nerves horribly. Once I began my descent there would be no more hesitation. I knew; but dear God, I thought, let that train come quickly, let me begin my descent into the abyss now, at once, before my strength fails me.

The stroke of one o'clock cut through the stillness like an axe.

Had an hour passed so quickly? The sentries' footsteps, echoing up to us with monotonous regularity, seemed to be counting out the seconds. There could not be so very many trains at this time of night.

Gimenez was showing signs of impatience. I told him to keep still. The words were hardly out of my mouth when a distant whistle broke the silence. Quickly it swelled in volume.

"This is it," I said.

I shuffled back towards the edge of the cat-walk. Then, holding my breath, I slid myself over, gripping the rope between my knees, and holding the ledge with both hands to steady myself. At last I let go. The rope whirred upwards under my feet, the wire binding tore at my hands. I went down as fast as I could, not even using my legs.

As soon as I touched the ground I grabbed the parcel containing the second rope, and doubled across the courtyard to the low wall. I released the rope, swung the grappling iron up, hauled myself over, and dropped down on the other side, behind the doorway, leaving the rope behind for Gimenez.

The train was fading away into the distance now, towards the station. The drumming of its wheels seemed to be echoed in my heaving chest. I opened my mouth and breathed deeply to ease the pressure on my lungs. Above me I saw the dark swinging line of rope, and the sharp outline of the roof against the sky.

I stood motionless, getting my breath back and accustoming my eyes to the darkness. The sentry's footsteps rang out behind the wall, scarcely six feet away. They passed on, only to return a moment later. I pressed both hands against my beating heart. When all was quiet again I worked round to the doorway, and flattened myself against it. I felt all my human reactions being swallowed up by pure animal instinct, the instinct for self-preservation which quickens the reflexes and gives one fresh reserves of strength.

It was my life or his.

As his footsteps approached I tried to press myself into the wood against which my back was resting. Then, when I heard him change direction, I risked a quick glance out of my hiding-place to see exactly where he was.

He did exactly the same thing twice, and still I waited.

I got a good grip on the ground with my heels; I could not afford to slip. The footsteps moved in my direction, grew louder. The sentry began to turn . . .

I sprang out of my recess like a panther, and got my hands round his throat in a deadly grip. With frantic violence I began to throttle him. I was no longer a man, but a wild animal. I squeezed and squeezed, with the terrible strength of desperation. My teeth were gritting against each other, my eyes bursting out of my head. I threw back my head to exert extra pressure, and felt my fingers bite deep into his neck. Already half-strangled, the muscles of his throat torn and engorged, only held upright by my vice-like grip, the sentry still feebly raised his arms as if to defend himself; but an instant later they fell back, inert. But this did not make me let go. For perhaps three minutes longer I maintained my pressure on his throat, as if afraid that one last cry, or even the death-rattle, might give me away. Then, slowly, I loosened my blood-stained fingers, ready to close them again at the least movement; but the body remained slack and lifeless. I lowered it gently to the ground.

I stared down at the steel helmet which, fortunately perhaps, concealed the sentry's face; at the dark hunched shape of the body itself, at the sub-machine gun and the bayonet. I thought for a moment, then quickly drew the bayonet from its scabbard, gripped it by the hilt in both hands, and plunged it down with one straight, hard stroke into the sentry's back.

I raised my head, and saw that I was standing immediately below the window of cell 45. Old memories fireworked up in my mind: hunger and thirst, the beatings I had suffered, the handcuffs, the condemned man in the next cell, Fränzel spitting in my face.

My revenge had begun.

I went back to the doorway, near the infirmary, and whistled twice, very softly. A dark shape slid down the rope. It creaked under his weight. I went to meet him. Gimenez climbed the low wall, detached the light rope with its grappling-iron, passed them down to me, and jumped. In his excitement, or nervousness, he had left our coats and shoes on the roof. At the time I said nothing about this. Clearly his long wait had depressed him; he was shivering all over. He gave a violent start when he saw the corpse stretched out near our feet.

I clapped him on the back. "You'll really have something to shiver about in a moment. Come on, quick."

Our troubles had only begun. We still had to cross the courtyard in order to reach the wall between it and the infirmary. Then there was the roof of the covered gallery to surmount, and, finally, the crossing of the perimeter walls.

I carried the rope and the fixed grappling-iron; Gimenez had the loose one. We doubled across to the wall. It was essential for us to get up here as quickly as possible. The light left on in the infirmary was shining in our direction, and a guard could easily have spotted us from a first-floor window of the central block as we made our way towards the inner wall of the perimeter.

Gimenez gave me a leg up, and I managed to reach the top of the wall and hang on. But I was quite incapable by now of pulling myself up; all my strength had drained away. I came down again, wiped my forehead and regained my breath. If I had been alone I should in all probability have stuck at this point. As it was I bent down against the wall in my turn, and Gimenez got up without any trouble. I undid the bundle of rope and passed him the end with the grappling-iron attached. He fixed it securely. Then I tried again, with the rope to help me this time. Somehow I scrambled up, using hands, knees and feet, thrusting and straining in one last desperate effort. Gimenez lay down flat on his belly to give himself more purchase, and managed to grab me under the arms. Eventually I made it.

My heart was hammering against my ribs and my chest felt as if it was going to burst. My shirt clung damply to my body. But there was not a minute to lose. We coiled up the rope again and crawled along to the covered gallery. From here it was a short climb up the tiles to the ridge of the roof. We had to hurry because of that damned light; once we had got over the other side of the roof we were in shadow again.

Unfortunately I made a noise. Two tiles knocked against each other under the sliding pressure of my knee. Gimenez reproved me sharply.

"For God's sake take care what you're doing!" he hissed.

"It wasn't my fault—"

"I haven't the least desire to be caught, even if you have!"

Since this was a sloping roof, we only needed to climb a little way down the far side to be completely hidden. If we stood upright we could easily see over the wall. Soon we were both crouching in position at the end of the covered gallery, our equipment beside us.

I was not acquainted with the exact details of the patrols in the perimeter. When I went out to be interrogated, I had observed a sentry-box in each corner, but these were always unoccupied. Perhaps the guards used them at night, however: it was vital to find out. We already knew that one guard rode round and round the whole time on a bicycle; he passed us every two or three minutes, his pedals squeaking.

We listened carefully. Gimenez was just saying that the cyclist must be alone when the sound of voices reached us. We had to think again.

Perhaps there was a sentry posted at each corner of the square, in the angle formed by the outer wall. If this turned out to be so, it would be extremely difficult to get across; nothing but complete darkness would give us a chance. That meant we must cut the electric cable, which ran about two feet below the top of the inner wall, on the perimeter side.

I half-rose from my cramped position and took a quick look. The walls seemed much higher from here, and the lighting system enhanced this impression. A wave of despair swept over me. Surely we could never surmount this obstacle?

From the roof it had all looked very different. The yawning gulf had been hidden. But the perimeter was well-lit, and the sight of it—deep as hell and bright as daylight—almost crushed my exhausted determination.

I craned forward a little further. The sentry-box below on our left was empty. I ducked back quickly as the cyclist approached. He ground round the corner and started another circuit. A moment later I was enormously relieved to hear him talking to himself; it was this curious monologue we had intercepted a moment earlier. He was alone, after all.

Behind us rose the dark shape of the main block. We had come a long way since ten o'clock. Another six yards, and we were free. Yet what risks still remained to be run!

Little by little determination flowed back into me. One more effort would do it. Don't look back, I thought. Keep your eyes in front of you till it's all over.

Bitter experience had taught me that over-hastiness could be fatal; that every precipitate action was liable to bring disaster in its train. Gimenez was eager to get on and finish the operation, but I firmly held him back. I was as well aware as he was of the dangers that threatened us; I knew that every moment we delayed increased our risk of recapture. I thought of the open cell, the rope we had left hanging from the wall, the dead sentry in the courtyard, the possibility of his body being discovered by a patrol or his relief. Nevertheless, I spent more than a quarter of an hour watching that cyclist. Every four or five circuits he turned round and went the other way. We were well-placed in our corner: he was busy taking the bend, and never looked up. We were additionally protected by the three shaded lights fixed on each wall. All their radiance was thrown down into the perimeter itself, leaving us in shadow. We could watch him without fear of discovery.

Three o'clock.

Gimenez was becoming desperate. At last I decided to move. Holding the end of the rope firmly in one hand, I coiled it across my left arm like a lasso. With the other hand I grasped the grappling-iron. As soon as the sentry had pedalled past, I threw the line as hard as I could towards the opposite wall. The rope snaked up and out, and the grappling-iron fell behind the parapet. I tugged very gently on it, trying to let it find a natural anchorage. Apparently I had been successful; it held firm. A strand of barbed wire, which I had not previously noticed, rattled alarmingly as the rope jerked over it. After a little, however, it was pressed down to the level of the wall.

I gave one violent pull, but the rope did not budge. It had caught first time. I breathed again.

"Give me the other hook," I muttered to Gimenez. I could feel him trembling.

The cyclist was coming round again now. I froze abruptly. For the first time he passed actually under the rope. When he had gone I threaded the rope through the wire loop and pulled it as tight as we could. While Gimenez held it firm to prevent it slipping, I knotted it tightly, and fixed the grappling-iron in a crevice on the near side of the parapet. In my fear of running things too fine I had actually overcalculated the amount of rope necessary; over six feet were left trailing loose on the roof. That thin line stretching across the perimeter looked hardly less fragile than the telephone-wires which followed a similar route a few yards away.

I made several further tests when the cyclist was round the other side. I unanchored the grappling-iron on our side, and then we both of us pulled on the rope as hard as we could to try out its strength.

If the truth must be told, I was horribly afraid that it would snap, and I would be left crippled in the perimeter. When I pulled on it with all my strength I could feel it stretch. One last little effort and the whole thing would be over; but I had reached the absolute end of my courage, physical endurance, and will-power alike. All the time the cyclist continued to ride round beneath us. Four o'clock struck.

In the distance, towards the station, the red lights on the railway line still shone out. But the first glimmer of dawn was already creeping up over the horizon, and the lights showed less bright every moment. We could wait no longer.

"Over you go, Gimenez. You're lighter than I am."

"No. You go first."

"It's your turn."

"I won't."

"Go on, it's up to you."

"No," he said desperately, "I can't do it."

The cyclist turned the corner again. I shook Gimenez desperately, my fingers itching to hit him.

"Are you going, yes or no?"

"No," he cried, "no, *no!*"

"Shut up, for God's sake!" I said. I could not conquer his fear; I said no more. Still the German pedalled round his beat. Once he stopped almost directly beneath us, got off his machine, and urinated against the wall. It was at once a comic and terrifying sight. As time passed and the dawn approached, our chances of success grew steadily less. I knew it, yet I still hesitated. Gimenez shivered in silence.

Abruptly, as the sentry passed us yet again, I stooped forward, gripped the rope with both hands, swung out into space, and got my legs up into position. Hand over hand, my back hanging exposed above the void, I pulled myself across with desperate speed. I reached the far wall, got one arm over it, and scrambled up.

I had done it. I had escaped.

A delirious feeling of triumph swept over me. I forgot how exhausted I was; I almost forgot Gimenez, who was still waiting for the sentry to pass under him again before following me. I was oblivious to my thudding heart and hoarse breath; my knees might tremble, my face be dripping with sweat, my hands scored and bleeding, my throat choked, my head bursting, but I neither knew nor cared. All I was conscious of was the smell of life, the freedom I had won against such desperate odds. I uttered a quick and thankful prayer to God for bringing me through safely.

I moved along the top of the wall towards the courthouse buildings, where it lost height considerably. I stopped just short of a small gateway. Workmen were going past in the street outside, and I waited a few moments before jumping down. This gave Gimenez time to catch up with me.

At five o'clock we were walking down the street in our socks and shirt-sleeves—free men.

The two men were stopped by the Germans a day or two later, but Devigny was able to dive into a nearby river and escape again. He eventually made it to Switzerland and rejoined the war, distinguishing himself in many battles. He became one of France's greatest war heroes.

Escape Strategy

PAT REID

The imposing castle at Colditz became the German dumping ground for Allied prisoners who had proven troublesome in their efforts to escape during World War II. The idea was to keep an eye on all the most recalcitrant prisoners by placing them in an impregnable fortress and guarding it extremely well. More than five hundred German troops were posted as guards, and tight security measures were observed.

Unfortunately for the Germans, they had brought together the best minds for escape ever assembled under one roof. The men quickly formed an Escape Committee and elected an Escape Officer, Pat Reid, to coordinate and assist with various attempts and discourage some of the less-inspired plans. By war's end, twenty-seven prisoners had successfully escaped and made it back to Allied lines, and many more broke out, only to be recaptured on their way to neutral territory. As Colditz was widely considered escape-proof, this was a magnificent feat. The prisoners built tunnels, picked locks, scaled walls, and even walked out the front gate dressed as German officers—anything to be free. One enterprising prisoner used a game of leap-frog to work his way close to a fence. When the right moment came, his friends helped him vault right over and off he went.

Prisoners of many nationalities were housed in Colditz, and it took considerable effort for the different groups to work together. The Dutch, in particular, made some interesting escapes, and they were famous in the prison for their lifelike dummies, which were used to fool the Germans during roll calls (*appells*), thereby giving escapers a little more lead time.

There are several good books about the escapes from Colditz, including Pat Reid's *The Colditz Story*, from which this escape in 1942 is taken. Virtually every chapter of his book contains an ingenious escape. After helping dozens of others, Reid eventually escaped and made it to safety in 1944.

I was lying on my bunk one hot day in August 1942. "Lulu" Lawton (Captain W. T. Lawton, Duke of Wellington's Regiment), was lying in another nearby. Lulu had one short break from Colditz and had been recaught after a few hours' journey outward bound. He was a Yorkshireman and he naturally preferred the smell of the fresh air outside the precincts of the camp. He lay ruminating for a long time and then in a sad tone of voice, turning towards me, he said:

"As far as I can see, Pat, it's no good trying any more escapes from Colditz—the place is bunged up—a half-starved rat wouldn't find a hole big enough for him to squeeze through." Then he added soulfully: "I wouldn't mind havin' another go, all the same, if I could only think of a way."

"You've got to consider the problem coldly," I replied. "The first principle for success in any battle is to attack the enemy in his weakest quarter, but what is always confused in the question of escape is our understanding concerning the enemy's weakest quarter. It isn't, for instance, the apparent weak point in the wire or the wall, for these are his rear-line defences. We have to go a long way before we reach them. It's his front-line defences that count, and they are inside the camp. Jerry's strongest weapon is his ability to nip escapes in the bud before they are ready. This he does right inside the camp and he succeeds ninety-eight per cent of the time. His weakest quarter inside the camp has therefore to be found; after that, the rest is a cakewalk."

I added: "For instance, if you were to ask me where the German weak spot in this camp is, I should say it's Gephard's own office. Nobody will ever look for an escape attempt being hatched in the German R.S.M.'s office."

"That's all very well," said Lulu, "but Gephard's office has a cruciform lock and an ugly-looking padlock as well."

"All the better," I answered. "You won't be disturbed then."

"But how do I get in?"

"That's your problem," I concluded.

I never dreamt he would take the matter seriously, but a Yorkshireman's thoroughness is not to be denied.

There was a Dutchman in the camp, the red-bearded Captain Van Doorninck. He used to repair watches in his spare time, and he even repaired them for the German personnel occasionally, in return for equipment with which to carry on his hobby. Thus, he possessed a repair outfit consisting of miniature tools and various oddments in the way of materials, which were rigorously denied to other prisoners. He never gave his parole as to the employment of the tools.

Van Doorninck was brainy. He had a wide knowledge of higher mathematics, and at one period he gave me, along with one or two others, a university course in Geodesy—a subject I had never thoroughly grasped as a student.

Besides tinkering with watches Van Doorninck was not averse to tinkering with locks, as Lulu Lawton found out, with the result that the former devised a method of lock-picking that any Raffles might have been proud of.

I have described the outward appearance of the cruciform lock before as resembling a four-armed Yale lock. Its essential internal elements consisted of between six and nine tiny pistons of not quite one-eighth of an inch diameter each. In order to open the lock these pistons had to be moved in their cylinders by the insertion of the key. Each piston moved a different distance, the accuracy of which was gauged to a thousandth of an inch.

The principle involved was the same as that employed in the Yale lock. The keyhole, however, was like a cross, each limb being about one-sixteenth of an inch wide, whereas the Yale has a zigzag-shaped keyway. The latter keyway might have presented more difficulty to Van Doorninck, though I am sure he would have overcome it. However, he solved the cruciform problem by manufacturing a special micrometer gauge, which marked off the amount of movement that each piston required. He then made a key to conform, using his gauge to check the lifting faces of the key as he filed them. The key looked rather like a four-armed Yale key.

Van Doorninck succeeded brilliantly where I had failed miserably. I blushed with shame every time I recollected the tortures I had inflicted on so many wincing sufferers in the dentist's chair! The new key was a triumph. Moreover, Van Doorninck was in a position to "break" all the cruciform locks, though each one was different. Thereafter, like ghosts we passed through doors which the Germans thought were sealed.

Returning to the door of Gephard's office: once the cruciform lock was broken the other lock, the padlock, presented no difficulty.

The plan evolved. Lulu Lawton had teamed up with Flight Lieutenant "Bill" Fowler, R.A.F., and then made a foursome with Van Doorninck and another Dutchman. Dick Howe, as Escape Officer, was in charge of operations. He came to me one day.

"Pat, I've got a job for you," he said. "Lulu and three others want to break out of Gephard's office window. Will you have a look at it? I'd also like you to do the job for them."

"Thanks for the compliment," I replied. "When do we start?"

"Any time you like."

"I'm not so sure of the window idea, Dick," I said, "but I'll check up carefully. It's pretty close to a sentry and it may even be in his line of sight."

"Kenneth Lockwood will go sick whenever you're ready," Dick continued, "and he'll live in the sick-ward opposite Gephard's office and manipulate all the necessary keys."

"Good! There's no German medical orderly at night, so I can hide under Kenneth's bed after the evening *Appell* until lights out. Then I can start work. I'll take someone with me."

"Yes, do," said Dick, "but don't take Hank this time. He's an old hand. We've got to train more men in our escape technique. Choose someone else."

I had a look at the office. It was small and oblong in shape, with a barred window in an alcove at the far end from the door. Gephard's desk and chair were in the alcove. The remainder of the office was lined with shelves on which reposed an assortment of articles. Many of them, such as hurricane lamps, electric torches, dry batteries, and nails and screws, would have been useful to us, but we touched nothing. The window exit was thoroughly dangerous. I saw by careful inspection and a few measurements that with only a little more patience we could rip up Gephard's floor, pierce a wall eighteen inches thick, and have entry into a storeroom outside and below us. From there, by simply unlocking a door, the escapers would walk out on the sentry path surrounding the Castle. There was one snag. Did the storeroom have a cruciform or an ordinary lever lock?

This was checked by keeping a watch from a window for many days upon the area of the storeroom. The storeroom door was not visible, but a Jerry approaching it would be visible and, in due course, a Jerry was seen going to the door holding in his hand an ordinary lever key! Van Doorninck would take a selection of keys and there should be no difficulty. The alternative, which would have taken much longer, would have been for me to construct a camouflage wall and examine the storeroom at leisure. This escape was to be a blitz job. The hole would be ready in a matter of three days. Experience was proving that long-term jobs involved much risk due to the time element alone. I often mused on the chances of the French tunnel which was advancing slowly day by day. . . .

The work would have to be done at night; Gephard's office was in use all day. The office was situated near the end of a ground-floor corridor, on the opposite side of which was the camp sick-ward. This ward was across the courtyard from our quarters, so that the undertaking involved entering the sick-quarters before the main doors were locked up for the night and hiding there under the beds, until all was quiet—there was a sentry in the courtyard all day and night nowadays. The hospital beds were not high off the ground and were rather crammed together, giving ample concealment for superficial purposes.

I chose Lieutenant Derek Gill (Royal Norfolks) to come along and help me; he was the right type—imperturbable. We started operations as soon as Kenneth was snugly ensconced in his sick-bed, with serious stomach trouble. When the doors were locked and the patrols departed, Kenneth manipulated the keys, opened the sick-ward door and then Gephard's door, locked us in for the night and returned to bed.

I removed the necessary floorboards underneath the window and also, incidentally, under the desk at which Gephard sat every day! I started work on the wall. The joints between the stones were old, as I suspected, and by the morning the two of us had reached the far side. I noticed there was plaster on the other side. This was what I expected; it was the wall-face of the storeroom. That was enough for the first night. Most of the larger stones were removed in a sack, and in the under-floor rubble a passage was cleared at a forty-five-degree angle so that a person could ease himself down into the hole. Blankets were laid down so as to deaden the hollow sound, and the floor under Gephard's desk was then very carefully replaced. Nails were reinserted and covered with our patent dust-paste. All cracks were refilled with dirt. In the early hours, Kenneth, by arrangement, let us out and locked up. We retired to the sick-ward, the door of which also had to be locked, and rested comfortably until the German medical orderly arrived on his morning rounds, when we retired under the beds.

The next night Derek and I went to work again. This time the job was more difficult; the hole in the wall had to be enlarged enough to allow a large-sized man's body (Van Doorninck) to pass through. At the same time, the plaster on the further face was to be left intact. I knew the hole was high up in the storeroom wall, probably eight to ten feet from the floor-level. We finished the task successfully and in the morning retired as before.

The escape exit was now ready. Dick, Lulu, Bill, and myself worked out the plan together. It was based on the fact that German N.C.O.s occasionally came to the storeroom with Polish POWs who were working in the town of Colditz. They brought and removed stores, baskets of old uniforms, underclothing in large wooden boxes, wooden clogs and a miscellaneous assortment of harmless soldiers' equipment, as far as we could see. They came at irregular hours, mostly in the mornings, sometimes as early as 7 A.M. and seldom more often than twice a week. These habits had been observed and noted over a period of a month. It was agreed that the escape party should be increased to a total of six. Two more officers were therefore selected. They were Stooge Wardle, our submarine type, and Lieutenant Donkers, a Dutchman. It was arranged that Lulu should travel with the second Dutchman, and Bill Fowler with Van Doorninck.

Sentries were changed at 7 A.M., so the plan was made accordingly. Van Doorninck, who spoke German fluently, would become a senior German N.C.O. and Donkers would be a German private. The other four would be Polish orderlies. They would issue from the storeroom shortly after 7 A.M. Van Doorninck would lock up after him. The four orderlies would carry two large wooden boxes between them, the German private would take up the rear. They would walk along the sentry path past two sentries, to a gate in the barbed wire, where Van Doorninck would order a third sentry to unlock and let them pass. The sentries—with luck—would assume that the "fatigue" party had gone to the storeroom shortly before 7 A.M. Once through the barbed wire the party would proceed downhill along the roadway which went towards the park. They would, however, turn off after fifty yards and continue past a German barracks, and farther on they would reach the large gate in the wall surrounding the Castle grounds; the same over which Neave and Thompson had climbed in their escape. At this gate, Van Doorninck would have to use more keys. If he could not make them work, he had to use his wits. Indeed, if he managed to lead his company that far, he could probably ring up the Commandant and ask him to come and open the gate!

The plan necessitated the making of two large boxes in sections so that they could be passed through the hole into the storeroom, and yet of such construction that they could be very quickly assembled.

The day for the escape was fixed shortly after a normal visit to the storeroom, in order to lessen the chances of clashing with a real fatigue party. We prayed that a clash might not occur, but the visits were not accurately predictable and we had to take this chance.

The evening before the "off," after the last *Appell,* nine officers ambled at irregular intervals into the sick-ward corridor. There was other traffic also, and no suspicion was aroused. The sections of the wooden boxes had been transferred to the sick-ward at intervals during the day under coats. Eight officers hid under the beds, while Kenneth retired to his official one and saw to it that the hospital inmates remained quiet and behaved themselves. They were mostly French and were rather excited at the curious visitation. Kenneth had a way of his own of dealing with his brother officers of whatever nationality. He stood on his bed and addressed the whole sick-ward:

"I'll knock the block off any man here who makes a nuisance of himself or tries to create trouble. *Comprenez? Je casse la tête à n'importe qui fait du bruit ou qui commence à faire des bêtises."*

Of course, Kenneth knew everybody there intimately and could take liberties with their susceptibilities. He continued:

"What is going on here is none of your business, so I don't want to see any curiosity; poking of heads under beds, for instance; no whispering. When the patrol comes round, everybody is to behave quite normally. I'll be sitting up looking around. If I see the slightest unnecessary movements, I'll report the matter to General Le Blue as attempted sabotage."

Kenneth's mock seriousness had an edge to it. Among those in the sick-ward were a few more or less permanent inhabitants—the neurotic ones. They were capable of almost any absurdity and a firm line was the only one to take in their case.

The sick-ward was duly locked and night descended upon the Castle. Quietly the nine arose, and as Kenneth unlocked one door after another with ease, we "ghosted" through. Eight of us squeezed into the small office and Kenneth departed as he had come.

"Derek," I whispered, "we've got a long time in front of us before we start work. There's no point in beginning too early in case of misfires and alarms."

"How long do you think it will take to break out the hole?" he questioned.

"About an hour, I should say, but we'll allow double that amount."

"That means," said Derek, "we can start at, say, four A.M."

"Better make it three A.M. We must allow much longer than we anticipate for pushing this crowd through, along with all the junk. There's also the hole to be made good. Have you brought the water and the plaster?"

"Yes. I've got six pint bottles and enough plaster to do a square yard."

"Good. What time to you make it now?"

"Nine-forty-five," Derek replied. We sat around on the floor to pass the vigil.

At midnight there was an alarm. We heard Germans unlocking doors and the voice of Priem in the corridor. He went into the sick-ward for five minutes, then came out and approached Gephard's office door. We heard every word he said as he talked with the night-duty N.C.O. The latter asked:

"Shall I open this door, Herr Hauptmann?"

"Yes, indeed. I wish to control all," answered Priem.

"It is the office of *Oberstabsfeldwebel* Gephard, Herr Hauptmann."

"Never mind. Open!" came the reply.

There was a loud noise of keys and then Priem's voice:

"Ah! of course Herr Gephard has many locks on his door. I had forgotten. Do not open, it is safe."

The steps retreated and then died away as the outer door was relocked. We took several minutes to recover from this intrusion. Eventually Lulu Lawton, who was beside me, whispered into my ear, "My God! You were right, and how!"

It was uncanny the way Priem scented us out and nearly caught us in spite of all our precautions.

In the dog-watch, I started work quietly by making a small hole through the plaster and then cutting and pulling inwards towards myself. Minute pieces fell outside and made noises which sounded like thunder to me, but which were not, in reality, loud. In due course the hole was enlarged for a hand to pass through, then the rest was removed with ease. I had a sheet with me to help the escapers down into the storeroom beyond. Van Doorninck went first. He landed on some shelves and, using them as a ladder, descended safely to the floor. A few minutes later he reported that the outside door of the storeroom had a simple lock and that he had tried it successfully. This was good news. The other five officers followed: then the sections of the two boxes; the various bundles of escape clothing; the Polish troops' uniforms; the German soldiers' uniforms, and lastly, the plaster and the water. We could have made good use of a conveyor belt!

Derek and I wished them all good luck and, wasting no time, we started to refill the hole in the wall as neatly as possible, while Van Doorninck on the other side applied a good thick coat of plaster. The wooden boxes would come in very handy for carrying away the empty water-bottles and surplus plaster as well as the civilian outfits! Finally, as the last stone was ready to go into place, Van Doorninck and I checked watches and I whispered, "Good-bye and Good luck," and sealed the hole.

Derek and I then replaced blankets and floorboards carefully. By 6 A.M. the operation was finished, just as we heard Kenneth whispering through the door: "Is all well, are you ready?"

"Yes, open up."

Kenneth manipulated the locks and we retired to the sick-ward.

From there we would not see the rest of the act. The escapers would leave at 7:10 A.M., while the sick-ward would not open up until 7:30 A.M. Morning *Appell* was at 8:30 A.M. This was where the fun would start!

At about 7:30 A.M. we sallied forth unobtrusively. Dick was waiting for us and reported a perfect take-off!

Van Doorninck's uniform was that of a sergeant. The sentries had each in turn saluted smartly as the sergeant's fatigue party wended its way along the path towards the barbed-wire gate. Arrived here, the sentry in charge quickly unlocked it, and the party passed through and was soon out of sight of our hidden watchers in the upper stories of the Castle.

As minutes passed and there were no alarms, we began to breathe more freely. By 8 A.M. we could almost safely assume they were away.

The *Appell* was going to cause trouble. We had for the time being exhausted all our tricks for the covering of absentees from *Appell*. We had tried blank files, with our medium-sized R.A.F. officer running along, bent double, between the ranks and appearing in another place to be counted twice. We had tried having a whole row of officers counted twice by appropriate distraction of the N.C.O.s checking off the numbers. We had tried bamboozling the Germans by increasing the returns of officers sick. The Dutch dummies were no more.

If the escape had been in the park, we had a greater variety of methods from which to choose. Park parades, in the first place, did not cover the whole prisoner contingent. We could add bodies to begin with; as we had done, for instance, by suspending our medium-sized officer, on occasion, around the waist of a burly Dutch officer, whose enormous cloak covered them both with ease! On another attempt, we had staged a fake escape to cover the real one, by having two officers cut the park wire and run for it—without a hope of escape, of course. The deception, in this case, was that the two officers acted as if a third was ahead of them among the trees. They shouted encouragement and warning to this imaginary one, whom the Jerries chased round in circles for the remainder of the day!

By now we had temporarily run out of inspiration. We might manage to conceal one absence, but six was an impossibility. So we did the obvious thing. We decided to lay in a reserve of spare officers for future escapes. We concealed four officers in various parts of the Castle. There would be ten missing from the *Appell!* With luck the four hidden in the Castle would become "ghosts." They would appear no more at *Appells* and would fill in blanks on future escapes. The idea was, by now, not unknown to the Germans, but we would try it.

The morning *Appell* parade mustered and, in due course, ten bodies were reported missing. There were hurried consultations, and messengers ran to and fro from the *Kommandantur*. We were counted again and again. The Germans thought we were playing a joke on them. Guardhouse reports showed there had been a quiet night, after Priem's visit, with no alarms.

The Germans kept us on parade, and sent a search-party through all the quarters. After an hour, they discovered two of our ghosts. This convinced them we were joking. They became threatening, and finally held an identification parade while the Castle search-party continued its work. Eventually the latter found two more ghosts. By 11 A.M., not having found any further bodies, they concluded that perhaps six had escaped after all. The identification parade continued until they had established which officers were missing, in the midst of tremendous excitement as posses of Goons were despatched in all directions around the countryside.

We were satisfied at having increased the start of our six escapers by a further three hours. Later in the day we heard that the Jerries, after questioning all sentries, had suspected our fatigue party, and working backwards to the storeroom, had discovered my hole. There was much laughter, even among the Jerries, at the expense of Gephard, under whose desk the escape had been made! I leave it to the reader to imagine the disappointment and fury of Priem at our having eluded his grasp so narrowly during the night!

Before the evening was over, we had our disappointment too: Lulu Lawton and his companion were recaught. I was sorry for Lulu. He had put so much effort into the escape. It was largely his own idea and he had displayed cleverness and great pertinacity. These qualities, I thought, deserved better recognition than a month of solitary in the cells.

Lulu told us how Van Doorninck led the fatigue party past the German barracks and onwards to the last gateway. As he approached it, a Goon from the barracks ran after the party and asked Van Doorninck if he wanted the gate opened. "Naturally," replied the latter!

The Goon hurried off and returned shortly with the key. He opened the gate and locked it again after them!

A day later, Stooge Wardle and Donkers were recaptured.

Bill Fowler and Van Doorninck carried on happily. They slipped through the net and reached Switzerland safely in six days. That was in September 1942. Two more over the border! We had no reason to be ashamed of our efforts!

Bid for Freedom

WALTER THOMAS

The full story of Lieutenant Walter Thomas's adventures in escaping is told in his World War II memoir *Dare to Be Free*. Thomas was captured during the German invasion of the island of Crete. Despite being seriously wounded, he tried repeatedly to escape from the German field hospital where he was held.

Thomas made such a nuisance of himself in the hospital camp that he was marked for transfer to a regular POW camp in Germany. But while being held in a temporary camp in Greece, he made a run for it. His escape took extreme courage, as his companions all backed out and he had to go it alone while still healing from his injuries. Not many men would have risked it.

Soon after midday on 30 October with snow-capped Olympus on our left, we steamed up the Gulf of Salonika to tie up in that historic port. Above the harbour the old stone city walls, the towers and the fortresses standing out on the hill gave a medieval atmosphere, but around the docks things were modern enough. There was a small amount of German and Italian shipping about, with here and there a cruiser or a destroyer from Mussolini's fleet. German Marines, none of whom seemed more than eighteen years old, paraded on the wharves, constantly saluting their smart-looking officers. Everybody seemed busy, but all were very interested in the Englanders as we were off-loaded and shepherded into Red Cross vans. We were driven along the water-front, past the great circular tower of Salonika and in a few minutes were at the gates of the prison camp.

My heart sank at the sight. Here was no hospital wire. This was a real prison camp. High mazes of barbed wire ran at all angles. Throughout the camp were great towers on which sentries could be seen fondling their machine-guns. From behind the wire near the gate a crowd of unkempt and undernourished prisoners gathered to gape forlornly as we were formed into ranks and our luggage checked.

It was almost dark by the time all our personal belongings had been strewn on the gravel and the Guard Officer satisfied that we carried no implements for escape. The great gates opened and we poured in, to be ushered into various buildings.

In a large dormitory I met again quite a few of the officers who had come up from Athens in the hospital ship. We all fell to exchanging experiences, and I felt quite at home amongst them. Two in particular I came to respect immensely. Lieutenant-Colonel Le Soeuf, tall, dark and quietly spoken, had been captured with his unit, the 7th Australian Field Ambulance, when they were overrun at Heraklion in Crete; Major Richard Burnett, a regular officer, had been CO of his unit on Crete and had been captured while making a reconnaissance in the dark.

Salonika was a bad camp in every way. In the past many shocking atrocities had been committed by guards who had been former members of the Nazi Youth Movement. Burnett was even then investigating a horrible case—a German sentry had thrown a grenade into a latrine packed with dysentery cases and the carnage had been frightful. The only explanation given on Burnett's protest was that the men were whispering in a suspicious manner. The authorities supported the sentry's action.

In a recent unsuccessful attempt at escape, three men had been shot out of hand and their bodies left for days in the hot sun, while for other escapes soldiers had been bound with barbed wire and whipped as a warning to all. Drunken guards had been known to walk into the compound and cruelly maul unarmed prisoners, while it was said that the officer in charge of the young Nazis would ask daily of his guard how many English swine they had killed and congratulate the murderer effusively.

It was an alarming picture, quite different from the treatment I had experienced in Athens. Listening to it all I regretted much that I had ever left the hospital.

The camp had been an old Greek Artillery barracks, but the Germans had allowed it to deteriorate badly, so that now it was in a terrible state of sanitation, with practically no drainage at all. Millions of flies swarmed around the latrines and cookhouses and formed ugly black heaps where refuse was dropped. Scores of mangy cats slunk among the barrack-rooms.

The prisoners in the compound were the stragglers of the large army which had already passed through to Germany. There were thirty officers and some two hundred men, one hundred and fifty of whom were maimed in some way.

About fifteen were men who had lately been caught in and around Salonika. These were a grand crowd of fellows, and I made a point of talking to them and gaining much valuable information.

Some had been out and recaptured four or five times; indeed, the greatest joke amongst them was the case of the Australian who was picked up as a matter of course by a German patrol each Friday at a house of ill fame. Others with higher motives for escape had been free for long periods, only to be recaptured either on the very borders of Turkey or at sea moving south to freedom.

One, a tall New Zealand sergeant with a sense of humour, had seen his chance on a day of pouring rain, when a German officer had visited the camp hospital. The officer had walked into the lobby, and hung up his dripping coat and hat before entering the German guardroom. The sergeant had donned these quickly and marched out into the rain. The sentries had all, one by one, frozen into a salute. Thereafter, he walked down into the streets of Salonika. It was truly an escape to fire the imagination.

A long-haired lad from Sussex had clung to the bottom of one of the contractor's drays and had been carried out of the camp. A very young Cockney told us of his adventure in going out in a bag of rubbish.

The prisoners were even then working on a mass escape plan. But they had the shrewdness of experienced escapists. It was some days before I was to be allowed into their confidence.

Meanwhile, the atmosphere in the officers' mess was unpleasantly strained. There were bickerings over food all round, and quarrels between the Medical Corps and the combatants over such futile things as seniority and the post of Senior British Officer in Captivity. On one occasion feeling ran so high that one side actually asked a German NCO to consider and settle the dispute.

It was not a pleasant place. Consequently I was pleased when Dick Burnett asked me to share a room accorded him because of his rank.

Burnett was keen on escape. He had been free on more than one occasion in Crete and in spite of his forty years was determined to risk all the hazards to get back to his regiment. For as long as he was to be a prisoner he was firmly resolved to cause as much trouble for his captors as possible.

For the first three or four days, I think, he was weighing me up as a possible partner for the months we might have to spend together before reaching British lines.

Then we began to lay our plans.

The section of the camp we were concerned with was only a small part, a sub-section, of the main Salonika Prison Camp. Most of the other sub-sections were now empty and unguarded, with the exception of the one immediately to the west of ours. This held political prisoners from Greece and Yugoslavia. In there one day we had seen an old lady awaiting execution for aiding British escapers.

The sub-section was an oblong, some three hundred yards by two hundred, containing seven large barrack huts, a cookhouse and a large new building. The only exit was the gate at the north-west corner and apart from the roving sentries within the compound, the Germans relied mainly on the guard posts immediately outside it. At the southern end these consisted of two twenty-foot towers, each with two sentries, a machine-gun and a movable searchlight. At the northern end there were the sentries on the gate, those on a tower by the gate, and two sentries with machine-gun and searchlight on the roof of a small shed used for storing horse fodder. The south and west sides were bounded by other sub-sections, the north by an open space and the Salonika road, and the east side had a wide gravel road which separated the compound from rubbish and salvage and which led along to the stables.

A whole morning spent watching guards, drawing innumerable diagrams and getting annoyed with one another disposed of the front, the west and the rear sides as quite impossible. Only the east side was left and we had little hope that it would produce the answer. In common with the others it had some three hundred yards of wire tangle, ten feet high, ten feet wide, but there was one difference. There were two buildings which broke the obstacle, that is, the wire tangle ran in between them, and rambled up and over them. It did not run along the back.

One of these was the cookhouse. It had a thick cement wall for a back and, furthermore, was less than a stone's throw from the southern sentry tower. We mooched around it for half an hour after lunch and rejected it as impracticable.

The second building was a fairly new three-storied building. A preliminary examination revealed no possibilities; all the windows facing out were heavily barred with steel and barbed wire, while even if work could free them it would be too dangerous to be lowered to the road below in full view of the searchlights at either end.

But just as we were deciding dejectedly that a tunnel was the only solution, we espied a staircase winding down from the ground floor to hide what must be a back doorway onto the gravel road below. The passage down was blocked by large empty crates. The door was of itself unimportant. There were still the searchlight and machine-guns covering the road outside. But Dick had an idea and we climbed again onto the first floor to discuss it.

The two searchlights which concerned us covered the road very efficiently. The one at the south end from the tower had an unobstructed view, while the other one on the roof of the hay shed was only limited by its position from seeing the actual back of the building in question. But, and on this our plan depended, these posts had the additional task of covering the south and north wire respectively: their searchlights were on swivels and they would swing from one task to the other every few seconds. For the most part one or other of the posts would have its light focused on the gravel road, occasionally both would play together along it for minutes on end. But with an understandable human error, often for a few seconds, both crews would switch simultaneously onto their secondary task. This would leave the road in darkness until either of them realized the position and swung his searchlight back. Burnett and I considered that, given luck, this erratic few seconds would give us a chance to make the initial dash across the road and use the scant cover of a shallow culvert before the searchlights swung back.

And so we examined the door.

The crates barring the steps down from the first floor were really no obstacle and would afford good cover for any work we should do. The steps ran down in two short flights onto a very small landing, and the door-frame was set firmly in stone. There were steel and wooden bars across it, both bolted and nailed, and the whole was covered with barbed wire on staples. Formidable certainly, but, provided we were not hurried, we thought it could be done.

One remarkable thing about our work on this project was the complete absence of the adventure spirit and the elation of imaginary success. Every step we took in this venture was coldly methodical. We took very few into our confidence.

Amazingly enough, the tools for the work were no trouble at all. I brought a pair of excellent pliers from a Greek electrician working in the barracks; Burnett made some useful crowbars from sections of our beds; and Fred Moodie, a camp doctor, provided a strong pair of plaster cutters. Fred also arranged for me a good supply of the German cod liver oil salve which had proved very soothing and beneficial to my wound.

We started work that night. Immediately after the evening check we made our way to the building with innocent unconcern and talked to various orderlies until curfew, when we slipped behind the crates under the first flight of stairs until all was quiet.

The work was necessarily slow, and not a little nerve-racking. Each nail, each bolt had to be worked out slowly and with great caution; a loud squeak would leave us perspiring and fearful for long minutes. Every now and then the crunch of heavy feet on the gravel outside would hold us up, and on three occasions during the first night two of the guards talked for a long time just outside the door.

By four o'clock we had removed all the wooden bars and two of the six more formidable steel bars. We tacked the bars back loosely into their old positions and generally tidied up the evidence before setting off on the quite hazardous trip back to our barracks. The two sentries detailed to prowl round inside the compound had orders to shoot on sight after curfew, and though the twenty minutes they took on their regular rounds provided ample time for us there were the searchlights to pin us down occasionally and always the chance that the sentries might vary their tactics.

We reached our room without incident and were sound asleep for the six o'clock room check. Having previously convinced the Germans that it was less trouble not to order us out to stand by our beds each morning (as laid down), we were left to slumber on until almost lunch time.

Our progress on the second night did not compare with the first night. There were too many interruptions—stable-hands coming home late from leave and arguing out on the road, restless sentries and irregular changing of guards. And we were discovered at work by a group of Australian and British medical orderlies, and it took us some little time to impress on them the need for absolute secrecy. However, we worked out two more steel bars and managed to loosen a third before an early rooster, crowing beyond the stables, warned us of approaching day.

On the third night we made very good progress indeed; by eleven o'clock the last of the steel bars was disposed of. We had brought a rough chisel and a screwdriver to remove the lock, but, to our amazement, we found that it was not, in fact, locked. A few nails had been hammered at random around the edges, however, and just after midnight the last was worked out and we were able to move the door.

It opened two or three inches and then stuck. We realized that there was an apron of barbed wire stapled onto the outside. With some difficulty it would be possible to worm a wrist with pliers through the opening. After a short consultation we decided to leave it as it was until the night of the break, knowing that it would only take a few minutes to open it.

We made our way carefully back to our room, secreted our tools under our mattresses and in the stove, and undressed in the dark. It was only about one o'clock and, tired as we were, the prospect of a few extra hours' sleep was very pleasing.

No sooner had we said good night, however, than we were suddenly startled by the tread of heavy feet in the passageway outside. There was a guttural order, our door burst open, and three soldiers rushed in. Torches flashed in our faces, our blankets were pulled off roughly, and the room quickly but not thoroughly searched. Then, as if satisfied, the officer barked an order and the party clattered out and away, leaving two very shaken men behind.

Now that visit was unfortunate. The explanation was quite beyond us, particularly as ours was the only room searched. Perhaps someone had discovered and reported that we had not been sleeping in our beds at night; or perhaps it was merely a check on me as a known 'bad lad'. But the effect was this: Burnett decided not to come. Three nights' work had taxed his nerves badly and now he thought our whole plan was discovered. Even when daylight proved that no attempt was made to re-fix the door, Burnett saw the possibility of a trap—a machine-gun covering the exit to make an example of anyone who attempted to escape. He was still as determined as ever but with the caution of forty years he weighed the chances as too dangerous, and started straight away on a new plan to throw ourselves from the train on the way through Yugoslavia.

His pessimism shook me not a little. I spent the morning watching the area near the cookhouse, and after lunch sat down and tried to come to some decision. His arguments were very sound; the plan had been hazardous enough without the new threat. Yet at the back of my mind was a conviction, however unfounded, that the plan was still secret.

Finally I took out a piece of paper, and ruling a line down the centre, wrote in two columns all the pros and cons I could think of.

That was a poignant half-hour. I knew well that the wrong decision might cost me my life. Yet I felt very strongly that it was a case of 'now or never', that, if I let this opportunity pass, I might never be presented with another.

As the page filled up, Burnett sat quietly watching me. I knew that he was apprehensive, but, having stated his arguments once, he made no attempt to dissuade me further.

Before I could make up my mind we were besieged by some five or six of the more hardened card players and I was quite willing to procrastinate an hour for a game of pontoon. Perhaps it was my abstraction, but within half an hour, without effort, I had taken every *drachma* off the whole school. After a drink of cocoa from my Red Cross parcel they all departed very disgruntled, threatening that they would come back on the morrow to get it all back. As soon as they had gone, at Burnett's suggestion, I entered under the 'Pros' the fact that I now had 8,000 *drachmae* for escape purposes.

At six o'clock I made my decision. It was, I am sure, the decision of my life. Our original plan had been to get some greatly needed rest that night, Saturday, and escape on Sunday about nine when the guards not on duty were on leave. But now, as things appeared to be moving rapidly and because my nerves were so tense that I could not sleep, I decided to go on my own that night.

When Burnett saw that I was determined, he gave me everything he had; all his bread, condensed Red Cross food, a civilian coat, and all his savings, including some English money. He cooked me up a wonderful farewell meal and set himself to do a thousand and one little things to help me to get ready.

It was now after curfew. It was therefore necessary to move with great care over to the building. Soon after eight-thirty, I said goodbye to Burnett. He was terribly apprehensive of the risk I was taking and heartily miserable that he was not coming with me. I realized I was going to miss his company very much.

It took me almost an hour to go the two hundred yards from our barracks. The searchlights seemed particularly restless and the roving patrol sat down and talked for nearly half an hour while I lay in what shade a wire-netting fence afforded. When finally they moved off I ran quickly up the steps and through the door into the hall of the medical building. As soon as I latched the door behind me a startled voice greeted me.

'Are you *mad*? Surely you know that it's dangerous to be out at curfew?'

It was an Australian medical orderly. When I told him of my plans he immediately offered his help.

We moved onto the first landing, from where we could look through the barred window down onto the road. Everything seemed quite normal. We watched for half an hour, but, with the exception of a team of horses being taken out from the stables, only the usual movement was apparent.

The orderly and a friend appointed themselves to keep watch while I worked. We arranged a code of signals whereby, should they wish to warn me, they would throw something small down the steps leading to the escape door. The 'all-clear' would be one or the other whistling from *Rigoletto*.

The door was as we had left it. I removed all the loosely held bars and convinced myself that no one had tampered with them. The door opened noiselessly some three inches and even with great caution it only took me twenty minutes to cut the eight or nine restraining wires on the outside.

As I cut the last one and felt the door suddenly swing easily towards me, the first alarm signal in the form of a leather slipper clattered down the stairs behind me. I closed the door quickly, my heart in my mouth. Outside I could hear heavy feet crunching slowly down the road. As they approached the door I held my breath in apprehension. With the searchlights full on I felt that no one could miss the tell-tale loose ends of wire. But, although I could have sworn there was a slight pause just level with the door, the danger passed and in a few seconds I heard a soft but unmusical attempt to whistle the arranged all clear.

I opened the door a few inches and studied the ground. The road was only some fifteen feet across, but I realized that unless the searchlights settled down I would never get over without being seen. The sentry in the tower on the south end was unusually restless; his light was flickering to and fro every few seconds. I decided, as it was then nine-thirty, to wait until the ten o'clock change of sentries with the hope of getting someone more placid. During the wait I worked out each step across the road, and the point where I should get over the low wall into the rubbish on the other side.

Just before ten the team of horses, which had gone out earlier, returned noisily up the road, and, although I did not look, I imagined they were towing some vehicle. When they had passed up towards the German stables I stole a look out. I thought for a moment that the opportunity was ideal, for one of the searchlights was playing on the stable yard, probably to help the unhitching of the horses. I had just made the decision to go and was in the act of opening the door when some object clattered down the stairs behind me. A second later came the sharp order of the Corporal of the guard as he turned his ten o'clock relief up the road—I shivered as I realized how very nearly I had run right into them.

For fifteen minutes after the old guard had clattered past the door on their way to the guard-room, the searchlights on both ends were seldom still for more than a few seconds, but soon after that the new sentries began to tire of their vigilance. Sitting back on the stairs I could count up to four seconds while no light shone through the keyhole or under the door. So I opened the door cautiously and looked out.

Looking across the road, I realized that although the tower at the south end shone direct onto the exit, it would be the light from the roof of the hay shed which would be most dangerous, as it shone over the rubbish. I started counting the irregular breaks of darkness. Sometimes there would be one or other searchlight shining on the road for over ten minutes, then for an erratic five minutes it would be in darkness every few seconds.

'One—two—three,' I counted, 'one—two—three—four getting better now, one—two—three—four—my word, I could have made it that time, one—two—three—phew, just as well I didn't then . . . ' and then there would be another period of light. The most unnerving thing about it all was the fact that there was no way of knowing how long any particular period of darkness was going to be. I knew that whenever I made the decision it would be final. The success or failure of the whole plan depended on nothing more than luck.

I think perhaps I must have been poised there for half an hour. But it seemed years to me. I alternated between self-reproach for having missed a good chance and a chill of horror when a period of darkness lasted only one second.

And then I went. Not running, but carefully over the road, my stocking-covered shoes making little noise on the gravel. But as I prepared to throw myself over the low wall on the other side of the road, I sensed the return of one of the lights and involuntarily dropped to the ground, realizing instantly that I must present an ideal target to either sentry post.

First the light from the hay shed played idly up and down the road, and so brilliant was it that it shone right into the gravel where my face was buried. Then I sensed the other one flashing over my shoulder. My body tingled with terror and for the first time in my life I felt the hairs on the nape of my neck pricking and rising.

I could hear two of the sentries talking quite clearly. They did not sound at all excited and yet surely they must have seen me. My body began to flinch and cringe as I imagined a bullet striking home. My mind went numb, and I had no idea how long I lay there, but at last, one after the other, the lights swung away.

I sprang up. Instead of vaulting the low wall I passed along it, turned into the courtyard of an MT garage. I dropped behind a large oil drum as the first light swung back. Here I was not so frightened, for the low wall now shielded me completely from the one searchlight and the drum from the other. I must have been pinned there for all of ten minutes. It was uncomfortably cramped, and I was apprehensive lest some driver or later-returning guard should discover me.

But when darkness came I was able to slip over the wall, and worm through the rubbish towards the outer ring of wire. There was no need to stop even when both lights were playing down the road, for there was sufficient shadow amongst the rubbish and small scrub to mask cautious movement. There was thirty yards of this cover stretching over to the outer ring of doubled apron barbed wire. This presented no problem with my wire-cutters. But

I was surprised when I was through it to run into a wire-netting fence. Following it along, I came to a break covered by a sheet of iron, which I crawled through to find myself in a small cleared space littered with large boxes. I was just passing one of the latter when a movement somewhere near stopped me. I hugged the ground, my heart in my mouth. All was quiet for a few minutes, then just as I prepared to continue, again came the small movement, much closer this time. I placed it as just behind the box. I was becoming really scared when from inside the box came the unmistakable clucking of a disturbed hen. I was inside the guards' chicken run.

I crossed the run to the rear corner of the garage and cut a small square to let myself out. I found myself in a grass enclosure, bounded by two very high stone walls, which ran into a corner some two hundred yards away. Very clearly I could hear the rumbling of the trams on the main Salonika road.

The wall bounding the road was about ten feet high and I could see glass glistening along its length. But it didn't present any great obstacle—the Germans had attempted to make it more formidable by giving it an apron of barbed wire—thus making an ideal ladder.

I climbed up it carefully. The road was still very busy for that time of night. In addition to the trams and army vehicles there was a steady stream of civilians and soldiers on both sides of the street. I waited ten minutes and was thinking of retiring for a few hours to let things settle down when I fancied I heard a single shot from back in camp. I listened for a full minute. Although I heard nothing further and was almost convinced that it was my over-taxed mind playing tricks, I decided to push on and take the chance of discovery.

With the glare from the lights of the prison camp there was quite a shadow on the road side of the wall, and as soon as there was a perceptible break in the traffic below I lowered myself so far as the lowest strand of barbed wire would allow me and dropped the remaining four feet, falling in a heap on the footpath.

My first reaction was one of acute pain. The jar was considerable. But almost immediately I became aware of two figures standing some fifteen paces away arguing volubly. They were both soldiers and I saw by the rifle he had slung over his shoulder that one of them was on duty. But as I picked myself up I knew I had not been seen. The second soldier was obviously very drunk and was abusing the sentry roundly.

I moved quickly up the street for two or three hundred yards, stopped and removed the spare pair of socks which I had worn over my shoes, and walked very quietly into Salonika.

The whole of the venture up to this stage had been cool and methodical. A desperate fear of the risks had numbed my mind against any anticipation of success. But now at every step I felt welling within me a glorious exhilaration, an ecstasy so sweet that my eyes pricked with tears of gratitude. All the oppression, all the worry and boredom, which had so weighed me down, seemed to disappear as though they were taken like a heavy cloak off my shoulders. The air was pure and free.

Escape or Die

PAUL BRICKHILL

Charles McCormac was an English planter's son living in Malaya when World War II came to the Pacific. He was captured by the Japanese in the early days of the war. Few escapers have made such a bold, direct move in their desperation to be free. The tale of his miraculous escape is told in *Escape or Die*, by Paul Brickhill—himself part of one of the most famous escapes ever made, the Great Escape from Stalag Luft III in Germany.

A fter they pushed him back into the compound, bleeding, McCormac knew that the next time the Japanese took him to the Y.M.C.A. for interrogation they intended to torture him, presumably to death. What made it worse were the impossible alternatives.

The change had been so swift. A few weeks before, he and Pat had moved into their new house near the aerodrome in Singapore. He was twenty-six and she, twenty-one, was having their first baby. In that same week the Japs landed in Malaya. At first, people in Singapore did not think the Japanese would get very far. Pat was frightened when Charles, as a sergeant wireless operator-gunner, flew in the Catalinas on bombing raids, but when he was not flying he came home at night. And then the defenses seemed to crumble and the Catalina squadron was wiped out in a single, devastating Jap raid and the remnants were evacuated to Java.

McCormac did not go with them. He had lived many years in Malaya, where his father had been a planter, before he joined the R.A.F., and because he was an "old hand" the C.O. gave him permission to stay behind and see Pat safely evacuated by ship; the Japanese had unpleasant ways of dealing with

Eurasian girls who married Europeans. They said they were renegades and gave them special treatment. She was lovely in the exotic Eurasian way but to McCormac, standing on the wharf, she looked tearfully forlorn leaning over the rail as the ship pulled out.

He went back briefly to the house, a sinewy man with a bitter downward twist to his mouth, moving from room to room methodically smashing all their things so the Japs would not get them. Then he put on a clean, white shirt that Pat had left out for him and went out to join up with the army in the ground fighting.

Singapore fell a week later and two days after that the Japanese caught McCormac, still on the island, fighting from the roadblocks with a band of volunteers. Out of touch with other troops they had not known the island had fallen, and that was the start of the trouble. It had pleased the Japanese to regard them as saboteurs and they shot two of the band on the spot. Then they noticed McCormac's dirty white shirt. If he had been in the R.A.F. as he claimed, they said, he would be wearing a khaki shirt. He must be a spy and they would deal with him in a suitable way quite soon.

The hell of the cage had started then. Isolated in a banana forest, the Pasir Panjang cage was a hot clearing a hundred yards square, fenced by coils of barbed wire and circled by the trunks and broad leaves of banana trees, a screen round the degradation. Inside the wire the Japanese crammed hundreds of British and Australian soldiers and civilians, giving them each a couple of spoonfuls of rice and a sliver of dried fish most days. Starvation and dysentery are an unpleasant combination and the cage was a focus of sweaty putrescence. By night, arclamps round the wire threw a glare over them, though by day the Japanese sent them in heavily guarded batches down to the docks to clear bomb rubble.

The Japanese commandant warned them that they could not hope to escape, but if they tried the punishment would be extreme, not only for the man who tried but for others, too, as a deterrent.

One day, three of them tried. They did not return with their party and it was rumored that friendly Chinese had hidden them. The thin men in the cage waited for the reprisals, but nothing happened.

A few days later an army sergeant slipped away. Still nothing happened. After another few days seven more did not return from the docks one evening.

At dawn the men in the cage were paraded at attention. They were still at attention at 4 P.M., many held up by friends after collapsing and being clubbed to their feet.

At that hour a party of Japanese officers arrived and a Japanese sergeant wandered thoughtfully among the prisoners as though he were inspecting cattle and picked out eleven men, mostly Australians, all about six feet tall. Japanese soldiers dragged them to the middle of the parade square and lashed their hands behind them. Another squad of Japanese soldiers marched briskly up to them and bayoneted all of the eleven in the throats and stomachs. It was quite quick and they were all dead within a minute.

A growl started swelling from the captives. Some of them shuffled a pace or two forward, almost involuntarily; the machine guns opened up and as three of them toppled to the ground an Australian lieutenant jumped forward and faced them, waving his arms and yelling: "Hold it, you fools. We can't do anything yet."

He turned and walked warily towards the Japanese officers and the captives heard him saying in English that they had violated the rules of war. A Japanese soldier hit him in the back with his rifle butt, the commandant signalled to his men and three of them grabbed the Australian and started to drag him away. The lieutenant managed to twist his head round to the parade again and shouted to them: "Mark these lice for future reference."

They never saw him again.

The commandant announced that he would not kill any more men at random. If anyone else escaped they would execute every remaining man on his working party.

The following morning they took McCormac to the Y.M.C.A., standing him in a room in front of a Japanese officer wearing baggy khaki pants, puttees, shirt and a sword. He had a flattish head and a Mongoloid, moon-like face, and for the first hour he made McCormac walk in and out bowing and hissing to show respect. They questioned him for the next hour, beating him occasionally with fists.

In interrogations by the Japanese, Western soldiers are absolved from the normal obligation to give name, rank and number only. To avoid torture one is permitted to answer a few questions. For an hour McCormac fended off some questions and answered others. They left him (under guard) for four hours, presumably to let fear work on his morale, and then two Japanese soldiers took him into a room in front of another Japanese officer, clearly a senior one.

Teruchi was short and very broad. He spoke English with an American accent and looked almost European.

"You lived in Cairnhill Road?" he said.

"Yes," said McCormac.

"Then your wife was Eurasian?"

McCormac stared at Teruchi and did not answer.

"Do not deny it," Teruchi said. "We have been to the house." He took a couple of steps forward and the Japanese soldiers gripped McCormac's arms rigidly. Teruchi said coldly, "You're the curse of the East, you people. And you're a saboteur." He kicked and his boot caught McCormac in the stomach. Teruchi kicked again and again till McCormac collapsed on to his knees, arms still tightly held, feeling he was going to vomit.

"Where is your wife?" Teruchi said.

"I don't know."

Teruchi said more slowly: "Where . . . is . . . your . . . wife?"

"Evacuated."

"When, and how? And to where?"

"By sea. The third of February. I don't know where to."

"Ah," said Teruchi. "The *Wakefield*." McCormac was startled again. Teruchi seemed to know nearly everything.

"We sank her," Teruchi said with satisfaction, and added unemotionally, "I regret to assure you that there were no survivors. You can believe me when I say that. I know."

McCormac felt he wanted to be sick again.

"Where is your wife's family?"

Pat's parents, her sister and brother were in Kuching, Sarawak, where the father was postmaster. McCormac had a terrible certainty of what would happen to them if the Japanese located them.

"I don't know," he said.

Moving deliberately, Teruchi pulled his Samurai sword out of its bamboo scabbard. He held it with two hands clasped round the long handle and waved the blade in front of McCormac's eyes.

"Where is your wife's family?"

"I don't know," McCormac said stubbornly. "I just have no idea."

Teruchi jabbed but McCormac, tensed and waiting, managed to jerk his head aside in time to save his eye. The point speared through the fold of skin at the corner of his eye, grated on the bone and tore through and out. Teeth bared with shock, he twisted his face down and to one side, trying to hunch it protectively between his shoulders while the blood dripped on his thigh.

"Where is your wife's family?" he loudly demanded.

"I don't know." McCormac lifted his head to watch.

Teruchi jabbed again and once more McCormac ducked and the point sliced across his cheek by the corner of his mouth, but did not go through into the mouth. Teruchi smiled and McCormac, reckless from rage and pain, snarled: "You do that again and I'll bloody well choke you."

Teruchi, still smiling, said gently, "I will see you again. We will have adequate time and arrangements." He jerked his head to the Japanese guards; they yanked McCormac to his feet and handed him over to two guards from Pasir Panjang cage, a lean one with a bony face known to the prisoners as "Kinching" (a very rude Malayan word) and a plump one known with crude but satisfying malice as "Fatso." They walked him the four miles back, opened the wire gate and roughly and maliciously kicked him through.

The working parties were back from the docks and an Australian called Donaldson, with whom McCormac had become friendly, swabbed the gashes on his face with a strip torn off McCormac's shirt while he listened to what had happened.

In the morning they marched McCormac to the docks again with the working party and on the way Donaldson edged alongside and said quietly:

"I got an idea last night. Supposing all the working party escaped, all seventeen of us. They'd have no one left to take reprisals against."

McCormac felt a moment of hope but then knew it was no good. "No go," he said. "They wouldn't do it. If they weren't killed in the break they'd die sooner or later in the jungle."

"Worth trying anyway," Donaldson said. He had a few words with each member of the party at the docks that day; two or three liked the idea, a couple were tepidly interested and the rest not interested.

A Portuguese Eurasian in charge of the party directed rubble clearing and they found he was a friend, though necessarily a guarded one. When the Jap guards were watching he bellowed and snarled at the prisoners, but when the guards' backs were turned he whispered in a friendly way out of the corner of his mouth, advised them to go slow on the work and now and then slipped them a cigarette or a little rice from his pocket, which they accepted with gratitude.

About five days after the affair with Teruchi the man said to McCormac: "Don't you remember me . . . Rodriguez. I worked on the aerodrome."

Then McCormac remembered him as one of a local, hired labor force building huts and runways and pens for the planes. They talked warmly for a while and McCormac told Rodriguez of the grim position he was in.

Rodriguez hesitated and then said. "My brother is in Malaya. He is with some Eurasian and Chinese guerrillas in the hills around Kuala Lipis. They raid the Japs. I could tell you where there is a boat for crossing the Johore Straits and you could probably all reach them and join them."

"Why are you offering all this?" McCormac asked. "We can pay you nothing and only endanger you."

"I want no payment," Rodriguez said. "The Japanese raped my eldest daughter and took her away."

Fatso and Kinching were in a good humor that night, and so were the other guests, Flatface, Lofty and Harry, the little Korean, cruelest of them all. They had been to watch the mass beheadings of some recalcitrant prisoners and of some Malayans and Chinese suspected of being anti-Japanese. They told the men in the cage that scores of heads had rolled and described the scene with gestures and laughter.

"We'll probably all die anyway," Donaldson said. "Look, let's try the gang again about escaping. If Rodriguez'll help us they might come at it."

Once more they approached the others but there were still half a dozen who refused. McCormac thought of the solution.

"Look, Don," he said, "there's no roll call here; only numbers. So long as there're seventeen on the gang the Japs don't give a darn. There are some other tough blokes in this compound. Why not fix some changeovers till we have seventeen blokes all game for it?"

That evening they fixed it, crawling among the wretches lying on the filthy ground, talking in whispers till they had six men willing to join them and had arranged for the six they replaced to join other parties. They would make for the hills near Kuala Lipis and join the guerrillas.

Next day they faced the problem of how to escape, and down at the docks, manhandling the crushed concrete and debris, they conspired in whispers whenever they could. Rodriguez, a little fearfully, consented to help them all, but only on condition they did not escape during the day when under his care. He had a wife and six more children to consider.

"If you can get out of the compound at night," he said, "come to my house at Paya Lebar and I'll lead you to the boat."

Back in the cage they made a plan for the following night. The lights always came on at six-thirty, and then the tropical night fell with its usual swiftness. If they could somehow smash the lighting system they could rush the gate when it was dark and scatter into the banana trees and lalang grass.

They were keyed up to it now, scared but resolved. There was no going back. Anyone who backed out now would be bayoneted in reprisal after the escape. Donaldson had a last grim word before they tried to sleep: "If anyone's wounded or falls behind, there's no going back for them. They'll have to be left."

They all agreed. McCormac, eyeing them, thought what a desperate team they looked—dirty and stinking all of them, with cropped heads and thick beard stubble, hungry and skinny-ribbed, dressed in filthy, ragged shorts and brutalized by circumstance.

He sweated more than usual at the docks next day in case Teruchi should send for him, but the day passed much as usual, except that most of them managed to walk back to the cage with thick sticks hidden in their shorts. Donaldson had found a lump of lead and a couple of feet of thin rope. He knotted the lead to the end of the rope to make a "bolo" club.

About a quarter past six Donaldson and a couple of others stood round McCormac while he reached through the barbed wire and yanked two electric leads out of a junction box. In ones and twos they were all wandering over to the front gate. Six-thirty came and nothing happened. Dusk was gathering in the hot clearing. A Jap soldier walked out of the atap guard hut and crossed to another little atap hutch where the power plant was to switch on the lights. As he pulled the switch, a flash lit the hutch from the inside; there was a puffing explosion and the roof burst into flame. "Christ, it's blown up!" One of the prisoners nearly shrieked it in hysteria.

Donaldson bellowed "Now!" and jumped forward, the others streaming after him. The bamboo gate burst in front of them as they trampled through, and at the same moment Jap soldiers came running out of the guard hut and screamed at the sight of them. Two had guns and raised them, but only three or four shots cracked before the prisoners were on them. McCormac smashed a lump of wood in the Korean's face and Harry the Korean dropped. He tugged the bayonet out of the Korean's belt and ran for the banana trees. Dim figures were running with him. He looked back and saw bodies on the ground and Donaldson struggling with one of them. "Come on, you bloody fool," McCormac screamed.

Machine guns opened up on the other side of the cage, and then they were stumbling through the lalang grass, zigzagging between the banana trunks and the huge green leaves that slapped against their faces.

McCormac found himself with Donaldson; they ran on for several minutes till the crashing noises near them in the jungle grew fainter. They slowed to a walk for a while, sweating, hearts pounding, and breathing noisily, probably as much from tension as the exertion.

It was several miles to Paya Lebar, and when they were out of the rubber trees they moved warily, hunched low with only their heads peering nervously over the dry tips of the lalang grass, which rattled with a terrifying noise as they brushed through. Some time after ten o'clock Donaldson picked out the loom of the big tree that Rodriguez had said was about fifty yards down the track from his house. The darkness was heavy and still, almost cool after the steamy heat of the day, but they were both sweating and trembling and sat down by the trunk of the tree.

Ten minutes later the grass rustled; they crouched silently, and as two shadows neared they recognized two of the party. During the next quarter of an hour several more arrived, and McCormac crawled off round to the back of Rodriguez's house and knocked quietly on the door. In a few seconds Rodriguez opened it, dressed in slacks and a dirty singlet. Somehow he had heard of the explosion by the cage and was nervous.

"I think there is an alarm," he whispered. "I cannot risk my family by taking you to the boat." He told McCormac exactly where it was, hauled up on the mud of the mangrove swamp near Kranji Point, about three hundred yards west of the spot where the Causeway threaded across the narrow strait to Johore. He took McCormac's hand and pressed some paper into it (it was three hundred and fifty Jap dollars), squeezed the hand, whispered "Good luck," and vanished behind the door. McCormac crawled back to the tree and found that fifteen of the party had arrived.

They waited nearly half an hour for the other two, but they never came, and three or four said they thought they had seen them shot or bayoneted in the escape. It seemed fairly sure that two of the Jap guards were dead too, and probably at least one more. They all knew now that if they were recaptured there would be no simple ceremony such as a bayonet in the stomach, but a more prolonged business—probably the bamboo treatment, where a man is lashed down, tightly spreadeagled over some young bamboo shoots. The bamboo grows some five inches a day and the tips are sharp enough to be neither stopped nor diverted by a human body.

In twos and threes they set off for Kranji Point, the groups keeping about twenty yards between them, led by McCormac, who brought them on to the mud flats. Over to the left by the water's edge lay two small boats, and almost in the same instant he and the others in front saw dark shapes moving about ten yards away.

Those in front tried to back; a shout came from the dim shapes and one of the escapers yelled "Japs!" More startled shouts, and McCormac was running with some of the others at the dark shapes. There were two or three orange flashes and the jarring cracks of point-blank rifle shots, and the two groups tangled in struggle. McCormac hacked like a maniac with his bayonet; a Jap fired two more shots from a machine pistol and McCormac crashed into him and they both went down, the Jap underneath. McCormac was stabbing him and suddenly it was all over.

There were eight escapers left on their feet, and the bodies of six Japanese soldiers and several escapers on the ground. Someone said in a hoarse whisper, "Come on, for Christ's sake. There'll be hundreds of them here in a minute." They ran over to one of the little boats and shoved it down toward the water; it slid fairly easily over the slime into the oily water and they tumbled in, found a paddle lying in the bottom, and one of them dug the blade into the water and drove the little boat slowly out into the strait.

They were about two hundred yards out, when a searchlight flicked into brightness on the Causeway; one moment they had been thankfully marooned in the husk of darkness, and then, full-grown from birth, the beam lay flat and dazzling on the water. It started to sweep and McCormac whispered sharply, "Down."

Flat on the floorboards they huddled under the level of the gunwales, conscious of soft light as the beam slid across the boat, then darkness and light again as the beam swung back. It played around them for a long time and they waited in terror for the sound of an approaching launch. It seemed to be hours before the light flicked off. The Japanese must have thought it was an empty boat adrift, because no launch came. When at last they sat up again the scattered lights on the shore and the Causeway had retreated into the distance and they did not know which way they were facing.

"We've been drifting," McCormac said. "There's a whale of a strong tide and we're moving out to sea."

"Thank God for that," said Donaldson. "The farther the better."

There was no point paddling when they did not know where they were going and they spent the time investigating the boat. It was small and old, and on the floorboards up in the bows they found a small drum of water, some strips of dried fish and some rotten fruit.

Dawn seemed a long time coming and as the light grew stronger the land showed as a dark line low on the sea in the track of the sun. In turns they tried to paddle toward it when Donaldson noticed two dots in the sky over the land. In seconds they knew that the dots were aircraft heading their way. The planes were quite low and flew steadily toward them.

"Zeros," McCormac said tersely. "Overboard!" And he dived over the side into the water, which was quite warm. Someone said, "Jesus, the sharks!" Two or three of the others jumped over and the rest stayed in the boat, warily watching the fighters, which curved in and slid, roaring, low over the water to one side of the boat, dropping wing-tips to watch. In line astern they climbed a little, turned steeply, slanted down and ran in for the kill.

In panic, the last men in the boat were tumbling over the side and, as the first flashes came from the leading fighter, McCormac, who had swum about twenty yards from the boat, took a deep breath and went under. When he came up the water was lacy with foam torn up by cannon shells and the boat was upside down. The leading fighter was turning in again. He saw a couple of other heads on the water and then he went under once more. When he surfaced with the strain of trying to hold his breath the water was frothing again as the second fighter slammed in a blare of noise overhead. Each fighter made two more firing passes; then they circled once briefly and turned off back to the land.

McCormac swam over to the upturned keel moving sluggishly in the water. Donaldson reached it at the same time, and two more heads bobbed beside them, the owners panting and splashing. They were two British soldiers— Roy and Skinny. The foam lashed up by the shells was dissolving but there were no other heads in sight.

Donaldson panted, "Let's turn this dumb thing over again," and they reached up clumsily to the keel, heaved on one side and the boat came slowly over, full of water and with the gunwales just above the surface.

Someone said, "Get in, for Christ's sake, away from the sharks," and they floundered over the gunwales, nearly turning the boat over again. Virtually floating inside her, they looked for the other four. There were no signs. McCormac said laconically, "Sharks or bullets." There seemed to be nothing more to say.

When they had their breath they started bailing with their hands and slowly the gunwales lifted so that the water stopped slopping into her. Shells had torn a chunk out of the bow, but otherwise, by some miracle, there were only two neat holes under the water-line, and McCormac plugged these roughly with strips torn off the remains of his shirt.

Away to the east the land still lay thinly on the horizon and they hoped the turning tide would swing them in again to the Malayan coast, where they could get ashore unnoticed. By noon they knew unmistakably the line was getting fainter, and after about three hours they could not see it anymore.

Now thirst was worrying them. The heat was heavy and endless and they lay in the water on the floorboards; it was cooler like that, but by dusk McCormac could feel his tongue swelling. Darkness brought coolness but they could not sleep. Miraculously, round about midnight, rain poured for nearly an hour, fresh and cool, and they lay on their backs with their mouths open and also soaked it up in their filthy rags and squeezed it into their mouths.

At dawn they were alone on the sea. By noon their tongues were swelling again and McCormac knew that they, the last four out of the seventeen, were probably going to die too. They lay there quietly.

About four o'clock Skinny, a wiry little gunner from Wales with a broken nose and two teeth missing, said sharply, "God, here they come again." His voice was frightened and his rigid face stared over the gunwale. They looked and saw the dot low in the air. No one spoke until McCormac said, "It's coming this way." In a few seconds there was no doubt.

Someone, either Skinny or Roy, said, "Only one this time," and Donaldson growled. "That's quite enough."

They watched it growing larger, undecided whether to chance the sharks or the bullets. McCormac, the airman, suddenly said, "That's not a fighter. It's too big. It's a multi-engined job."

The plane grew swiftly and McCormac saw that it was a big flying boat. He recognized it and said, surprised, "It's a Dornier. A Jerry!"

Skinny said excitedly, "Let's wave. They might pick us up. We'll have a chance with the Germans."

"They'll hand us over, you fool," replied McCormac.

The big aircraft swept straight towards them, engines swelling louder. Skinny jumped up in the boat, waving his singlet and shouting. A wing dipped as it roared over and then it turned very slowly and suddenly the nose dipped. It landed in a shower of glistening spray and turned towards them.

McCormac was planning to jump over the side and swim away, remembered the sharks and changed his mind. Almost hypnotically they watched the flying boat approach. A sudden burst of engine and the hull swung against the boat. A door in the side snapped open and in the frame stood a white man. Grinning at them, he shouted something in a foreign tongue. McCormac caught the word *"Komm!"*

The man leaned out and caught Skinny's arm and heaved him into the lane. One by one the others scrambled after him, helped by the man in white. They all collapsed on the floor and McCormac started vomiting. He lifted his head after a while and saw the white man and a little brown man looking down at him. For a moment he did not comprehend, and then a wild thrill shot through him.

He said in Malay, "Who are you?" and the white man answered in a language very like Malay:

"Royal Netherlands Air Force."

Of the seventeen men who made the attempt, just two escaped to freedom in Australia after five long months wandering through the jungle. McCormac eventually reached England where he learned that his wife and newborn baby were alive and well. He had the satisfaction of witnessing Teruchi's execution at war's end and was presented with the very sword that had been used to cut his face.

The War Journal of Major Damon "Rocky" Gause

MAJOR DAMON GAUSE

Major Rocky Gause was trapped on Bataan with 70,000 other American and Filipino troops when the Japanese overran the Philippines in World War II. The scene on the American side was complete chaos, with starving troops fast losing their will to fight as they realized that they were trapped. For most, the infamous Bataan Death March awaited. But Rocky Gause chose to escape against impossible odds.

He made it to Corregidor and then escaped as that island eventually surrendered. After weeks in hiding, he and another American escapee made a daring voyage to Australia in a leaky, 20-foot boat with only a one-page map, pulled from an old *National Geographic,* to guide them. It took them 159 days, dodging Japanese fighter planes, tropical storms, and coral reefs, to reach their destination. They were quickly hailed as war heroes in a time when America desperately needed heroes, but after a short tour of the United States, Gause was desperate to get back into the fighting. He died while on a training flight over England before he got his wish. The memoir of his harrowing escape lay in his soldier's footlocker for 50 years before finally being published in 1999 as *The War Journal of Major Damon "Rocky" Gause.*

The story here begins during the rout at Bataan when Gause is first spotted by the Japanese while attempting to get a truck full of food across a bridge to other American troops. His bravery and tenacity allowed him to stay free while many of those around him simply quit.

The steel bridge across the Lamao River was one of the most important links in the slender American line of communications and supply. I drove our truck onto the span and looked blankly at the Japanese gun carrier blocking the bridge exit, only fifty feet away. The Nips were equally surprised to see us and, for a second, neither party budged. I thought, later, that I might have had time to turn our vehicle around and escape.

At least one of the Japs shouted something that we knew meant "Halt!" or "Surrender!" Baker leaped out the left side of the truck and I was on his heels. The Japs stirred from their lethargy and opened up with their forward machine gun, but it was two steps to the bridge rail and we both went over and into the water—twenty feet below. The river was low at this time of the year and bedded with rocks. I don't remember how I landed, but I didn't feel a bit of pain in spite of the rocks and boulders I must have landed on. The sergeant later told me that he felt no pain from the leap either. Guess we were too scared.

Although low, there was still a swift current in the river, and in a few moments we were carried a hundred feet downstream. The Japs were unable to bring their mounted machine guns into play over the bridge rail and, before they could unlimber their rifles and begin shooting, we were beyond the range at which they could hit anything smaller than a blimp. They did try to shoot us, though, their bullets spattering harmlessly into the water and trees that towered canopy-like above us.

It was late in the afternoon when we did our Steve Brodie act, and I have never longed for darkness as I did during the next half hour. The Japs knew that I was an officer, because of the garrison hat I had been wearing, and were anxious to make me either a captive or mincemeat. I had worn the hat ever since I was awarded my wings at Kelly Field and it was a kind of good luck charm. It had been pierced by bullets and flying shrapnel several times on Bataan, but I lost it forever as soon as my feet left the bridge rail.

The squad from the gun carrier quickly divided, a few taking each side of the stream, and a hurried search was begun before darkness closed in. We were only a couple hundred feet below the bridge, hiding close to the bank beneath the protection of heavy overhanging foliage. Sgt. Baker had lost his revolver in the plunge and mine was wet and useless. "How in hell are we going to defend ourselves?" the sergeant whispered. That was the $64 question for which I had no answer.

As the soldiers came closer, cursing and swearing, and hurrying from one open place to another along the bank looking for our heads in the water, we stretched out and buried ourselves in the mud and water to our necks. My heart was pumping violently and my mouth was dry, although I was immersed in dirty river water. The quick footfalls approached, then stopped a few paces away. I imagined a man peering into the gathering dusk. Was he looking in my direction? What if I should have to move? Then he walked on, and his companions hurried right past and joined him.

Soon after, the heavy jungle night swept across the peninsula, but we still heard distant bodies crashing through the jungle. A patrol was coming back up the river, brandishing torches and lights and talking and shouting across the stream. Sgt. Baker and I were afraid to talk for fear one might be listening close by. We burrowed deeper into the mud and pressed close against the bank. Bushes and tree branches dangled in our faces. From 30 feet away, we could hear the searchers' bayonet blades swishing through the brush and water along the bank. They were giving the river zealous scrutiny.

Spotlights were cast upstream every few seconds, and from their strength I knew that in a minute the Japs would be on us. I planned to make a grab at a rifle barrel, pull the soldier into the water, and strike out downstream, holding him for protection. I hoped Baker would escape detection in the melee that would follow.

The bank above my head quivered from the weight of the approaching soldiers. The bayonet steel slicing the water is the most annoying sound I have ever heard. Then they were over us, talking eagerly in Japanese. A white beam flashed straight out across the creek, and a bayonet and gun muzzle poked down into the water a foot in front of my eyes. I watched it hypnotically and was preparing to dodge its slashes, when it was withdrawn and the searchers moved a few feet farther upstream, and another bayonet cut through the water.

They were near the bridge before I dared turn and look at Sgt. Baker. He puckered his nose as if to sneeze, and I bit my heart, but he ducked his head under the water, stifling the urge. All that night, parties of soldiers moved up and down the stream looking for two nice, but not so fat, Americans.

Two things stuck in my mind as the water began to chill my body. I wondered what old Admiral Dewey would have thought if he could see the fall of Bataan. I was certain that the peninsula was doomed, and I knew that Corregidor could not hold out much longer. I thought, too, of my mother who was along in years and probably praying for me. She would always wonder, I thought, how her son died. So I tried to be brave and await the end. I was so certain that this was "the end" that I could feel the cold steel of a bayonet being pushed through my innards.

About midnight, a large group of Japs forded the river just below our hiding place. They were shouting jubilantly, sensing the complete victory, and once on the other side set up their field pieces and began pouring shells into our rear area at random. We could hear their officers shouting commands. In an hour they moved farther down the peninsula in pursuit of the broken and fleeing Filipino and American soldiers.

About four in the morning, there was little noise except rifle and small arms fire. Crickets still chirped in the midst of the holocaust and the inevitable mosquitoes had feasted on our faces. The sergeant and I removed our shirts, I carefully tucked my silver wings into my trouser pocket, we unlaced our shoes and buried them in the mud; then we proceeded cautiously downstream, keeping in the covering shadows of the bank. We hoped to get back through our own lines.

When we drew near the mouth of the river we smeared mud afresh over our faces and began wiggling across a sandbar that blocked the entrance to the bay. The river, when it was low, flowed beneath the sandbar. As we drew upon the bar I noticed how pleasingly warm the sand was. The water was warm, of course, but after lying in it for so many hours, I was shivering. In fact, the sergeant was shivering so hard, I was sure the Japs would see the ripples on the quiet water near the banks. I was to notice many times again the comforting feeling of warm sand after long stretches in the water.

We had crawled a half a block when we heard footsteps sucking into the sand. The rattling of gear indicated about a dozen men, and I felt sure it was a Jap patrol. I instinctively pressed my arms to my side and prayed that I resembled a log. Sgt. Baker did the same, I later discovered, and the soldiers passed twenty feet away, talking among themselves. I didn't look, but from the boisterous sound of their voices and laughter they were not expecting any live Americans to be within miles.

I had been leading the two-man expedition, and when the Japs passed I inched my way slowly backwards. I drew abreast of the sergeant and we both retraced our path into the water. The sky was beginning to turn pink in the east, so we went a little deeper and buried ourselves once again in the mud.

Neither of us had eaten for a day and a half, although our truck was loaded with food when we abandoned it so unceremoniously. Our primary purpose, unfortunately, had been to get food back to the men and then eat. Baker, however, stuck a can of iron rations in his pocket sometimes before we reached the Lamao River, and lying in the brackish creek water, we twisted the can open and devoured the contents. Then the shadows disappeared entirely and we settled deeper in the mud, prepared to spend the day. Time never dragged so slowly. We heard great activity above the bank and at noon saw Japs washing their mess kits on the bank of the river within a few paces of us. We planned to wait for night and make another attempt to escape, but the sun moved ever so slowly across the sky to dip into the China Sea. Water lapping gently against Baker's face was the only indication he was within touching distance when I at last whispered, "Let's go!" but the sergeant and I were so weak from lack of food and sleep and lying in the luke-warm water for twenty-four hours that it was a struggle to crawl once more to the mouth of the creek.

When we huddled in the shallow water on the river side of the sandbar, I saw that getting across and into the ocean was impossible. During the day, the Nips had established a bivouac area at the mouth of the river. Several big bon-fires were sending up large clouds of sparks, and by moving back to the protection of the river bank and poking our heads up above the bank at intervals, we saw that the warriors were having a merry time. The camp was enlivened by women and everyone was drinking sake and cavorting about like the victory-crazed devils they were. We didn't realize it at the time but they were celebrating the fall of Bataan.

We crept up the stream against the rippling current, slipping along near the bank, and about ten o'clock the merrymakers quieted down. Our plan was to encircle the camp and get back to the beach and Manila Bay. Baker and I helped each other up on the wooded slope above the river, and he picked up a heavy stick. We rested then, both so dirty from the mud that we looked as vile as the Japs. I finally ventured a few steps and saw that our enemies were covering the entire area. There must have been a regiment encamped.

The soldiers were lying on mats, most of them sleeping, and some were covered with a light tarpaulin. They were exhausted from the hard fight and the celebration. The fires had died down, and the snores from the men closest to us were the only recognizable sounds. We had been without water and food for so long that we both must have been slightly insane because in one motion, Baker who had come up behind, and I darted out, and each of us picked up a canteen and returned to the underbrush to flop down and drink long and deeply.

When empty, we laid the cans down carefully, and I beckoned the sergeant to follow me through the Jap encampment, stepping over prostrate soldiers and dodging others. Some turned and looked at us, but none recognized the two dirty and near-nude figures as Americans. We had traveled perhaps three hundred yards in the general direction of the beach and were nearly out of the camp and breathing almost normally, when a harsh voice broke the night with a gruff and strident command to halt—I think.

In a flash I dropped down on a sleeping mat beside sprawling Jap soldiers, and Baker, without any hesitancy, followed my example. I pulled the tarpaulin slowly off the Jap next to me. He gave a groan and turned over, and I covered my head with the sheet. I lay tense, straining every nerve, but the sentry never even investigated and my bedfellow snored on blissfully. After perhaps an hour I dared to poke my head out from beneath the cover and glance at the sergeant, who was lying on his stomach, shielding his head with his hands.

He saw me crawl away, wriggling a few feet and lying still as if sleeping, and then sliding another few feet. The camp was in deep darkness by this time, and, after another hour, we reached the beach on Manila Bay and waded into the water up to our necks.

We had heard much about sharks and I couldn't shake off the thought of their rows of sharp, even teeth. The water was warm but I was shivering violently and Sgt. Baker told me he also was unable to control his muscles. We were standing on coral, and as the waves pounded in they would throw us against the rocks and jagged bottom until we were cut in a dozen places. Blood attracted sharks, I recalled uneasily. Moving slowly, hiding whenever we could behind rocks, we waded slowly along the Bataan shore toward the tip of the peninsula.

The moon rose about midnight, and Jap patrols ranged the beach, directing searchlights out into the sea, but we followed the beam with our eyes, and just before it would flash across us, we ducked our heads beneath the water.

An hour before daybreak we were near the village of Cabcaben, near the tip of Bataan, where I thought our lines might have been reformed, so we decided to go ashore. As we came out of the water the waves bashed us down innumerable times and in the struggle to reach the beach Sergeant Baker and I became separated. When I missed the sergeant, I recalled hearing a commotion behind me and paddled around a few minutes searching, but I saw nothing in the black water. I was afraid to call because the area was honeycombed with Japs. The sergeant either died from exhaustion or was attacked by a shark, but he made no outcry, fortunately for me. He has never been heard from since.

There were streaks of gray in the east when at last I dragged myself up on the beach, praying the Americans would be holding a line here. I was without shoes, famished, and tired, and my eyes were almost closed from the saltwater. The water, too, had washed into the gashes from the coral, and every bone and muscle ached. If your hands and fingers have ever become puffed and crinkled from immersion in dishwater, you can imagine how my skin looked.

After resting for perhaps twenty minutes on the sand, I staggered up on the beach through a hundred yards of underbrush to a road that skirted the shore. It was littered with household goods, clothing, military supplies, and every other evidence of flight. I must have been slightly delirious by this time. I was able to think only in streaks, and every few minutes the road, jungle, sky—everything—would merge into a kaleidoscopic mess. I was standing motionless and bewildered in the road, immersed in one of my trances, when a Filipino approached and beckoned to me. I rocked back and forth unsteadily, absolutely unable to function, but he led me off the road perhaps a hundred steps to a thatched shed where his wife and two children were resting. Seeing that I was an American, the bronzed little man blurted out that Bataan had been surrendered and that the Japs were everywhere—"All around!" This latter observation with a wave of his arms and widening of his eyes. Understanding somehow—I was unable to speak coherently—that I must get away, he gave me a shirt and his wife brought me food, native rice, and bread. I rested about an hour with them, and my strength returned miraculously so that I was able to thank them before leaving.

I went back to the beach and the water and tried to work my way farther down the peninsula, but I discovered I wasn't as strong as I thought, and I finally came ashore after perhaps a hundred yards. I located a narrow trail and was stumbling aimlessly along it when two Japs loomed up in front of me. They gibbered at me and laughed in my face. They probably were saying very uncomplimentary things about Americans, but I was helpless. Jap fashion, they took my watch—it was useless to me anyway—snatched my ring off my finger, removed two hundred dollars from my money belt, and administered a kick that sent me sprawling into the grass along the trail. They laughed and left. I was mad as hell.

I had been told that the Japs made a distinction between officers and enlisted men after capture, so I sat up, fished my flyer's wings out of my pocket, and fastened them carefully to my shirt. I hadn't moved ten yards from where I had flattened the grass when a lone Jap carrying a rifle with fixed bayonet stopped me. He ripped the silver wings off my shirt as I told him, with as much dignity as I could muster, that I was an American officer. His answer was a slap in the face and he stepped back with his rifle pointed, daring me to act. I thought he was going to shoot regardless of whether I moved or not. Instead he prodded me in the stomach with the needlelike point and kept alternately shoving me with the butt and sticking me, until we reached a clearing where about 300 American soldiers were huddled together in a prison enclosure.

I was given a final mighty push and landed face-first among a group of men who were too sick, exhausted, and weak to even move out of the way of my falling body. These men, I learned, had been there since April 9th—two days—without food or water. They were bewhiskered, ragged, and thoroughly beaten, and in serious physical condition because of continued exposure to the tropical sun. The Jap guards lorded it over these silent, hopeless creatures like slave masters of old, beating some and bayoneting others on the slightest provocation.

I had been there only a short time when a flight of Jap dive-bombers began circling the prison area and I thought to myself, "These bastards are going to eliminate all of us with a few well-placed bombs!" But the camp was on a narrow runway and the planes were readying to land.

It was a hot, stifling day and the dust, even in early morning, rose in blinding clouds covering everything, grinding between your teeth, clogging motors, getting into your hair. I walked slowly through the prison area so as not to attract attention. Men were lying with flies buzzing around and dipping into wounds. The captured soldiers groaned and begged for water, but the Jap sentries stalked past, spitting at them. Several buzzards floated ominously overhead.

The beach road paralleled the runway and carried a horde of straggling Filipino citizens. When the Japs took control of Bataan, their first act was to force all civilians into the interior. Now the Japs were stopping all of them who passed, taking everything of value. It was a disgusting exhibition by these victory-crazed, sadistic devils.

Children clung pitifully to their mothers' skirts, and lines of fear and fatigue marred the usually bland faces. The Japanese demanded many things, and their cruelty and ruthlessness made me turn away. Any Nip whose bayonet was unbloody soon corrected that oversight. They ripped clothing, ostensibly in their search for valuables, but the poor people who were being accosted possessed nothing of value but their spirit. That the Japs could not break or take. A single word of protest was insurance for a bayonet thrust in the belly. Husbands, wives, and children were separated, with one or more members of the family lying dead or dying beside the road. I decided that a Jap prison pen was no place for me.

On the shore side of the prison enclosure was a two-hundred-yard strip of jungle and then Manila Bay. I decided I'd better make a break before the Japs stopped their looting and became fully organized. I spoke to several of the healthiest appearing Americans, inviting them to accompany me. They shook their heads in refusal and said I'd never get out alive, and if I did I'd have to swim to Corregidor. I couldn't blame them. They had performed their duty valiantly, and were disillusioned and sick of fighting a hopeless, one-sided fight.

It was now about eight in the morning. The sentries were careless, considering us a bunch of helpless creatures, and their primary interest was looting the people shuffling past the camp. I edged over toward the runway. One sentry was sauntering along with his back toward me, a hundred yards away. Another was approaching, holding his gun carelessly on his shoulder. My first thought was to try for the gun, but it might not be loaded. As he drew abreast, I glimpsed a sheathed knife at his side. There was not time to plan further. He passed, and I leaped on his back, pressing my left forearm against his throat with all my strength and grabbing for the knife with my right. He twisted and writhed, screaming. At last the knife came free, and I slid it into his back as far as it would go. I felt his body relax and let him drop.

With the knife in my hand I sprinted into the bush. The captured soldiers had watched my act without a sound, but the Jap's cries had brought other guards. As I ran I heard them shouting and crashing through the underbrush behind me. I suddenly had superhuman strength and leaped over boulders and fallen trees with ease. A few shots fired from the rear encouraged me to increase my lead. Jesse Owens wouldn't have had a showing with me on this dash. When I burst out on the beach I picked up a driftwood plank and kept right on running with bounding leaps into the waves. I was a hundred yards out in the water when my pursuers appeared on the sand, and I was already churning the water in the direction of Corregidor, three miles away. They fired volley after volley in my direction, but they fortunately were no better riflemen than other Japs I encountered.

Swimming rapidly, I saw an inter-island steamer halfway to Corregidor that had somehow escaped sinking. I pushed my plank in its direction, and several hours later pulled myself up on the hot and weather-beaten deck. I didn't even bother to conceal myself, but fell asleep where I first dropped. It was late in the afternoon when I awakened with the skin on my back cracked and blistered. Feeling sure that the Japs had forgotten about me, I cut loose a lifeboat, jumped over the side, and clambered in. Using an oar, I pushed off from the steamer and rowed away from its protection when I heard the rat-a-tat of machine guns. Looking toward shore I saw that my friends of the morning had mounted three machine guns on the beach and were taking pot shots at me. They must have seen me crawl aboard the ship, and the only reason I could imagine why they didn't come out after me was that they had wagered on who would kill me. It was the usual Jap conceit.

After a dozen bursts they found the range and soon had punched a score of holes in the lifeboat. One slug took the right oar out of my hand and I decided I'd better go overboard again. I unfastened the other oar to use as a float, and plunged into the bay water. The Japs continued firing but couldn't get a good shot at my bobbing head and flailing arms, so, about sundown on April 11, I crawled ashore at Corregidor. My eyes were nearly closed, and I was bearded, cut and bruised, literally broiled from the sun and water, and entirely spent.

Down in Korea

WARD MILLAR

Ward Millar's story, told in *Valley of the Shadow*, is one of supreme determination. After serving in World War II, Millar was studying nuclear physics when he was called back to active duty by the Air Force to fight in Korea. On his thirtieth mission, his plane caught fire and he was forced to bail out over North Korea. He broke both ankles in the fall and was quickly captured. After being hauled half-starved from one camp to another, a Chinese medical corpsman in a makeshift hospital finally tried to set his ankles. Following another move, he convinced a "doctor" to remove the poorly set casts as he knew he could never escape with them on. The results left him with both feet frozen with the toes pointed down at almost 45 degrees. Despite this formidable handicap, Millar was determined to escape before being taken farther away to a regular POW camp.

He was left without boots and was only able to take short walks with the aid of two sticks that served as crutches. But as a result of his predicament, he was left virtually unguarded. After all, who in that sad condition would try to escape from deep behind enemy lines?

A week passed, and then another. I ate like a hog, and I could feel my strength returning, bit by bit. This was all to the good, but I still needed the boots, so every time one of the Chinese nurses came into the room, I made a big to-do about them, always bringing up the phony Chinese claims that they did not take POW possessions. At night I prayed that I would get them.

I guess I literally wore them down, for one day one of the "nurses" finally said, "O.K. Have shoes for you. American boots." When he went away to get them, I thought, Thank God. My prayers have been answered. But when I saw what he referred to as "boots," I was bitterly disappointed. His "boots" turned out to be an old, beat-up pair of four-buckle galoshes—Heaven knows where they came from originally—designed to fit a 10½ shoe. Since I wore an 8½ shoe, and had no shoes, my feet literally swam inside the huge gunboats. I shook my head and frowned, then I tossed the galoshes into the straw alongside my pallet. I made it clear to the nurse that the galoshes were a poor substitute for boots.

It was not until two days later that I realized that the galoshes were exactly what I needed.

The thought occurred to me late one evening while I was lying on my pallet, legs crossed high in the air, griping to myself about the way the Chinese doctors had butchered my feet. If I ever get back to the States, I thought, I will either have to have the ankles rebroken and reset, or get a pair of shoes with some kind of built-in heel. Then suddenly I remembered the galoshes. *There was enough room inside them to build a false heel! Was it possible?*

I sat bolt upright and rummaged through the straw, searching for the discarded galoshes. When I found them, I looked around to make sure the other soldiers were asleep, and then I slipped the right galosh on my right foot. I wobbled it around to see how much room I would have inside, then I grabbed a bunch of straw, wadded it up, wrapped it in a rag, and placed it inside the galosh over the heel. I put my foot back inside. Now it fitted rather snugly against the top of the galosh. Then I had another idea: if I wrapped my ankle and the lower part of my leg with rags, the upper part of the galosh would also fit snugly and provide some support for my ankles.

Within about an hour, I had manufactured a second heel cushion for the left galosh and collected enough rags to serve as ankle supports. Without wasting any further time, I put them all together and snapped the buckle shut. I grabbed my two walking sticks, crawled to the doorway, and then outside for a test run. It was still early, and there was a possibility that some of the Chinese were up, but I knew that if they saw me, I could tell them I had had an attack of dysentery and had gone outside because of it.

The trial run was a success. The false heels inside the galoshes allowed me to stand upright. Moreover, the space inside the galoshes permitted a sort of mechanical ankle action by allowing my legs to move with a minimum of ankle bending when I took a step. Using the two sticks as ski poles, I found I could hobble along, at least for short distances. I covered the ten yards to the outhouse in record time, compared to crawling or to my performance in the borrowed tennis shoes. When I got back inside the hut that night, I was trembling with excitement because I knew I now held the secret to escape.

My galoshes had turned out to be a blessing in disguise.

I knew it was important to keep this new discovery absolutely secret because the minute the Chinese found out I could walk, however clumsily, they would either post a guard over me or ship me posthaste to the POW camps. So, during the daytime, I kept the galoshes hidden under the straw. But at night, after everyone was asleep, I put them on, crawled outside, and hobbled up and down behind the hut, "getting in shape," so that I would be ready for long-distance travel.

Meanwhile, I began assembling my final "escape kit," which by then consisted of a handful of rock salt, a few scraps of soap, my piece of toweling, the top of a tin can bent double to form a crude knife, and a small can of tinned meat that one of the soldiers had given me when my stomach trouble had been at its worst. I was saving that until I reached the west coast and open water. In addition, I still had the two hundred won stuffed inside the lining of the Mae West, as well as my empty escape vest, G suit, and leather jacket. This was not much equipment, admittedly, but I had one factor that overcame any shortcomings—high morale and confidence inspired by the fact that I was at least able to hobble upright.

This ability was doubly important because the Chinese did not even dream I had it, and therefore I was sure that when I did finally turn up missing, they would be amazed and would perhaps limit their search simply because they thought I couldn't walk. This gave me, in effect, an added advantage.

On the afternoon of August 14, the rains stopped. Later that evening I heard the lashing of gears and roaring of engines as several Russian trucks skidded through the mud, air brakes hissing, and pulled to a stop outside the huts a little down from my own. Almost immediately there was excitement among the Chinese patients; at long last the trucks had come through to take them to the rear. Soon the word spread down the line: everyone was to be evacuated! The Chinese were jubilant, but my heart sank! Once again, on the verge of escape, I was to be evacuated to the rear.

I knew I had to think fast or I would soon find myself looking at North Korean countryside through the barbed wire of a POW camp. By the time the nurse came by our hut, I had worked out a stratagem; I told him that I had developed a very bad sore throat. Knowing that they wanted me to be "all well" when I was sent to the POW pen, I thought they might delay my departure long enough to give me an opportunity to escape. He seemed very upset about the throat and rushed out to get some kind of white, crystalline powder for me to take. Later he talked to me, felt my forehead to see if I had fever, and agreed that I ought not to be moved while I was sick.

That evening most of the Chinese patients were loaded aboard the trucks. But there was not room enough for all of them, so the decision was made to send one of the trucks back the following evening to pick up the stragglers. The nurse said to me, "You stay one night. Then go Pyongyang."

I said, "O.K.," but thought to myself: That's what you think. I'm leaving here tonight, and not the way you expect!

The nurse told me to get my possessions together, because he wanted to carry me down to the hut where the straggler patients were billeted. I knew this would make my escape more difficult, but there was nothing I could do about it, so I started picking up my stuff. However, just at that moment, the nurse who looked like Robert Montgomery came in with another white powder, and when he saw me "packing," he asked where I was going. When I told him, he said, "No, no, you stay." He did not want me to go out in the damp night air. To obey him was to stay in an empty hut, so I lay back down in the straw, thinking that this was just the kind of confusion I needed.

I suspected that the Chinese nurse who looked like Robert Montgomery would come back about eleven for a final bed check, so I had to delay my escape until after then. While I lay on the straw pallet waiting, I went over my plans one last time.

On the theory that it would be the last direction the Communists would follow in their search for me, I had decided that when I left the village I would travel due north, away from U.N. lines. After two days of moving at night and sleeping during the daytime, I would then turn due west, and head directly for the coast, which I figured to reach on the third or fourth night, depending on the speed I could make. If possible, I would steal a boat and sail out to sea; otherwise, I would inflate my Mae West and swim and float with the current until rescued.

I believed the odds for success were in my favor, mainly because I could move far better than the Chinese knew. I figured that on the first night, even though I could not leave before midnight, I would make at the very least, four miles, probably three and a half miles more than the Chinese would give me credit for. The Chinese, I hoped, would spend the first day searching only in the immediate vicinity of the hospital—looking thoroughly in each hut in the village, the huts in the outlying areas, and through the fields and streams. On the second day, they might broaden the search considerably, but by then, I would be at least ten miles from Na-han-li, moving steadily away in a direction they were least likely to search.

At about eleven o'clock, "Robert Montgomery" came into the hut, filled my water bottle, and gave me another white powder. My throat never felt better, but for effect I grimaced as I swallowed, coughed a couple of times, and groaned, holding my hand to my forehead. The nurse sympathized with me, explaining that the powder would help clear up the infection. He said conditions would be better in the POW camp in Pyongyang, and that I probably would not get another infection. Then he bade me good night and walked out of the hut. I started getting myself ready immediately.

I dressed hurriedly, putting on my Chinese tan cotton trousers, over which I stretched the half-laced G suit. For a moment I considered removing the suit and throwing it away, but I knew that the rubber bladders inside might be useful as flotation equipment in case I was unable to steal a boat, so I kept the suit on. I zipped up my flying suit, now little more than a jacket, tucked my blue silk scarf around my neck, and climbed into my deflated Mae West. Then I put on my brown leather jacket, and last, over that, I strapped the many-pocketed escape vest.

I stuffed the pockets of the vest full of various "escape" items, including the small can of tinned meat, a handful of rock salt, several small green apples, my brass spoon, the chunks of G.I. soap, and the piece of white toweling. Last of all I wrapped rags around the lower part of my ankles, and then buckled on the big, black galoshes, making certain that the straw under each heel was in place and nicely tamped. I felt under my pallet to be sure the two walking sticks were on hand, then I lay back to wait a few more minutes until "Robert Montgomery" had had time to get to sleep. It was about midnight when I finally got up and hobbled out of the back door of the hut.

In order to have cover as I made my way around the village, I walked straight into a cornfield behind the hut. There was a slight wind rustling through the corn stalks, which served to drown out the scuffing noise I made with the gunboat galoshes and sticks. As I moved along, I looked through the stalks for ripe ears, but there were none. The corn was too young.

I stayed in the cornfield until I had cleared the end of the village, then I cut back and got on a narrow, dirt road that led out to the north. It was my plan to follow roads whenever and wherever possible. The Koreans and Chinese rarely used their roads at night, except the main supply routes near the front, so for my purposes they were comparatively safe. I was afraid that if I tried to move through the hills and fields in the dark, I might fall and seriously twist my ankle. As I walked along, I noticed that my galoshes left enormous tracks, with the "U.S. Royal" emblem clearly visible.

Though I was now well out of the village, I kept a constant watch for Chinese soldiers, because I was not sure whether or not the hospital was guarded on the perimeter. During my two weeks at Na-han-li, I had seen a great many Chinese soldiers who were not patients. Some of them were attached to a unit that was working on a project in the nearby hills, digging revetments and storage bins. But for all I knew, some of them may have been assigned to the hospital. I hurried on, passing first one and then another hut alongside the road. There were burlap bags stacked on the front porch of the second hut, and for a brief moment I considered foraging in them for food, but I gave the idea up when, thanks to the increasing moonlight, I saw two small, Korean children sleeping on the ground in the yard.

A few minutes later, I spotted what I had hoped I wouldn't—the perimeter guard. There were two soldiers, each with a rifle slung over his back, standing in the middle of the road, smoking. I saw the glow of their cigarettes before they saw me, ducked off the road, and slid down into a drainage ditch. Inching along on my hands and knees, I made my way out to a cornfield that paralleled the road, plunged through the stalks for some distance, then turned and walked north once again, making, in effect, a wide detour of the check point. While in the corn, I searched for some ripe ears, but the field had already been stripped, a fact that caused me some anxiety since I was depending completely on the corn as my food supply. Suppose all the fields were stripped. What could I do about food?

During the second hour of travel, the little strength I had began to leave me. My breath became short, my steps hesitant. The dull, throbbing pain in my ankles, which I had tried to ignore, suddenly became a major problem. I sat down to rest on the shoulder of the road, and took a long swig from the canteen. Then I ate an apple. But when I got ready to get up and go, I realized it had been a mistake to rest. My legs were so stiff that I could hardly get to my feet. An almost overwhelming desire to sleep engulfed my senses, and I thought how foolish it was of me not to have tried to sleep during the previous day.

Somehow, I got upright again and wobbled along, holding on to the two sticks, all the while fighting off a feeling of panic. My God, Millar, I thought, don't give up now. You have gone scarcely a mile. Perhaps not even that. The Chinese will find you if you try to hide here. You must push on. I slogged on, holding an image of Barbara and Adrian before me as incentive. I wanted to take out my cross and pray, but both my hands were riveted to the sticks, so I just prayed to myself, saying the "Our Father" over and over.

The road, or oxcart trail, dipped down and forded a stream, and having no choice, I waded in. The water pressing against the outside of the galoshes was refreshingly cool, and I paused for a moment in midstream to enjoy the sensation. For a moment, I was gripped with a desire to lie down in the water and sleep, somewhat like a man weary in snow, but I fought to stay awake and hurried out of the creek. Time was passing. I still had miles to go before I could feel safe. Moreover, if I did not find corn soon, I would have to go all the following day without food.

After leaving the stream, I struck up a kind of steady pace, albeit a slow one, and moved off down the road. Hardly a minute or two passed before I stopped, my ears fully alert. Was that a voice I had heard? My heart was beating loudly, making a "cush-cush" noise in my eardrums, but above this I could hear, now definitely, voices, and they were someplace behind me, not too far away. They have discovered my escape already and they are following the galoshes tracks, I thought to myself. What to do?

I plunged down the embankment of the road, flailing my sticks wildly, slipping and sliding, until I came to a rest on my hands and knees in soft, damp grass. Then, crawling as fast as I could move, I struck out at a ninety-degree angle to the road. I soon reached a point where I could go no farther, and I collapsed, face down in the wet grass. Absolutely motionless, I waited, listening as the voices came on, and on, and on.

Suddenly out of the oncoming babble, I picked up the unmistakable strains of a woman's voice. What was that? Had the nurses come along with the guards? Logic argued against it. Well, then, who? My curiosity was so aroused that I had to take a look, so I very carefully turned my head until I could see the road with one eye. Now the voices were very close, and I saw that they belonged not to Chinese soldiers but, of all things, to a group of a half-dozen Korean civilians, all dressed in white, each carrying a large straw basket on his head. I watched as the procession went by, wondering who they were and why they were out so late. I could not find an answer to those questions, important as they were to my future plans, but I knew at least one thing: they were not looking for me, and the relief following this realization was enough to make me limp all over.

I waited in the grass at least a half hour to let the Koreans get a head start and to make sure none of their friends were following behind; then I crawled back out on the road and got up rather shakily on my feet. The side excursion had consumed my little remaining strength. I was now so tired I could hardly keep my eyes open or put one foot in front of the other. Sheer fear—or perhaps it was some supernatural force in answer to my prayers—kept me going a few minutes longer, until I reached the edge of another cornfield, which seemed to contain some ripe ears. On the first stalk, I found three, and with much creaking and cracking, I managed to break them off and stuff them in the pockets of my C-3 vest.

Now that I had food, I knew I must find a hiding place because I could go no farther, so I kept in the cornfield, pushing toward a hill that rose out of the opposite end. The two army sergeants, Ward and McPherson, had advised me that the safest place to hide in daytime was on a hill. The Koreans, busy in the fields, or in the villages, came into the hills only to collect firewood. Some-how—I really am not sure how—I reached the end of the cornfield and crawled some fifty or sixty feet up the hill until I came to a group of bushy shrubs into which I burrowed like a rabbit. I took a long swig on the canteen and then fell sound asleep.

I woke up a few hours later, at dawn, Thursday, August 16, a free man! From my slightly elevated position I could see some distance through the valley. Breakfast smoke was curling up from the chimneys of the huts. Several Koreans were already out in the fields, working between rows of corn and beans. The road down which I had come was clearly visible and, so far, empty. I got out an apple and took a bite, thinking, This is the crucial day. Within a few hours, or even minutes, the alarm will be spread and the searching parties will be out, and the whole countryside will be alerted. I must be very careful.

Not seeing any better hiding place, I went back to sleep, hoping to build up my strength for the long journey ahead. When I awoke again, it was late af-ternoon. I sat up and peered out. There was no sign of excitement or alarm. The scene was much the same as before, with Koreans working in the field, the road empty, and smoke drifting lazily from the chimneys of the huts. Luck is with me, I thought. The Chinese, for one reason or another, possibly because they couldn't believe I had gone far, had not alerted the Koreans. Phase one of the plan was working. The Chinese would not find me that day, and therefore I had another night to put distance between them and myself.

My morale zoomed, and after eating another apple, I began to feel a little cocky. The thought that I was accomplishing absolutely nothing by sitting still made me impatient to move on. Was it safe? I looked out into the valley. There were no Koreans nearby, certainly none close enough to tell I was American. From a distance, I thought, I probably looked like a Chinese, what with my brown clothes. Would a Korean go out of his way to approach a man he believed to be a Chinese soldier? I asked myself. "No," I answered out loud. "Then what's holding you back?" "Nothing," I answered myself again, eyeing the hill above and mentally laying out a route. Minutes later, I was on my feet, moving across the partially screened hillside in broad daylight.

The hill was not steep, and I was able to reach the top without crawling, although I found my ankles were more stiff and sore than ever. There were no fields on the other side of the hill, so I dropped down just below the crest and continued walking along the ridge, well out of sight of the farmers. I was quite warm and perspiring heavily, losing valuable salt from my system, so I took off my leather jacket and tied it around my waist the way I used to do in grammar school, unzipped my flying suit at the neck, and put my scarf in one of the pockets. Every two hundred feet or so, I paused and took a swig from the canteen, and every few swigs I took a little salt.

At dusk I stopped again in the cover of bushes for a good rest. For the first time, I took off the galoshes to inspect my feet and, as expected, found big blisters and raw spots along the top and the heel where they came in contact with the galoshes. I would have given a million dollars for a pair of socks. Lacking them, I laid tassels of corn silk over the raw spots and then packed it throughout the galoshes. Afterward, I ate my last apple and broke open one of the ears of corn, but it was like unraveling a "Chinese package," which finally turns out to be nothing. The "ear" of corn was a tiny thing about five inches long, the kernels not yet clearly formed. Nevertheless, I ate it, soft cob and all. It tasted starchy.

Part of my plan was to get back near the road before it became completely dark, so as soon as all the Koreans left the fields, I got up and pushed on, moving down a hillside into yet another cornfield, where I stopped and ate a half dozen of the miniature ears. Then, thinking the stalks offered as good cover as any, I lay down to sleep until dark. I awoke a few hours later, with raindrops splashing in my face. I got up, picked a dozen more ears of corn, stuffed them inside the C-3 vest, then hobbled out onto the road, and once again headed north.

I walked on in the rain, stopping often to rest or to drink a swig from the canteen. It was a very dark night, and I lost a lot of time hiding from and dodging imagined soldiers.

Later I began to get weak, so I stopped and gobbled a few more ears of corn, since eating seemed to restore my strength, at least temporarily. About midnight it began to rain very heavily, and I thought I had probably gone north far enough to throw off any pursuers who might be foolish enough to be out in this weather, so I cut to the left, following a rough trail, and headed almost directly west. Later, I turned to my left again, and headed somewhat or, at least, what I figured was southwest, the direction to the nearest reach of the Yellow Sea. I was very tired, and my speed had dropped off to practically zero miles per hour. In effect, I was pulling myself along by the poles with blistered and aching hands, chanting with each slogging step: "Slowly, but surely . . . slowly but surely. . . ."

Somehow, I kept going until dawn Friday. Then I found a group of shrubs shaped like an umbrella, and I crawled under them, prepared to spend the day. I took off my wet galoshes, dumped out the pulverized corn silk, rubbed my feet, and doused them with a little water from the canteen. Then I made a pillow of my Mae West and C-3 vest and lay back comforted by the knowledge that my umbrella-shaped hovel wasn't quite as wet and muddy as outside. Before going to sleep, I took out my wooden cross and thanked God for getting me through one more day and asked His help and guidance through the next. When I awoke at about ten o'clock in the morning, the cross was still in my hands, resting between two blisters. I had been too tired to put it away.

I ate a few ears of corn, saving the silk tassel for galosh lining, then peeped out at the country around me to find that I was still more or less up in the hills, surrounded by thick underbrush and rocky ravines. The day was beautiful, bright blue, and the overcast gone. There was no sign of human life—no huts, no fields, no people, no noise, save the chirping of birds. Where was I? Which way was the Yellow Sea? Navigation in the air, with charts, computers, and radio aids, was reasonably easy. But now, down on the ground moving across hills at a snail's pace, my visibility reduced to a few feet, I was uncertain, not to say lost, and haunted by the thought that perhaps an inlet or bay of the Yellow Sea lay only a few miles away, hidden from my view by the hills.

There was only one answer to this; in spite of my limited ability to move, especially up, I simply had to climb a high hill and take my bearings. I looked around me. About half a mile away in the north, I saw a cone-shaped, tree-covered knob jutting up into the sky. I judged the hill to be about eleven or twelve hundred feet, not much, but perhaps enough to provide the information and intelligence I needed. There seemed to be little danger of being seen in these hills, so feeling I could not afford to lose a minute of time, I made the decision to move out and climb the hill that very day. I ate a few more ears of corn to give me added strength, put on my galoshes and vests, and then I was on my way.

The hill turned out to be much steeper than it looked from a distance, and I had a very difficult time climbing it. This is the procedure I used: First, I dug both sticks into the hard ground, using them like alpenstocks, after which I put my right foot forward, about one good step. Then, leaning back on the sticks, I brought my left foot alongside my right foot, and gave a big push, enough to swing myself over the balance point. As I swung forward, I pulled the sticks out of the ground, and jabbed them in front of me so that I would not fall forward on my face. Then I resumed the starting position again.

About midday, when I was halfway up the hill, I stopped on a grassy plateau and stretched out to rest, falling asleep as usual. I was not worried about cover or concealment, because I knew no Korean in his right mind would climb the hill on such a hot day. It was late in the afternoon when I awoke. I picked up my sticks and pushed on, crawling the steep rise of the last hundred feet on my hands and knees. I finally reached the summit about five o'clock in the afternoon. I sat down on a rocky ledge and dangled my feet over the side, observing the broad expanse of countryside with more than the casual tourist's interest.

I realized immediately that there was something drastically wrong with my dead-reckoning navigation. There was no water to the west or south-west—only rolling hills as far as the eye could see! Where was I? Suddenly I remembered Ho's wooden replica of Korea, and his mark indicating our po-sition. *Poor little illiterate kid . . . he doesn't even know where we are. . . .* But was he right? Was I really in the middle of Korea, some seventy miles from the coast? Was it possible?

Just at that moment, a flight of four United States Air Force F-84 jets whis-tled overhead, heading north. I watched them as they flew on a few miles, then turned abruptly and began circling. Suddenly the sky around them was dotted with black puffs of smoke—flak. The planes dove down one at a time on some target hidden from my view by a hill, and I heard the bombs as they went off— *BOOM—BOOM—BOOM—BOOM!* Several minutes later after further at-tacks the planes, pursued by the puffs of black, climbed out, formed up, and then flew south, passing directly over me. I waved, knowing full well it was fu-tile and they would never see me. In less than twenty minutes they would be landing at Taegu. How long would it take me?

My trip to the top of the hill had produced negative results; all I knew was that I wasn't near the coast, that somehow I had completely miscalculated. However, I refused to believe I was, as Ho had indicated, in central Korea. I knew I must be somewhere near the coast, perhaps a few miles farther inland than I had thought originally. In the light of this new information, there was only one thing to do—head for a line of taller hills barring my path to the southwest, where I might get an even better idea of my position and, with luck, spot one of the hoped-for bays or inlets. I was discouraged but not whipped. I intended to walk to the west coast, no matter how far away it was, or how long it took me.

There was no alternative.

Millar was eventually recaptured, but a Korean, desperate to make his way to South Korea, helped him secretly signal passing U.S. planes for several days. They were spotted at long last, and an American helicopter was able to land nearby and rescue them.

Escape from Laos

DIETER DENGLER

Escapes by American soldiers during the Vietnam War were almost nonexistent because of the rugged jungle and the impossibility of blending into the local population. For the few that made it, immense suffering would come before a bold move and incredible luck allowed them to beat long odds and escape. Conditions were horrendous and torture a way of life. Most POWs were so weak from illness and starvation that escape wasn't even a remote possibility.

In the following episode, taken from his memoir *Escape from Laos*, Lieutenant Dieter Dengler makes his break after several months of captivity. He had been shot down while flying his first real mission and captured soon after. Beaten and driven to exhaustion, his captors pushed him on a long, disorienting journey through the jungles of Laos. After one early escape attempt he was hung upside down, beaten, and smeared with honey and ants. Nightly, he was staked out spread-eagle, bound at wrist and ankle.

Eventually, he was taken to a small prison camp deep in the jungle where two other Americans were being held along with several other prisoners. The guards were cruel and conditions abysmal, but even so it took everything Dengler had to convince the other prisoners to attempt an escape. The story begins after a starving Dengler is beaten for stealing a chewed-up corncob a guard had thrown to a small pig nearby. It was the last straw, and the other prisoners finally agreed to attack the guards and escape. Unlike most escapes, this one was direct and violent.

No one said anything, and my mind raced with questions and worries. As it was, the three Thais were better adapted to survive in this jungle than we were. Phisit had been a paratrooper in Malaysia and he really knew the jungle well. With the added burden of

Y.C., we three Americans were now at a real disadvantage. I waited until the three of us were alone in our own hut to bring up the topic again.

"Gene, we just can't do it," I told him. He remained silent.

"Leave him be, Dieter," Duane said.

"Nah, he's right," Gene said, "so we don't go with the two of you."

"Don't be a fool—we want you with us," I said.

"And I want Y.C." Gene's determination was unwavering. Though the darkness hid his face from me, I could tell that he was worried but also dead set on his plan.

"Listen, you guys," he said, "Y.C. and I will go together by ourselves and then after we make it over the one ridge, we'll lie in wait for air contact. Y.C. has his white shirt to use for signaling and we'll have enough food. I'm sure we'll make it. If you guys make it out before we do, be sure someone looks for us, and tell him where to look. Okay?"

For a while all three of us remained silent, then began to chatter in our usual way. We were all nervous and sleep did not come easily. Tomorrow we would be alive and free—or dead.

In the morning I didn't want to wake up. I'd slept well in spite of the thought of escape, and I wanted to cling to sleep a little longer. Gene rousted me out. "The C-130—it flew over again last night!"

That was good news. "Man," I said, "if it comes over tonight, we're home free."

The Old Man let us out for a few minutes. While the others were milling about, I went around to the latrine behind our hut, dug up the stolen machete buried there and got it back into the hut without Nook seeing me.

After we were put back inside, the day dragged intolerably, minute by minute. The more I thought about the escape, the more it scared me. Was it the right thing to do? Should we wait until more of the guards were gone? If anything went wrong, we'd all be killed. Was the slim chance of freedom worth the high risk of death? No matter how bad the conditions were in the camp, at least I was still alive. The moment I committed myself to escape I gave up that firm grip on life. I knew that as soon as we were on the other side of that fence and into the jungle, the rest would be up to us. It would have been so much easier and more secure to stay where we were and give it another six months or a year, hoping the war would end and we'd be released.

Duane was sitting by the door looking out.

"What're you thinking?" I asked him.

"That tomorrow we'll be free men!"

That did it for me. From then on I tried to think only positively.

Phisit came over to our hut after getting permission from the Old Man. He brought Y.C.'s can along. Gene took down the bamboo containers full of rice and we used the can to measure out each man's portion. The rats had been into one container and little bugs crawled around in the rest, but there was more rice than we thought there'd be and it was all hard and dry. We gave Gene an extra portion since he was going to lay low with Y.C. and would probably spend more time in the jungle than we would. We put on our escape clothes. Gene got his rucksack ready while Duane gave his hat a greening with leaves. We pushed my bed of leaves aside and lifted the light mat covering the hole. We pried the bamboo pieces a little farther apart and tied them back with some rattan so that the hole was wide enough for a man to get through easily.

The sky looked great, not a cloud in sight, and we were sure we would make air contact. That thought alone kept us going. I felt like screaming out loud, just to settle the butterflies in my stomach.

Almost as if they knew what was happening, Moron came over to our hut and just stood outside looking in, while Phisit and I pretended to be playing on a makeshift chess board. Moron stood there for close to an hour and my heart was going a few beats too fast all the while. "Damn it, why doesn't he leave!" I said under my breath to Phisit. Procet was pretending to sleep in the darkest corner of the hut but actually was hiding a couple of containers of rice under his shirt. I was sure that despite the bad light the guard could see that we were wearing different clothes. We'd worn these clothes a few times before to accustom the guards to the change, but I wasn't at all sure that the ruse had worked. I felt a foreboding—that he must have known we were up to something.

Phisit said something to Moron, then faked a smile as he said to me, "I told Moron to move a piece, so act worried, as if his move hurt you."

I scowled at Moron's dumb, random move, pretending to be losing the game. I moved and Moron quickly countered.

"Good boy," Phisit said, and I didn't know if he meant me or Moron.

After a few more moves, I gave a deep sigh and shook my head, throwing my hands up in defeat. "You won!" Phisit told Moron.

With a wide, silly grin spreading over his stupid face, Moron nodded his head, awed by the whole thing, and strode off hooking his thumb under the rifle sling on his shoulder. My heart was still pounding and both Gene and Duane had turned a shade whiter. "Good thinking, Phisit," I said.

Thani was keeping a constant eye on the guards as Y.C. called to us, "The guards are in the kitchen."

"But chow time hasn't been called!" I said. It was too early for them to be there. Was it a trap?

"They're probably hungry, like us," Gene said. That seemed logical enough and I dismissed my negative thought.

We all looked at each other. The moment had come. Duane brought out the water container and filled our cups. "To freedom!" we toasted. "To freedom, dead or alive!" I thought to myself.

I let myself down through the hole and crouched under our hut. While I waited for the word that all of the guards were in the kitchen, I worked my way to the logs I'd loosened previously and began removing the dirt. Then I heard: "All in the kitchen."

This was it. I grabbed the logs, lifted them out and laid them down alongside the hut. I bellied out to the fence and started to work on it. Then I heard Phisit mumble and I knew that something had already gone wrong. My body worked faster than I could think. In a split second I crawled back under the hut, sloppily replaced the poles and climbed up through the hole, putting my mat and leaves in place and flopping on top of them. My face was flushed and my heart was pumping hard, the blood pounding at my temples, as Phisit sat there just as calm as could be.

"What the hell is going on?" I demanded between breaths.

"Two of the guards were missing." Phisit said, with no hint of excitement in his voice. "I didn't think we should do it."

Anger came out of me like steam, exploding from a safety valve. Here was the second man deciding at the last moment that it was too risky, but waiting until my ass was on the line to let me know about it. I was in a murderous mood. "Damn you, Phisit, if you ever pull that again, I'll keep going and get a gun and come in and let you have it, believe me!" I was boiling mad now and he knew there was nothing idle about my threat.

We just finished putting the rice back into the hollow roof poles when Nook walked up with a bowl of rice broth. He let us out to sit at the table. When he left, I slipped around the hut and finished the job of replacing the logs and fastening the bamboo poles. I sat down at my place and noticed that the rest of them had hardly touched their broth. Out of spite, I ate all of mine. Without looking my way, Phisit left the table and went back to his own hut.

We were locked up for the night and the blocks and cuffs seemed more unbearable than usual, a cruel reminder of the imprisonment we seemed incapable of escaping. It was a miserable evening. I kept thinking how close I had come to being killed. Then we found out from eavesdropping on the guards that the two missing men, the ones Phisit was so worried about, had left to spend the night in the village. Phisit's supposed problem wasn't a problem at all, only an advantage, as the odds would have been five to seven, in our favor.

Almost as if to rub it in, the C-130 circled over the camp several times. We resolved we would try again tomorrow and would succeed. Then we fell silent. I stared at the ceiling without seeing it, my mind far away—thinking of Marina, of my parents and friends, and freedom.

Morning came and we readied ourselves for the escape in near silence. We divided the rice and changed our clothes once more. Phisit grew worried and cautious again. He thought that the guards knew we were up to something.

"Maybe we should wait until tomorrow?" he suggested.

"Not on your life," I replied, giving him a dirty look.

We watched carefully to see if the guards would keep their weapons with them. As long as they parked the guns as usual in their hut, the escape was on.

At about 4:00 P.M. we took our footblocks off. We sat around, waiting for the word to come from Thani and Y.C. in the other hut. Thani again kept the watch, relating what he saw to Y.C., who would then call out in a hushed voice to Duane who was stationed at the door of our hut.

"Guards entering kitchen," Y.C. called.

"Guards entering kitchen," Duane repeated.

"Don't have weapons," Y.C. informed Duane who repeated it.

"Great," I whispered to our group. "We'll have them. It's on."

Y.C. mumbled something. "What did he say?" we asked.

"All in the kitchen, but one's missing!" Duane said.

I knew if we were ever going to go, we had to go now. "Hell, let's go. He's probably not back from the village, yet," I said. Gene, Phisit, and Procet agreed. Duane said it was okay and called back, "It's on."

With the practice of the previous day's false start, I was confident I could go even faster this time. I let myself down under the hut, pulled out the two loosened logs and crawled out. I glanced back and saw Phisit's head and shoulders coming through the opening. I untied the rattan holding the fence together and slipped the cross-hatched bamboo pieces upward to make a hole through which to crawl.

There was no fear now. Like a cat, I jumped up to the porch of the guards' hut and made my way across it, the bamboo poles squeaking uneasily at my every step as I let myself in through the side entrance. There were two Chinese weapons leaning against the wall. Then I spotted an American M-1 in the far corner. I looked out through the front entrance of the hut and realized I was standing in full view of the kitchen, about a hundred feet away. I jerked myself back against the wall, and when no one was looking, I jumped across the open doorway to the M-1 on the other side. I heard Duane's name called, the signal for him to leave the hut and join Procet and Phisit. I grabbed a full ammunition belt and ran across the hut and out onto the porch. Without stopping, I tossed the two Chinese rifles toward Procet and Phisit, then jumped to the ground, checking my M-1 to make sure it was loaded.

So far, everything was working as planned and even going faster than we had anticipated. Less than a minute had passed. Phisit, Procet, and Gene were already in position and Duane was running toward the two Thais. I ran after and past Gene and he quickly followed me to the bamboo cluster, where we waited for a few seconds.

A noise on the other side of the compound indicated that Phisit and Procet were moving out of their hiding place. I ran out from the cluster as Gene took off for the second guards' hut to get the Thompson submachine gun and to cover me from the side door. The kitchen was in full view now and I yelled, *"Yute, yute!"*

The world turned over before my shout had stopped echoing. We had expected the guards to be so surprised by the attack that they would just sit there, stunned, and let us take over without a fight. But just before my shout, they all started to run toward me. They must have seen Procet and Phisit on the other side just before I yelled. They had gone about fifteen feet when a shot rang out and I felt the air swish past my head. I hadn't expected any of them to have a rifle and the near miss seemed unreal. I then realized that it had to be the missing guard or Papsco. Our plan to take the place over without firing a shot had gone right down the drain.

Screaming and yelling filled the air. Someone was shooting wildly in my direction, and I wondered what had happened to the other guys, especially Gene, who was supposed to be covering me from the hut. I seemed to be all alone, out in the open.

Only three feet away, Moron was coming on at a full gallop, his machete cocked high over his head. I fired from the hip point-blank into him. The force of the blast hung him in the air, his machete still raised, and then spun him backwards to the ground. There was blood gushing from a huge hole in his back. I stood over him with my mouth wide open, amazed that a single slug could do such damage and mindful of nothing but the horrible-looking back.

Screams and shots snapped me back to reality. I spun around just in time to see Nook trying to outflank me. "Damn you, Gene! Where the hell is everybody?" I yelled into the air as I fired at Nook. The bullet hit him in the side and he collapsed, still yelling at the top of his lungs. I shot again to finish him off, but he kept on yelling.

The guards were running every which way now and I opened up at the fleeting forms. I saw one man drop, and then everything became a confused blur. I reloaded my M-1 and through it all still heard screaming. Out of the corner of my eye I saw someone trying to get into the jungle. I aimed from the shoulder and fired. The man dropped, then rose, holding one arm. It was Sot! I fired round after round at him, but he was already gone. Then suddenly, everything was eerily quiet.

Duane came running to me, carrying a gun and yelling, "The clip, the clip, it keeps falling out!"

"You're pushing the clip release instead of the safety," I yelled at him. His face was snow-white.

"Everything's going wrong!" he screamed. "I got Papsco's carbine but he wasn't in the hut."

Sot had gotten away, and God knows where Papsco and the Old Man were. That meant at least two, maybe three men had gotten away. I had a sudden paranoid vision of one of the guards looking down the sights of his rifle at me. I started running and shouting, "Let's get moving!"

I could hardly believe it when I realized that Nook was still alive and groaning. I aimed at him and pulled the trigger but the gun didn't go off. For a moment I stood there stupidly, and then realized the chamber was empty. I left him and ran around the corner of the fence toward the entrance to the compound, which was our prearranged meeting place in case of a change in plans. Duane came running toward me.

"Where in the hell are the rucksacks?" I yelled.

"In the hut!" he hollered.

"Get them, I'll get the mosquito nets!" I dashed by him to Papsco's hut, only to find it picked clean. Even the shoes that had been hanging underneath the hut were missing. Apparently the Thais had been there before me.

I met Duane with two rucksacks at the entrance to the compound. As I swung one rucksack up on my back, one of the straps broke. The pack was very heavy, far heavier than my own pack. I could barely lift the thing with one hand. "Whose rucksack is this?" I asked Duane, but he shook his head.

Duane began running toward the jungle. He, too, was dragging a rucksack. "Whose is that?" I hollered, but he kept on running, stopping briefly to vomit from the unusual exertion.

Suddenly, a piercing pain in my foot stopped me dead. I had snagged rattan, bristling with fishhook-like thorns. The cuts were deep, baring the white of bone. The pain shot from my foot to my head and I pulled off the rattan and kept running, despite the pain, until I caught up with Duane. We heard the sound of someone coming to our left. Duane and I ducked into the bush and froze. The familiar red head appeared and there were Gene and Y.C., making their way through the jungle. Duane and I jumped up and ran until we caught up with them.

"Hey, Gene, this must be Y.C.'s," I said, dragging the rucksack forward. But Gene was confused, as we all were, and didn't know what I was talking about. Y.C. caught up with us and took the rucksack with a bewildered look. We started to move off together but Y.C. held us back. Then Duane ran on ahead, while I stopped and took hold of Gene's hand.

"Go on, go on," he said. "See you in the States." I looked into Gene's face and got all choked up. I tried to say something but the words wouldn't come. I pumped his hand, began running, then stopped and waved at him and Y.C.

I found Duane all tied up in some thick foliage. "It's no use, it's just too thick," he said. "Let's get out of here!"

We turned and ran back to where we had seen Gene and Y.C. All of a sudden we were at the tiny cornfield we had never seen but about which we had heard the guards talking. The cornstalks towered over us and it was easy running between the rows until we arrived at a huge, natural barrier of thorns. It was about twenty-five feet high and impenetrable. We ran all along the thorn row, looking for a hole, but it was solid as a castle wall. I tried to pry through the heavy thorn bush with my rifle but it was just too thick. Duane stood looking at me and I stared back. On the other side of the ridge lay a reasonable chance of freedom. But the thorns had us cut off. There was nowhere to go.

We were startled by a dog barking close by and turned to find Malay standing beside us. He must have witnessed the whole breakout and then left when we did.

"That dog's going to give us away!" Duane grumbled. He started to move toward Malay to shut him up and instantly Malay turned, ran up a few yards, and disappeared into the supposedly impenetrable thicket. We ran over to where he had vanished and Malay was standing on the other side, whining.

"He's dug a hole right through this thing to go hunting," Duane mumbled behind me as we crawled through the thicket, crossed a slimy creek on the other side, and a few yards beyond that, the base of the ridge. Duane was ecstatic. Somehow I felt that Malay, who was still standing at the fence with his head cocked, had known what was going on.

A few yards up the bank we fell on our knees, folded our hands around each other and closed our eyes in prayer. "God, please help us now. Please let us live!"

Now that we were relatively safe, all my adrenaline seemed to ebb away. When I stood up after praying, I nearly blacked out. The rifle became a heavier burden than I thought possible as it kept digging into my shoulder. The ammunition belt around my waist dragged me down as we moved up on the ridge.

The ground was pocked with hundreds of animal tracks leading toward a puddle on a small shelf. We were both thirsty and I told Duane to cover me as I slowly crawled on my stomach toward the puddle. As I came near, I heard something on the other side. In an instant I was back with Duane in the bush. We both lay there motionless and Duane held his finger across his mouth in a gesture of silence, nodding his head in the direction of the sound. It was quiet there now. I touched Duane lightly, pointing to the M-1 lying out of my reach, and he slid it to me silently. I slipped off the safety and pointed the muzzle toward the noise.

The bush rustled again. There were some whispers but I couldn't see anyone. The bamboo moved and I heard the voices again, only much closer and clearer this time. Duane slid down toward me, his carbine aimed at the sound. Then Procet walked into view. Relief flooded over us but we still didn't dare move, thinking that they, also, were on guard and the slightest noise might draw a bullet from them.

Duane kept his head pressed close to the ground while he waved his hand in the air. Procet saw him and waved back. The puddle was too exposed to be a safe meeting place so we joined the Thais about fifty feet above it.

It was not exactly a meeting of friends, as there had been plenty of hatred between us in the past, and both groups were now armed. We eyed each other suspiciously, alert for any false move. Procet kept looking at my belt. "How about some ammo?" he asked.

"Okay, but give me a machete in trade. You've got three," I said. I wanted to ask them why they had left me all alone back at the camp, but I kept silent, not wanting to risk a shoot-out. However, all on his own Procet offered an explanation.

"I saw the Old Man and shot him in the leg so he couldn't go for help. But then all the guards ran your way and I couldn't get a single shot off at them. So we got the shoes and let Y.C. and Thani out, and by that time it was all over. Then we left."

They were all wearing shoes and when I asked for mine, Procet said that Y.C. had them. "Oh, yeah, your rucksack," Procet said, holding the bag out to me.

We moved on. Thani cut a way through the foliage with the point of his machete. It seemed stupid to me to make such a trail because trackers could easily follow it, but I didn't say anything. We came across an animal track and followed it, single file, through a long series of switchbacks up the side of the mountain.

The trail was a hotbed of leeches, but there was no time to stop and pull them off. Our only hope was to cover as much ground as possible before dark.

The leeches were nothing compared to the worms we came across next. They were everywhere, and it was difficult to walk without stepping on the awful things. Their orange bodies were fat and gleaming with slime and from their backs rose a spiny fin like a dragon's. From their heads grew another horn, similar to a spear. They were as much as a foot long and a half inch thick. Some of them stretched out full length across the trail, while others lay sprawled in various curves. The sight of these creatures turned my stomach more than some of the offal I'd gagged down at Hoi Het. I flicked them out of my path with my rifle.

As we came to the top of the ridge, Thani heard water running some-where. We were all eager to find it; dehydration had my head spinning. Thani moved ahead and walked down along fallen trees and stopped. We all followed him, hoping to see a valley below, but to our great disappointment the trail wandered downhill for a while and then climbed yet another ridge. We gath-ered what strength we had and continued walking.

Night had fallen and we were cold, but we kept going. The jungle canopy above us separated from time to time and as I glanced up now and then at the millions of stars above, I wondered if anyone back home sensed that I was now a free man.

The going got steep and rough and we frequently slipped and fell. The ground ripped my bare feet and my clothes snagged constantly on branches and thorns. I didn't know who was in front of me and who was behind. Fa-tigue had struck us all dumb. What we all needed was water.

We finally came upon a spring, and I stood knee-deep in the ice-cold mountain water and drank thirstily. Every few seconds I lifted my head and looked around like an animal on the alert for predators. As I rubbed my arms I felt the slimy leeches covering them and could make out their dark bodies glis-tening in the faint light of the moon. I noticed that one of my tobacco pouches was missing but I used the other to rub my face and the rest of my body.

We talked very little but agreed on spending the night together. We quietly searched for a place to bed down on this first free night, and then collapsed on an animal trail, with a rock wall to lean on behind us. Duane sat down next to me and it was good to feel the warmth of another human being nearby. I fell asleep quickly.

I awakened with Duane calling my name. I sat up, alarmed. Duane pointed to the sky, the little we could see of it through the heavy foliage. The C-130 was making her evening circles. We looked at each other and lay back down, but I couldn't sleep until the drone of the engines died in the distance.

Something was disturbing my sleep and I awoke to find rain spattering in my face. Duane and I crawled under some huge leaves and held them over our heads to keep off the rain. Soon the drizzle became a downpour and little streams falling off the leaves found their way down our necks. We huddled over our rice, which we knew would mold in a day if it got wet. The downpour turned the dirt into mud so slippery that I slid down the slope for several feet before I could find a root to grab. The noise of the rain in the jungle drowned out every word of panic we yelled at each other. It rained all night. The gray dawn finally brought some relief.

As we slowly made our way down the trail, we noticed that the Thais were wearing plastic rain sheets. "Those damn guys," I muttered. "They were stealing everything they could lay their hands on while I was shooting it out."

"Hey, how about one for us?" Duane asked Procet. Procet shook his head and then Duane asked Phisit, who also refused.

"Then how about enough to cover our rice?" I asked, trying to keep the anger out of my voice. Procet and Phisit talked this over, and Phisit ripped off a piece about a foot square, barely enough to cover the rice in my pack.

The ground was very muddy, making traveling extremely difficult. We clambered up the slope by holding onto vines and roots. At the top we confronted each other to say goodbye, and I saw exhaustion and fear in their eyes as we quietly shook hands. Then Duane and I took a right, and the jungle swallowed us up in a matter of seconds. We never saw the Thais again.

That was the morning of June 30, 1966—the first morning I had seen as a free man in over five months.

Duane Martin and Dieter Dengler wandered in circles for three weeks, barefoot and fighting starvation, illness, leeches, and mosquitoes. Duane, too disoriented to even speak, was finally killed after stumbling upon a local villager wielding a machete. Dengler managed to elude the villagers and, by the merest chance, was spotted by a passing American plane. Near death and barely recognizable as a human being much less an American soldier, he was pulled into the helicopter sent to rescue him. He had malaria and a variety of other ailments and had lost 70 pounds, but he was alive and free.

Out of a Turkish Prison

BILLY HAYES WITH WILLIAM HOFFER

Billy Hayes was just another young American who had dropped out of college to knock around Europe when he was arrested trying to board a plane in Turkey with 2 pounds of hashish strapped to his body. He was just twenty-three years old. He spent the next five years trying to survive the infamous Turkish prison system before making his escape in 1975. Originally sentenced to four years, the Turkish government inexplicably changed his sentence to thirty years just months before he would have finished his time.

He endured filthy, nightmarish conditions, beatings, and sometimes near-chaos during his imprisonment. At one point, hoping it would present better escape opportunities, he got himself placed in the prison insane asylum. The depravity and brutality he saw there seems beyond comprehension.

His story was publicized by *Time* and *Newsweek* and the U.S. State Department worked for his release, but the Turkish court system was an impenetrable morass. In desperation, Hayes eventually got himself transferred to an island prison 20 miles off the coast of Turkey, and despite the betrayal of a trusted friend on the outside who had taken money and promised assistance, he plotted his escape. His incredible story was eventually published under the title *Midnight Express*.

In the evening after work I raced back to the barracks to make my preparations while the other men went to dinner. I changed into dark clothing—my blue jeans and the sneakers I had inked for my window escape with Harvey Bell. I took my precious map of Turkey; now tattered from much handling, from its hiding place and wrapped it in wax paper, then put it in my leather carrying pouch, along with my address book. I counted my meager supply of money and cursed Joey; he had taken most of it. I now had only about forty dollars in Turkish lira. I put the money into my wallet and the wallet into the pouch too. I strapped the pouch tightly to my side, and pulled on a navy blue turtleneck sweater.

I went to the window and double-checked to see that no one was coming. Then I went to my bed and drew a knife from under the mattress. I was scared to death to be caught with that knife; to possess a weapon was an extremely serious offense. I had stolen the knife from the conserve factory. It was short and pointed, the kind used for paring fruit, and its wooden handle was splintered and just barely held on by worn screws. I had hidden it under a rock in the orchard and the day before had transferred it to my bed. All night long, even when I was asleep, I was conscious of that forbidden knife under the mattress. Now I wrapped paper around it to sheathe it and slipped it into the pocket of my jeans. And then I put on my lucky hat.

I couldn't just sit out on the dock waiting for a boat to appear. So the plan was this: Up a slight hill from the harbor was the tomato paste processing area. Five large concrete bins were used to store the paste. I knew from working around them that the one on the end was empty. I could hide inside each night, whenever the weather looked right, watching the harbor while avoiding the guards on patrol. Sooner or later the Marmara would churn up another storm, and the boats would appear.

I waited till dusk. Then I took a walk along one of the trails. That was normal enough. Just another prisoner out enjoying nature. My path took me near the tomato paste bins. I checked around me. I looked into the empty bin. Then I jumped inside.

It was cool and dark. I huddled in the bottom. The sky slowly turned black above me. At times I checked the harbor, not really expecting to see any boats there in good weather, but hoping.

I heard footsteps, the measured pace of a guard. I sat motionless. If he looked inside, what could I say? I thought of the knife. I prayed he wouldn't stop. He passed by.

I waited quietly until 9:45. Not tonight. I jumped out of the bin and dashed back to the barracks before the curfew. No one really counted us until morning, but I didn't want to take chances.

I watched and waited for a full week. Lazy Indian summer days were followed by calm quiet evenings.

And then on Thursday, October 2, I awoke to the sound of wind and rain beating against the window pane of the barracks. I looked out at the gray sky and my heart began to pump. I knew it was the day. The storm grew worse during the evening. I worked furiously at my job until lunchtime, then raced to the harbor. A half-dozen fishing boats had already dropped anchor. More were heading my way! If only the storm would keep on until after dark.

I worked more easily that afternoon, trying to save my strength for what I hoped was a full night of rowing. At 5:30 the guards released us from work. The rain had stopped but the sky was dark and low and the wind was strong. I ran to the harbor. The sea was rough and choppy. Boats were strung out all over. I headed back to the barracks to prepare.

When darkness closed in on Imrali island I climbed into the tomato bin. A prison spotlight routinely swept the area. By now I knew its pattern. Crazy shadows rose on the wall of the bin whenever it passed over. There were lights on the boats in the dark harbor.

I wanted to wait until after the curfew. Then I could be sure that other prisoners were not around. So I crouched and planned. I would swim out to the farthest fishing boat and untie its dinghy. And then row for the Asian shore.

Time passed slowly. I realized that I had to relieve myself. I crawled to a far corner of the bin and peed. The urine mingled with the rain puddles, then trickled back across the floor of the bin and settled in the corner where I'd been hiding. If I changed my position I might be more exposed to a patrolling guard. So I had to squat in the liquid. The smell hardly bothered me anymore.

Time crawled now. I felt as if I'd been waiting for days. My watch only showed eight o'clock. I tried to relax. My thoughts flew to all the things I would do when I got out. I thought of Lillian. I thought of Mom and Dad. I imagined myself walking down a street in a city. Any city. A free man. I was so close. I *had* to make it.

A noise! Footsteps. I didn't dare breathe. A guard moved up the pathway toward the bins. I could hear him stop next to my hiding place. A bright orange glow flared up, flickered in the wind and went out. The guard coughed. Then he moved on.

The rain began again. It soaked me to the skin. The wind was icy. I huddled in the bottom of the bin and waited.

Finally my watch showed ten-thirty. I eased my head up over the top of the bin and listened. The sounds of the storm filled the night. I took a couple of deep breaths and raised one leg over the edge of the bin.

What was that?

Quickly I dropped back down inside. I huddled against the wall. Off in the distance a dog barked. I thought of the guard tower and its machine guns.

I waited another ten minutes, listening. Again I poked my head over the edge of the bin and looked through the driving rain. Then lifted one leg up. Again I thought I heard a noise and dropped back down. I shivered in fear.

I decided it must have been my imagination. My hands shook. I wondered if I really had the nerve to go through with this.

For a third time I gathered my courage. I took several deep breaths. "All right," I said to myself. "All right. Let's just go."

The bank down to the harbor was covered with a mixture of broken stones and rotting tomato pulp. The earth was muddy and puddled. Slime covered me as I crawled carefully down the bank on my belly. I was in the open, exposed to the searchlight. Each time it passed over I dug deep into the slime. I lay motionless. I prayed.

Slowly I worked my way down to the bank. Now for the hard part. The first fifty yards of water lay directly in front of the guard tower. I could see one soldier in it operating the searchlight. Another paced quietly with a machine gun. I was thankful for the noise of the wind and waves. Even so, I would have to be careful.

I slipped into the cold water. Above me the searchlight moved across the harbor. I pushed off from the shore, my heart pounding with the knowledge that my escape, so long dreamed of, had begun, and that there was no going back now. I had committed myself.

I swam slowly, afraid to splash. The heavy clothes weighed me down. A wave caught me in the face, driving salt water down my throat. I fought back a cough. I tensed for the bullets to rip into my back.

I swam breaststroke so that only my head would break water.

When I could swim no farther without a rest, I stopped and looked back. The dim lights of the harbor had fallen behind. Ahead I could see bobbing lanterns, each one indicating a fishing boat. I would swim to the farthest one.

I fought against the storm. Several times I stopped, treading water, checking my position, gulping air. Then I started again, heading for the last fishing boat.

There it was, a tiny dinghy tied to the rear. Would it hold up in this sea? It had to.

I hoisted myself over the side of the dinghy. It took every bit of strength I had left. Exhausted, I sank onto the wet floorboards. I lay there for several minutes, shivering in the cold, trying to catch my breath. Then I raised my head slowly until I could see over the side of the boat. I studied the shore, expecting to see a patrol boat bearing down on me. But there were no lights following me out.

The front of the dinghy was covered over, offering maybe three feet of shelter. The rest of the boat was totally exposed. I felt in the dark for the oars. I found them. They were thick and heavy.

Bang! A window crashed open right over my head. I froze. Above me a Turkish fisherman gargled the poisons out of his throat and spit across my head into the water.

My heart had stopped beating.

The window creaked on its hinges and banged shut.

Slowly I slid up under the covering in front of the boat. I shivered in a puddle of cold water. I curled up as tightly as possible, but my legs still lay exposed. I wanted to get out of there before the fisherman opened his window again.

I glanced up at the underside of the covering. Over my head I could dimly see a large knot, the end of the rope that tethered the dinghy to the fishing boat. The knot was thick and tight—impossible to untie. I reached into my blue jeans for the knife. My pants were soaked. They clung to my legs. Finally I reached the knife. The rope was wet and sinewy. The knife cut through it at an agonizingly slow pace. I hacked away until my muscles ached and my arms and back were bruised from rubbing against the ribs of the boat. I desperately had to cough, and the effort of holding back the spasms wracked my chest. A damp chill settled in my lungs.

I drew numb fingers back and forth, back and forth. And then only a few strands of rope were left. I stopped. Once more I looked around me. I listened. I held my breath and slit through the final strands.

The knot fell. The severed end of the rope trembled and moved an inch up through the hole in the covering. And then it rasped out through the hole and disappeared. The boat was free!

I was adrift. As quietly as I could I crawled to the center of the dinghy and got up on the seat. I looked out. I was drifting toward the prison shore! I grabbed for the oars, and then discovered there were no oarlocks, none that I could see. There was no light now. My hand touched a twist of rope at the center of one oarshaft. It was shaped like a figure eight. I realized that the loop of the pretzel must fit over something. I felt the gunwale. Ah, yes. There were pegs on the sides of the boat. The rope-twists slipped over the pegs.

Hurrying now, I was scared to death because the dinghy was drifting not just toward shore but toward the hulk of another fishing boat. I jammed the oars into position. I pulled. One oar failed to catch the water, and the boat lurched, and I pitched around in the darkness. The second fishing boat loomed larger. I centered myself on the seat again and adjusted the oars until I could tell both blades were at the right angle. And then I pulled, and again. And the drift slowed, then stopped. The dinghy began to move in the other direction.

It was hard rowing. The tossing sea kept me bobbing at different angles. The oars often failed to bite into the water. I had to shift my balance quickly to keep from being thrown off the wet bench. I braced my feet against the bottom and gradually after several minutes, a rhythm developed.

Now I had to steer a careful course down the inside of the horseshoe-shaped island. There were huge rocks in the breakerline. And there were many more fishing boats anchored further south, I discovered. I had to weave a path for the dinghy between the two sets of hazards. The rain lashed down in sheets, driven by the wind. Its ferocity scared me. But the rain also gave me cover.

My muscles were hardened from yoga and from hefting sacks of beans. I pulled and heaved on the oars. Slowly, the edge of the island slid past.

I watched the lights of the harbor. They receded to a small cluster, pinpoints of brightness in the dark night. I knew I wanted to steer a course in line with the lights and the edge of the island. If I lost sight of the lights I'd be too far over to one side. I strained against the wind to keep the boat in line.

The current was much stronger in the open sea. It pushed the dinghy to the west. Waves slammed the boat broadside, and the wind threw salt spray into my eyes. Quickly I grew exhausted. The island lights had focused down to a single point when I stopped rowing and checked my position. Behind me, somewhere through the storm, was the Turkish mainland. Twenty miles south.

I rowed till I thought I'd collapse. Then I checked again. Did I see lights in the direction of the mainland? I looked again and there were none. More rowing, back breaking. Another look, lights! Three pale lights. But they were off to one side. I was being pulled far off course.

A wave of self-pity swept over me. I loosened my grip. One of the oars caught the current. It lifted from its peg and nearly pulled from my hand. I jerked it into the boat. I threw both oars to the bottom of the dinghy. The tiny craft veered off down the waves.

This would never work! It might take me days to row to the shore. If I didn't drown first. My breathing came in heavy sobs. I held onto the seat and sat still for a moment. The dinghy rode up the face of a long swell. It hung suspended for an instant, then rushed down the other side. Another long swell rolled under me. Again the boat rose and then plunged. I was terrified.

But it was a strange sort of fear. I could die out here in the open sea, but at least I'd die free. Just the word filled me with new strength. Free! I was free!

The lights of Imrali had faded behind me. For the first time in five long years I was beyond the bounds. My heart leapt up. I was free! All that remained was to stay alive. To finish this boat ride and set my feet on solid ground.

I grabbed the oars and set back to work. I pulled on them angrily, wrenching the boat around, back on course. Then I worked to resume my rhythm. I chanted aloud to myself as I struggled.

> "If they catch me . . .
> They'll beat me . . .
> Shoot me . . .
> If I make it . . .
> I'm free . . .
> I'm free . . .
> I'm free . . ."

I had waited five years for this ride. I wouldn't give up now. *I would not!*

Still the current pulled me to the west. I rowed twice as hard with my right arm, trying to get back on course for the three pale lights.

I sang to myself. I yelled at myself. I cursed myself in Turkish and English.

Hours passed in dark wet agony. My right hand ached where, long ago, Hamid had smashed it with his *falaka* stick. Then it cramped. The skin of both hands was raw, and salt water stung in broken blisters.

I stopped rowing. Carefully I pulled the oars into the boat. The fingers of my right hand didn't work. I had to pry them off the oar with my left. I grabbed my soggy handkerchief and tied it around the throbbing hand. I pulled the knot tight with my teeth.

Then back to work. I rowed. I rowed with fixed determination. All that mattered was to keep pulling, keep going, keep the rhythm. My body stopped complaining. I was beyond pain. I exulted in the movement. I was free.

The lights were closer now. They were! I could do it. Even the sea began to cooperate. The storm seemed to calm. The first hint of light blue glow tinted the sky to the east. Another hour.

Thud. The oar scraped something. Then the bottom of the dinghy scratched across sand. A small wave lifted the boat and sent it forward a few more feet, then set it down again. I rolled over the side and found myself in one foot of water. I rushed up the beach and sank down on my knees.

But I was still in Turkey.

My next goal was the city of Bursa. I knew from the map that it lay somewhere along the coast to the northeast. It had about 250,000 people. I could lose myself there. And from Bursa I could get transportation to Istanbul. Then, Johann. He would hide me for a couple of weeks until the search died down.

The search! The rising sun in front of me reminded me that fishermen would soon be stirring. One of them, when he opened his window for his morning gargle, would certainly miss his dinghy. It would take the prison guards little time to make a head count. I had to move fast.

My watch still worked. It was after five A.M. I got up and sucked salt air deep into my lungs. Then I set off trotting toward the sun. The warm orange light gave me new strength. Ahead of me stretched the deserted north coast of Asia Minor. This was the finest morning of my life.

I ran on. I should have been tired. I should have been hungry. But my legs pumped without stopping. Each step took me farther from prison. How much time did I have? When would they find the dinghy?

I ran on and on. Still the shore was wild and deserted. The sun dried my clothes. My face and arms were caked with salt. My mouth burned.

Then I came to a huge outcropping of rocks that jutted into the sea, blocking the beach. I waded into the water up to my waist and worked my way around the rocks. As I moved past the point my eyes caught sight of what looked like a modern village in the hills up ahead—a strange cluster of buildings here in the middle of nowhere. I saw three towers. Were they the three glowing lights I'd sighted on during the night?

Oh, no! An army camp!

I melted back behind the rocks. I waded back around to the beach and walked inland to the cover of the woods. In a long circle I moved past the army base.

Another hour of walking. I knew I must be very careful. Surely the alarm was out by now. Why hadn't I shaved my blond moustache before I left? I should've brought shoe polish or something to dump onto my hair.

I came to tilled fields. In the distance I could see a few peasants working. Around a bend, a small village.

Careful. Don't blow it.

I followed a dirt road until it entered the town and became a cobblestone street. An old man with a stringy gray beard leaned back on his heels against a wall. He sucked on a pipe.

"I must get to Bursa," I said.

The old man looked at me. *Turist,* obviously. Dirty, wet, crusty, muddy, bandaged right hand. Floppy hat pulled low. "How do you know Turkish?" he asked.

I answered hesitantly. "Twenty months in Istanbul prison. Hash."

He grinned. "What are you doing here?" he asked.

"I was on the beach with some friends. We had a jeep. I drank a lot of *raka* last night and got lost. Now I need to get to Bursa." With the tip of his pipe he pointed up the narrow road to an old Volkswagen bus.

"Bursa," he said.

The roof was piled high with burlap bags filled with onions, olives, other produce. The inside was packed with peasants. I found someone who looked like the driver.

"Bursa?"

"Six lira."

I paid. Then I squeezed into a back seat against the window. I pulled my hat even lower and tried to keep a hand over my moustache.

The bus bounced along the muddy coast, up mountain roads winding toward Bursa. The old driver whipped around turns at high speed. I hadn't ridden in an open vehicle for years, and it was frightening. On the outside turns gravity pushed me out over the edge of the cliffs. *How ridiculous it would be to die here, I thought. Now. When I'm finally free.* But there was nothing I could do. And the driver had to know the roads.

We stopped at markets along the side of the highway. Peasants tumbled out to sell their wares. Gradually the load lightened. The bus driver increased his speed.

Finally Bursa came into view. It was a city of about 250,000 people, I knew, the only city of its size along this coast. Its streets were hot and dry and dusty, lined with crumbling buildings of the old Turkish architecture, with an occasional Western-style office building that was also falling apart. I checked my watch. Nine-thirty. I knew they had missed me now. I hadn't showed up for work.

A battered cab sat at the curb. I approached the driver carefully.

"Istanbul?"

"Seven hundred lira."

"Four hundred fifty." It was all I had.

"*Yok.* Seven hundred."

I shrugged. The cabbie pointed to the bus station. "Twenty-five lira," he said.

Yes, but I didn't want to go near the bus station. They'd be looking for me there. For sure. As I peered down the street I could see two policemen standing out in front of the bus station. I wondered whether they had a description of me and were watching for me in particular.

But I had no choice. I had to get to Istanbul. To Johann. The longer I waited, the greater the risk.

I walked toward the station. As I passed the entrance one of the policemen yawned.

I bought a ticket to Istanbul. The bus would leave in a half hour. I sat down to wait and was suddenly exhausted. Hungry, too. I found a snack counter and bought a chocolate bar and a big bag of pretzels.

The bus arrived. Again I had to walk past the policemen. They seemed to ignore me. I climbed in and took an aisle seat. My heart raced. Please, please let me get to Istanbul.

I waited for the bus to leave. I thought it never would. But at last it began to move. It left the station and headed for the open road that swings around the eastern edge of the Sea of Marmara to Üsküdar. I began to breathe again.

The trip was bumpy. The bus buzzed with Turkish chatter. Flies fought for my pretzels.

We came to Üsküdar. Across the Golden Horn, rising steeply from its shores, I saw Istanbul, with the spires of minarets crowning its hills. There was where it had all begun. The bus crossed the Yeni Kopru bridge, and once again I was in Europe.

It was nearly noon. I was frantic. No doubt at all, the Turkish police were after me now. I could only hope to blend with the other *turists* who crowded the Istanbul bus depot.

I stepped off the bus and kept my eyes low to the ground. I moved into the middle of a group of people and walked with them out onto the streets. Only from a distance did I stop to look back at the station. Two policemen stood outside the front entrance. There was no sign of alarm.

Now, Johann's hotel. It was almost over. I found a cab driver and gave him the name of the hotel. We wound through back streets until we arrived at the door. Not the Hilton, that was for sure.

I wondered about my lucky hat. It covered my blond hair, but the hat was conspicuous, too. Maybe it was more obvious than the hair. Before I stepped into the hotel, I pulled off the hat and shoved it under my arm.

I walked into the lobby. Behind the desk was a bald-headed Turk. He looked up.

"Johann?" I asked. "I'm looking for Johann."

"Johann?" He eyed my clothes. "Johann left yesterday for Afghanistan."

Despite this setback and a few more scary moments, Hayes was able to sneak across to freedom in Greece the following day and eventually make his way home.

Dark, Deep-Laid Plans

MARK TWAIN

First published in 1884, *The Adventures of Huckleberry Finn*, by Mark Twain, defined the "great American novel." In this entertaining scene, Huck and Tom Sawyer are plotting the best way to free their friend Jim, who is being held as a runaway slave. It quickly becomes obvious that Tom has read a few too many tales of escape in his young life.

It would be most an hour yet till breakfast, so we left and struck down into the woods; because Tom said we got to have *some* light to see how to dig by, and a lantern makes too much, and might get us into trouble; what we must have was a lot of them rotten chunks that's called fox-fire, and just makes a soft kind of a glow when you lay them in a dark place. We fetched an armful and hid it in the weeds, and set down to rest, and Tom says, kind of dissatisfied:

"Blame it, this whole thing is just as easy and awkward as it can be. And so it makes it so rotten difficult to get up a difficult plan. There ain't no watchman to be drugged—now there *ought* to be a watchman. There ain't even a dog to give a sleeping-mixture to. And there's Jim chained by one leg, with a ten-foot chain, to the leg of his bed: why, all you got to do is to lift up the bedstead and slip off the chain. And Uncle Silas he trusts everybody; sends the key to the punkin-headed nigger, and don't send nobody to watch the nigger. Jim could 'a' got out of that window-hole before this, only there wouldn't be no use trying to travel with a ten-foot chain on his leg. Why, drat it, Huck, it's the stupidest arrangement I ever see. You got to invent *all* the difficulties. Well, we can't help it; we got to do the best we can with the materials we've got. Anyhow, there's one thing—there's more honor in getting him out through a lot of difficulties and dangers, where there warn't one of them furnished to you by the people who it was their duty to furnish them, and you had to contrive them all out of your own head. Now look at just that one thing of the lantern. When you come down to the cold facts, we simply got to *let on* that a lantern's resky. Why, we could work with a torchlight procession if we wanted to, *I* believe. Now, whilst I think of it, we got to hunt up something to make a saw out of the first chance we get."

"What do we want of a saw?"

"What do we *want* of a saw? Hain't we got to saw the leg of Jim's bed off, so as to get the chain loose?"

"Why, you just said a body could lift up the bedstead and slip the chain off."

"Well, if that ain't just like you, Huck Finn. You *can* get up the infant-schooliest ways of going at a thing. Why, hain't you ever read any books at all?—Baron Trenck, nor Casanova, nor Benvenuto Chelleeny, nor Henri IV., nor none of them heroes? Who ever heard of getting a prisoner loose in such an old-maidy way as that? No; the way all the best authorities does is to saw the bed-leg in two, and leave it just so, and swallow the sawdust, so it can't be found, and put some dirt and grease around the sawed place so the very keenest seneskal can't see no sign of its being sawed, and thinks the bed-leg is perfectly sound. Then, the night you're ready, fetch the leg a kick, down she goes; slip off your chain, and there you are. Nothing to do but hitch your rope ladder to the battlements, shin down it, break your leg in the moat—because a rope ladder is nineteen foot too short, you know—and there's your horses and your trusty vassles, and they scoop you up and fling you across a saddle, and away you go to your native Langudoc, or Navarre, or wherever it is. It's gaudy, Huck. I wish there was a moat to this cabin. If we get time, the night of the escape, we'll dig one."

I says:

"What do we want of a moat when we're going to snake him out from under the cabin?"

But he never heard me. He had forgot me and everything else. He had his chin in his hand, thinking. Pretty soon he sighs and shakes his head; then sighs again, and says:

"No, it wouldn't do—there ain't necessity enough for it."

"For what?" I says.

"Why, to saw Jim's leg off," he says.

"Good land!" I says; "why, there ain't *no* necessity for it. And what would you want to saw his leg off for, anyway?"

"Well, some of the best authorities has done it. They couldn't get the chain off, so they just cut their hand off and shoved. And a leg would be better still. But we got to let that go. There ain't necessity enough in this case; and besides, Jim's a nigger, and wouldn't understand the reasons for it, and how it's the custom in Europe; so we'll let it go. But there's one thing—he can have a rope ladder; we can tear up our sheets and make him a rope ladder easy enough. And we can send it to him in a pie; it's mostly done that way. And I've et worse pies."

"Why, Tom Sawyer, how you talk," I says; "Jim ain't got no use for a rope ladder."

"He *has* got use for it. How *you* talk, you better say; you don't know nothing about it. He's *got* to have a rope ladder; they all do."

"What in the nation can he *do* with it?"

"*Do* with it? He can hide it in his bed, can't he? That's what they all do; and *he's* got to, too. Huck, you don't ever seem to want to do anything that's regular; you want to be starting something fresh all the time. S'pose he *don't* do nothing with it? ain't it there in his bed, for a clue, after he's gone? and don't you reckon they'll want clues? Of course they will. And you wouldn't leave them any? That would be a *pretty* howdy-do, *wouldn't* it! I never heard of such a thing."

"Well," I says, "if it's in the regulations, and he's got to have it, all right, let him have it; because I don't wish to go back on no regulations; but there's one thing, Tom Sawyer—if we go to tearing up our sheets to make Jim a rope ladder, we're going to get into trouble with Aunt Sally, just as sure as you're born. Now, the way I look at it, a hickry-bark ladder don't cost nothing, and don't waste nothing, and is just as good to load up a pie with, and hide in a straw tick, as any rag ladder you can start; and as for Jim, he ain't had no experience, and so *he* don't care what kind of a—"

"Oh, shucks, Huck Finn, if I was as ignorant as you I'd keep still—that's what *I'd* do. Who ever heard of a state prisoner escaping by a hickry-bark ladder? Why, it's perfectly ridiculous."

"Well, all right, Tom, fix it your own way; but if you'll take my advice, you'll let me borrow a sheet off of the clothes-line."

He said that would do. And that gave him another idea, and he says:

"Borrow a shirt, too."

"What do we want of a shirt, Tom?"

"Want it for Jim to keep a journal on."

"Journal your granny—*Jim* can't write."

"S'pose he *can't* write—he can make marks on the shirt, can't he, if we make him a pen out of an old pewter spoon or a piece of an old iron barrel-hoop?"

"Why, Tom, we can pull a feather out of a goose and make him a better one; and quicker, too."

"*Prisoners* don't have geese running around the donjon-keep to pull pens out, you muggins. They *always* make their pens out of the hardest, toughest, troublesomest piece of old brass candlestick or something like that they can get their hands on; and it takes them weeks and weeks and months and months to file it out, too, because they've got to do it by rubbing it on the wall. *They* wouldn't use a goose-quill if they had it. It ain't regular."

"Well, then, what'll we make him the ink out of?"

"Many makes it out of iron-rust and tears; but that's the common sort and women; the best authorities uses their own blood. Jim can do that; and when he wants to send any little common ordinary mysterious message to let the world know where he's captivated, he can write it on the bottom of a tin plate with a fork and throw it out of the window. The Iron Mask always done that, and it's a blame' good way, too."

"Jim ain't got no tin plates. They feed him in a pan."

"That ain't nothing; we can get him some."

"Can't nobody *read* his plates."

"That ain't got anything to *do* with it, Huck Finn. All *he's* got to do is to write on the plate and throw it out. You don't *have* to be able to read it. Why, half the time you can't read anything a prisoner writes on a tin plate, or anywhere else."

"Well, then, what's the sense in wasting the plates?"

"Why, blame it all, it ain't the *prisoner's* plates."

"But it's *somebody's* plates, ain't it?"

"Well, spos'n it is? What does the *prisoner* care whose—"

He broke off there, because we heard the breakfast horn blowing. So we cleared out for the house.

Along during the morning I borrowed a sheet and a white shirt off of the clothes-line; and I found an old sack and put them in it, and we went down and got the fox-fire, and put that in too. I called it borrowing, because that was what pap always called it; but Tom said it warn't borrowing it, it was stealing. He said we was representing prisoners; and prisoners don't care how they get a thing so they get it, and nobody don't blame them for it, either. It ain't no crime in a prisoner to steal the thing he needs to get away with, Tom said; it's his right; and so, as long as we was representing a prisoner, we had a perfect right to steal anything on this place we had the least use for to get ourselves out of prison with. He said if we warn't prisoners it would be a very different thing, and nobody but a mean, ornery person would steal when he warn't a prisoner. So we allowed we would steal everything there was that come handy. And yet he made a mighty fuss, one day, after that, when I stole a watermelon out of the nigger patch and eat it; and he made me go and give the niggers a dime without telling them what it was for. Tom said that what he meant was, we could steal anything we *needed*. Well, I says, I needed the watermelon. But he said I didn't need it to get out of prison with; there's where the difference was. He said if I'd 'a' wanted it to hide a knife in, and smuggle it to Jim to kill the seneskal with, it would 'a' been all right. So I let it go at that, though I couldn't see no advantage in my representing a prisoner if I got to set down and chaw over a lot of gold-leaf distinctions like that every time I see a chance to hog a watermelon.

Well, as I was saying, we waited that morning till everybody was settled down to business, and nobody in sight around the yard; then Tom he carried the sack into the lean-to whilst I stood off a piece to keep watch. By and by he come out, and we went and set down on the woodpile to talk. He says:

"Everything's all right now except tools; and that's easy fixed."

"Tools?" I says.

"Yes."

"Tools for what?"

"Why, to dig with. We ain't a-going to *gnaw* him out, are we?"

"Ain't them old crippled picks and things in there good enough to dig a nigger out with?" I says.

He turns on me, looking pitying enough to make a body cry, and says:

"Huck Finn, did you *ever* hear of a prisoner having picks and shovels, and all the modern conveniences in his wardrobe to dig himself out with? Now I want to ask you—if you got any reasonableness in you at all—what kind of a show would *that* give him to be a hero? Why, they might as well lend him the key and done with it. Picks and shovels—why, they wouldn't furnish 'em to a king."

"Well, then," I says, "if we don't want the picks and shovels, what do we want?"

"A couple of case-knives."

"To dig the foundations out from under that cabin with?"

"Yes."

"Confound it, it's foolish, Tom."

"It don't make no difference how foolish it is, it's the *right* way—and it's the regular way. And there ain't no *other* way, that ever *I* heard of, and I've read all the books that gives any information about these things. They always dig out with a case-knife—and not through dirt, mind you; generally it's through solid rock. And it takes them weeks and weeks and weeks, and for ever and ever. Why, look at one of them prisoners in the bottom dungeon of the Castle Deef, in the harbor of Marseilles, that dug himself out that way; how long was *he* at it, you reckon?"

"I don't know."

"Well, guess."

"I don't know. A month and a half."

"*Thirty-seven year*—and he came out in China. *That's* the kind. I wish the bottom of *this* fortress was solid rock."

"*Jim* don't know nobody in China."

"What's *that* got to do with it? Neither did that other fellow. But you're al-ways a-wandering off on a side issue. Why can't you stick to the main point?"

"All right—*I* don't care where he comes out, so he *comes* out; and Jim don't, either, I reckon. But there's one thing, anyway—Jim's too old to be dug out with a case-knife. He won't last."

"Yes he will *last,* too. You don't reckon it's going to take thirty-seven years to dig out through a *dirt* foundation, do you?"

"How long will it take, Tom?"

"Well, we can't resk being as long as we ought to, because it mayn't take very long for Uncle Silas to hear from down there by New Orleans. He'll hear Jim ain't from there. Then his next move will be to advertise Jim, or something like that. So we can't resk being as long digging him out as we ought to. By rights I reckon we ought to be a couple of years; but we can't. Things being so uncertain, what I recommend is this: that we really dig right in, as quick as we can; and after that, we can let *on,* to ourselves, that we was at it thirty-seven years. Then we can snatch him out and rush him away the first time there's an alarm. Yes, I reckon that'll be the best way."

"Now, there's *sense* in that," I says. "Letting on don't cost nothing; letting on ain't no trouble; and if it's any object I don't mind letting on we was at it a hundred and fifty year. It wouldn't strain me none, after I got my hand in. So I'll mosey along now, and smouch a couple of case-knives."

"Smouch three," he says; "we want one to make a saw out of."

"Tom, if it ain't unregular and irreligious to sejest it," I says, "there's an old rusty saw-blade around yonder sticking under the weather-boarding behind the smokehouse."

He looked kind of weary and discouraged-like, and says:

"It ain't no use to try to learn you nothing, Huck. Run along and smouch the knives—three of them." So I done it.